What Others Are Saying about Andrew Malone

The Master Song is the closest thing I have found that approaches the magic, depth, and wonder of the *Lord of the Rings* trilogy. The characters are real and believable; the story, though fantastic, never pulls any of those "amazing coincidences" I find so annoying. No, this is the real deal—the situations are serious, the reactions are real, and there   You go through it properly, or you simply dor   ask from a master storyteller? And this is ex   lrew Maloney.

—   affer
Dictionary editor, textbook author, and English professor at
Shizuoka University, Japan

There are writers, and then there are storytellers. Andrew Maloney is both! When an author can open a new world and describe it as if you had been there before, then you know you are in good hands. From the opening line, you are whisked into a new realm and then ushered into a wonderful story hard to put down. With fantastic description blended within the realistic dialogue, *The Master Song* is one of those books that you will dwell upon much after it is over. You will relive the epic adventure in your mind and find yourself lost within your imagination sparked by a talented author—Andrew Maloney. Well done, Andrew, well done.

—Brae Wyckoff
Author, the Horn King Series (*The Orb of Truth* and *The Dragon God*)
Host, *Broadcast Muse* radio show
President, LR Publishing and Destiny Authors
Cofounder, The Greater News international ministry

The Master Song

The Master Song

Andrew Maloney

WHITAKER
HOUSE

Scripture quotation is taken from the *New King James Version*, © 1979, 1980, 1982, 1984 by Thomas Nelson, Inc. Used by permission. All rights reserved.

THE MASTER SONG
Blue Time ~ Verse 1

Andrew Maloney
www.bluetimebooks.com

ISBN: 978-1-62911-176-6
eBook ISBN: 978-1-62911-177-3
Printed in the United States of America
© 2014 by Andrew Maloney

Whitaker House
1030 Hunt Valley Circle
New Kensington, PA 15068
www.whitakerhouse.com

Library of Congress Cataloging-in-Publication Data

Maloney, Andrew, 1977–
  The master song / by Andrew Maloney.
    pages cm. — (Blue time ; verse 1)
  Summary: "On a cold, stormy evening in Ireland, five teenagers suddenly find themselves lost, separated, and unprepared for a dangerous quest 'beyond the Veil' into Morsden Forest, a secret world hidden from ours"—Provided by publisher.
  ISBN 978-1-62911-176-6 (alk. paper) — ISBN 978-1-62911-177-3 (eBook) [1. Supernatural—Fiction. 2. Adventure and adventurers—Fiction. 3. Music—Fiction. 4. Imaginary creatures—Fiction. 5. Green Man (Tale)—Fiction. 6. Ireland—Fiction.] I. Title.
  PZ7.7.M26Mas 2014
  [Fic]—dc23
                        2014018096

1 2 3 4 5 6 7 8 9 10 11   W   21 20 19 18 17 16 15 14

For my wife, my kids, and my parents, as always:
whatever I know of virtue, I've learned from them.

* To view complete collection of maps pertaining to Blue Time, visit www.bluetimebooks.com.

Contents

Prologue

Horses and Hunters

A Nightmare galloped through the woods—an obsidian, foam-flecked whirlwind with hooves as immense as any elephant's—and the Forest inhabitants recoiled from her poisonous darkness. She was a Nightmare in the truest sense of the word: smoky tendrils curled up from her nostrils as she ran; her eyes were violent, glowing red. But her mane was the most fearsome thing. It smoldered, and in the glint of the occasional, somber moonbeam that was able to penetrate the canopy, the Treeman who was watching her trample through the Forest would have sworn the Horse's mane looked like it was in flames.

The vantage point was sixty feet off the ground, nestled between the boughs of an ancient oak. No one could see the Treeman, this *Coeduine*, because he was made of virtually the same substance as his perch. He curled his five long, slender fingers around his staff, and the slight creaking of wood might have been his hand or the staff itself. His feet dug into the bark—a person would be unable to distinguish where his toes ended and the tree began. Standing on the ground, he would be as tall as the Nightmare, about eleven feet, with shaggy hair like oak leaves tied back behind broad shoulders, and a stern, intelligent face carved out of wood. This Coeduine was a tracker and a warrior, a *Sealwyr* in his language. His speed rivaled the Horse's, as did his power. He moved like water—an odd sight to the unaccustomed eye, because he looked like he was made of rigid bark. And he was, after a fashion; though he looked human, especially in the face: yellow eyes, white teeth, and lips pursed in deep thought.

The question was, should he confront the Nightmare alone? Or should he get reinforcements? But that would mean tracking the beast, and who knew how long that would take, or what damage she could do in the meantime? There was a human settlement just a day's journey from here.

No. No time for reinforcements. He would do this himself.

Twirling his staff and nestling it under his armpit, he slipped out of the tree, uncoiling like a timber serpent, lithe and silent. The Treeman's dexterity would appear astonishing to a human, though it was average for his race. Muscles rippled as the Coeduine tightened his body for the chase.

He broke into a run, wind-swift, but quieter. A human's eyes would have deceived him, had one been around to watch. Was the Forest moving?

An ear-splitting neigh, almost a demonic shriek, shattered the inky quiet of the woods, for all sounds from the local inhabitants had been silenced. It was almost as if the Nightmare was calling attention to herself.

It was preternaturally still, dark, eerie. Fog twirled around the Treeman's long legs. He leapt over fallen trunks, stones, brambles, and plants; under branches; over branches; sometimes swinging into the trees like a monkey, sometimes on the ground like a pursuing tiger; slinky and fast, never breaking stride. He was on the beast in moments.

"Leave me be, Treeman. I've no quarrel with you," the Nightmare snorted as the Coeduine pulled up short, not even breathing hard. He twirled his staff and slammed one end into the damp earth, a gesture of warning. The Horse was speaking his language.

They were now in an odd clearing, surrounded on all sides by a nearly impenetrable Forest from ancient times: the Morsden, which Translates as "the Covering." For the most part, the Forest was a wall of foliage, unless someone carved out space for a village. But here was a natural clearing about a mile in circumference, exactly circular, with soft grass ankle-high to a human. No human hand had made this; perhaps one of the *Coedaoine* had, but in all his time in the Covering, the Treeman had never seen this clearing before. Above their heads, brilliant starlight streamed down, overpowering a wan sickle moon. The heavens were watching, and the Treeman felt a stirring in the ground that he could not explain—but it didn't concern him at the moment.

Yes, he was *sure* the Nightmare's mane was burning now. How was that possible? Who among the Corrupted knew such evil Singing? He had never seen anything like it.

"Who Awakened you?" the Sealwyr demanded.

"Please," the Nightmare scoffed, stamping her hoof and sending up a plume of acrid-smelling smoke. "Don't insult me with questions you know I won't answer."

"Were you sent by Agenor?" the Treeman persisted.

The Nightmare whinnied, which he interpreted as a mocking laugh. "Agenor? Is that the Pig?" The Horse's eyes narrowed. "No. He's out of favor, from what I hear. His incompetence is a source of much derision. I answer to a higher power."

If the Nightmare were to be believed, it meant only one thing. The Coeduine blanched. "Bàsisolc," he whispered. Yes, it must be true. Only an evil as great as Bàsisolc could or *would* Awaken a Mare into something like this. She was not the work of an underling.

The beast widened her eyes in surprise, and golden sparks leapt out of her mane, showering the misty grass. "You're not just any Sealwyr if you use the Ancient's name without trembling. Let me pass. I'll give you no more free information."

"You're not welcome here."

"Then let me leave!" the Mare exclaimed. "You're blocking my way." She cocked her head in puzzlement. "What is your name?"

The Treeman was silent. He pulled his staff out of the ground and held it in a defensive position.

"What, you're going to fight me with a stick? Sealwyr, you are braver than most, but maybe not as smart. Need I remind you? Wood *burns*. Now come, I've told you more than I should; what will it hurt to tell me your name? I would know who it is I am going to trample."

"What's *your* name, monster?"

"Arsoíche." The Horse bent one foreleg and lowered her head in a mocking bow.

"*Night Terror.* Interesting."

"Thank you. I thought it was fitting."

They started circling each other, the Treeman swinging his staff in long, slow arcs. Every step Arsoíche took left a puff of smoke, and her long mane flickered with embers.

A realization came to the Treeman as they circled. "You're searching for a Verse!" he exclaimed.

"I told you I'm not playing these foolish games. I do not answer to you."

She *was* looking for a Verse. The Treeman *knew* it. The Horse was in the Forest for a specific reason, not just running amok to scare the inhabitants.

"You know, you could just let me walk out of here, Sealwyr. I've no fight with the Morsden."

"You should know my name is Ysgafn Droed," the man of wood said in reply.

"*Light of Foot.* Interesting." The Horse snickered, and her volcanic eyes were narrow slits.

"Thank you. I thought it was fitting."

Arsoíche charged Ysgafn with a war cry, ears flat against her head, hooves sending a shower of sparks into the air. Her teeth were bared in two sets of fangs, and her mane was truly a flame of fire now, flying five feet behind her head. She brought her entire bulk to bear upon the Coeduine, but Ysgafn was not named "Light Foot" for nothing. Leaping to the side like a bullfighter, he brought the staff down on the Mare's snout with such reverberation that it startled the birds out of their sleepy nests and sent them screeching into the night sky.

The Nightmare roared in pain and anger. She turned much too quickly for a normal Horse, biting the arm of the hunter and tearing a deep chunk of wood-flesh away. The Coeduine let loose a sharp cry. The gape in his forearm seeped something akin to blood and bubbled with hissing yellow foam. Venom! As if the Nightmare wasn't formidable enough!

Arsoíche spit out the flesh of the Treeman.

They faced off again. The seriousness of the first attacks had drained any sarcasm out of their demeanors; now they panted, each waiting for the other to move and make a mistake. But Arsoíche was impetuous again, striking out with her hooves once, twice, three times.

Ysgafn blocked the jolts as best as he could with glances of the staff now held in his good arm. Every kick felt like his arm would shatter. He needed to do something, or the Nightmare would crush him. The poison was affecting his vision, and he felt himself weakening.

Whirling the staff in an arc under Arsoíche's forelegs, Ysgafn brought the beam straight in between the back legs and twisted it around, throwing himself in the dirt as he did so. The attack knocked the legs out from under the Horse.

With a bellow and a curse, Arsoíche collapsed. The Coeduine had less than a second to tuck and roll, or he would have been pinned by her. Before she could recover, the Treeman untangled his staff and rolled to his knees in one fluid motion.

With his uninjured arm, he brought the butt of the staff down on the Horse's rib cage like a vertical battering ram. He heard something snap and crack, and Arsoíche howled. She lost her breath, gasping and rolling onto her feet, red eyes wide in pain. Her mane was extinguished and smoking in ratted wisps.

Good. Ysgafn didn't think he could stand another assault. The wound in his arm was running blood, a jagged, footlong gash with the imprint of the Nightmare's fangs. He was beginning to feel light-headed. He patted out some flames that had caught his oak-leaf hair alight and leaned on his staff.

Arsoíche coughed and sputtered, trying to recapture the lost breath, stumbling and falling as she loped away from the Sealwyr.

"No more." Arsoíche choked and spat lavalike blood on the ground. It cooled in seconds and crusted over. "Leave…me be, Woodman."

Now Ysgafn had a dilemma. It was against Coedaoine law to leave something like *that* alive in the Forest, but if Bàsisolc had risked sending a fiend as rare and powerful as the Nightmare in search of a Verse, then he was closer to finding one than the Treefolk realized. The questions were, which Verse, and where was it? Ysgafn thought about asking Arsoíche those questions, but he knew what the answers would be.

No. Leave Arsoíche to make her way back to her master with a broken rib. Honestly, Ysgafn was unsure he *could* kill the Nightmare in this state.

The poison was crawling up his arm like a thick fire. It wouldn't kill him; no, not someone as powerful as a Coeduine. But he would be sick a couple days, and the fever would slow him down. He had to get information relayed to the Eldest as fast as possible.

"Arsoíche," he said through clenched teeth, "if I see you again, I'll break more than your rib. Get out of the Morsden. Now."

Just before the Nightmare disappeared into the blackness of the thick trees, she tossed her mane in an act of prideful defiance and glared over her shoulder with molten eyes. "Yeah, yeah." She gave a wheezing laugh and winced in pain. "Bàsisolc was right. Leave it to the Coedaoine to miss the forest for the trees!" And she hobbled off into the night.

Ysgafn collapsed cross-legged on the spot, using his staff for support. His vision danced, and perspiration beaded on his rough forehead. What the Veil did that mean, "Forest for the trees"? Or did it mean anything at all? Something hidden in plain sight? Not getting the bigger picture? Was that just a mocking statement to rile him, or was the Nightmare trying to share something important? Was she playing him?

Ysgafn winced as he sucked out venom from the bleeding wound, spitting the foul-smelling stuff on the ground in hissing drops. It blistered his mouth.

There was no way he'd make it to Rhydderch's cabin tonight. The *Pêllys* would have to help.

"Bassett?" Ysgafn called out moments after Arsoíche had disappeared.

A ball of light about ten inches in diameter burst into existence at eye level with the Treeman. It zoomed and zipped, whizzing in excitement, changing from whites to yellows to greens to reds. It was mesmerizing to watch, but with the poison haze, it gave the Coeduine a headache.

"Are you going to stop bleeding?"

"Never mind, I'll be fine," Ysgafn told the little person in the light. He unraveled a strip of black leather from his staff and clenched his jaws as he pulled it tight above the wound to make a tourniquet. "Did you hear everything the *Truillygru* said?" he asked the Pêllys, referring to the Nightmare as "Corrupted."

"Not a word escaped me, Ysgafn."

"Good, my friend. Make haste to Rhydderch and Fiorlen and relay what you overheard. If you happen upon one of the Thornsword Brethren, Boujòn should be notified that Arsoíche might try to return to the Morsden."

Bassett spun in an impatient whirl. "And then?"

"Have Rhydderch get word to the Eldest that Bàsisolc is looking for a Verse in southern Morsden Deep, and make sure to mention Arsoíche's statement about 'missing the forest for the trees.' I think that might mean the Verse is nearby. I will work on healing and see if I can't uncover a lead. Can you remember to make your way back to this clearing? Meet me here at tomorrow's nightfall."

"You will be all right?" the Will-o'-the-wisp asked.

"I won't die."

"Good enough, then. Hail, Sealwyr Ysgafn!" The ball went dark and was gone.

After Ysgafn had dressed the wound as best he could, he pulled to his feet, leaning on the staff. Some venom was circulating through his body, and it made his brain dull. Still, he forced his mind to consider the possibilities. What was the forest? What were the trees? Was the Horse just mocking him? Or was it something deeper?

What if she wasn't looking for a Verse—what if she was looking for a *Demeglwys*? Here, in the clearing. The forest for the trees. Missing the bigger picture.

The last thought shocked his head clear. Really? Could it be? He spun on his heels, taking in the clearing in one panoramic glance. Could a Sanctuary be hidden here? How could Bàsisolc have found it? Why, Ysgafn wasn't sure if even Crannhyn knew where all the Temples were. They had been covered in the Veil so many centuries ago.

But, yes, Ysgafn thought. *I can feel* something *here.* It was subtle, but it was there. Perhaps the small amount of venom still in his system was playing tricks with his brain, but he didn't think so.

And now he cursed himself for sending Bassett off so soon. If there truly was a Sanctuary here, time was of the essence, and mighty Crannhyn must come. Ysgafn wasn't sure he knew enough of the First Tongue to open the Temple alone. Hmmm. And what of the Temple's guardian? Could he deal with it on his own?

If only it were dusk, he could find out....

As he searched for a suitable spot in the trees to hide and recover, he thought of the human girl from so many years ago. A small smile spread across his face, in spite of the dull ache of his wound. It had been decades since he'd thought of their times together in the Morsden, seeking the Love Verse. She would be, what, sixty and some summers by now? What she wouldn't give to be here, if there really were a Sanctuary hidden in the Morsden!

Ysgafn selected a low branch and eased himself against the trunk. Whatever the mystery would reveal, tomorrow evening couldn't come quick enough.

Part I

Audrey's Diamond

1

Pretty Odd

Talking to plants was something of a secret pleasure for Nolan. Not that he expected them to talk back or anything, but it had been an odd habit of the boy's, since he was old enough to walk, to pretend that trees were his imaginary friends. He conversed with them in his mind and gave them names from fantasy stories he had read. The poplar by the school playground was Edmund; the willow whose branches wept over the small creek that ran behind his house was named Wendy; there was a tall, ancient oak in the front yard named Cornelius.

In real life he had only one friend. That was Stanley Stewart, who was just as peculiar as Nolan but for different reasons. According to IQ tests, Stanley was the smartest kid in three states. But, of course, being *smart* is something entirely different from being *cool*. Nolan didn't think Stanley talked to plants, although he'd never asked him; and obviously he would never, ever, admit to anyone publicly that he talked to trees and flowers more than he talked to real people. People thought he was odd enough as it was.

Adolescence had exploded in Nolan's life when he was twelve years of age. Overnight, it seemed, a heavy cloak was thrown over his shoulders, a dreadful burden that led to a breaking voice and a complete lack of any kind of motor skills. He was pale skinned, uncoordinated, self-conscious, freckled, graceless, short, and skinny. Most often, the emotional scars of the teen years fade, leaving behind a perfectly normal, well-equipped young adult; but to someone like Nolan, it seemed awkwardness would always be a fellow traveler.

He'd yet to have a growth spurt, just a bit over four foot eight; but his arms, legs, and neck were longer than they should be. Or so he imagined. He weighed seventy-six pounds—a massive difference from most of his classmates, who were, like, four inches taller and a good twenty pounds heavier. His voice cracked when he spoke, so his replies were terse to the few people who did talk to him. Most people thought he was stuck-up, or maybe just dumb; in actuality, he didn't want them to laugh at his squeaks. If he stood up too quickly, he got dizzy and almost blacked out. Apparently this happened to kids his age, something to do with starting puberty or whatever; but it seemed to happen more to him than to anyone else he knew.

Nolan was in sixth grade at Buckingham School, overlooking Dorchester Bay, next to an antique Catholic church; and the school was set up like a college campus: sprawling and intimidating, with century-old redbrick buildings and rolling hills of green grasses, complete with gnarled old trees for him to chat with. The private school hosted first through ninth grades, and there were about seventy children in his year. None of them (except Stanley) talked to him if he could avoid it.

It was the last day of school, and he was supposed to be taking his final exam in Intro to Economics, but his mind was wandering, as it often did. Out the window, he watched Edmund sway in the hot wind and wished he was outside, too, wearing a pair of dark sunglasses. Nolan hated Economics, so he was repeating a poem to himself in his head and tapping a pen on his leg to the meter. Might be a little weird for a boy his age to like poetry, but it was just the way his mind worked: economics, stupid; poetry, awesome.

Nolan, unlike Stanley, wasn't overly intelligent. He mostly maintained average marks in school, although this had more to do with a tendency to daydream than any lack of smarts. His best subjects were literature and biology, and he prided himself on knowing more about plants than anyone else in school, maybe even Stanley. His favorite hobby was botany, which was *very* odd for a boy his age. What kind of twelve-year-old knows the first thing about growing flowers, herbs, and fungi? But Nolan had a green thumb, and so he spent most of his time studying plants, when he should've been studying for things like his Intro to Economics test.

The problem with his being a plant lover was his asthma, meaning a lot of the pollen and fragrances that plants put off made it hard for him to breathe. In spite of that, his bedroom was overgrown by various foliage that could be smelled as soon as someone entered the house. Nolan wasn't about to give up the one thing he was good at for some silly reason like breathing.

The boy's eyes flickered between a lock of his red hair and the top of his desk, where his all but blank economics exam was taking up space. He sighed, blowing the strands of hair up in the air through thin lips stained purple from the grape candy he was illegally sucking on. (Candy was contraband at Buckingham School.)

Truth be told, Nolan despised his red hair because it was different from what most kids had. His classmates made fun of him, calling him "Fire Truck" and "Torchlight" and things like that. His mother had the same color hair, and although he would never tell her, he wished it were his father's dirty blond (like his lucky little brother got) or even just a mousy brown—something that wouldn't stand out as much.

It also annoyed him that his cheeks were covered in this ridiculous peach fuzz. He wished he could grow a beard, something manly. His nose was straight and long, maybe too large for his face, and that bothered him. He was convinced his teeth were oversized, and that bothered him, too. In fact, when he looked in the mirror, Nolan didn't like much of anything about his appearance.

Some would call him unique, as if that were some sort of compliment. To him, *unique* meant *weird*, and he didn't want to be weird; he wanted to be like everyone else. Just *normal*.

Now, lest someone think there was nothing redeeming about Nolan, for those few who acknowledged his existence, it was universally accepted that his eyes were his nicest feature. They were huge, bright, and green, like June beetles, he'd been told. Somehow the hazel of his father's and the blue of his mother's had mixed to produce an unusual shade that could be seen clear across the room. His vision was amazing, well over 20/20; but it was drawn against his will to minute details, like smudges of paint on the walls or little bits of dust floating in the air. It made his eyes hurt and gave him terrible headaches, especially if the day was particularly bright and sunny.

All of these inane thoughts were racing through his mind, along with the poem, as he alternated those green eyes between the lock of hair and the lonesome test in front of him, until:

"Mr. Marten, with your situation regarding my class, it might be advisable for you to pay attention and *take your exam!*"

Nolan jerked his head up, eyes fumbling for the source of the outburst. Oh, yeah. It was his Intro to Economics professor. Nolan's voice cracked as he said, "S-sorry, Dr. Whitefield. Just resting my eyes for a minute."

After a fashion, that was true.

The old woman's gaze bored holes into him, and she clicked a red ink pen over and over to show her agitation. "Perhaps you would do well not to drool so much when you are 'resting your eyes,' Mr. Marten."

Several kids chuckled. Nolan's eyes were drawn to the professor's double chin, and he noticed a mole on her neck that was turning purple with irritation, a long gray hair growing out of it. He blinked and shuddered. Yecch! Why'd he have to have such good vision?

"Yes, ma'am," Nolan mumbled, returning his attention to his exam. He scratched his leg through his navy blue shorts and sighed again. What did he care about the current financial situation of the Czech Republic? Where the heck was the Czech Republic, anyway? Geography was one of his worst subjects. Was it even a real country anymore? No, that was Prussia. Right? See, his mind was getting all cluttered now, thanks to the stupid, perchance nonexistent Czech Republic.

Nolan hazarded a glance to his left and saw Stanley Stewart gazing up into space, possibly working out some algebraic formula to count how many tiles were on the ceiling. He'd finished his exam thirty minutes ago, and since he had the highest marks in the class, there was no way Dr. Whitefield was going to call *him* out for daydreaming.

Maybe Stanley would let him cheat.

Making a slight jerking motion to get his attention, Nolan formed an expression with his eyes that said "Help me, help me!" and nudged his chin at Stanley's effortlessly composed paper. His friend scoffed and turned the paper over so Nolan couldn't read it. Nolan tossed him a savage, scandalized look.

The bell rang an excruciating fifteen minutes later. Nolan moaned and threw down his pen in despair. *Well, that's another test bombed.* His sole chance to pass this class hinged on Whitefield's really liking him. He looked up to see her glaring.

Aw, man. He was gonna fail.

As Nolan shuffled up to the front, past Stanley gathering his overflowing book bag, a thick boy named Jason Dupree shoved him aside and slammed his paper down on the professor's desk. "I am *outta* here!" the brute bellowed, then stomped off to join a jovial sea of students clambering for their lockers, eager to tear the place apart. *Well, I'll bet* he *passed the test*, Nolan thought. Even though Dupree had the mental capacity of a blade of grass.

"Have a good summer, Dr. Whitefield!" Nolan tried to sound cordial, maybe earn a few last-minute brownie points. Maybe she thought his hair was too long, and that was why she didn't like him. (It was questionably legal by Buckingham's standards.)

Or maybe it was because he thought her class was ridiculous and had turned in only half the homework assignments over the year.

Yeah, that was probably it.

Avoiding Dr. Whitefield's withering stare as he turned in his exam, Nolan then picked his way to his locker through a mob of students and dodged a wet clump of paper towels aimed at his head. Stanley shuffled up next to him, smirking.

"So how d'ya think ya did?" he asked.

"Oh, shut up. That was so weak! You could've let me copy!" Nolan's voice cracked.

Stanley pretended to give his comment serious consideration for a second. "Ummm, no. See, cheating is wrong, and cheaters never prosper, and it's your fault you skipped studying with me last night so you could bowl on Wii." He offered a smug grin. "Besides, Whitefield was watching you like a hawk. You'd've been caught, so you should thank me for being stalwart in refusing to let you copy."

Nolan had to surmise what "stalwart" meant, but he wasn't sincerely mad at Stanley. He pretended to glower for a few seconds as some tall kid threw a pile of papers in the air, singing, "School's out for summer! School's out forever!" Nolan and Stanley were littered with about two reams' worth of math homework as if they hadn't been standing there, talking like real people. Stanley brushed away a stray sheet, unconcerned, as the rude kid tramped by, still spouting old rock-and-roll lyrics.

Stanley was a pudgy boy. No one would call him obese, but a bit on the heavy side, sure, with kind of a blotchy face and nerdy glasses that almost hid his soggy gray eyes. His thin blond hair was cut short and parted on the side, and he had the worst fashion sense ever given to a geek. He unbuttoned the scarlet jacket of his Buckingham uniform to expose a wrinkled, dirty T-shirt boasting that iconic photo of Albert Einstein and his wild hair with a caption underneath that said, "Brains matter." With hefty white calves glowing beneath knee-length shorts, and red socks sticking out the tops of his Converse sneakers, he looked preposterous. Nolan couldn't help letting a little giggle escape.

Appearing at Nolan's elbow with a wave was his brother, Emery, a fourth grader, who sported the very normal-looking dark blond hair and hazel eyes of their father. Emery was popular among his little friends, unlike his older sibling. He waved a second time to Stanley, who gave him a superior nod of the head. Emery was the typical younger brother, rather annoying to the older boys but tolerated from time to time when they coerced him into bringing drinks and snacks and stuff, which, of course, Emery was only too happy to do because it meant he got to hang out with the "big kids."

"I'm sure I got an A in Physical Science," Emery said by way of hello. He'd threaded his way across campus to Nolan and Stanley's building.

"Good for you, squirt," Nolan replied in a put-off mood, his pride still smarting from the disastrous Econ exam. He unbuttoned his own uniform and shrugged out of the shirt, then started unpacking his cluttered locker. "Oh, well. Just a nice, quiet summer ahead of us, filled with my plants and your science journals, eh, Stanley?"

"Yeah, uh, except for the part about us all leaving for Ireland the day after tomorrow. Remember?"

Nolan's shoulders slumped.

Stanley smirked. "Ha! You forgot!"

"I'm so excited!" Emery interjected.

Nolan moaned, and his forehead slammed the locker door shut. He'd forgotten, in the agony of today's miserable exams, that his parents were taking them to spend the better part of the summer in Ireland. His aunt Florence, who lived there, was getting remarried the first of July, and that meant he'd have to spend most of his time away from his plants and books, in the presence of his snotty, conceited cousin Genevieve. Yuck. She was two-and-a-half years older, and she lorded that fact over the boys like a queen. She also thought herself very pretty, and so did most people. But Nolan couldn't stand her. It was lucky she lived on the other side of the Atlantic Ocean, and that he saw her only rarely, like when his aunt came visiting on random Christmases.

Both Stanley and Emery were beside themselves at the prospect of traveling to Ireland, but Nolan just knew the whole thing would be a nightmare. He'd been trying to push it from his mind for weeks, so as not to ruin the excitement for his friend and his brother.

Of course, Nolan's parents were ecstatic about the thought of spending a few weeks in Ireland; they believed it was a good excuse to take a long break from the rat race of Boston. "You an' Emery're old enough now to enjoy the cult'ral heritage," his mother had said. She'd been raised there and still had a soft accent. But what did *he* care about his cultural heritage? Wasn't Ireland just a dinky island out in the middle of the ocean? Who cared about some thousand-year-old country inhabited by shepherds?

"Well, I can't wait!" Emery put in, his enthusiasm undampened.

Nolan scoffed. "Don't the men there wear skirts?" he asked Stanley, looking sideways with his forehead still resting against the metal grate of his locker.

"Nah, that's mostly Scotland. C'mon, bro, cheer up. It'll be fun. At least I get to come with you. What if you had to stay with your cousin and I was stuck in Boston?"

"Well, I think it's a waste of a summer!" Nolan's voice squeaked again, so he fell silent.

"Well, I think it'll be very cool to go, and you should be thankful your parents have enough money to pay for all of us," Stanley said. His parents were much poorer than Nolan's and were rather lazy people. Their paying for a monthlong vacation in Ireland would've been as likely as paying for a trip to the moon.

It was Stanley's grandparents who funded his education, spending almost all their finances on the astronomical tuition fees of Buckingham, because this was the kind of education their brilliant grandson would need to get a scholarship to attend MIT. Nolan got the distinct impression Stanley's own parents couldn't have cared less whether their son went to college at all. It was kind of sad, and Nolan felt guilty whining about a trip that Stanley had been dreaming about for weeks.

"Yeah, at least you'll get to come with us." Nolan sighed and opened the locker again, removed his belongings, and slammed it shut as a throng of eighth graders surged past, many of them bumping into him. The three boys allowed themselves to be jostled along the buffalo herd of students toward the front doors of Buckingham's Stringfellow Hall and out into the stifling summer air.

Boston was experiencing a strange heat wave that had killed something like four old folks whose houses didn't have air-conditioning. It was all over the news, along with tips on how to stay cool and keep hydrated—something most Bostonians usually didn't worry about. But now, the asphalt was scalding hot, and the three boys started sweating. Smog hit Nolan's lungs, and he gagged on a cough. He plunged a hand into the pocket of his shorts to retrieve his inhaler, took a deep hit of the medicine, and waited for his lungs to stop itching. His head swooned a bit, and his eyes began to throb in the harsh sunlight. Where were his sunglasses?

"You okay?" Emery asked. He pointed to Nolan's backpack pocket, and Nolan reached for his sunglasses.

He nodded. "Just hard to breathe in this heat."

"Yeah, let's get some shade," Stanley said, looking around. "Your mom's late. Must be traffic."

They stood underneath the gigantic tree Nolan called "Cristo" and watched the other students clamber onto buses or into their parents' cars. Stanley leaned his broad back against the tree trunk, chewing on his pinky finger and wiping sweat off his glasses with his free hand. Emery was talking to a couple of other kids in his grade. Nolan squatted down.

"Hey, dork, the short bus is filling up quickly—you'll miss your rides!" Jason Dupree sniggered, sucking down a Coca-Cola while he tormented a helpless nerd just across the way who was struggling to get on his bike. Nolan would've ignored him, like usual (Buckingham didn't even *have* short buses), except Stanley retorted:

"Don't be an idiot, Dupree. You realize that doesn't make any sense, right? I mean, considering I've got an IQ of one seventy-five, and you're in remedial *everything*, maybe *you* should get on the short bus, you doltish troll!"

Nolan was quite sure Dupree had no idea what "doltish" meant, and he supposed it took several seconds for Stanley's rejoinder to register in the dunce's dull brain, anyway, because there was a marked space of silence before the bully's ears turned red with rage.

"Uh-oh. That's probably a little less polite than he's used to." Nolan scrambled to his feet as Dupree hopped off the other kid, who gave a wild look of respect mingled with sympathy to his soon-to-be-murdered fellow geeks and then sped away from the scene of the crime. "Aw, man, here he comes," Nolan muttered. "Emery, keep away."

That was all Nolan needed just before his mother pulled up—to get himself and/or his brother pummeled by this bozo five minutes into summer break. He coughed on the smog again and waited for the attack. He was scared enough to cry, but he didn't want Stanley to see it, so he made to go stand in front of his brother. It would look like he was trying to protect Emery, and maybe Stanley wouldn't see his shaking knees. It felt like ice-cold water was poured down his back.

But they were saved the beating by his mother materializing out of nowhere, hair aflame in the sunlight, oblivious to the bully bearing down on her children. She pulled Nolan into a sideways hug while calling to Emery, who came running over, leaving Dupree to crack his knuckles and slink off to wherever sweaty trolls went for the summer.

Darla Marten was the ol' block from which the Nolan chip came off, except her eyes were blue instead of green. She was in her late thirties. One glance from any passersby, and they would say, "Yep, mother and son."

As Dupree slunk away, a sense of calm flooded Nolan, who was not a very brave boy at all. Realizing he had been saved by his mother's sudden appearance, he sneered and waved at Dupree's back until his mother began to squeeze him and placed a reassuring hand under his elbow, trying to both shield him from the sun and stroke his hair at the same time. He coughed.

"What's wrong, Nolan? Yore asthma? Lor', it's devilishly hot out here. Get in the car quick-like, lads!" she was saying as Stanley laughed, either at their good fortune of escaping Jason Dupree or at Nolan being pampered by his mother in front of the whole student body. The boy tried to squirm out of his mother's grip.

"Gedoffme, Mom," he managed as he freed his head from her arm, mussing his hair. "You're embarrassing me in front of the whole school!" She released him as though shocked by his embarrassment, then turned her mothering to a more-than-willing Emery as Stanley looked around the campus. No one was paying them any attention; they were as invisible as always to the rest of the school, no matter what Darla Marten did to her sons.

She herded the three boys into her Nissan Armada, Nolan in the passenger seat. His mother continued to fuss over him until he said, with a crack in his voice, "I'm *fine*, Mom. Get a grip." His mother clicked her seat belt and pulled out in front of several other cars and buses, prompting a few drivers to beep their horns angrily. She drove like a maniac.

"Are ya breathin' all right, Nolan? How's yore lungs?" she persisted, placing a hand on his chest as she weaved in and out of rush-hour Boston traffic like hers was the only car on the road. Stanley gripped his armrest with white knuckles, and Emery hooted at a near miss with a semi.

"Mom, I'm okay," Nolan replied sharply. "Let it go!"

"Smog's a plague in this heat. Not surprised yore asthma's actin' up." Another jolt as the driver of a van laid on the horn, but Darla was oblivious. "So 're ya lads excited about the trip?"

"Absolutely, Mrs. Marten," Stanley replied, still audibly recovering from the near miss.

"Nolan's not," Emery tattled. "He doesn't want to see Genevieve."

Nolan's mother gave him a sidelong glance, which almost put the SUV into the guardrail. She ignored the screeching brakes of the cars behind her. "Well, I suppose you and yore cousin don't have much in common—"

"She's a stuck-up squid!"

"Nolan!" His mother burst out laughing but swiftly stifled it. "Genevieve can be a little, er, self-centered now an' again, but she's a nice girl in spite of it. And jus' think of the experience, takin' in all that Irish culture!"

"Dad says Irish culture's nothing but beer and boiled meat," Nolan persisted. "And seeing as how I don't like either...."

Stanley chuckled.

"Well, yore father liked the Irish enough to marry one, so he's full o' hot air, that man. You'll have fun enough, I promise, without boiled meat *or* beer." Nolan's mother turned off the freeway, cutting across three lanes of traffic and almost sending a mass transit bus onto the shoulder. "T'tell ya lads the truth," she continued, oblivious, "I'm a little nervous about this trip meself. Sister gettin' married to some Welshman she hardly knows.... And you *know* how the Welsh are!"

"It's 'myself,' Mom," Nolan inserted. "'Myself.' You sound like a fruit when you say 'meself.' You've been American long enough to say it right. And no, Mom, actually, we don't know how the Welsh are, seeing as how we've never met anybody from Wales before," he pointed out. "Where is Wales, anyway?"

"On the island with England, to the west," Stanley supplied.

"Well, then, why not call them English?"

"It's an entirely diff'rent country, Nolan!" his mother said, exasperated.

"That's like saying Rhode Island's an entirely different country from Massachusetts."

"Rhode Island *is* an entirely different country from Massachusetts!" Stanley deadpanned, and everyone laughed as Darla turned onto their street, the tires squealing as she took the turn at least twenty miles an hour faster than legally allowed.

"Well, boys, I can tell ya this," she said, recovering the Nissan as she steamed ahead toward their house. "Yore goin' to thoroughly enjoy yoreselves out there."

Nolan rolled his eyes, unconvinced. "Yeah," he murmured with a squeak in his voice. "I can hardly wait."

2

Parental Relations

Stanley would be spending the night. It wasn't uncommon for him to eat and sleep at the Martens' home four or five nights a week, as he generally avoided his parents as much as possible.

Somehow they made it to the Martens' home on Hydrangea Circle in one piece. The SUV skidded to a stop in the circular drive, and the passengers lurched forward as Darla threw it into park. Their home was a two-story colonial boasting four bedrooms, a study for Nolan's dad, a theatre/game room for the kids with an air hockey table, and a saltwater pool out back that Nolan didn't use because he hated to swim. Emery, however, was a fish. Still, as Nolan was such a plant lover, the landscaping in the large backyard would've won awards in any gardening magazine, and each of the trees had been given a secret nickname.

As soon as Nolan's mother opened the front door, a powerful smell of mulch and blooming flowers hit everyone's nostrils. The house was dark and cool compared to the blinding scorch outside.

All three boys dropped their school things in the entryway, and the two brothers began shedding what little of the Buckingham uniforms they were still wearing: loafers went flying; clip-on ties, belts, and shirts lay forgotten by the front door. Emery was down to a pair of Sponge Bob boxer shorts and a white T-shirt before padding off barefoot to his room for his summer clothes.

"Now, don't leave yore clothes lyin' 'round, lads, right?" Nolan's mother set her keys on the table by the front door, stepping over the pile of uniforms, and called out, "Maribel? Can ya start dinner now, dear? Mr. Marten'll be home early tonight."

Maribel was a maid who came over a couple times a week to straighten the home, do some laundry, and cook dinner. She appeared from another hallway with a load of dirty clothes under one arm.

"No problem, Mrs. Marten. The chicken tonight?"

"Please do."

Stanley followed Nolan upstairs to his bedroom.

Nolan collided with the door, turning the handle as he did so, and fell into a large room painted green (his favorite color) that was filled with various planters of greenery. Because bright lights hurt Nolan's eyes, the room was kept dark, and all the plants were low-light vegetation: some mushrooms, certain herbs, a few vines, a fern, a couple hanging pots, and even a rare night-blooming flower that could grow in black light.

His full-size bed was situated underneath the corner windows, over which the heavy shades were pulled down to block out as much of the offending sun as possible. There was a built-in bookshelf of oak along one wall, showcasing several hundred hardbacks and scores of gardening magazines. On a matching desk with a soft white light glowing sat a tank that contained a Halloween crab nibbling on bologna near a small bowl of clean water. Due to Nolan's asthma, the Martens didn't have any furred pets, so Emery kept a massive Pacman frog in his room.

"Hey, Houston." Stanley greeted the black, orange, and purple crab by thumping it on its shell. It scurried sideways, still chowing down on the lunch meat. It was a peculiar name for a pet, but then again, it was a peculiar pet.

Nolan tossed his school shorts on the bed and pulled on a pair of comfy, baggy basketball shorts, scrunching his bare toes in the Berber carpet and stretching. His lungs still ached a little. He turned to the crab. "I see Maribel fed you." The maid was terrified of the crab and of Emery's frog, but she fed them dutifully whenever she was over.

He and Stanley spent the next couple hours bashing his cousin Genevieve, playing Nintendo, and waiting for Nolan's dad to get home. They were starving when they heard him come in, and the little light that slipped in under the window blinds was very blue, fading fast.

This was Nolan's favorite time—that brief period when it was no longer day but also wasn't quite night. The hour around dusk. When he was a little boy, tearing up the neighborhood on his skateboard (well, as much as his asthma allowed), it was understood that his curfew was when the sky just began to darken, as it was now. Right after sunset, when the easternmost horizon turned the deepest blue, a strange feeling of exhilaration would come over Nolan, and it was then that he felt most alive. His mother told him it was the "time between times," the magic hour; and, as weird as it sounded, it *was* magical to him.

Ever since he could remember, Nolan had called it Blue Time. It became a bit of a joke with his parents. "Make sure yore home at Blue Time!" his mother would holler as he hopped on his skateboard to go dig in the dirt around the park. He'd always bring her back a handful of tiny flowers, just as Blue Time approached—

"I'm starving!" Stanley announced, breaking his reverie.

Nolan nodded. "Yeah, let's eat!" His voice cracked.

"Later, Houston. Keep it real." The colorful pet was floating up to its eyes in the water bowl, occasional bubbles escaping its underbelly. Again Stanley thumped the crab on its shell, and the two boys headed downstairs and slipped barefoot across the hardwood floor onto the tile of the kitchen, then into the dining room, where Nolan's parents were seated at the large hand-carved wooden table.

"I thought ya were comin' home early tonight," his mother was saying to his father, who waved hello to the two boys. "Maribel was keepin' the chicken warm for an hour."

Nolan Marten Sr. shrugged. "Couldn't be helped. Too much work the day before leaving on a three-week vacation. I tried." Turning to his namesake, he said, in his Bostonian accent, "Ever notice that it smells like cow manure in this house?" He smiled. All of Nolan's plants left a faint odor of fertilizer, which his father never failed to point out. He winked at Nolan's friend. "Evening, Stanley. I see we're having you for dinner again. Spending the night, too?"

Stanley nodded.

Nolan loved his father and looked up to him, but he was closer to his mother, in spite of her fussing. His dad had a tendency to be blunt, and if someone didn't know him well, he might think he was a little rude. His sense of humor was very dry, almost mocking, but he didn't mean it disrespectfully; it was just a reflection of the particular way he looked at the world.

When Nolan was younger, he'd thought his dad was a bit scary, but deep down, he knew the senior Nolan was a loyal man under a gruff exterior. He loved his children with all his heart, even if he sometimes had difficulty showing it.

Mr. Marten wouldn't have admitted to himself that he was vaguely embarrassed by his oldest son's peculiarities and awkwardness. Every father wants their son to be "popular" in school, to be good in sports, to be smart and manly. He loved his oldest boy, even with his oddities, but Emery was more the type of child that he could throw a baseball to and talk about the Red Sox. Often Mr. Marten had trouble relating to Nolan.

Still, Nolan Jr.'s relationship with his parents was healthy, compared with most twelve-year-olds. He almost never argued with them, unless his mother was harping on him too much in front of others. His folks didn't overburden him with chores and were content as long as he passed his classes and stayed out of serious trouble. Nolan didn't understand why most kids his age were at such odds with their parents. What were they protesting against? Nine o'clock curfews? Big deal.

Not that Nolan had anywhere to be after nine o'clock, anyway; it wasn't as if he had a bunch of friends begging for him to come hang out at all hours of the night.

Emery bounded into the dining room, slid into his chair, and started wolfing down his roasted chicken without a glance at anyone.

"Hi, Son. Why, my day was great, thanks for asking. How was yours?" Nolan's father snickered. If Nolan looked like his mother, then Emery was a copy of his father.

"'T—was—fine," Emery responded around a mouthful of yams.

"Mmm-hmm, and how were everyone's exams?"

"Fine," Nolan lied abruptly, so that his parents wouldn't pressure him about the Intro to Economics test. He took a satisfying slurp of fruit punch and eyed up his plate, piled high with chicken roasted in fresh garlic and lemongrass (from Nolan's garden), brown-sugared sweet potatoes, and wilted spinach, with a side salad of wild greens smothered in bleu cheese dressing.

Another of Nolan's odd quirks: he loved veggies and probably would've gone vegetarian if his mother didn't insist he eat meat for muscle development, to which his father had once quipped, "What muscle?"

Between mouthfuls of vinegar and spinach, Nolan slurred, "I think I passed my econ exam."

Stanley choked on a bite of chicken.

"Good to hear, considering how much that school costs me a year!" Nolan's father downed the rest of his cranberry-peach iced tea. In his early forties, he was already a partner in a prestigious law firm, and his work ethic was something he tried to forge into his children. Good grades were as important to him as good batting averages.

He slapped Stanley on the back, sending the chunk of chicken flying, and eyed Nolan's hair. "Although you could probably do with a haircut. Don't you think, Darla? He's looking a bit bushy, right?"

Because he had her red hair, Nolan's mother kept it as long as Buckingham would allow him to grow it, down to his collar. She was proud to show it off. But his dad thought it was girly and hinted at least once a week that his mother should get the shears after his "unruly mop." Nolan wouldn't've minded if his dad won that case—to him, the less red hair, the better! But so far, shaggy was the way of the day.

"Aw, Nolan, it's fine," his mother protested. "Leave the boy alone. If he likes his hair a little longer, what's it matter? School's out now, anyway."

Nolan's father narrowed his eyes at him. "Something tells me it's not *you* who wants hair that long, eh?" He gave the boys another little wink as Maribel brought him a fresh glass of tea before wishing them a safe journey to Ireland and excusing herself for the night.

After dinner, Nolan's father drove the two older boys over to Stanley's house, a peeling white-framed row house dangerously close to being in Southie proper. Stanley's parents were not too friendly to Nolan's dad, probably because they considered him a snobbish yuppie; but, truth be told, Mr. and Mrs. Stewart would've done better for themselves with more ambition. Nolan Jr. had known them both to be unemployed from time to time, and Mrs. Stewart always smelled like wine.

Stanley, looking sheepish, hurried to throw his suitcase together while Nolan's father, shifting his weight from one foot to the other, tried to engage Mr. Stewart in conversation about this disgusting weather. He assured the man that his son would be quite safe in his protection, and he thanked him for letting Stanley come along, as Nolan Jr. was sure to be despondent without his partner-in-crime. Then he laughed at his little joke. Mr. Stewart did not.

Nolan Jr. felt that twang of discomfort he always got when over at Stanley's house, looking at the cramped, dirty living room and smelling that nasty odor from the basement that threatened to close up his lungs. He felt bad for his only friend. Stanley was embarrassed by his folks' idleness, especially since everyone knew he was five times smarter than both of his parents put together.

Stanley returned from his bedroom, lugging a large suitcase his grandparents had purchased for the occasion, looking self-conscious amid the surroundings and especially with his parents' obvious dislike for Mr. Marten's "uppity ways." Mrs. Stewart made a big show of planting a wet, wine-laced kiss on his forehead, although it didn't appear to Nolan that there was any real affection. Mr. Stewart nodded to his son and said, "Watch yourself there, kiddo," to which Stanley murmured a hasty good-bye and headed out the door even before Nolan and his father had bidden the Stewarts good night.

It was awkward.

"Well, your folks certainly are a pleasant couple, aren't they, Stanley, my boy?" Mr. Marten quipped, sliding into the driver's seat with a fake smile plastered to his face as he waved to the Stewarts.

"They don't seem too shaken up at me leaving for three weeks, huh?"

Nolan's father grunted and didn't say anything further, giving his son a cheerless smile. They drove home in near silence.

3

Rathdowns Manor

Two days later, Nolan Marten left Logan International Airport in Boston, scheduled to land in Dublin, Ireland, near Blue Time. The seven-hour flight was uneventful, and he entertained himself by reading the vomit bag, like, fifty times and skimming the "So You Know You're Going to Die in a Fiery Plane Wreck" safety pamphlet. There were pictures of stupidly calm people in a flaming airplane, surviving an emergency landing in the Atlantic Ocean. He wondered if his oxygen mask would work, figured it wouldn't matter anyway if the plane *did* crash, and then began to occupy his time with studying the elderly man next to him. The poor old soul had more hair in his ears and nose than he did on his head.

I bet his oxygen mask would work.... Nolan snorted.

On his other side, Stanley, who was beside himself with excitement, kept up a slow, consistent monotone of Ireland's history, which bored Nolan to tears. He wished he could have slept, like Emery, through the whole flight, except the fat man in front of him squashed his seat back as far as it would go so that Nolan could count the flakes of dandruff on the back of his head.

His parents, in the row behind him, were watching a boring news program on little TVs installed in the backs of the seats. Just as Nolan was starting to doze, Stanley broke into a monologue about the 1845 Potato Famine, and Nolan's mind danced to disjointed thoughts, wondering such things as whether Maribel was going to remember to feed Houston, or if Mr. Sanders (the poplar in the backyard) would brown under the grueling Boston heat.

The only thing that remotely interested Nolan was when Stanley told him about a local legend that the Bog of Allen was inhabited by werewolves. Nolan's mother scoffed at this and said the Bog of Allen was a "ruddy great peat swamp" that couldn't be home to werewolves because it was flatter than a pancake, so Nolan tuned out.

He had quite convinced himself this trip was going to be the most mind-numbing three weeks of his life when the plane started to descend. Disembarking through one of those moving ramps that attach to the plane's doors, Nolan stretched and yawned, almost tumbling over in the process as that blackout feeling stole over him. He took a few deep breaths to clear his head, and when he had recovered, he glanced at his watch, which he'd already forwarded by five hours. *Well, that's twelve hours of your life you can never get back,* he thought to himself.

It was getting dark, and a cool breeze played across the orange, green, and white of the Irish flags and the blue/gold of the EU flags stationed every few hundred feet. It was a stark change to the oppressive heat in Boston, and he shivered in his shorts and black T-shirt with Edgar Allan Poe's gaunt face printed on the front and a sarcastic quip underneath that said, "You'd be depressed, too, if *you* lived in Baltimore."

The drive out of Dublin was miserable for Nolan. It was almost dark, so there wasn't much to see of the city except for lights on the billboards and in the buildings, and the rented car was about the size of a riding lawnmower. After being stuck on an airplane all day, and now with all their luggage and five bodies crammed into this toy-sized car from the Czech Republic (of all places!), the drive to their final destination seemed like a never-ending nightmare.

They were heading to a town called Edenderry, about an hour or so outside Dublin. One of the most famous landmarks of Edenderry was the Rathdowns, the sprawling estate where they would stay for the duration of their trip. The grounds belonged to an old lady named Audrey Redding, a client of Nolan's aunt Florence, who had agreed to hold the wedding at her manor.

Rathdowns was famous enough to have its own Web page, so, of course, Stanley had memorized its entire history and proceeded to recite it for the cramped Marten family, whether they wanted to hear it or not.

"The main house was built in eighteen seventy-one," he was saying, "and it's since been modernized three times: once at the turn of the century, again during World War II, and then just recently…well, like, ten years ago…when Grahame Redding—that's the old lady's husband—passed away, leaving the estate to his widow, Audrey."

"So it's kind of like a castle?" Emery interrupted the monologue. "Never seen one in real life. Does it have water around it?"

"No, there's no moat; it's just a big house," Stanley replied. "It's got seventeen bedrooms, and it's redbrick. I should've printed out a picture of the place—"

"We'll see it soon enough, Stanley," Nolan's mother said, evidently not interested in an old mansion. The long flight and cramped drive seemed to have put her in a grumpy mood, too, and Nolan thought she also might be a little nervous about meeting her sister's husband-to-be.

Stanley continued, unperturbed. "It's got a bunch of barns, stalls, greenhouses, and a conservatory. But it's known for the ancient forest bordering the grounds. Oh! I forgot why the forest is so famous: there's a *cairn* on the property."

"What's a cairn?" both Emery and Nolan asked at the same time, shoving each other for a few more inches of room.

"An old pile of rocks," their mother answered flatly.

"Yeah," Stanley said, deflated. "It's like a marker from the Celts."

"Celts with a *k* sound, Stanley," Nolan's father corrected him. "You watch too much Boston basketball."

"Right. Celts. Anyway, this cairn's famous because it's, like, as old as Stonehenge or something, and none of the history buffs knows what it means or why it was put there. So, like, hippies come from all over the world to see it."

"Hippies?" Nolan's father blurted out with a smirk.

"Well, you know, those people that worship the earth, or whatever."

"Right." Nolan's dad nodded, looking at his wife. "Hippies, Darla. Continue, Stanley."

"According to the Rathdowns Web site, Audrey Redding's known to be 'eccentric and reclusive,' but she gives lots of money to historical societies and save-the-forest kinds of places."

"What's 'eccentric' mean?" Emery asked. He had an annoying habit of asking about words he didn't know.

"Crazy," Nolan's mother said. "And we're spendin' the next three weeks at the old loon's castle so's my *eccentric* sister can marry some Welshman with tattoos and earrings...."

"Now, now. Tell us how you *really* feel." Nolan's father laughed again, and his wife shot him a sour look. He held up his hands, steering with his knees, which were already near the windshield. "Hey, you *wanted* to come! Who'd want to miss out on the luxury of driving a motorized shoebox on the wrong side of the road, all across the Irish countryside? Ah, lighten up, Darla. You're as tetchy as Genevieve. And before you ask, Emery, *tetchy* means 'cantankerous.'"

"Wait. Aunt Florence's fiancé has tattoos and earrings?" Nolan snorted. "Nice."

"That is *so* cool," Emery agreed. "Can I get my ear pierced?"

"If Emery gets a piercing, I get a tattoo," Nolan demanded. However, he was terrified of needles; it was more about proving a point that it was only fair.

"No," his mother said. "Only idiots and hoodlums have tattoos and earrings."

"Dad has a Notre Dame tattoo, and he wore an earring in college," Nolan pointed out.

"That proves my point," his mother retorted.

An hour later, Nolan's first view of Rathdowns was obscured by a bouncing Emery, who was trying to get a glimpse of the "castle." An electronic gate boasting a wrought-iron crest was open, and the little car proceeded through to the winding drive beyond, surrounded on both sides by evenly spaced linden and cherry trees. Off in the dark distance of rolling meadows, lit by rows of lanterns, dense copses of shadowy trees could be seen with patches of cultivated flowers everywhere.

But on the north end of the estate, domineering and oppressive, stood the centuries-old Rathdowns Forest. It was so dark, no light seemed to penetrate to the forest floor, and it looked like a great wall of black, wild and unkempt, ominous, threatening the manicured gardens nearby. For the first time in his life, Nolan felt a little nervous about trees, and he was quite sure he had no desire to speak to any of those in this particular wood.

When the manor itself came into view, even Nolan's mother gave a low whistle of appreciation. The place was huge. Three stories, maybe four, all windows, widow's walks, and stately redbrick, with flower boxes, porticoes, and pillars. Warm lights glowed from the windows, as if to welcome the Americans.

The car circled the massive marble fountain before the impressive steps leading to the front door.

All three children clambered out and stood dwarfed by the building before the adults could disentangle themselves from the car. Several footpaths were marked with white wooden signs, pointing out walks to the barns and gazebos. A large pond was off in the distance, illuminated by a spotlight beneath a fountain that changed colors as it sprayed water into the air.

The double oak doors opened, and Aunt Florence bounded down the front steps as if it were her mansion they had just pulled up to. She must have been watching for their arrival.

She seized her sister in a tight hug and exclaimed, "Lord bless me soul, you've arrived!" She was shorter than Nolan's mother (who was not a tall person) and a bit plumper. The same bright red hair fell past her shoulders, but her eyes, like her sister's, were blue, not green like Nolan's.

Florence gave Nolan's dad a sideways hug and greeted Stanley, then turned to face Nolan and Emery. Her hands flew to her mouth. "Lord bless me soul!" she exclaimed again. "Is this wee Nolan? And teeny Emery?" They were both crushed in a tight hug. "Why, they're regular weeds, aren't they? My word, they've grown, Darla, haven't they?"

Emery shrugged out of her embrace, mumbling a hello.

"Nice to see you again," Nolan managed, his voice breaking as Aunt Florence let him go. Something faint in the damp Irish air reminded him of mildew, and it bothered his lungs. His aunt's overpowering perfume didn't help, either. He turned his head and took a quick puff from his inhaler.

"Kent's waiting, Mother. And no one can find Audrey."

Everyone turned to see Genevieve Eleanor standing in the doorway, looking impatient.

Nolan's cousin was a bit over fifteen. She was taller than her mother, and much thinner, with light honey-brown eyes and long auburn hair that hung to her waist. Genevieve was graceful and confident, with a complexion overdone in makeup that Nolan could see from down by the driveway. She was dressed in fancy designer jeans with glittering fake diamonds on the pockets, a wide black belt, and a frilly white blouse. Nolan almost burst out laughing when he saw her, all dressed up to welcome the guests, but then he realized that, as conceited as she was, she probably *always* dressed like that.

"Are you lot just gonna stand outside in the dark? Food's gettin' cold." Genevieve had a very high-and-mighty-sounding accent that wasn't quite Irish and wasn't quite American; it was like an aristocratic, nasal twang that made Nolan's skin crawl. He caught Stanley's eye and made a nasty face that was half hidden by the dark. Emery giggled.

"Right," Nolan's mother replied, sounding a little put off. "Just come down here and help us carry in the luggage, Genevieve, dear."

"How're you kids?" Genevieve offered to the three boys as they gathered the luggage. She carried one small handbag.

"Kids?" Nolan fired up. *Where does she get off…?* But Genevieve had already disappeared inside the residence, looking high-handed. Nolan gave Stanley and his younger brother a foreboding look and muttered, "This is gonna be a long three weeks."

Rathdowns Manor was elegant and rather cold. It reminded Nolan of a museum where a person must not touch anything for fear of contaminating it with germs. It was sterile and opulent at the same time, and it would've been impossible to feel comfortable there. It was the size of four shopping centers stacked on top of each other, but with a labyrinth of corridors and staircases chopping them up into a bunch of different rooms. He wasn't sure he liked the place.

Florence showed them to their rooms on the third floor and said she would give them a few minutes to get settled. Nolan's parents were across a long hall lined in rich, red carpet. The boys were placed in a huge bedroom with a walk-in fireplace and two four-poster beds. Tudor-style leaded windows overlooked a well-lit garden unlike any Nolan had seen before. There was a small goldfish pond, a reflecting area with a white gazebo, hundreds of flowers, and topiary mazes made out of bushes. And that was just what he could see in the light of the lanterns.

"This place is spooky," Emery decided, throwing his suitcase on the overstuffed black leather sofa that would be his bed.

"Yeah, but it'll be cool to explore the grounds," Nolan said, trying to make out more details.

"We're kinda like the Pevensie kids," Stanley put in, unpacking his suitcase into an ornate white armoire with gold trim. "You know, staying at the Professor's house."

Before Nolan could reply, a strong knock on the door startled him. As he pulled it open, he came face-to-face with a giant-sized man who laughed and stuck a massive hand in the boy's face.

"There's the lads!" the huge man chortled. "Name's Kent Taylor. I'm ta marry yore aunt!" His accent was almost impossible to understand, and he rushed all his words together in excitement.

Kent must have been six feet six inches tall, which, to Nolan's limited knowledge, was rare for a Welshman. He had dirty-blond hair that fell well past his shoulders; right now, it was gathered in a ponytail. His crystal blue eyes peered out above a well-groomed beard surrounding a muscular face—something Nolan had never known it was possible to possess. The man had tattoos on the meaty part of both arms; they were sayings in a language Nolan guessed was Welsh (which seemed to be comprised entirely of consonants). A silver earring dangled from his left earlobe, and in his right ear were two silver hoops, one up high in the cartilage.

Behind Kent stood Florence, beaming. She wasn't much taller than Nolan, so the two were an odd couple, Kent towering over his fiancée by more than a foot.

Nolan's parents came out of the bedroom across the hall and drew up short at the mountainous man in front of them. The pictures they'd seen didn't do Kent justice.

Nolan's father collected himself and offered his hand to Kent. "It's really very nice to meet you, Kent. Nolan Marten. And this is my wife, Darla. I see you've already met our sons, Nolan Junior and Emery. That's our son's friend Stanley."

Nolan's mother shook Kent's hand. "I believe congratulations are in order."

"Thank ya, thank ya. I feel like the luckiest man alive, to be sure," Kent responded. "Can't tell ya what it means to me and Florence havin' ya here for the weddin'." He motioned to the children. "My daughter, Quinn, 'll be joinin' us tomorrow. Comin' from her school in France."

"Oh? So…you've a daughter, then?" Darla glanced at her sister. "Florence must've forgotten to mention that."

If Kent thought it was odd his fiancée hadn't mentioned his daughter to her family, he didn't show it. "She's me pride and joy. Let's see, she's, what, thirteen now? 'Bout the age of yore oldest there. My, how quickly they grow, eh? Wonderful Christian girl, superb morals, keen on schoolin'. She's gettin' top marks this year."

"Wonderful," Nolan's mother replied, casting another glance at her sister, who was wearing a lovesick grin. "So, are you Catholic?"

Kent burst into laughter. "Nah, nah. I'm a Protestant pastor."

Emery blurted out, "You're a preacher?"

Everyone chuckled, and Kent said, "That's right, my little man."

"You look like a biker."

Kent roared another laugh and tousled the nine-year-old's hair.

Genevieve came up the stairs at the end of the hall. "Audrey's joinin' us in the dining room. Let's eat."

Nolan thought she might have given Kent a dirty look, and he wondered if she didn't think too much of her mother's decision to marry the Welshman. But he wasn't entirely sure that the sneer wasn't aimed at him, Stanley, and Emery. He fought the urge to stick out his tongue at her as she glided regally back down the stairs.

They all followed her, up and down little flights of narrow stairs, through many different rooms, each one more elaborately decorated than the previous, until they came at last to the first story once more and entered the dining room, which looked like the Oval Office of the White House. There were statues and plush carpets, a huge, cold fireplace, and man-sized portraits of old people on white horses chasing red foxes. The table itself was at least fifteen feet long, solid wood, with carved legs and chairs almost too heavy to move. It reminded Nolan of something out of the *Dracula* book, maybe, confirming that he didn't like Rathdowns. The other boys were awed by the place, and the adults were talking about the architecture and furniture.

"There's a suit of armor in our bedroom," Nolan's father told his boys. "You'll want to see it."

"Really, Audrey's not overly fond of the place," Kent was saying. "But it's an historical landmark 'round here, and her husband ran the place for forty-some-odd years. Addie was raised here, which is me reasonin' for her turnin' out the way she did!" He laughed.

"Sorry. Addie?" Nolan's mother asked.

"Adelaide is Kent's ex-wife," Florence supplied. "She's Audrey's daughter."

"Oh, right. S'pose ya wouldn't know that," Kent said.

His mother looked even more puzzled. "Wait. So, Kent's daughter—"

"Quinn," Florence provided.

"Yes, Quinn. So, Audrey is Quinn's *grandmother*, then?"

"That's right." Kent nodded as if there were nothing unusual about this.

"But that means Audrey is hosting the wedding for you—her own daughter's *ex*-husband—to remarry Flo—"

Aunt Florence cleared her throat, looking a little embarrassed. "That probably seems a bit strange, right? But Audrey does not get along well with Addie—"

"And why are we talking about my wayward daughter when we should be celebrating a wedding?"

Everyone turned to see Audrey Redding enter, dressed in the wildest-looking outfit Nolan had ever seen. The woman was probably in her sixties, with her gray hair pulled up in a bun and tucked under what could only be a paisley nightcap with a dangling tassel. She was dressed like she was heading for a safari in khaki trousers with lime-green hiking boots and what Nolan took to be a maroon riding vest over a white bullfighter's shirt. She wore no jewelry, no makeup.

She seemed strong-willed but easily distracted, like a poet who could box. Her skin was very wrinkled, and age spots covered her weathered hands. Nolan figured she had been a tomboy in her youth. Her accent was very soft and easy to understand.

"Audrey, these're Florence's family from America," Kent said, introducing Nolan's parents. Audrey's manners were impeccable; she greeted them cordially.

Nolan's mother looked like she didn't know quite what to say. "Er, thank you very much for bein' willin' to have us all here."

Audrey's smile seemed genuine. "A trifle, dear, a trifle. This old, decrepit money pit has not been put to such a good use in a hundred years. I'm very fond of Kent and my granddaughter Quinn, and Florence has made them both happy. Thus, her family is more than welcome, more than welcome. *Fy nghartref yn eich cartref.*"

"Whoa!" Emery exclaimed. "What does *that* mean?"

"It means 'my home is your home,' young man," Audrey replied, turning to face the boy. "And who might you be?"

"Emery Wyatt Marten, ma'am. I'm nine years old." And he gave a little bow like he was meeting royalty. Genevieve rolled her eyes, and everyone except Audrey burst out laughing.

"Well, Emery Wyatt Marten"—Audrey returned the bow—"*céad míle fáilte*. That means 'one hundred thousand welcomes.'"

She introduced herself to Nolan and Stanley, then said, "I believe the cook has prepared a scrumptious meal. I've been told something with seafood and duck. I'm sure everyone is starved. Would you care to sit down?"

A butler, whom Nolan had not even seen standing at attention in the corner of the room, nodded and disappeared to summon the meal. Nolan couldn't help but be impressed. This lady had *servants*.

As they sat, Audrey said, "Again, welcome, all. And please forgive me for not being there when you arrived, but the leeches—alas, that's my entourage of worthless doctors—demand an inordinate amount of my time, and since there are too many witnesses around Rathdowns for me to kill them and bury their skeletal remains out in the forest, you see, I must allow them to waste my time. My apologies."

The Americans gave a nervous laugh. It was an odd thing to hear from such a polite woman as they'd seen so far. Nolan couldn't tell if the old lady was joking or perhaps a little crazy. At any rate, with her around, perhaps the three weeks there wouldn't be quite *so* boring.

During dinner, Genevieve didn't deign to look at the "kids" the whole meal. She excused herself about fifteen minutes later to make an "important phone call," and they didn't see her the rest of the evening.

Once everyone had finished the dessert of bananas foster and the adults had enjoyed a cup of coffee, the children were dismissed for the night, but Nolan knew he wouldn't be able to sleep at all. It was just too creepy, the old, cold mansion in a foreign country, and with five hours of jet lag, it was late afternoon to his internal clock. He could tell it would be a sleepless night and he'd be a zombie in the morning. On top of it all, he felt like he might be coming down with a head cold, which was worse for him than for most people due to his asthma. Typical.

Even after sleeping on the plane the whole flight, Emery was curled up with a down-filled coverlet on the overstuffed black leather sofa in the boys' enormous bedroom, snoring even before Nolan and Stanley had climbed into their four-posters.

The two boys spent an hour or so bashing Nolan's snobbish cousin before Stanley drifted off to sleep, leaving his friend to stare at the pale indigo alarm clock on the nightstand until the sun started peeking over the Irish horizon.

Feeling exhausted and floaty, Nolan rolled out of bed at six thirty in the morning and sighed as that strange, adolescent blackout feeling rolled over him. *Great*, he thought as he waited for the feeling to pass. *One day down, twenty-something more to go.*

4

The Snob and the Tomboy

The boys' first day in Ireland passed away in a jet-lagged daze. Nolan was definitely feeling a head cold coming on, but he didn't tell his mother. She would overreact and demand that Audrey's doctors take a look at him, or do something else that would embarrass him.

That afternoon, they were in what one might call the backyard, but it was about ten times larger than any backyard Nolan had ever seen, surrounded by a low wrought-iron fence. The Irish called it a "garden," and it certainly was, with lush green grass, shadow-throwing birches, red oaks, and smaller apple trees, a bird bath, and at least twenty different flower varieties. A cool breeze blew through, and Nolan was in heaven, in spite of the jet lag and looming cold.

Genevieve had been barricaded in her room most of the day, on the phone. But right after teatime, she condescended to speak to the boys in the garden, only because she was tired of all the wedding talk going on in the informal parlor. She came out still dressed as if going to a ballet, and milled around by the French doors for several moments in silence while the boys attempted to ignore her.

Emery was dangling over the lowest branch of the birch tree Nolan had named Isolde, while Nolan leaned against its thick trunk, studying the petals of a bright yellow rose he'd picked from a massive bush along the iron fence at the back of the garden. Stanley was sitting in a wicker chair, finishing his cup of tea and reading a book. Nolan realized Blue Time was getting closer.

"What're you three up to?" Genevieve broke the silence from the back doors, apparently put out that they had ignored her presence for so long.

"Hanging out," Emery responded, laughing at his own joke.

"Not a lot to do around here," Nolan put in, setting the rose on the ground next to him.

"There's loads to do in town, if you're old enough to go."

"Well, too bad for us *kids*, huh?" He focused on not letting his voice break.

Genevieve made an ugly face. "That's not what I meant."

"Yes, it was," Stanley stated, not looking up from his book.

"No, it wasn't. I just…oh, never mind." Genevieve made a dramatic move for the back doors but didn't go inside. When she realized the boys weren't distraught at the impending loss of her presence, she thought better of leaving and addressed Nolan. "Don't you think they're makin' this wedding out to be something bigger than it is? I mean, how can they talk so long about a thirty-minute ceremony?"

Nolan shook his head. "No idea."

Why doesn't she go away? he thought. *She can't actually* like *talking to us.*

"And isn't it completely crazy to have the wedding at Kent's ex-wife's mother's estate? There's something wrong with that, right? Honestly, I think I'm the only one in the family who's not gone nutters."

"Could've fooled me," Nolan said.

She ignored him. "You lot'll like Quinn, though. She's more of a boy than a girl, anyway. And don't buy that rubbish that she's 'so pretty,' and 'so smart,' and 'so wonderful.' Kent could never speak a negative word about his 'pride 'n joy.' He's obsessed."

Nolan rolled his eyes at Stanley, who had stopped reading. "Genevieve, we don't care," Nolan said. "Seriously. Don't you have some more makeup to go put on?"

It was a rather nettling thing to say, but Nolan thought she was trying to pester them on purpose, and he was determined not to let her get started. It didn't occur to him that perhaps she was attempting to start a conversation because she was bored and, deep down, was excited to talk to new people.

The fifteen-year-old curled her lips back in a sneer. "Oooh. That stung. No, really, ya cut me deep there." She snorted. "Yeah, real mature, but what did I expect from a *kid?*" This time she turned around with a flip of her perfumed hair and headed inside.

Nolan should've kept quiet, but he couldn't resist a final shot. "Oh, and *you're* such an adult. Like, barely two years older than me. Big whoop!"

"Just let her go." Stanley waved his hand, disinterested, and returned to his book.

Emery seemed excited about an argument breaking out. His head snapped from his brother at the base of the tree to Genevieve, who now whirled around with her finger in the air.

"You're just jealous 'cause my friends've got driver's licenses, and I won't be stuck here all summer with these stupid people talkin' about some stupid wedding."

"That's the second time you've mentioned the wedding," Stanley pointed out. "Now who sounds obsessed? Perhaps the wedding's bothering you, mmm? Maybe you don't like Mr. Taylor."

Genevieve turned to look at Stanley as if she hadn't realized he was there. "What are you talkin' about, little boy? Like I care who my mother traps herself with this time."

"Abandonment issues," Stanley told Nolan with a wise nod. "From her real father leaving her mother. She's got a gender bias and a distrust of authority."

Genevieve snorted again, and it was quite an unpleasant sound, something like a cross between a horse and a pig. "You're a chunky little munchkin, and you're gonna psychoanalyze me? Kent Taylor's a git, his daughter's a stuck-up imbecile."

"What's a git?" Emery asked.

"A contemptible fool," Stanley supplied.

"Talk about the pot and the kettle," Nolan jibed.

Emery laughed, even though he probably didn't know what *that* meant, either.

"She's got jealousy issues, too. With the stepsister." Stanley appeared unfazed at Genevieve's remark about his weight.

"Oh please, tubby, as if you know."

But now Nolan was getting angry. "Hey, don't make fun of my friend!" His voice cracked as he got flustered.

Genevieve laughed. "Why don't you keep quiet, pip-squeak, till your voice changes?"

"Why don't you go pile on another inch of zit cream, you puffed-up prima donna!" Nolan jumped to his feet and swooned in a mockery of Gen's theatrics.

"What's a primo-donner?" Emery asked, evidently not wanting to miss the finer points of older kids' name-calling techniques.

"Prima donna," Stanley corrected him. "First lady in an Italian opera, but we mean it like an egotistical, obnoxious brat."

"Oh!" Emery nodded.

Genevieve whirled on Stanley. "You keep outta this, fatty."

"I said, don't make fun of my friend!" Nolan took a menacing step toward his cousin.

Emery, overcome with excitement that they had degraded to terms he understood, like "brat" and "fatty," leapt off Isolde's branch.

"You're a disgusting little boy," was all Genevieve said to Nolan.

"And you're a bitter, toffee-nosed hag who's angry 'cause her daddy ran off and left her, and her mom's marrying a professional wrestler."

Nolan might as well have slapped her in the face from the way she reacted. She recoiled, and her bottom lip quivered as if she might cry. He felt awful. He'd gone too far, and he knew it. But before he could apologize, Genevieve raced back into the mansion, telling her mother to "clam up" when she chided her for slamming the French doors like she'd been raised in a barn.

There was several seconds' silence before Emery asked, "What's 'toffee-nosed'?"

"Means stuck-up," Stanley told him. And then to Nolan, "Well, that went well."

"I didn't mean to make her cry."

"At least she'll leave us alone now," Stanley pointed out.

"Yeah, but that's not right to make fun of her parents like I did. Not her fault."

"No, it's not the kids' fault their parents are weird."

Nolan realized Stanley wasn't talking about just Genevieve. "Yeah, but she called you fat," he reminded him

"I *am* fat." Stanley didn't seem hurt to say this.

"You're not fat," Nolan protested, "you're—"

"What, big boned?" Stanley smirked.

"*Elephants* are big boned," Nolan said with a smile.

"He's husky," Emery offered seriously.

The two older boys laughed. As Nolan opened his mouth to suggest they go find Genevieve to apologize, more shouting was heard coming from inside the house. The boys peered in through the windows to the informal parlor to see if Genevieve was laying into her mother again. Stanley pulled open the door to the kitchen and let Emery run in first.

"And you said the trip would be boring!" Stanley shook his head.

Nolan followed him inside. But it wasn't Genevieve who was yelling. There was a young woman standing just inside the informal parlor, yelling into a cell phone in what Nolan was sure must've been a foreign language, except that he understood pieces of it now and again. The four adults and a wedding planner were sitting on antique chairs, all eyes glued on the girl who was red in the face with frustration as she stamped on a magnificent Persian rug.

In all the tangle of the argument with Genevieve, Nolan had forgotten that Kent's daughter would be coming home from school that evening. Truth be told, the thought of meeting a new girl had been cause for slight concern with him, and he'd made it a topic of conversation with Isolde the tree.

A girl his age hanging out the whole summer.... If one thing—any one thing—made Nolan feel awkward and nervous, it was girls. (Genevieve didn't count, of course. She wasn't human.) He'd had zero experience with girls, except for a few bossy, overweight ones in class who were always making fun of his red hair.

Earlier, Nolan had tried picturing what Quinn might look like, based on her father; and in his mind's eye, he'd imagined a girl six feet tall with dangling crocodile's teeth for earrings and a bunch of tattoos.

The real-life Quinn was much different.

She was taller than him by a few inches, though certainly not six feet. Her eyes were a liquid blue, huge under light eyebrows, and her skin was tanned. Her sunny blonde hair, straight like her father's, was pulled back in a simple ponytail that fell to the middle of her back, with wisps sticking out here and there. She was dressed in a pair of ratty blue jeans and a faded gray T-shirt that was too large for her, probably her dad's. Her sneakers were shabby, and she wasn't wearing makeup at all. Nolan's first impression was that Genevieve was right: Quinn was a tomboy, like her grandmother seemed to have been.

Her suitcase and backpack had been dropped on the rug, and she was still yelling at someone on her cell phone. Her accent was ten times worse than her father's, and Nolan forgot his nervousness as he strained to understand what she was saying.

"Ya've completely lost yore mind, Mum. I'm not jokin' here! I'm perfectly capable of decidin' for meself t'go to Gran's—"

Quinn's mom, Addie, must have interrupted her daughter with a colorful slew of words, because Quinn's eyes got larger and larger the longer she was silent, her face going from red to purple as she tried to control her anger. Finally Quinn cut her mother short.

"Mum, that's enough! I'm already here, and yore makin' a scene. What's done is done, no use tryin' to change it. Da's lookin' at me, and there's all these nice Yanks sittin' 'round thinkin' yore a complete loony."

There was another interruption on the other end.

"I don't know what else t'tell ya, Mum. That's between you and Gran and Da. No, I don't really care. I have to go now—I love ya, but yore drivin' me crazy. Bye."

Without waiting for another tirade, Quinn hung up the phone and glanced around at everyone, her face returning to a normal color. "Right. Sorry 'bout that," she said.

Kent clambered to his feet, the antique chair creaking with relief, and he gave his daughter a bear hug.

"She's layin' into ya as well, eh?" he asked as she extricated herself from his grip.

Quinn nodded. "She'll get over it. Introduce me to the Americans."

"Friends, this's my daughter, Quinn. These're Florence's family." Kent pointed out each one in turn. "That's Nolan, Darla, and their son Nolan Junior, and his friend Stanley—they're yore age, 'round about. And that's Emery, the younger Marten boy. This is Jacoby, the weddin' planner."

Quinn raised her eyebrows and offered a smile. "Pleasure."

Everyone said hello, except for Nolan, who simply waved, that awkward feeling starting to creep up his neck again. He caught Stanley's eyes, the expression of which seemed to say to him, "*She's cute!*" Nolan frowned as if to respond, "*If you say so.*"

"Genevieve's skulkin' in her room, I s'pose?" Quinn hauled up her belongings and started to thread her way upstairs to her bedroom.

Nolan wondered if she liked Genevieve or not, as that would go a long way toward proving whether Nolan would like Quinn. As the adults settled back into their boring conversation, Kent lauding his daughter's qualities, the trio of boys traipsed back outside, since there was nothing better to do. It was full-on Blue Time now, and Nolan felt that rush of excitement he always felt as dusk fell. For a moment, he forgot that he hadn't slept in thirty-six hours and that he was fighting a summer cold.

"I think she's nice-looking," Stanley said.

Emery agreed, but Nolan merely shrugged, trying to appear cool to his best friend and brother. Deep down, he was afraid of making a fool of himself in front of Quinn.

As if on cue, she slinked outside moments later, closing the kitchen door with a soft click. Nolan willed himself to look unruffled.

"Can I join ya fellas?"

"Sure you can," Stanley answered for them.

Nolan watched her lanky frame bound onto the same branch Emery had occupied earlier.

"Ta. Adults talkin' nonsense, and I don't feel like answerin' Dad's questions about Mum, so I thought I'd come meet ya, seein' as how we're s'posed to be cousins, right?" Quinn drew a knee under her chin and perched like a bird. She had good balance, and Nolan noticed she was barefoot because she began picking at the chipped purple nail polish on her pinkie toe. She seemed so collected and self-assured, the exact opposite of himself, but he could hardly understand what she was saying because of her accent. The Welsh one was much stronger than the Irish.

"Well, I'm not a cousin." Stanley apparently wanted to make that clear.

"So, what'd ya guys do to make Gen so cross? She wouldn't tell, but I think ya made her cry." Quinn gave a wicked smile and then added, "Good one, that, by the way."

That settled it. Nolan knew she was all right, accent or no.

"She came out here and called you a toffee-nose and said Stanley was fat," Emery supplied, eager to show his mastery of the newly learned word.

"She didn't!" Quinn appeared shocked, but she laughed. "Talk about throwin' stones in a glass house. She's the most stuck-up berk I know! And don't ya worry 'bout her overmuch, Stan-o. She starves herself 'cause she thinks she's a heifer. Girl lives on rabbit food."

Stanley smiled.

"What's a berk?" Emery asked.

"Like an idiot." Stanley, of course, would know. "We don't use that word in the States."

Quinn nodded. "I wouldn't say it 'round the adults—some get offended by it, though I've no idea why." She paused, looking down at Nolan. "Oi, what's yore name—Nolan? You don't talk much, huh?"

Nolan started, and his palms were instantly sweating. "Oh, I—well, no, uh, I talk—"

Yeah, like a caveman, he thought to himself. He was deathly afraid his voice would break.

"That's good, Nols. Ya seem like a smart one." The others laughed, but Nolan wasn't quite sure she wasn't making fun of him. Her sense of humor reminded him of his father's, and he absolutely *hated* "Nols."

"Actually, Stanley's the smart one," Emery said.

"Oh, stop it, you're making me blush." But Stanley wasn't blushing. "You speak any other languages besides English?"

Quinn nodded. "I attend school in France."

"That's sweet," Stanley said. "*J'apprends le français aussi.*"

"*Votre prononciation est bonne*," she responded, and it annoyed Nolan a bit because he had no idea what either of them had just said. Quinn continued, "I take Latin at school, but it's a silly language, and I know some Italian words, too, but mostly not the polite ones."

Nolan didn't want to be left out of the conversation, so he ventured, "And Gaelic, too?" His voice squeaked, and blood shot from his neck to his ears, probably matching his hair in the failing Irish light.

She shrugged but didn't make fun of his voice, and Nolan thought that was pretty considerate of her. "Well, a tiny bit. Like 'hello' and stuff. Ya probably mean Welsh. We hafta take it in primary school—back home in Wales, I mean, not in France. Welsh's different 'an Irish, mind ya, but I know some words in both."

Now that she was expecting him to respond, Nolan didn't want to appear flustered, so he cast his mind around for something to say, hoping his voice wouldn't break again. "So, why's your grandmother allowing your dad to get remarried here at her home after he divorced her daughter? Shouldn't she hate him?"

Quinn was thoughtful for a second. "Hmmm. That's kinda confusin'. Mum left Da after she stepped out on him, and that made Gran really cross. So Gran's havin' the weddin' here to spite her. My mum tried to keep me from comin', but I like Florence, and I'm here to support me da."

Nolan thought the whole thing was odd but didn't say anything. What her weird grandmother did at her own mansion was her business.

The girl did remind Nolan of her grandmother, easily distracted, jumping around topics like her mind was running ahead of her mouth. "This yore firs' time in Ireland?"

The boys nodded.

"Dunno why Gran's so fond of it here. 'S a dreadfully borin' place, innit?"

"Not so far," Stanley sniggered. "You ever been to the States?"

Quinn looked up from her dirty feet and rested her chin on top of her knee, tucking a lock of yellow hair behind her right ear. "Nah. Don't really care to. Not overly fond of Yanks. Seems most of the ones I've met are all prats."

"What's a prat?" Emery asked.

"Same as a berk," Quinn answered before Stanley could. "Like, some'un dumb an' arrogant."

"Well, why not call him 'dumb and arrogant,' then?" Emery wanted to know. "And, hey, not all Americans are dumb and arrogant. I mean, some Irish people are dumb and arrogant, too!"

"You've only met, like, three Irish people in your whole life, Emery," Stanley said.

"I'm not Irish anyway," Quinn pointed out. "The ginger's more Irish 'an I am," she said, referring to Nolan's red hair, of course.

"Or you're English." Emery shrugged. "Whatever."

"Not English either. I'm Welsh. That's like sayin' yore Californian when ya live in New York."

"We're from Massachusetts."

"Whatever." Now Quinn shrugged, and all four of them laughed.

Blue Time faded away, but they continued talking in the garden through the evening until it got too cold. Nolan was exhausted and quite sure now that he was getting a stuffed-up head.

When they went inside, Nolan's mother started fussing over him, saying he should've worn a jacket. What if he caught cold? And was he having trouble with his asthma? He turned beet red as he caught Quinn, Stanley, and Emery snickering at him. "It's *summertime*, Mom," he said, pushing her off. "I don't need a jacket."

When his mother kissed him and Emery good night, Nolan's cheeks flamed with more embarrassment as he looked sidelong at Quinn, who was stifling a laugh. Her eyes twinkled at his discomfort.

Once the parents disappeared to their bedrooms, Genevieve skulked down into the parlor. She shot a wounded, angry look at the boys.

"Quinn." She said it like a curse word. "I'm not your messagin' service, but your grandmother would appreciate if you'd join her upstairs before goin' to bed. She was displeased you didn't come up to say hello before." Genevieve turned to go back upstairs, apparently put out that she'd been tapped to run errands for the old woman.

"Sure thing, Gen," Quinn called to her back.

"Don't call me Gen!" The fifteen-year-old stomped up the stairwell.

"Sure thing, Gen," Quinn repeated, and the boys tried not to laugh too loudly.

"She's liable to murder you in your bed," Stanley said.

Quinn shrugged. "She needs ta get over herself. I'm jus' takin' the mickey." And with that she saluted the boys. "See ya in the mornin', *kiddies*." She trotted after her future stepsister without another word.

"What's 'taking the mick—'"

But Stanley cut Emery off before he could finish his question. "You'd think your mother wasn't from here. I'm going to have to get you a dictionary or something, Emery. We can't be translating for you the whole time. It means 'making fun of.' Now let's go to bed."

"I like her," Emery decided as they started the long walk to their bedroom. "She's funny."

"Me, too," Stanley voted.

"She seems a little gruff, and sorta bossy," Nolan pointed out.

"Nah. You're just mad 'cause she called you 'ginger.' At least the summer won't be boring with her around," Stanley said with a yawn. He stared at his friend a few seconds. "Did you know you looked terrible, Nolan?"

"Gee, thanks, buddy. I think I've caught a cold."

"Shoulda worn a jacket like yore mummy tol' ya." Stanley was pretty good at faking accents.

The boys tromped up to their room, and Nolan felt like he would be able to fall asleep at last. That would be the best thing for his oncoming cold—a decent night's rest. When he dropped off, he was thinking he agreed with Stanley—the summer might not be so bad with Quinn around, as long as he could get her to stop calling him "Nols" and "Ginger."

And at least she'd be good at pestering Genevieve.

5

Storms and Sickness

Nolan was dreaming. He was in the spooky forest bordering Rathdowns Manor, and he was conversing with a slender silver birch tree when he realized he was thirsty. Deathly thirsty. The kind of thirst that cannot be quenched by soda or Powerade, only by fresh, ice-cold water. And it woke him up.

Rubbing his eyes, he sat up in the four-poster and glanced at the glowing face of his wristwatch. It was three thirty in the morning. He felt terrible. His forehead was beaded with sweat, his palms were clammy, his eyes were watery, his nose was stuffed up, and his chest wheezed. He reached for his inhaler in the dark and heard Stanley's rhythmic snores from the other bed across the room. Emery sounded asleep, too.

Nolan was sick. His cottony mouth and throat demanded water. He slid out of the bed and into his shorts and a pair of slippers. That adolescent swooning came over him, and he waited until the light-headedness passed and his eyes adjusted to the dim light.

The night was cold. His soft steps echoed as he clicked open the huge door and shuffled down the hall toward the bathroom. Fancy electric sconce lights flickered on the walls, casting a soft glow along the hallway. It was a little spooky.

He was startled to see Quinn, and a shriek caught in his throat. She was leaning against the wall by the door to her room, still dressed. Even in the low light, he could see she'd been crying. Her face was puffy and her hair disheveled. Something was wrong. She sniffed and wiped the back of her hand across her nose, grasping something that glittered.

"Quinn, are you okay?" he whispered.

She squealed so loudly that Nolan jumped back, his skin crawling. "Cor, Nolan!" she hissed loudly. "Ya scared the—" Her empty hand flew to her mouth, evidently to keep herself from swearing.

"I'm sorry!" Nolan felt stupid. Of course she would freak in this house, in the middle of the night, with some moron calling out to her in a dimly lit hallway.

She took a few deep breaths. "Don't do that. My heart stopped, really!"

"I'm sorry," he said again, not knowing what else to say.

Quinn shook her head. "Why are ya up?"

"I'm sick," he replied. "I needed water. Why aren't you sleeping?"

Her face fell, and she looked distraught, his question having brought back to her mind why she'd been crying. "I've been talkin' with Gran all night. She's…she's not doin' good. She, uh, she told me she thinks she's dyin'."

Nolan was taken aback, his cold forgotten. "Oh, wow, Quinn. I'm really sorry. That, uh…." *What do you say to something like that?* he wondered.

The teenager rubbed her face. "I jus' thought it was one of her ridiculous stories, but she gave me this, so I think she's serious." She held up the thing that Nolan had seen glittering in the pale light and handed it to him.

It was like a large, clear jewel. Very heavy, not like thin glass, which was Nolan's first thought. It was solid, about the size of a walnut, attached to a thick, sturdy silver chain. Even with the little light there was in the hallway, its facets sparkled, cut like a pear-shaped diamond—except that a real diamond this size would be worth millions of dollars, he guessed. Maybe hundreds of millions.

"It's beautiful," Nolan whispered, handing the pendant back to Quinn.

"It's real," she said, slipping the chain over her head and tucking the gem under her shirt. "I mean, Gran says it is, at least."

Nolan's eyes got wide. "You mean like a real diamond?"

Quinn shrugged. "Unless Gran's tellin' one of her stories, but I would think in this case she'd tell the truth." She reached down and picked up a book on the floor by her bare feet. It was wrapped in thin brown straps of leather. "She even gave me her journal." Her eyes misted again, and she looked away from Nolan.

"Quinn, I...." But he didn't know what to say; everything in his head sounded brainless. "Did she say how long she thinks she has?"

Quinn spoke in a rush, like she was getting it off her chest, and Nolan struggled to understand her. "Few months. A little more. I don't think it's cancer; she's just...ill, and she knows it. Y'know, like one of those feelings. That's why the solicitors and doctors are all over the place, and why she's havin' the wedding here. She told me it was an excuse to bring me here, to give me the pendant and her journal. Without some elaborate event, Mum wouldn't let me see her alone. She told me the diamond was a precious heirloom from ages past, and I should guard it with my life. It must be worth millions of pounds, don't ya think? I don't know why she didn't give it to Mum." Quinn cocked her head and rolled her eyes. "Well...yes, I do. But Mum's gonna have a stroke when she finds out."

Nolan coughed, which reminded him of his illness.

Quinn's expression softened. "I forgot ya said ya weren't well. How'd ya take sick? Seemed all right today."

Nolan shrugged. "From the flight over? I dunno. Maybe breathing all that dry, recycled air on the plane. And not sleeping, like, two nights in a row. Could be the damp air, out in the country. Who knows?" His voice cracked. "I need a drink of water."

"Come with me." Quinn led him to a lavish bathroom larger than most bedrooms. She filled a glass with tap water and handed it to Nolan. "I had jet lag once. Went to Australia on holiday with me folks when I was eleven. Couldn't sleep for two days."

"Yeah." He drained the glass, then handed it back to her, and she filled it up again. "I still feel kinda floaty."

After his third glass, he felt satiated. He wanted her to leave so he could use the toilet, but she just hung around, like she didn't want to go to bed. Nolan felt bad for her, even though his head hurt, so he tried to think of a way to get her mind off her grandmother. He coughed and wished he'd brought his inhaler.

"I have asthma," he said out of the blue, like it was a confession.

"Heard yore mum frettin' about it. That's gotta be difficult. Sometimes ya feel like ya can't breathe, huh? D'ya have one of those inhaler things?"

Nolan nodded.

"When's yore birthday?" Quinn had a habit of jumping around topics like a restless cat with a twitching tail.

"October fourth."

"Mine's the sixteenth of May. I'm older 'n you!"

"By, like, five months—big deal. You sound like Genevieve."

"Yeah, but five months means I'm in charge; ya gotta do what I say."

"That's the stupidest thing I've ever heard."

"Aye. It's just the rules. Like havin' me very own slave."

"Whatever! Give me another drink of water." They both giggled as she handed him the empty glass for him to fill.

They were silent for several seconds, and Nolan was about to excuse himself, blaming his aches, and head back to bed.

Quinn kept him by asking, "What's yore middle name?"

"Elliot. What's yours?"

"Can ya keep a secret?" Quinn's eyes glittered.

"Yeah."

"So can I."

"You're a git," Nolan retorted. And they giggled again. "I should probably go—"

"Do ya read?"

"Yes, I can read! Can you?" Nolan felt like she was making fun of him. Here he was, sick, trying to cheer her up because her grandmother was ill, and she was asking him if he could read!

She cocked her head. "No, I know ya can read. That's not what I meant. I mean, d'ya like to read?"

"Oh." Now he felt a little guilty. She was just trying to keep from going to bed so she could quit thinking about her grandmother. But her inflection was as confusing as her accent. "Y-yeah, I love to read. I mean, I'm good at reading. Reading's okay."

Quinn pushed her lips together and wrinkled her chin. The Welsh accent disappeared as she spoke in a guttural, Tarzan-like voice, "Yes, Nolan can read. Nols like bookees." She beat her chest like a gorilla and flashed a grin.

"Ha ha." Nolan rolled his eyes. "And I hate 'Nols,' by the way."

"All the more reason to call ya it, then."

"Whatever. I'll start calling you 'Q-ee' or something."

"Sorted."

There was more silence, and Quinn looked out the bathroom window. Rathdowns Forest was black along the horizon. Fog slithered along the ground. Even the lanterns around the gardens couldn't penetrate the inkiness of the forest.

She bent and washed her face in the sink. As she dried her skin with a plush hand towel, she asked, "Ever hear about the Greenmen?"

"Yeah. Maybe." A person couldn't love plants as much as Nolan and never have heard of Greenmen. Folks made wood carvings of them to sell at Celtic festivals in Boston. "They're, like, Treepeople who watch over the forest. Only come out at Blue Time."

"Blue Time?"

"Uh, the magic hour of dusk, right?"

Quinn nodded. "Gran's nuts over 'em. See, this estate is famous. The trees in the heart of the forest are hundreds of years old, maybe a thousand or more. It's why they built a cairn here, she says, to honor the Greenmen."

Nolan remembered Stanley talking about the cairn, but he didn't remember him saying anything about Treepeople.

"She actually believes in Greenmen?" he asked.

Quinn shrugged. "Who knows what Gran really believes? Probably, yeah. She talks to the trees. I've heard her. Calls 'em by name."

Nolan started. "Uh, do you believe in Greenmen?"

"No." Quinn thought for a second. "Well, I never did before tonight. I just read some of her journal—it's full of facts 'bout her adventures in a secret world back when she was a girl. Been there hundreds of times, she says. Calls it the Otherworld, like in the Irish myths—a part of our world that's hidden behind a magic Veil. Spent all this time with Greenmen, thinks they're comin' back for her, she was on a quest to find a magic song or somethin'…. I s'pose she could be out of her mind, but the details are incredible, she's got maps and everything—"

A knock on the bathroom door made them jump nearly out of their skins. They both squealed as Genevieve barged in. "It's four in the morning. What the—"

"Genevieve! Is everyone tryin' to give me a heart attack? Flippin' knock, for Pete's sake!" Quinn threw the hand towel at her future stepsister.

"I did knock. Why are you two awake? And shut in a bathroom?"

"Mind yore own business," Quinn said.

"I'm sick," Nolan hastened to explain, realizing the situation was a little weird-looking. "Quinn got me water." He coughed for emphasis.

Genevieve ignored him. "Quinn, you been cryin'? Your eyes are all red and puffy."

"Hang it, Genevieve. Mind yore own business!"

"I'm trying to—but you're both in the way, gigglin' like little kids! Surprised you've not woken the whole house!"

Quinn muttered something that might have been a bad word, but Nolan couldn't be sure with her accent. When she was angry, he lost almost any chance of understanding her speech. She waved good night to him, shot Genevieve a nasty look as she pushed past her, stomped down the hallway, and slammed the door to her room.

Genevieve scoffed. "Well, that was pleasant. Little brat and her 'Christian morals.' Needs a bar of soap in her mouth." She looked down at Nolan and frowned, seeming surprised he was still there. "Nolan. Get out. I need to use the loo."

"Ewww. That's so gross, Gen." Without another word, Nolan shuffled down the hallway to the boys' room and climbed back in his bed. Stanley and Emery were oblivious that he'd been gone. He punched his pillow. Four glasses of water, and he hadn't used the bathroom.

But that's not what was making him feel agitated. He felt awful from the sickness, and for Quinn. He had no idea what it would feel like to find out he was about to lose someone he loved.

And what about these Greenmen, and Audrey running around with them as a little girl? Nolan wanted to dismiss it as the ranting of an old lady with a cracked imagination, but he couldn't. No matter how much he tried to rationalize that Audrey was losing her mind, he found himself wanting to believe her about the existence of this Otherworld. And it seemed like maybe Quinn did, too.

And, yeah, maybe Stanley was right. Quinn was sort of cool. Kinda. Maybe.

He was able to fall into a fitful sleep with that thought swirling around in his clogged head.

The next morning, Quinn frowned as Nolan wandered into the kitchen. He knew he didn't look very good: greasy hair, bloodshot eyes, blotchy skin, kind of pale green.

"Ya better not get me sick, mate!"

Nolan's father felt his forehead as his mother popped a thermometer in and out of his mouth.

"Thirty-eight point two degrees," his mother pronounced with a worried frown. "We'll hafta cancel the trip into town."

"Darla, we can't do that," Nolan's father protested. "Florence and Kent have got a million things to do, and we promised to go with them. They need our help. Otherwise they'll be stuck with that fop Jacoby all day."

"Then you can go with them, Nolan. I've got to stay and watch over him. He's got a fever over a hundred."

"Mom, I'm not dyin'. It's just a cold." Nolan's voice sounded ridiculous with his stuffed nose.

"Florence, what d'ya think?" Kent turned to his fiancée. "We could go into Dublin coupla days from now."

Quinn frowned. "That's stupid, Da. Really. With the weddin' so close? You lot should go. It's not like there aren't people in this house who can take care of him if he needs somethin'. Right, Nols?"

Nolan nodded. "Her grandma's here, too."

His mother reluctantly gave into the pressure from the other adults to leave Nolan in Audrey's care. The grandmother hadn't been downstairs yet, but she sent word through Genevieve that if it would make Darla more comfortable, she'd be delighted to send for her personal doctors to have the boy looked over. Nolan was marched upstairs to his room, where he undressed and climbed into bed.

His mother left the butler about seven thousand instructions and then allowed herself to be piled into a Land Rover belonging to the Rathdowns. At least they'd be traveling to Dublin in style.

The other kids decided to stay at the manor, although they were given strict instructions not to be in close proximity to Nolan. After noon, two doctors showed up and gave Nolan a once-over. They deemed it nothing more than the common cold but said that Nolan should be looked after with his asthma, in case it settled in his lungs. Other than that, rest and warm liquids were the treatment prescribed.

Grandmother Audrey made an appearance in his room soon after the checkup to wish him a speedy recovery and revealed she'd had weak lungs as a child. Nolan made no mention of his conversation with Quinn from the night before. Audrey looked to be in reasonably good health, and he wondered if her sickness was more mental than anything else. But she seemed distracted, maybe even nervous.

Nolan dropped off to sleep, wondering if Audrey knew something they didn't, even as unbelievable as her story was.

A peal of thunder startled him awake. His cold medicine was clogging his head. What time was it? He'd taken off his wristwatch, but the indigo clock on the nightstand said half past seven. Blue Time. The sky was turbulent and shredded, a gloomy blue-gray with low thunderheads, and a ghostly mist crawled through the grounds of Rathdowns. Summer rain fell in a solid, soaking sheet, and Nolan shivered.

The door burst open, and Stanley came into the room, with Emery hot on his heels. Genevieve came in a few seconds after with a scowl on her face and a cell phone in her hand.

Nolan recoiled, drawing the comforter up to his chin. "Genevieve, get out! I'm not dressed!"

She rolled her eyes. "Don't be an idiot, Nolan."

Stanley said, "Quinn's gone running off after her grandmother, barefoot, in a nightgown."

"They're both outta their minds," Genevieve proclaimed.

Nolan was confused. "In the rain? Why's Audrey in a nightgown?"

"Not Audrey. Quinn!"

"I'm about to call her dad," said Genevieve. She started punching numbers into her phone.

"Hold on. Why's Quinn in a nightgown?"

"Said she wasn't feeling well after lunch," Stanley answered. "Wanted to lie down and read. Been by herself all day. I thought maybe she was sick, too."

"Her grandmother just jumped down the stairs while we were eating dinner, and she ran out into the storm," Emery said. "Quinn must've saw her out the window. We heard her yell, and then she tore after her before we could ask what was going on."

Lightning lit up the window. Seconds later, there was a crash of thunder, and the lights flickered.

"Where's the butler?" Nolan asked as he grabbed his bathrobe at the end of his bed. He sucked back mucus dripping down his nose and held a hand to his forehead. He felt like garbage.

"No clue," Stanley said.

Genevieve went out into the hallway, still dialing a number, while Nolan cinched his robe and stepped into his slippers.

"The house seems deserted," Stanley continued. "We tried to find someone."

"Voice mail." Genevieve made an impatient sound. "Mum, everybody in this house has gone stupid. Give us a bell." She ended the call. "What's your parents' mobile number, Nolan?"

"They can't do anything from Dublin. My mom'll just panic and get in an accident, driving in this storm."

Genevieve huffed and called another number. "Oh, come on, Kent! Answer your flippin' phone." She paused. "Kent, Genevieve. Call us."

Nolan glanced at his brother, who was trembling with excitement, but Stanley seemed perturbed.

"I don't like this, Nolan," his friend said. "You're sick. Just wait for them to come back on their own."

Nolan shook his head. He knew what Audrey was thinking. "It's Blue Time," he said, as if that explained it.

"What?" Genevieve looked at him as if he'd lost his mind, too.

Nolan didn't explain further. He led the troupe out the bedroom and down the winding steps to the foyer. The house was dark, except for the dining room and the repeated flashes of lightning outside. The windows rattled and fogged from the pounding rain. He wrenched open one of the front doors and was greeted by a blast of cold, wet wind. Branches were tossed willy-nilly along the front lawn; leaves swirled as if they were caught up in tiny tornadoes. It was downright creepy.

Should've put on shoes, Nolan thought. "They're at the cairn. We've got to hurry. Come on." He plunged out into the storm, followed by Emery and then Stanley, who was still trying to reason with him.

Genevieve trailed last, as if against her better judgment. "This is so stupid!"

Nolan broke into a run, which was hard to do in slippers that sank into the muck. He was drenched to the skin in moments, and his lungs burned like fire.

Dang it. He'd left his inhaler next to his wristwatch. Maybe this wasn't such a hot idea.

The four children raced down footpaths toward the forest's bristling edge. Moans and creaks and shrieks from protesting trees reached their ears, and Emery drew up short.

"We're not going into the forest, are we, Nolan?" But the nine-year-old had to jump into a run to keep up with his brother and Stanley. Gen brought up the rear, complaining about the rain.

"There they are!" Stanley shouted over the wind.

The cairn really *was* just a pile of old black rocks stacked in a roughly circular fashion, about eight feet high. Nothing much to look at. But standing there for centuries at the mouth of the gaping, ancient forest, backlit by forks of lighting high overhead that were answered by rumblings of rolling thunder, it held a certain solemnity; and the air crackled with energy as they approached Quinn and Audrey, who were engaged in an argument that could be heard over the gale.

"Have ya completely lost yore mind, Gran? Are ya tryin' to kill yoreself? We're gonna get struck by lightnin'!"

"What's going on?" Nolan yelled, his voice cracking, as they stopped in a semicircle around the two women at opposite points of the cairn. Rain streamed from their long hair. Quinn was barefoot, standing in an inch of mud, wearing a tartan nightgown that fell to her ankles. Audrey was dressed for a safari in a leather bomber jacket and fedora, like some elderly female Indiana Jones. She raised a finger at Quinn.

"You have no idea what you are talking about, child! He is coming for me. Finally! Watch and see."

"What are you two doin'?" Genevieve stamped her foot, sending a spray of muck into the air. "We need to get inside the house this instant! Quinn, I'll call your father!"

"Gran, there's no such thing as talkin' trees!" Quinn insisted. "Yore ill. Yore mind is dimming. You know Dad'll help ya. Let's get inside!"

"I am not senile, girl! You can't possibly believe that—did you read the journal? What about the diamond? Haven't you put it together? Do I look crazy?" Audrey's eyes flashed with fiery passion.

"It's a story, Gran! A children's fairy tale! There's no secret wor—"

The sky split, and all six were thrown on their faces as twin arcs of lightning struck the cairn and rippled out into the forest. Nolan's ears popped, and he went momentarily deaf. Who knows how they escaped electrocution? He sensed it wasn't normal lightning. The hair on the back of his neck and his arms stood at attention as he staggered to his hands and knees, shaking his head, his unkempt red hair slicked to his cheeks, rivulets of cold rain skewering his back.

His first thought was for Emery, and then everyone else followed a half second later. He was about to call out when Genevieve screamed like someone was pulling out her fingernails with a pair of pliers.

Stanley swore, and Emery cried out, "Nolan! Look!"

As Nolan jumped to his feet, his head threatened a blackout, and he couldn't catch his breath. He turned when he saw five other rain-soaked people rooted to the spot, mouths gaping, eyes focused in stark terror over his shoulder. He turned, and his mouth dropped open.

There, coming out of hiding from behind the tree line, was the massive form of a Greenman.

6

Tírcluddaithe: It Begins

Genevieve and Emery would not stop shrieking; Stanley stood frozen in silent terror; even Quinn was overwhelmed. She stood wide-eyed in defiant disbelief, babbling over and over, "This isn't happening. This *can't* be happening. None of this is real!" Audrey just stood there, looking justified, face beaming in the rainstorm. And Nolan stared up at the Greenman with a sense of not shock or even fear, but something more like, *"Haven't we met?"* He somehow knew that this was not a hallucination. He watched the Greenman as it strode into the clearing by the cairn.

Long fingers curled around a tall staff as the Treeman sank down to his knees. Even kneeling, he was seven feet tall at the shoulders.

What surprised Nolan more than anything wasn't the fact that a living Treebeing had just walked out of Rathdowns Forest—he'd somehow expected that as soon as he'd left the manor, oddly enough. What was incredible was just how *human* the Greenman looked. It wasn't like a tree had just sprouted to life and uprooted. To have called him a "walking tree" would've been insulting. He was as distinct from a tree as Nolan was from an ape. Images of the Ent Treebeard from the *Lord of the Rings* movies raced through his mind.

This wasn't like that at all.

It was like a man clothed in supple, sinuous wood. It seemed quite natural: his skin, his arms, his legs, his chest, his hair, his toes, his beard, his clothing, his...face. He had a face! A very normal-looking, handsome human face, only made of oak. His eyes glowed a warm, intelligent yellow.

Nolan realized the Greenman was in pain. That startled him back into the moment. The Treeman was wounded, his forearm bandaged with a black leather strip with dried blood around the edges.

And then he started singing.

That was weird.

At first, it was a slow, haunting, unintelligible melody that spoke to something deep inside Nolan of magic and antiquity; it shifted keys, moving from major to minor and back again. Somehow Nolan could feel it, even though he didn't know anything about musical theory. The Treebeing's voice was a rich, mellow baritone, and the tune reminded Nolan of the Celtic music they played at Irish festivals in Boston.

He felt the music first in the pit of his stomach, and the feeling climbed slowly up his body and into his brain. It was then he started to understand what the Treeman was singing. It rhymed. In English. That was weirder than the song itself.

But it wasn't *just* English. It was also still in the Treeman's language. Nolan heard the foreign terms as they were spoken, and his brain mysteriously filled in the appropriate words in English, just half a beat later. Soon Nolan's brain began to categorize vocabulary in the First Tongue; it wouldn't be that hard to learn the language with the Translation going on in his head simultaneously.

Emery moved to stand by Nolan, entranced and silent. Even Genevieve had stopped screaming. From somewhere behind him, Nolan felt Stanley. He wanted to look at Quinn and Audrey, but the song was telling him something that seemed important.

> *"The words we release, and the power they contain,*
> *Serve to build kingdoms, or destroy what remains.*
> *Among the vast and twisted, tangled lands,*
> *Each stained with twisted, tangled tongues,*
> *Chaos and confusion freely pass*
> *From careless lips, darken'd minds, and dirty lungs.*
> *But my Song is the key to unlock them all;*
> *Knots unravel, let true meanings fall.*

So my words, upon reaching the hearing ear,
Impart new strength and dispel all fear."

As the magic took effect, a last, lingering note was carried on the winds of the storm, and the Treeman fell silent. No one knew what to say. They all looked at each other, stunned that they'd understood the end of the Greenman's Song.

Nolan didn't even register that the mystical storm had stopped, and the twilight sky was very, very blue.

Audrey broke the silence with a reverential whisper. "Ysgafn Droed."

The words came across as "light of feet" in Nolan's brain. Odd name.

"Audrey," Ysgafn replied with a smile. "You look…different. Have so many summers passed?"

"You've come too late," she replied, bitter tears coming to her eyes. "It's not like when I was a child, all those times. I am old now, and I am dying."

"Yore *not* dyin'!" Quinn shouted. "Tell her she's not dyin'!"

Ysgafn studied Quinn for about five seconds. "She *is* dying. Everyone is dying. Well, nearly everyone is dying. But she might not be dying just yet."

"Okay, wait. Hold on just one blankin' minute here. Is this a joke?" Genevieve pushed her way to the front of the group and placed one hand on her hip. With the other hand, she pointed accusingly at Ysgafn. "What is going on here? What is that *thing*?"

Nolan was surprised she wasn't afraid of the massive Treeperson. After all, in his hand was a serious-looking staff twice as thick as Nolan's arm and at least ten feet long, tapered on the ends, its thick middle wrapped in black leather. The wood was intricately etched with ferocious, jagged symbols that looked like a warrior's handwriting. The Treebeing meant business. If he had the notion, he could finish them all with one sweep of that staff.

Genevieve, if she had half a brain, should've been paralyzed with fear. But then again, it *was* Genevieve.

"Gen," Stanley murmured, "let's try not to agitate the ten-foot-tall magical being from another world, okay? What d'ya say?"

Ysgafn sat down cross-legged so he could view the smaller ones, ignoring Genevieve, who huffed and placed both hands on her hips.

He said, "It's not really *another* world, just the *Otherworld*. It's the same as this one; it's just Veiled. They are called the Hidden Lands." He smiled at Stanley. "Your kind would call me Coeduine; my people are shepherds of the Forest. What's your name, wealth of Aossí?"

What does that mean, 'wealth of Aossi'? Nolan thought. The word for "Hidden Lands" was *Tírcluddaithe.* Coeduine meant "Treeperson," but Nolan's mind rendered it "Greenman." Ysgafn called himself a *Caevnaóir,* "Shepherd"; although, with that staff, Nolan would've called him a warrior.

But "Aossi" took Nolan's mind a second longer to decipher, like it had to search for an equivalent because the term didn't directly translate. Finally his brain registered: "Fair Folk."

But "wealth of the Fair Folk"? That still didn't make sense. Maybe the magical Song was broken….

"My name is Stanley Stewart," Stanley replied, mustering his courage. Nolan wasn't sure he'd be able to speak to Ysgafn without his voice trembling.

"Always a pleasure to meet Audrey's friends," Ysgafn said, extending a large hand toward the twelve-year-old. Stanley gulped and looked at Nolan with nervous, uncertain eyes. He cautiously reached up and shook one of the Coeduine's long fingers.

"I'm Emery Marten." And Emery shook the Treeman's finger.

"Have you all gone *insane?*" Genevieve shrieked. "You are talking to a *Tree!* I'm callin' the police—"

"Touch that mobile, and I'll beat ya with it, Gen; I'm not even jokin'," Quinn bit out, supporting her grandmother by the arm.

"How dare you threat—"

"Shut up, Genevieve," Nolan said.

"Did you find it? Did you find the Temple?" Audrey wiped her tears away and gazed up at Ysgafn with a look of wild longing.

"Yes," the Coeduine replied, smiling. "The Sanctuary was Veiled in Morsden all along. And not far from a village of Aossi."

The word *Morsden* became "Covering" in Nolan's head, and *Temple* was "Demeglwys." It was an odd sensation to hear a foreign tongue and yet have it convert into English inside one's brain. It took some getting used to.

Audrey clapped her hands and giggled like a young girl. "Morsden! Let's go!"

Ysgafn frowned. "Audrey, I don't know. I'm sorry. You do not seem well. Will your strength hold up?"

She nodded. "Yes, of course it will. My whole life I've waited for you to return. I am strong enough for this. And Quinn will go with me."

All the children started talking at once: Genevieve complaining about how everyone was loony, Stanley asking for clarification on what Ysgafn was talking about, Emery just jabbering, and Nolan arguing with Audrey and Quinn at the same time.

Finally Ysgafn slammed the butt of his staff into the wet earth three times, and silence fell.

"Please, my friends. I am wounded. I have very little time before the Veil is closed for the night." Here he glanced up at the sky, which was bluer with each passing moment. Looking down at Quinn, he addressed her regally. "Hail, last daughter of the Embroidery Queen. Would you accompany your grandmother and me on a quest?" He asked it so simply, as if he were inviting her to go get a cup of coffee with him.

"Who's the Embroidery Queen?" Stanley asked, but before the Treeman could answer, Quinn looked from Ysgafn to her grandmother, incredulous, and said, "Ya've gotta be—"

"We'll be back directly before the hour is up, and I assure you you'll be perfectly safe," Ysgafn said. "We can dismiss the guardian, open the Verse at the Sanctuary, and be back in a mere moment. You see, it takes someone of your bloodline to open it"—he turned to Stanley—"a daughter of the Embroidery Queen, Stanley. She was one of the first queens of Men, thousands of years ago."

"So Quinn's a princess," Stanley concluded.

Genevieve scoffed. "Oh, please."

"Then if Quinn goes, I go," Stanley demanded, looking to Nolan with an uncharacteristically fierce expression that told Nolan all he needed to know without any Translation in his head.

It was probably the bravest Nolan had ever been. He nodded to his best friend. "Me, too."

Ysgafn looked troubled. It took the Song of Translation a couple of seconds to find the right words for his reply. "Erm...well, rather...I mean, I suppose I could. But really, I don't think it's necessary for—"

"I'm not staying if you're going, Nolan." Emery looked like he was about to throw a fit.

"Hold on," Quinn put in. "I've not said I'll go."

"Of *course* you'll go, dear," Audrey responded, shocked. "Quinn, love, it's a fifteen-minute stroll in the woods."

"You haven't even told me what we'll be doing!"

"Why, the diamond, of course, Quinn. The diamond is a Verse of the Master Song."

"What diamond?" Genevieve wanted to know.

"What is the Master Song?" Stanley asked, talking over her.

"That would take more time than we have to explain," Audrey replied. "Suffice to say, it is important to the safety of our world as we know it. And *theirs*, as well." She inclined her head toward the Greenman.

"But last night…you said the diamond…" Quinn began.

Audrey waved her hand. "Do you think I'd let people know I possessed a fifty-carat diamond that contained a Song of indescribable power from a hidden world? I hadn't a chance to explain the whole truth to you, dear. Your miserable mother's held you from me for months."

"*Fifty* carats?" Genevieve's eyes widened.

"You mean, Mum knows about…?" Quinn said.

"My friends, we don't have time for this," Ysgafn interjected. He adjusted the wrapping on his wounded arm and winced. "Once the Veil drops, I won't be able to open it again until tomorrow evening, and I must un-Veil the Temple before the hour of dusk is through."

Genevieve tried a different approach with Quinn and adopted a motherly, caring timbre to her voice. "Quinn. Honey. Diamond or no, listen to me. You *can't* go traipsing off through the forest with this *monster*—"

"Excuse me!"

But Genevieve held up a cautionary finger toward Ysgafn, and the Treeman shrugged, letting her continue.

"Do you realize how utterly cracked this is? You are talkin' to a mystical mon—*person*—about going to some temple on some fairy-tale quest to recover an old piece of music no one took enough care to remember in the first place! It's rubbish! Now please, think clearly here. Your grandmother is not well, *you* are in a nightgown, and your father would birth kittens if he knew you were thinking about leaving with this, uh, *person*. Let's go back to the house and call a psychiatrist."

"They'll be perfectly safe," Ysgafn said.

"Then you can come back tomorrow when everyone is medicated and under shock therapy," Genevieve told him. "Does that sound like a deal?"

"I'll do it," Quinn said, staring directly and defiantly into Genevieve's eyes.

"Wonderful!" Audrey exclaimed.

Genevieve looked scandalized.

Quinn turned to face the Coeduine. "Yore name is Ysgafn?"

The Treeman nodded.

"Ya promise me, on yore friendship with my grandmother, a daughter of this Embroidery Queen, that I'll be safe, and we'll be gone only a couple minutes?"

Ysgafn nodded again.

"Yore certain ya can bring me back to this spot right here?"

"Yes, on my oath."

"Then I'll do it." She turned to the others. "You lot stay here. Keep an eye on Gran." She marched to the edge of the forest while the other children and Audrey erupted into a heated row, protesting.

"I'm not staying behind!" the old woman shouted.

"Gran, yore in no condition to go on a *quest*!"

"We must hurry," Ysgafn said. "The Veil will fall in less than half an hour. Who is going, and who is staying?" He pulled himself to his feet, towering over the humans.

"I'm going," Nolan shouted over the arguments, his voice squeaking. The others fell silent. "Stanley and I are going with Quinn," he said again. "Genevieve, you and Emery stay here with Mrs. Redding."

"Now you listen to me, young man," Audrey spouted, pointing a finger under his nose.

"I'm sorry, Mrs. Redding, but we'll be faster with just Quinn, and you know that. Stay here, and when we get back, you can explain all this stuff."

The grandmother looked ready to fall apart, but she swallowed her tears and nodded.

"Nolan, if you leave, I'll call your parents," Genevieve threatened.

"Please do. I don't really care."

"Nolan, please!" Emery whined. "You can't leave me here when you're going *there*. That's not fair."

"I'm sorry, squirt. Do you realize what would happen to me if something happened to you?"

"Ysgafn just said it's perfectly safe. Twice," he pointed out. "Quinn's grandma said she went over there loads of times when she was a kid, and she's come back all right."

"That's arguable," Genevieve muttered.

Nolan ignored her and said to his brother, "I'm sorry, Emery. No. Stay here and look after Quinn's grandmother."

Ysgafn was standing right at the forest's edge, his massive hand resting on Quinn's shoulder. The girl was looking pallid and scared, but she trembled with excitement. Or maybe it was a chill. She was soaked to the skin, after all. Nolan registered she was barefoot—how was that going to work?

But there was no time to comment on it; Ysgafn was walking into the forest, and the children started to follow. They instinctively knew to hold hands—Quinn, Stanley, and Nolan—and move in a straight line, like a preschool class crossing a New York City street.

"I always knew Blue Time was magical," Nolan whispered to Stanley.

"Would've been nice if you'd told me," Stanley rejoined.

Between the cairn and the entrance to the forest, a shimmering curtain-like Veil of mist rippled, causing the surroundings to blur and distort, like looking through a waterfall. Nolan started hyperventilating, and his lungs threatened to rebel.

The third to the last thing to reach Nolan's ears as they walked through the Veil separating Rathdowns from Tírcluddaithe was a panicked yell from Ysgafn as Audrey tried to rush the eleven-foot-tall mythical being, clawing for his leg. Nolan had no idea what happened next, but all the children broke handclasps in the confusion, almost as if they were flying apart, as they passed through the Veil. It all happened in a split second.

The second to the last thing he heard was Genevieve's cell phone ringing, then her shrieking, "Come back, you little brat!"

And someone small barreled into Nolan's back, toppling him forward; he saw a flash of Genevieve's polished fingernails on Emery's arm as the two of them fell through the Veil.

The last thing he heard was a curse as Ysgafn managed to grab Audrey. Their figures disappeared, but one of the Treeman's wooden hands hung in midair, and it clawed to grab Quinn's hand again. But it missed and shifted through the Veil with a ripple.

Stanley was pushed off to the side, alone, as he tumbled through it. Nolan scrambled to grab the nape of Quinn's nightgown; then something kicked him in the stomach, he fell into something like a vat of glue, and then he saw nothing but black stars.

They had gone to Another Place.

Part II

The Hidden Lands

7

Lost in the Woods

When Nolan regained consciousness, he couldn't breathe. His asthma was flaring up in the worst attack he'd had in many years. It didn't help that an insensible Quinn was lying rigidly on top of him. She must weigh as much as he did. Her dirty, wet hair was in his mouth, and his knuckles were white, fingers still clenching the collar of her nightgown. He pried his hands loose and slid out from underneath her. She moaned, but he was too panicked to worry about her. He needed his inhaler, but it was on the nightstand in his room at Rathdowns Manor. He rolled onto his bottom, tucking his head between his knees, willing his lungs to open, the air to go in and out. In and out. He wasn't suffocating. He was just fine. His lungs worked. He could breathe. Yes, he was breathing, in and out, in and out.

"Nolan? Nolan! Are ya all right?"

Through the dark red curtains of his matted hair, he looked sideways at Quinn, who was now kneeling next to him with wide, scared eyes. He made a wheezing sound, and she grabbed his hand.

"What do I do, Nolan? What do I do? How can I help?"

He shook his head. Nothing. In and out. In and out. His lungs felt wet and sticky. The air came in ragged gasps. But after several minutes, it began to get better. The attack was subsiding. His lungs opened a little, and more air rushed in; he swallowed, and his vision cleared. His pulse slackened to a more normal level of terror. His ears thundered, but the air went in and came back out.

At length he was able to say, in a hoarse gasp, "Fine. I'm okay. Where—where are we?"

Quinn looked around in a full circle. "We're alone. In some woods. It's kinda dark. I can't see anything but trees." She stood to her feet and began calling out names: "Gran? Ysgafn? Stanley? Genevieve? Emery? Anybody?"

"Don't. Yell." Nolan managed, holding up his hand to silence her.

"What? Why not?"

"The...Treeman...was wounded. His arm. Something...attacked him."

"He said it was perfectly safe."

"Safe...with him. Not...alone."

She looked around, bewildered. "Nolan, I'm scared. Where are we? Where are the others? What are we goin' to do?"

They were in trouble. Nolan took as deep a breath as he could and coughed. He remembered he was still sick, and soaked. The woods were freezing, silent, ominous—nothing except tall trees with the tops all but out of sight. There wasn't even a footpath, just everything dark and wet. They'd simply been dumped in the middle of some foggy forest. A light mist was in the air and clung to them like a sheet.

After falling through the Veil and finding themselves in a pile on the wet ground, they were covered with mud and grime. It had left them bruised and shaken. Quinn didn't even have shoes on. How had she planned on following Ysgafn through the Forest with no shoes? The absurdity of their situation would've made Nolan laugh if he hadn't been so scared.

He staggered to his feet, Quinn supporting him until he steadied. They were both trembling. Their teeth chattered, and their breaths left their mouths in wet clouds of mist.

Nolan knew he should be terrified, in a panic, screaming like a lost child, because he *was* a lost child. But something inside his stomach was bubbling warmth. It wasn't bravery, it was determination. He had to find Stanley and Emery. He had to get Quinn out of here. They had to get back somehow.

"Can ya make a fire?" Quinn asked.

"Everything's wet, and I don't have a lighter." And he didn't want to reiterate that there was *something* in this Forest that had injured a gigantic warrior made out of wood, and that fire might very well call it to them. They huddled close to each other for warmth, rubbing their arms. "We should start walking," he suggested. "Let's find the others. They can't be far."

"How d'ya know?"

"I don't," Nolan said.

"Where d'we go?"

"I don't know."

"How are we gonna get out of here?"

"I don't know!" Nolan snapped, then coughed.

"Don't yell at me, Nolan. This is not my fault!"

"Who in the world goes after a talking Tree into the woods with no coat, no shoes, no fire, no weapons, no food, no map, no *nothing?*" He coughed again.

"Ya did," Quinn retorted angrily. "And sick, to boot!"

"And had I not, you'd be all alone out here."

"I can take care of meself, Nolan."

"Bang-up job so far, Quinn." His voice squeaked, and his nose was running, dripping onto his bathrobe. The tension and fear of the moment, the panic of the lingering asthmatic attack, and the fiery drive to find the others got the best of his temper.

"This is *not* my fault."

"That's right, it's your *grandmother's.*"

"And *yore* brother's! He slammed into us, and the Greenman let go of me hand." She was yelling now, hands on her hips.

Emery! Nolan moaned. The fight deflated out of him as quickly as it had flared up. *Oh, no. Emery.* What would they do? He had to be all right—didn't he? Nolan and Quinn had made it through the Veil. So had Emery. He was just down the road. *What "road"? There's no road. There's a bunch of eighty-foot-tall trees and God knows what else slithering on the dirt!* What should they do? Nolan tried to think, but his cold made that next to impossible. His lungs were on fire. Well, standing here, they'd freeze to death. Better to move in circles than stand still yelling at each other.

"Is it too much to hope that you've got your grandma's journal?" The question was rhetorical; Nolan knew the answer.

Still angry, Quinn held up her grimy hands. "No pockets."

Nolan nodded. "She had maps." But he knew they wouldn't have been able to read the maps, anyway, without a point of reference. He was just stressed and scared, and he was taking it out on the only person around. In truth, he was glad he wasn't by himself. He thought of Stanley, who'd been pushed out of the way while going through the Veil. Chances were, he was alone right now, somewhere in these dark woods. *Oh, man....*

Quinn exhaled and dropped her hands. "Please, Nolan. I'm sorry, okay?" She reached out to grab his hand, speaking just above a whisper. "I'm so sorry. I'm sorry about Gran. I'm sorry about Emery and Stanley. I don't want to fight with ya. I wanna go home. I'm sorry ya came, and I'm sorry I don't have the journal. But I've got the diamond."

She pulled it out from under her nightgown and let it dangle on its thick chain. Even covered in mud, it glittered with what little light the dense Forest afforded. "Maybe we should look for this Temple thing—the others might be headed there, too. Maybe Ysgafn's with them, and we're the only ones who got separated."

Nolan doubted it and shook his head. "Your grandmother was the only one still holding on to Ysgafn when he went through. He also said the Temple was hidden by the Veil, and Blue Time's gone."

"Huh?"

"The magic hour, remember? The sky gets really blue at dusk. That's when magical things can happen, when Ysgafn can raise the Veil." He waved the comment away, not able to explain how he knew about Blue Time—it was something he could just sense.

"Look, let's try going that way." He pointed ahead of them. "There's got to be people living in this Forest somewhere. A village...or a camp. Even a stream we could follow. And we should move to keep warm."

So they started shuffling in a straight line; at least, it seemed straight to them. It was difficult because the forest floor was covered in rocks, pinecones, pine needles, ferns, broken logs, and mud puddles.

They walked in silence for about ten minutes, until Quinn let out a little yelp. She tried to hobble on, biting back tears, but Nolan told her to stop. He saw that the arch of her foot had a puncture wound that was bleeding, and he felt a twinge of compassion. At least he had slippers.

He plopped down on a wide rock, and she sidled next to him. He lifted her foot onto his lap, trying to study the wound in the low light. It didn't look too deep, but what did he know? He wasn't a doctor. He used the hem of her nightgown to try to wipe away the worst of the grime. Then he tore a length of the flannel to tie around the wound. Her foot in his hands was freezing, and, judging from the way she shivered, so was the rest of her. He was just as cold.

"Nice nail polish," he said, trying to smile.

Quinn didn't smile back. He could tell she was trying not to panic. She looked around and muttered, "It's dark, it's cold, we're lost...."

"Don't forget the whole traipsing through the woods in a nightgown thing, too," Nolan added.

This brought a small smile from her. "Yes, and perhaps the best thing to do would be to go in search of a proper cup of tea."

"What?" Now Nolan was confused. "Why on *earth* would we want to go looking for tea?"

"Precisely," Quinn said with a grin.

Nolan gave her one of those sidelong, raised-eyebrow looks, as if to ask if she'd broken something. Such as her head.

"Sorry, Nolan." Her momentary smile began to fade. "Kind of a lame joke. Ya said ya liked to read. Thought ya might know a little modern English humor, y'know? Arthur Dent? Ford Prefect? Zaphod Beeblebrox...?"

Nolan sat there with a blank look spread across his face.

"Er...forty-two?" she tried again.

Nolan shrugged, not following.

Quinn shook her head. "Yanks. Never mind." She gave a dejected sigh, taking a closer look at the shadowy trees that melted into the surrounding darkness. "Don't panic. Don't panic. Don't panic," she whispered to herself over and over.

Nolan didn't want her freaking out, but he didn't know what to say, so he pulled off his slippers and handed them to her.

"Nolan, I don't—"

"Just wear 'em, Quinn. Your foot's bleeding, for crying out loud."

She gave him another tiny smile as she put the slippers on. They were about her size. "Yore right, we *do* look like a coupla idiots runnin' 'round in our nightclothes."

"I'm in a bathrobe," Nolan pointed out. Then he sneezed, which made his lungs burn.

"That was the Arthur Dent thing," she tried to explain, but he was still befuddled. She squeezed his hand. "Never mind. Thanks...for the slippers. But what are ya gonna do? Yore feet'll be bleedin', too."

Nolan snapped off an enormous leaf from a plant behind the rock they were seated on. "This is like darmera, sort of." He sneezed again and wiped the back of his hand across his cold nose. His lungs were stiff, and he feared another asthma attack.

"We call those 'elephant ears,'" Quinn said.

Nolan shook his head. "No, those are colocasia—cocoyam. These are like rhubarb, but I don't think you can eat them. Normally they don't grow in forests, so this is some other kind of species. I'll use a bunch of them tied together with some of these." He pointed at several ropelike vines hanging from the boughs of a tree. They were green enough to pull and snap off. "I'll make an extra pair in case the first wears out."

"That's brilliant, Nolan. How d'ya know so much about plants?"

"Just what I'm good at," he said with a shrug. Deep down, he was flattered that she admired his plant knowledge.

With the materials to make an extra pair of sandals over his shoulder, they were on their way once again, whichever their way was. The early night air was chilled and thick with mist, but thankfully there was no strong wind under the trees. They shivered in their wet clothes as they walked at a snail's pace to avoid tripping over the uneven surface.

It seemed that the Forest's inhabitants had grown used to the new intrusion, for the sounds of night burst into a discordant symphony. Owls hooted, frogs croaked, the trees creaked, and there were drip-drip-drips from the moist leaves. The whole scene was creepy.

The children's own breathing sounded loud in Nolan's ears, and his was especially raspy as he drew air into his constricted lungs.

With his excellent night vision, peering warily into the darkness, Nolan thought he saw *something* move behind a twisted tree that was bowed down to the ground with age and under the weight of thick, shaggy tufts of Spanish moss. His blood ran cold, and he drew to a stop, forcing his breathing to remain under control.

Quinn must have sensed his unease, for she put her hand at his elbow. "What is it, Nolan?" she whispered, frightened.

He shook his head and whispered back, "Dunno. Something moved behind that tree. Something big enough for me to see."

Quinn strained her eyes, but the details of the Forest beyond fifteen or twenty yards turned into a hazy, dark mist.

Suddenly, with what little light the Forest provided, a large pair of yellow eyes glittered by the crooked tree. Quinn gasped and swallowed a scream, her fingers digging into Nolan's elbow. Their bodies tensed, and Nolan was afraid of another asthma attack.

"Let's walk," he whispered. "Don't run. It might charge."

Quinn seemed hesitant to turn her back to the glittering eyes, but Nolan shook her hand off his elbow and took it in his own. "Walk, Quinn. Don't bolt."

They had taken only a half dozen steps before they heard the creature slink away from the bent tree and begin following them. Whatever it was, it knew they'd seen it, and it wasn't trying to sneak anymore.

Nolan had the terrifying feeling of being *stalked*. His skin crawled and prickled; he glanced over his shoulder but saw nothing. Yet he knew it was *out there*, whatever it was. Following them in the dark Forest. He forced his legs not to break into a blind run. Quinn's fear was almost tangible; he felt it in her hand, feeding his own growing panic.

A howl rent the night air, silencing all the other Forest creatures, and both Nolan and Quinn screamed. He yanked her hand and pulled her after him as a crashing sound came through the woods. His lungs felt like they were covered in wool, but he hauled Quinn along, running in the opposite direction of the sounds of pursuit.

"Run!" he managed. "Run!"

"Nolan!" Quinn shrieked, pointing off to her left with her free hand.

He hazarded a quick glance and saw a flash of gray fur, a long, sleek tail, and a *humanlike* hand, though clawed and furred, grasping a tree branch as the creature pulled itself after them on two feet. Then it broke free, and they saw it clearly. The sight nearly caused them to stumble to a dead stop, but somehow they managed to keep running, although they had no idea where they were heading.

It was some kind of a dog, but much larger, about the size of a small horse, with slinky mottled-gray fur and a massive wolflike head with its ears pinned back against its skull. Its open mouth was red and slavering with long yellowed teeth, sharp enough to tear a child to ribbons.

But there was intelligence in its yellow eyes, which locked on theirs, and it howled a second time, taking up the pursuit. It wasn't simply a wolf; there was an almost humanoid shape to it, and in the flashes of movement Nolan glimpsed, it seemed to alternate between loping on all fours and leaping forward on two feet.

"Big—wolf," Quinn gasped as they flew deeper into the woods, heedless of their direction.

Of course, Nolan knew there was no way to outrun such a monster. It was just toying with them, enjoying the thrill of the hunt. Still, raw instinct had taken over, and adrenaline had overpowered his unyielding lungs, his cold forgotten in fear. He and Quinn kept running.

His leaf shoes were shredded in moments, but he ignored the pain in his feet as he hammered over the rough terrain.

And suddenly, they were falling.

In the dimness of the woods, and in their blind terror, they'd missed the muddy ravine. Nolan went down first, head over heels, Quinn a hairbreadth behind him, rolling, tumbling, and then sliding down a muddy drainage path for rain.

The two children banged over each other like two pinballs at full tilt, their handclasp breaking, and Nolan's arm slammed into a broken tree trunk; he flipped over once again, losing all sense of up and down. There was only the mud and the pain and the darkness. Quinn cried out as her leg snagged a large rock that continued down the mudslide with them, but miraculously it didn't crush the kids as they tumbled.

They came to rest at the bottom of the ravine, a full sixty or seventy feet below the top of the ridge where they'd tripped blindly into space.

A bunch of the debris littering the forest floor had traveled down the mudslide with them. At the bottom of the gorge was a tiny rivulet of rainwater, little more than a muddy ditch, with half an inch of water trickling along the contours of the earth.

They both lay dazed and in a heap, gasping for breath. Nolan's mouth was filled with muddy, leafy muck, and over the pounding of his heart, he could hear Quinn spitting out the same junk. Several seconds passed where they just lay in a jumble, listening for the sounds of pursuit.

But it was silent. A minute passed, and the two began checking themselves for injuries, unwinding from each other to assess the bumps and bruises of their filthy fall.

"Is it followin' us?" Quinn whispered, craning her neck to look up the steep hill they'd just plunged down. It was too dark to see much of anything. It all blended together.

"It might be trying to find a better way down here," Nolan spluttered, trying to breathe, but not so deeply that his lungs rebelled.

"Can ya stand?" Quinn still had Nolan's slippers on her feet.

Nolan nodded. The darmera leaves and green vines were still tied to the belt of his bathrobe. He lashed them to his feet, amazed that they were still usable, and that he and Quinn hadn't suffered worse injuries from such a spill.

It was much darker down here in the gully, but just a short distance away, on the other side of the ravine from where they'd fallen, the bank leveled out, and the misty Forest continued on.

They dared not run, and made as little noise as possible; but it was terrifying, thinking they were being pursued by the wolflike monster. And of course, Nolan knew being quiet didn't guarantee their safety—the beast would most assuredly be able to track them by smell just as easily.

But they heard nothing, and after a few minutes, Nolan began to let himself hope—just a little—that maybe it had given up chasing them for easier prey.

They'd gone maybe a quarter mile (there was no way to tell, it just *felt* about that far to Nolan) when he had a horrifying thought: He had no idea if they were walking in circles. They might be heading back *toward* the creature!

But the answer came when, up ahead, he saw something appear out of the gloom. It stood out as man-made, incongruous with the rest of the Forest. In the center of a small clearing, there were four long wooden poles and a rope ladder leading to a wooden landing some fifty feet overhead. It was a lookout tower, like those Nolan had seen dotting the mountain ridges on his skiing vacations to Montana. He thought they might be able to see above the tree line from its height and perhaps find a little protection from the beast.

He had no idea if it could climb rope ladders, but he prayed to God it couldn't.

"Question is, did friend or foe build that?" Quinn whispered as they hid in the trees. Her head darted this way and that, looking for any signs of the animal.

The tower appeared deserted, no lights and no sounds, but an enclosed, sheltered place up high away from the monster seemed like a godsend.

"If it's empty, perhaps it won't matter," Nolan whispered back. "Look, I'll go check it out, and if it's really deserted, I'll call down to you. If you hear anything, run and don't stop."

"That's a stupid plan," she hissed. "'Run and don't stop.' Like I could outrun that *thing*. No way. Let me go with ya."

Nolan thought for a second. Of course, she was right. They should stick together. Anything had to be better than getting eaten.

He nodded. She grabbed his hand, and they slinked as quietly as possible to the rope ladder.

It was difficult and painful to get to the top, with bleeding feet, bruises, welts, and sore, icy muscles. They pushed on the trapdoor, which swung back on loud iron hinges, and they scrambled inside, breathing heavily on the dusty floor.

The lookout tower wasn't very large, maybe fifteen by fifteen, like a one-room wooden cabin on tall stilts with a thatched roof. The only furniture, two cots and a hefty chest of iron and wood, lined three of the walls. Summoning the last of their strength, they heaved together to push the chest over the trapdoor, then collapsed for what seemed like an hour or more, just focusing on catching their breath, as they listened for howling. But all they heard were *normal* forest sounds.

When Nolan was able to roll over on his hands and knees, he crawled to the chest and worked the lid open. Inside were two massive gray woolen blankets that smelled of mold and, underneath them, a tinderbox and a small rusted dagger. Not what he had hoped for: a pair of shoes, or a first-aid kit for their numerous scratches and the wound in Quinn's foot.

There wasn't any glass in the long windows on each wall, but they offered a 360-degree view. It was too dark to make out much distinctly, except what was right around them—just more wet forest.

"All right, Quinn. You get some sleep first. I'll wake you in a bit. And in the morning, we'll see if we can find some civilization." He hefted the knife, taking some comfort in the knowledge that they were armed, although he knew the small implement would be useless against something the size of the monster that had chased them. And he also knew he wouldn't be brave enough to face down something like that, even with a bazooka.

Quinn didn't protest his offer to take the first watch. Nolan turned around so she could peel off her grimy nightclothes and tuck up in the smelly blanket, then she did the same so he could wrap up, too. Even though the blankets were itchy, it was much better than wearing wet, filthy clothes. Simple things like being warm and getting dry were a relief in their circumstances.

"'S only one thing I gotta say." Quinn was using a part of the blanket to try to dry her hair.

"What's that?" Nolan croaked.

"Ysgafn's full o' crap. Oh, it's 'perfectly safe.' Load'a codswallop, the flippin' git." And Quinn lay down on one of the cots without another word.

In spite of himself, Nolan smiled as he put his back to the chest and began spinning the handle of the knife with the point barely touching the wood floor.

It made a satisfying, small scraping sound, and the rhythm seemed to put Quinn to sleep.

He was surprised to find that his mind wasn't filled with the petrifying thoughts of being chased through the woods. Instead, it was filled with thoughts of Stanley and Emery, Audrey, and even Genevieve. Were they all right? They had to be. What were the chances of *them* running into some monstrous creature, too? They had to be fine. Right?

Yes, he thought as he sniffled, holding a grimy hand to his pounding head. They were all right. They were *all right*. He'd find them in the morning.

One thing Nolan was intensely aware of: He hated the Hidden Lands *and* talking Trees *and* freaking Wolves....

Quinn was soon snoring, and sometime during the darkest part of the night, Nolan fell into the exhausted sleep of someone ill who's done way too much when he should have been in bed. He stirred not at all, sleeping deeply.

8

The Otherworld

Perhaps Nolan's fever was affecting his dreams. They were filled with scenes of pain and loss, revolving around Emery and Stanley, strange wolves on two feet chasing them, and a pervasive fear of running in circles with no escape. His fever broke at dawn, and when his cooler body's dreams turned to protecting Quinn, he woke to sunlight streaming through the tower's glassless windows. Lazy motes of dust drifted through the still, warm air. Even through his stuffed-up nose, he could smell pine needles and green leaves. Birds were singing their summer songs, and a bee buzzed around the ceiling above his head. His throat and lips were cracked, his eyes were crusty with dried mucous and sweat, and he needed to use the bathroom. Except, there was no bathroom here. He still felt weak but not as sick as last night. His lungs felt heavy in his chest, but he didn't think he'd have another asthma attack as long as he didn't have to run from monsters. More than anything, he was hungry, and that was a good sign.

Quinn was already dressed in her nightgown, which was stained with filth. She also wore his slippers.

"Mornin'," she said. "There's a clear stream about fifty meters that way." She pointed to her right. "And some bushes with what look like red currants that way, but I didn't eat any, 'cause I thought ya should look at 'em first. And there's a village way down that way, or at least I think so, 'cause there's trails of smoke risin' out of the trees."

Nolan was about to toss off the blanket when he realized he was undressed, so he grabbed his bathrobe and waited for Quinn to turn around.

"I fell asleep," he confessed.

"No kiddin'," Quinn tittered with her back to him. "What happened to 'I'll wake ya up in a bit'? Some watchman. Lucky we didn't wake up as wolf burgers."

What she'd said just moments before finally sank in. "You left without me?" he asked as he dressed. He was staring out the window where she had pointed, and, yes, there was some kind of settlement or village to the west, away from the morning sun. But, as thick as the Forest was, it might well take them hours to get there. And who knew what kind of creatures *lived* in that village?

"In the daylight, there's nothing scary in these woods I can see, 'cept big birds and some squirrels with Elvis hairdos. Ya feelin' better?"

"A bit."

"Good! I felt better after I washed up some in the stream, but it's rubbish puttin' on dirty clothes again. Can I turn 'round now?"

"Oh, yeah. Sorry."

She whirled and smiled. "Still, now that it's daylight, I don't think Monsieur Fangs will be around, and there's somethin' over that way, so we should see if they can help."

"Do you think it's wise to just walk into a village?"

"Why not?" Quinn acted like she didn't expect any potential danger.

They climbed down the rope ladder and into warm sunlight, carrying their blankets, the tinderbox, and the dagger with them. It was obvious the clearing was man-made; it was just big enough to build the tower. The Forest encroached on all sides, and under the trees was a much darker green than the bright, sunlit area surrounding the watchtower.

Still, it was nowhere near as ominous as it had been last night, and, like Quinn, Nolan felt sure nothing *that* monstrous could be in the woods during the daylight.

To his right, he heard the brook burbling and wondered why he'd not heard it last night. It was swift and clear, about three feet deep. Strange-looking fish darted over large, smooth stones, and Nolan wondered how difficult it would be to catch one. He'd read about survivalists catching fish with their bare hands. Could he do that? Probably not.

And all in all, he wouldn't be able to bring himself to eat one; they were odd colors—pinks, reds, and electric blues. A few were black-and-white-spotted fish like nothing he'd ever seen on *his* side of the world before. There was also some kind of strange crayfish with oversized eyes, as big as any lobster, darting backward under a rock. He gave it a wide berth, thinking Houston the crab should get a load of this guy.

They were *definitely* in Another Place.

He excused himself to go find a tree, then returned to see Quinn tossing rocks into the water, scaring the multicolored fish. The scenery was quite beautiful, and Nolan would've been peacefully enjoying himself if there had been a car parked just a few yards away, or some people jogging with their dogs. He cupped his hands and brought a slurp of water to his lips. It was refreshing, cold, and very clean to the taste. He figured parasites weren't something they should be worried about, considering the alternative was dehydration, and he dunked his entire head in the stream. The shock of the water cleared his mind. He scrubbed his face, neck, arms, and hands while Quinn drew pictures with a stick in the black earth. Nolan wished he'd been smart enough to remember his inhaler—he felt like he was breathing through a cotton mask. But there was nothing he could do about that in the Otherworld.

Now, what had Quinn said about berries?

Turns out there *were* red currants on the bushes, and ripe ones, too. Although currants were not Nolan's favorite type of fruit, and these were a little too tart, he was hungry enough not to complain. They ate voraciously, devouring hundreds of the little berries until their fingers were stained red from the juice. Another rinse and a good, long drink out of the stream, and the two began walking toward where they had seen smoke rising out of the trees.

Nolan was by no means a junior woodsman; under the canopy, it was impossible to tell where they were heading, and he was sure he was going to lead them in circles. Sure enough, after thirty minutes, they doubled back to the tower somehow, and they stopped to figure out how to move in a straight line toward the village.

"Okay, in the books, they always follow the stream," Nolan said. "So we cross over, keep it on our left, and we're heading toward the smoke. I mean, the village, or whatever it is, has to be near the water. Does that make sense to you?"

Quinn rolled her shoulders. "Sounds good to me. Otherwise, we'll have to tie somethin' to the trees to make sure we don't walk in circles."

They started toward the village again, this time following the stream. After a couple miles, it widened to about a hundred feet between the banks, more like a river now; the current seemed swift. But it still headed toward where they'd seen the smoke from the watchtower.

The question was if the village was on the *other* side of the bank. Nolan didn't relish a swim under *normal* circumstances. Who knew what lived in the water? A giant octopus wouldn't surprise him. Perhaps they'd find a bridge if it came to that.

It got quite warm as the morning wore away, and they talked in soft tones, barely heard over the running water, carrying the blankets over their arms.

"Wild to think we're in some other world, huh?" Quinn asked, watching a jet-black bird with bright red and yellow shoulders, the size of the largest pelican, streak toward the water's surface, snapping at a cloud of gnats.

The Forest was full of life—some identical to animals found on their own side, some just slightly different. Some were oddly colored, others weirdly sized, and some had the same intelligent look in their eyes like the wolf-creature had last night. Nolan wouldn't have been too shocked to hear any one of them start speaking. So far, however, they all seemed like mute animals, only smarter, more aware of themselves and their surroundings. The birds and the squirrels, even a huge rabbit the size of a piglet, stared at the humans as they hiked by.

"Remember Ysgafn said it was the same as our world, just hidden," Nolan reminded Quinn. "Like a shadow world."

"So we're still in Rathdowns Forest?"

Nolan thought for a long second. "Yeah, I guess so. Well, sort of. 'Cept Audrey and Ysgafn called it Morsden."

It was then he realized that "Ysgafn" and "Morsden" were not Translating in his head like they had at the cairn last night. Maybe the Translation Song worked only when the Greenman was around, or maybe it wore off after a while. Great. Now they couldn't communicate, even if they did meet somebody. He doubted the Queen's English was the language of choice around here. That bothered him, but he didn't want to concern Quinn with it yet, so he didn't mention it.

Quinn said, "All the Celtic myths have stories about the Otherworld, but usually it's underground, populated by faeries, the *Aos Sidhe*. What was that word Ysgafn used to address Stanley?"

"Aossí. And it means 'Fair Folk.'" It was very similar word, but again, he noted that Aossí did not Translate.

"Yeah, Fair Folk. They're usually elves or faeries in the stories."

"I think it's literal," Nolan proposed. "Just fair-skinned. Or fair to look at. I mean, there's no such thing as faeries or elves."

"All in the perception. There's no such thing as Greenmen, either, Nols. *Or* giant wolves that run on two feet."

"Point taken." Nolan smiled to himself. She hadn't called him "Nols" in a while.

The sun, when they could see it through the canopy of trees, seemed just about overhead when the river branched off into an eddy where the current moved slowly around a small cove.

The little inlet was a scene out of a fairy tale. At least twenty species of healthy-looking trees surrounded the bay, some of them not native to a forest setting. But Nolan noticed teak and ceiba, mahogany and Eastern red cedar juniper, blackthorn and tilia lime trees. A few ancient magnolias spread their giant white flowers like oversized teacups. Smaller dogwoods and cherry trees, crepe myrtles, and crabapple trees seemed to be dashing toward the water as if in a mad race.

What was most beautiful were the dozens of willow trees lining the banks. Willows were Nolan's favorite genus, and here were purple willows, yellow willows, white willows, weeping willows, globe willows—just about every species he was familiar with. Their long branches dangled languidly over the cool, running water of the eddy. Lost leaves spun in endless, dizzying circles, racing each other in the current like tiny boats to head out into the main of the river, set free once again.

It occurred to Nolan that white willow bark would be a big help for all their aches and pains. It wouldn't do much if Quinn's foot got infected, but at least they wouldn't be hobbling around quite so much. Of course, chewing willow bark on a nearly empty stomach was a great way to make yourself puke.

Then Nolan saw the fig trees, and the tamarinds, too. *All right!* Finally a break. He grabbed Quinn's shoulder and started pulling her toward the water's edge.

"What?" she asked. To her, it probably just looked like a beautiful little cove with a bunch of pretty trees.

"Those are figs and tamarinds." He pointed to the fruit weighing down the boughs. "We can eat them."

"Thank God! I'm starvin'!"

They gorged themselves, reclining on the grassy bank in the warm sun. A strange bird similar to a blue heron, but maybe twice as tall, was standing on one leg along the bank. Its long beak darted now and again down into the water, each time coming up with a wriggling silver fish. Giant bullfrogs plopped into the current from the rushes, making splashes that sent ripples rolling out into the center of the pool.

Several families of different kinds of ducks paddled around, sticking their tail feathers up in the air as they fished for weeds along the river bottom. The drakes were marvelously colored: teals and mandarins, falcateds and mallards. They all seemed to get along together, quacking like good friends; even the loon, normally aloof, presided over the duck parade, belting out its eerie call as if sending marching orders down to the lesser waterfowl.

Nolan knew they should be getting on—there was no way he was going to spend another night out in the Forest. But the area was so peaceful, and he told himself another fifteen minutes wouldn't hurt.

Quinn tugged on the shoulder of his bathrobe. "What kinda plant is that?"

He followed her gaze and spotted a giant rhubarb, only it was many times larger than any he'd ever seen. The leaves were some twelve feet long, six feet wide, and *they moved on their own*. He sat straight up, staring at the plant to make sure it wasn't a trick of the eyes or an effect of the slight breeze blowing across the water.

No, that plant was moving on its own, as if it was *aware* of the water nearby and was stretching its leaves of its own accord to dip them into the pool. Nolan knew that plants were always moving, but normally you couldn't *see* them move, as you did other living creatures.

"It's a rhubarb, sort of. Kinda like what I made the slippers from, only ten times bigger."

Quinn's expression said that even she knew it wasn't normal for plants to move like that. "Have ya noticed that many things here seem more *alive* than they do on our Side? More...awake?"

Nolan nodded. "And there are several types of plants and animals that shouldn't be together. Arctic mixed with tropical...it's weird. I think the Greenmen really *are* Shepherds in this place."

"D'ya think that plant would let us use it as a slide into the water?"

He looked at her like she was crazy. "You're not scared the plant might attack you?"

"Well, I *have* eaten more 'n me fair share of rhubarb crumble, but *it* doesn't know that." She smirked. "Come on, Nols. 'S hot. Let's take a quick swim 'fore we head on." Quinn hauled Nolan to his feet and kicked off her slippers.

Truth was, Nolan was quite scared to enter the water—he hated swimming, and after last night, he was afraid some vicious sea monster would appear out of the pool and swallow them whole. But he knew that his worries were ridiculous—the water was clear enough to see to the bottom. He allowed Quinn to drag him over to the waving rhubarb, which seemed to recoil like a frightened animal at their approach.

"Shhh," Quinn told the plant. "'S okay, leafy." She reached out to stroke the fifteen-foot-long leaf, and it went rigid at her touch. She guided it like a long slide down over the edge of the bank.

"There's no way it'll hold your weight, Quinn," Nolan reasoned. "You'll fall on your tailbone."

"One way to find out, oh ye of little faith." She winked and then clambered on top of the leaf. It wavered but held her up. "See, I'm not *that* heavy!" And with a whoop, she let herself go, sliding down the length of the leaf to launch herself into the air before flopping into the water with a splash that sent the ducks quacking and fluttering off in protest.

She surfaced with a laugh that echoed across the lagoon. "Whew! That's refreshin'," she said after spitting out a spurt of water. "Come on, ya big baby. It's not scary. Take a dive!"

Nolan exhaled and mustered his courage. He couldn't let Quinn think he was afraid of a little water. He followed her example, running his hand along the rhubarb leaf and positioning it out over the water. It made a perfect slide shape, pointing downward, with a little upward tilt at the end to launch him into the air. He scrambled up on the leaf until he found his seat, thinking he'd look like an idiot if the plant did sense his fear and decided to drop him on his duff. But it held his weight.

Holding his breath, Nolan let go and felt himself sliding down the slippery leaf. With his eyes screwed shut, he felt his bottom leave the slide and hang in midair for a split second before he landed on his back in the cool water.

After scrambling for the surface, Nolan gasped and spit out a mouthful of water. But he found himself laughing instead of freaking out. This wasn't so bad!

"See! I knew ya'd like it, mate!"

They spent about ten minutes splashing and swimming—the pool was eight feet deep, at most. Quinn slid down the leaf a few more times; Nolan did it once more.

Time was getting on, and Nolan knew it; it had to be near one in the afternoon now. They forced themselves to the shore, and Nolan laced up his makeshift shoes with more leaves from a nonmoving plant. He also made sure the white willows weren't moving on their own before he used the dagger to scrape off a few squares of bark. He handed a square to Quinn, then chewed one himself, feeling the tingling sensation on his tongue. The bark was bitter but not unbearable, and within minutes, he could feel the pain from his numerous bumps and bruises lessen a bit. It was no Extra-Strength Tylenol, but it did help.

They dried off fast in the summer sun, and within a couple minutes, they unwillingly bid farewell to their little cove, following the contour of the river toward where they hoped to find some civilization.

Nolan could only pray his brother and the rest of them also had seen the smoke from the village or whatever it was. It was their best chance of being reunited, though he felt trepidation when he tried to imagine what they would find.

9

Thieving Princess

About two hours of hiking brought them to a path lined with large white stones that followed the river, which had widened even more. The dirt was tramped down, and the path seemed carved out of the Forest and well-maintained. They couldn't see the village yet, so they decided to keep to the tree line in case there were other travelers.

They hadn't decided whether to make their presence known to whoever lived in the village, but Nolan hoped that the others had also found this community, and that they all would be reunited with Ysgafn so they could get the heck out of here. He shuddered to think of what his mother was going through right now, with both her sons missing along with the other kids and Audrey. Would the police be involved? Knowing his mother, Scotland Yard was already on the case.

They heard singing and stopped, hunkering down behind a big clump of dense, bushy ferns. It wasn't Tree-singing; just normal human singing, like that of a man at work.

And that's what he was. A farmer was heading down the path, driving a yoke of oxen ahead of him. The oxen were shaggy with long, curling horns, and Nolan was reminded of a picture book he'd seen years ago about the aurochs, which was extinct on his Side of the world. The animals hauled a cart, laden with what looked like potatoes or rutabagas, toward the settlement.

The human was very normal-looking. He had light brown hair and tanned skin; Nolan guessed his age to be about thirty or forty. His clothes were old and worn but brightly colored with mismatched patterns of stripes and dots in blues and reds and greens. He wore stained leather boots that reached his knees, and at his side hung a naked short axe.

He was an Aossí—a man from the Otherworld—and the thought thrilled Nolan. While Nolan wouldn't swear to it, the farmer's ears *did* look a little pointy, but he was quite sure the man was otherwise human.

His cart rumbled by, and the aurochs sniffed the air where Nolan and Quinn were hiding, but the farmer paid no attention, clucking at the cattle and giving them a little swish with the willow branch he carried in his right hand. He broke into song again, singing in a language that Nolan could not understand.

Once he was ahead of them quite a ways, Quinn let out a deep breath, and Nolan realized he'd been holding his, too, which made his lungs burn.

"He seemed friendly," Quinn said.

"Yeah, but we don't look anything like locals, and what if they're not used to kids from the Otherworld—I mean, *our* world—coming into *theirs*? I think we should try to observe the village before making ourselves known. Maybe we can learn something about Audrey, Stanley, and Emery."

"And Genevieve."

"Her too, I guess."

Both sniggered.

They agreed to lie low and kept picking their way toward the village. "Did ya realize we couldn't understand what that farmer was singin'?" Quinn asked.

Nolan grimaced. "Yeah, I noticed. Either that Translation thingy works only for Tree-language, or the ability wears off when he's not around."

"So what do we do if we decided to introduce ourselves to the townsfolk?"

"Draw pictures, I s'pose. Know any sign language?" He snickered.

"I can spell me name and give 'em the Longbowman's Salute."

"The what?"

She showed him and then laughed sheepishly. "It's very rude."

"I don't get it. That means 'peace' or 'two' in the States," Nolan replied.

"Just don't show it to any Brit," she cautioned him. "Ya'll start a fight."

"Oh, so it's like the finger."

Quinn rolled her eyes. "Yes, Nols, it's like the finger."

They laughed and unexpectedly came upon the village. Just out of nowhere, the Forest cleared into a long, narrow meadow about a mile and a half long. The River ran right alongside the town and then disappeared off to the south, Nolan guessed, judging by the sun's position. Acres of level land were sown in fields of corn, potatoes, and other vegetables. About sixty log-and-earth cabins lined the river, and the town boasted three streets—a main and two cross streets. The signs hanging out front of the businesses were written in a foreign language that looked like "Irish mixed with symbols," Quinn said. It wasn't as rough-looking as the symbols on Ysgafn's staff, but there was some similarity, Nolan thought.

Over a hundred Aossí were out and about; many of them were children, playing games or helping adults carry supplies here and there. Everyone seemed happy and good-natured, a little poor but content, and at least well fed.

Nolan had expected some dreary, medieval huts and a few starving cows. This looked like a bustling pioneer town out of the 1800s, except that the townsfolk were dressed in loud, bright colors, and some of the adults had slicked back, bleached-blond hair. The people looked tall, even the children, and very pale-skinned, except for the ones working in the fields.

Fair Folk.

They could hear snippets of conversation in a wild, guttural language. As far as Nolan could tell, it was similar to the Treeman's tongue, and Quinn said it reminded her a little of Celtic languages, but neither of them could make out a thing from their speech.

"First things first," Nolan decided. "We need to steal some clothes and food."

Quinn gasped. "We can't *steal* from these people, Nolan! That's not right!"

"This isn't the time to be all moraled, Quinn. We have no money, and we've eaten nothing but berries and figs! We won't last another night in these woods without supplies of some kind."

Quinn looked hesitant, as if she were weighing his point. "But what're we gonna do? Sleep *in* the woods tonight? What if there's more of those Wolflings—or worse? At least the villagers are *human*. We could just *ask* 'em for help. We don't have to steal from 'em."

"Look, I don't know what else to do. We'll find a place to camp that's near the town. I'm pretty sure no wolves would attack this many people."

Quinn frowned, still unconvinced.

"Hey, I'm not a thief, either, Quinn, but I have a feeling if we make ourselves known to these people, they'll just keep us here or turn us over to the authorities or something."

"They might help us find the others," she pointed out.

"Or kidnap us and put us in the circus as 'freaks' from the Other Place. We can't just show up in their village, with no way to speak their language, and ask if they know where our friends are. And what if they don't know about the Greenmen? Or what if they're at war with them? It's all too risky right now. I promise, if we get a chance, we'll pay them back. Deal?"

She chewed on her bottom lip a second, then nodded. "Right. How d'we get 'round without bein' seen?"

Despite some very close calls, Quinn proved herself a better sneak thief than she probably would've liked to admit. Nolan was way too clumsy to be of much help, but by late afternoon, the teenage descendant of the Embroidery Queen had managed to pilfer a loaf of black bread, a small wheel of white cheese, a thin strip of what looked like venison jerky, two onions, four apples, and a leather skin full of dark red wine.

At least they wouldn't starve.

"Goodness, Quinn, I thought you'd take some peanuts or something," Nolan said, wiping his running nose with the back of his hand. He still wasn't feeling tip-top, but the worst of the cold seemed to be over. All he worried about now was getting a bronchial infection—that was murder for a kid with asthma.

They had selected a hideout of sorts in the woods about a quarter mile from the village. It was close enough to bolt into town, screaming their heads off, if something wicked this way came, but far enough out that no villagers would accidentally stumble over them. There were two boulders and a large berm that kept them invisible on three sides.

"It's not easy," Quinn said, throwing herself down on the dirt, exhausted. "Kids are runnin' all over the place in that town. Obviously they believe in havin' lots of children in the Otherworld. And there's not too many places to hide. I stick out like a sore thumb in this nightgown."

She took a hunk out of the bread and munched it after tossing the cheese wheel to Nolan. She also produced a chunk of soap and a small pouch filled with white powder. "I saw some kids at the river's edge brushin' their teeth with this. I couldn't find any of the little wooden brushes they were usin', so we'll hafta use our fingers."

"That's cool. 'Least our teeth won't rot." Nolan sniffed the powder. "It's like baking soda."

They ate fast and drank just a few sips of the wine. Neither of them was used to it, and they didn't want to get tipsy. Nolan thought it was pretty good, like bittersweet plums. Quinn made a face and said it tasted like rotted vomit.

After a brief rest, they brushed their teeth with the powder, then stowed the remaining food in their blankets suspended from a tree near their hideout, in case *normal* animals smelled the leftovers. Nolan said he'd seen that on *National Geographic* once, but he doubted it would be a deterrent for a walking wolf.

"And now for some real clothes," Quinn said with a burp. They snuck back to the village, Nolan on lookout, while Quinn slinked behind several cabins, under tables, and over barrels and troughs, where horses blinked at the newcomer, until she came to a small tentlike place made out of sheets dyed in wild colors—crimson, green, purple, gold, and silver—and embroidered with boars, harts, even a Treeman's wise face. At least these Aossí knew what Treemen were, and though the Coeduine's face didn't look *friendly*, it didn't appear that the Aossí thought they were monsters, either.

In front of the tent were clothes of all kinds hanging from rope tied between two trees. Under them were shoes made out of wood, cotton, and leather. There wasn't a person watching the clothes, but Nolan could hear chatter inside the pavilion.

"*Be careful,*" he mouthed to Quinn, who nodded nervously. Taking a gulp, she sneaked on one side of the tent, where no shadow would be cast, and then, lightning quick, a pile of clothes and shoes was in her hands. They crept back out of the village, and she tossed half the garments to Nolan.

They made it to the hideout sweaty and panting for breath. Nolan had to be very careful not to overexert himself with his asthma. They laid their piles on the forest floor and started going through them.

For herself, Quinn had grabbed a bright purple tunic, yellow trousers, and a pair of calf-length buckskin boots that fit perfectly, although it was impossible to know whether they were women's clothes. She'd even managed to filch socks and undergarments, like linen shorts, which made them both giggle.

Nolan would wear a forest green shirt that laced up the front with a leather strip. It would have to be tucked into the pair of black pants Quinn had brought him, the fabric of which was almost like denim, held up by a wide black belt with a silver buckle engraved to look like an eagle's head. His black leather boots were about half a size too big, but the socks helped fill up the space.

Grabbing the stolen soap, they bounced down to an eddy of the river that was deep and brown, surrounded by rocks and trees on all sides. A villager would have almost had to stumble over them to find them.

Taking turns, they bathed in the cold water, staying in earshot of each other but well out of sight for the sake of privacy. Quinn spent some time soaking the cut on her foot. When it was his turn, Nolan tried to clear out the leftover cold from his nose.

They hadn't been able to steal towels, so it wasn't much fun air-drying and putting on clothes while still damp. But they weren't going to complain. It was like a miracle, just being clean.

They buried their old clothes under the hanging blankets of food, and Nolan wasn't sorry to see the leaf slippers go bye-bye down the River.

One thing they didn't have was a hairbrush, so they both took strips of leather to tie their hair back. Quinn laughed at Nolan's tiny ponytail.

"Ya need a hair trim, mate," she said.

"Go steal me a pair of scissors, then," Nolan returned, putting on his boots. "My mom likes my hair long."

"And ya don't?"

"Not really. I don't like being a *ginger*." He used the word she'd called him the day before yesterday at Rathdowns. *Have we been here only a day?* Nolan was shocked.

"Aw, Mister Sensitive got his feelers hurt. That's cute." She smirked. "I was just havin' a go, Nols. One of me best mates at school's a ginger."

"It's fine, *Q-ee*."

She winked.

The brisk bath, the new clothes, and full bellies made them feel loads better. They were tired and a little sore, but Nolan's lungs seemed to be doing all right, and now the real adventure was to be decided. They sat down in their hideout to discuss strategy.

"We wait till it's dark and search the village for clues 'bout Gran and the others," Quinn planned aloud. "We use the coverlets like cloaks, act like we belong, try to blend into the shadows, don't draw attention to ourselves. If we don't find anything, maybe there's a map we can nick that'll show how to get to the Greenmen."

Nolan scratched his chin. "You don't think it's risky to go into the village again? I mean, just out in plain view? I'm sure people recognize strangers—there's only, like, sixty homes in the whole town. Everyone'll know everyone else. And what can we hope to learn if we don't understand what anyone's saying? We can't just eavesdrop at a pub. Sit in the shadows with a mug of ale and smoke pipe-weed."

"Now, see, how is it ya know 'bout Shire leaf and ya don't know anything 'bout Arthur Dent?"

"I have no idea what you're talking about, Quinn."

She shook her head. "Look, I'm open to other suggestions. We could just wander 'round the forest like lost puppies 'til somethin' nasty comes and eats us. But if Gran and the others have come across this town, I don't think it'll be too hard to find 'em. The Aossí will have them, or they'll be doin' the exact same thing *we're* doin', sneaking 'round to try and find *us*. Once people go to bed, we'll come back here, light a fire behind these rocks, and get some sleep. What d'ya think?"

What else could they do? "It'll be dark soon, anyway," Nolan acquiesced.

It was maddening, waiting the two hours until Blue Time. The magic hour didn't seem any different in Tírcluddaithe from in Boston or Ireland, but it *felt* different to Nolan because they were in Another Place. They'd seen Fair Folk and talked to a Greenman, been chased by a freaky creature, and swum with moving plants, all in twenty-four hours. Nolan had to admit, his summer trip hadn't been "boring" at all.

Wearing odd clothes, drinking wine, and playing with a tinderbox to get the hang of starting a fire outdoors, he was beginning to feel like a real adventurer, not some dorky sixth grader with a breaking voice and gawky limbs.

If they could just reunite with the others....

But sneaking into the village after dark proved to be a bad idea. The townsfolk had moved most of their wares indoors, and several bonfires were lit; people were laughing and making music, and the children were running in and out of the groups of adults, shrieking and playing games.

As Nolan and Quinn did their best to sneak into the settlement undetected, Nolan particularly noted the security of the small town. The doors to all the buildings were made of solid, heavy wood, many of them overlaid with iron. Most of the windows had strong metal shutters that could be barred over the glass, sealing the inhabitants inside. There even seemed to be entrances to underground shelters here and there. It was as if the people, while happy and relatively secure in their frontier home, were also prepared for invasion at a moment's notice. Maybe they were used to repelling Wolflings.

There also seemed to be a garrison of soldiers who all wore black ankle-length cloaks embroidered with a screaming eagle's head in silver thread over the left breast. The uniformed warriors seemed relaxed as they milled about the crowd, playing with the children, talking, and laughing, but one could not help but notice the swords they carried. A few had axes or crossbows.

Nolan decided these people weren't paranoid, just well prepared. It was probably the necessity of living in the shadows of such an imposing forest as the Morsden. If the strange creatures he and Quinn had seen so far were any indication of what the Covering held, these people were wise to be well armed!

Nolan and Quinn hunkered low behind the buildings, out of the light of the bonfires and the candles in many of the windows. Of course, they could understand nothing of the Aossí speech when they caught snippets from passersby. As far as they could tell, it seemed that neither the other children nor Audrey had found the settlement. None of the Aossí acted like anything was out of the ordinary. After thirty minutes, feeling more and more depressed, Nolan was about to motion to Quinn that they should head out.

They were now huddled behind the back wall of what appeared to be an apothecary. To their right, metal glinting in the glow of a bonfire caught Nolan's eye. A weapons seller had several swords and axes and bows standing in wooden rows in front of his shop. The windows were dark, and there was no one around. Odd how the weapons were left out, but a thought occurred to Nolan: They could use better protection than a rusted dagger, especially if they were to go hiking into the woods looking for Emery and the others. He motioned for Quinn to stay where she was, and he slinked along the wall on his hands and knees to get a better look at the closest sword.

"What're ya doin'?" she hissed, stamping her foot.

Nolan pointed to the swords. He raised himself into a crouched position, looking around for any Fair Folk.

A solid-looking, beautifully crafted leaf-bladed sword was at the end of the row closest to him. He grabbed the weapon and proceeded to tuck it under his makeshift cloak when a heavy hand clamped down on his shoulder. Nolan stifled a yell, and ice water raced down his spine. The powerful grip tightened, yanking Nolan to his feet. He was staring into the black eyes of a mountainous Aossí with braided muscles under his hairy forearms.

"Let 'im go!" Quinn raced out of her hiding spot, but the weaponsmith grabbed her arm and knocked her into Nolan with a fierce yell that caught the attention of just about the whole town.

Taking the sword, he grabbed both of them by the scruff of the neck and dragged them closer to the fire, where a dozen people were trying to see the commotion with puzzled looks on their faces.

"Get yore hands off me!" Quinn yelled, trying to stamp on the man's foot.

"Leyn tan maefuil saibhristyni? Fójurar!" the big brute thundered.

Nolan didn't need a Song of Translation to understand—"Thieves!"

10

Stanley and the Treegirl

When Stanley woke, he was on his side, staring at the largest fly agaric mushroom he'd ever seen. *Nolan should see this thing!* was his first thought. The cap was at least a foot in diameter. It was growing next to a huge pine tree, which made sense to Stanley. Even in his groggy state, his brilliant mind categorized the fungus as *Amanita muscaria*. Poisonous. And psychotropic. The theme to *Super Mario Bros.* popped into his head, because it was a red mushroom with white dots. Maybe he'd accidentally ingested some, and that was why he felt like he'd been kicked in the stomach. He knew he'd never be stupid enough to willingly eat a psychoactive, poisonous 'shroom.

He rolled into a sitting position, groaning. It felt like he was moving through glue. He placed his hands to his head, wondering if he was hallucinating, and then he realized his glasses were missing. His glasses! He couldn't see more than ten feet without them. *Oh, no!*

Stanley scrambled around, ignoring his pounding head and queasy stomach, desperate to find his glasses. The soft black earth had just soaked up a light rain. It smelled loamy and rich. His hand came down on a sharp pinecone, and he cursed. The ground did seem to vibrate with his vision. Was it the mushroom? No. No, that wasn't right—he'd just been pitched headlong through a magical portal to another world, hadn't he?

Boy, maybe he needed to take a bite of the mushroom. *Go ask Alice*, he sang to himself, *when she's ten feet tall*. Now all he needed was a White Rabbit and a Jabberwock.

"I'm late, I'm late! Goodness me, I'm late!" he said aloud, and realized something *must* be wrong with him. Perhaps he *was* hallucinating.

His glasses! There they were! He grabbed them out of the mud and tried cleaning them off on his shirt, but it was so filthy, it hardly did any good. He blew on the lenses, wiped them as best he could, and put them on.

What came into focus did nothing to put him at ease.

It was a dark forest. Rows upon rows upon rows of at least twenty or more different species of trees spread out in every direction, all of them like tall white ghosts. *Tales-from-the-Darkside* spooky. No path, no friends. He was alone. It was dark. How long had he been unconscious? They'd crossed the Veil at dusk.

Out of nervousness, Stanley muttered to himself, "It is pitch black. You are likely to be eaten by a grue." Although it wasn't technically pitch black, the statement brought a little comfort.

Where *was* everybody?

He was smart enough to know that screaming his head off would likely call every predator in the woods to dinner. If that giant Greenman (Ysgafn, wasn't it?) had been wounded by something in these woods, that would make Stanley seem somewhat of an hors d'oeuvre.

He needed some way to distract his mind to keep the panic at bay, so he ran through some French verb conjugations. *Meurs. Mourrai. Mourais. Meu—oh man, I'm gonna die!*

"Get a grip, Stanley," he told himself sternly. "People as smart as you don't die in the forest alone. It's *Swiss Family Robinson* time here!"

More like Lord of the Flies *time, Piggy!* the voice in his mind was mocking.

Dude, shut up! He murmured, "Ian Malcolm lived. The mathematician always lives in the end. It's a staple of chaos theory."

He died in the book, bro. Spielberg changed the story.

"Yeah, but he miraculously came back to life for *The Lost World*...."

You're reaching here, Stanley. Let's face it—you're no Jeff Goldblum.

Stanley often had conversations with himself in his mind. Of course, he would never admit that to Nolan. It made him sound crazy. But, at the risk of sounding conceited, Stanley reasoned he *had* to talk to himself to find his equal.

Yeah, 'cause Einstein and Planck are dead.

Don't say "dead." I'm gonna die in this Forest!

Oh, don't start this again. Just eat the mushroom and be done with it, my precious....

He sat down with his knees drawn to his chest and ran through some breathing exercises—the ones he was always trying to get Nolan to do with him but never succeeded, since Nolan argued it cut into their Wii time.

After a few minutes, the rush of hyper-oxygenated blood to his head shook him clear. Okay, he'd read enough survival guides. Logic dictated he should remain where he was until someone found him. If he went looking for the others, they could miss each other in this forest.

Is it a little chilly?

He did feel rather damp, and he wished he had a jacket. But at least he was in jeans and a T-shirt. Poor Nolan was in a bathrobe. Quinn didn't even have shoes. Talk about dumb.

How asinine could you be to go traipsing to a Hidden World in your boxers and a bathrobe?

Tell me about it. And with a cold, too! Never let it be said Nolan's the brightest bulb in the package.

Actually, you're the one who was pushing to come here. You wanted to impress Quinn.

Shut up, dude! So help me, I'll find a boulder and throw it at you.

The fat kid always dies in the survivor movies.

Great. Five minutes in the Otherworld, and he was losing his marbles.

Stanley pulled himself to his feet. It was too wet to get a fire going, and he didn't have a lighter anyway. He knew rubbing two sticks together was a cliché; it never worked. Maybe he could find a flint stone. *Flintstones, meet the Flintstones, they're the modern stone-age family....*

"Okay," he whispered to himself. "Logic aside, I can't just sit here and freeze. I'll do some circular searches from this central point here." He picked up a pointed stone and selected the pine tree with the mushroom as his starting place. He scratched a big X in the bark, then took twenty steps forward and marked another tree. Then he began walking in a wide circle, marking trees as he went, till he came back to the second tree he'd marked. He'd found nothing in his circuitous route except more trees. But then, he'd taken only twenty steps out from the pine tree and the mushroom. Okay, twenty more steps out. X's on the trees.

An hour later, he stood at the bank of a narrow brook that murmured around large, moss-covered stones. The break in the canopy overhead allowed starlight and the glow of the sliver of moon to splash down on the moving water with flashes of glittering white light. After the dark of the Forest itself, it seemed like a godsend. He couldn't see much of the horizon because of the woods surrounding the banks of the brook, but directly above his head, he did recognize several summer constellations.

Stanley knelt and drank the cold water. His stomach rumbled. Dinner at Rathdowns Manor seemed ages ago; and, being honest, he was used to eating a lot. But no such luck out here in the middle of nowhere. He'd yet to see a living creature or any edible plants, and the thought of hunger disturbed him more than being alone and lost. He wondered if he would see fish in the brook come sunrise, and he decided to spend the night by the river. In the morning, he would head downstream, hoping this brook met a larger river that led to some kind of civilization.

It was quite chilly in just a T-shirt, and the Forest was unnervingly quiet. He anticipated a wealth of night noises, but the babbling brook seemed deafeningly loud in the quiet surrounding him. He hummed "The Magic Flute" to keep from getting the willies.

He guessed that it was after midnight and that the moon would soon sink below the horizon; however, he had no real way to tell. He hunted near the brook until he found a massive hollow log that would provide some warmth and shelter. There were the requisite creepy-crawlies, but Stanley viewed all insects scientifically, so he pushed them out of the way. He curled up in a ball with the rotted bark against his back and a clear view of the brook before him. He didn't sleep the whole night, but he was proud of himself that he didn't cry once. There was a logical way out of this predicament—he just had to find it.

At sunrise, covered in ant bites from his night in the log, Stanley shuffled downstream. At least he had a clean water source. The banks of the brook were flat and easy enough to walk on. The sunlight was warm; under the canopy, it took on a muted gray-green color. Stanley saw some squirrels, several birds, and brown trout in the stream. The birds were chirping in the summer morning, and insects were busy darting to and fro. A light, warm wind caressed the leaves of the trees. Other than that, the Forest was silent. No humans, no larger animals; Stanley was alone in the world. No sign of civilization in any direction he could see. He started to despair, as much as he tried to fight it off. Perhaps he should've followed his logic and just remained where the Veil had placed him. The pine tree and its huge mushroom seemed ages ago, like a faltering dream.

He could devise no way to catch any of the trout—they were too fast—but his hunger was getting to the point that if he were lucky enough to catch one, he'd go all Gollum and just eat it raw.

By late morning (he guessed) Stanley was ravenous. He tried to eat the roots of the grasses that lined the banks of his stream, but they were inedible, bitter and tough. It got to the point that he considered hunting for duck eggs in the cattails by the banks, even though he had no way to cook them. Bacterial infection was far down his list of concerns, well below his rumbling stomach.

Around early afternoon, Stanley sat on a gray rock near the water's edge and cried. He knew, as a thirteen-year-old—one of the smartest alive, in fact—that crying was a pointless catharsis. He should be stronger, more mature, better able to keep his wits about him; he should be able to come up with a plan to reunite with the others so they all could go home.

But he'd been alone in the woods for hours and hours, and his stomach was starting to hurt. He'd not slept, and to all appearances, he might die here in the Forest without a miracle. So he cried.

It was his sobs that called the Coeduine maiden. She'd heard him nearly a mile away, such was their hearing; or maybe he was just being that loud. It was an odd sound in the Forest, for she knew the village of Arshúil lay twelve miles to the south. It was rare for her to see Men in this part of the woods—and they never cried.

In fact, she'd been on the point of tears herself, with Bassett off in one direction, Tintreach off in another, Rhydderch the monk and his sullen, quiet apprentice off in yet another. Fiorlen had gone south. They were spread far and wide throughout southern Morsden, looking for her father, Ysgafn. She'd seen no trace of him in two days. Here in the Covering, even for a strong warrior like her father, that was cause for alarm.

Bassett had said Ysgafn was injured. Fiorlen couldn't remember the last time her father had been injured.

And Bassett had said he thought a Corrupted mare was very near to finding a Verse. When they'd all met in the strange clearing the previous evening—and Ysgafn was not to be found—Rhydderch had dispatched Boujòn and his brethren to Crannhyn's domain. The monk had thought it serious enough to notify the Eldest. That worried Fiorlen.

Now, oddly enough, here was a Human youth dressed in peculiar clothing, sitting on a boulder, crying. Fiorlen thought perhaps this was not a coincidence. As she first set eyes on him, she had the overwhelming sensation he was from the Other Side. She walked from behind a tree and stood in silence about fifty feet from the lad, so as not to frighten him.

       ⌣

In his peripheral vision, through the tears, Stanley thought he saw something move. He lifted his head and rubbed his eyes underneath his glasses. His vision was blurred, and it took several moments to realize what he was looking at.

At first, he froze in fear and shock. His skin crawled, just like the audience watching a horror movie when the monster first appears on screen.

It would've been easier to handle if the monster came charging with a bellow. But this one stood stock-still, making not even the smallest movement. Just still. Staring at him.

But as Stanley's eyes adjusted, he saw it wasn't a monster. It was a Treeperson. Rather, a Tree*girl*. And a young one, at that. How he knew she was young, he couldn't explain. Perhaps it was her bark-skin, a rich mocha brown, not quite so rough-hewn as Ysgafn's had been. Perhaps it was her pale green leafy hair, thicker and longer than others'—it fell to her waist like willow branches. Perhaps it was her clothes—they were simple, like a child's: an earth-toned smock and no shoes, her bare feet, five toes on each, sticking out. Her legs were skinny, as were her arms, and quite long; she was taller than Stanley, it appeared, but not by much.

Or perhaps it was her eyes—yellow, catlike, betraying the inquisitiveness of a child. Yes, that was it. She was a little girl.

Neither spoke. They just stared at each other, barely daring to breathe.

Slowly, so she wouldn't bolt, Stanley raised his hand and waved hello. He struggled to keep his voice calm and friendly as he said, "Hi, Coeduine."

The Treegirl cocked her head as if she didn't understand. What about the Song Ysgafn had Sung? She had to understand "Coeduine." *God, please let her understand Coeduine!*

"I am a friend," Stanley said slowly. "I am friends with Ysgafn." That wasn't strictly true; they were barely acquaintances. But, given the circumstances, Stanley felt he could stretch the truth a little.

The Treegirl perked up. Her face brightened, and she gave a little gasp. "Ysgafn?"

Stanley nodded. "Yes. Ysgafn brought me here." Again, a slight stretch of the facts. "I don't know how to explain it. I am not from here." She didn't look like she understood. Did the Song wear off? "I am a visitor."

"You are from the Otherworld," the Treegirl stated.

"Yes, I am fr—hey! Oh, thank God! You can understand me?"

"Yes. Mostly." She took a step forward and stopped, as if waiting to see if he would run away. After another moment, she approached him. "I am Fiorlen. Ysgafn is my father."

Relief coursed through Stanley's veins, but he didn't jump to his feet because he didn't want to startle Fiorlen. "Outstanding! My name is Stanley. Where is your father?"

"He is missing. I've been looking for him for two days."

Stanley deflated. "Crap."

Soon the Translation Song quit working; but, using gestures, Fiorlen showed him that she would Sing again at sundown. In the meantime, they tried to teach each other their own language without magic. It was kind of fun for someone like Stanley, who picked up languages easily, but Fiorlen had difficulty pronouncing English words.

For some reason, it didn't surprise Stanley to learn that the magic wore off after a while—he had somehow anticipated that—but it worried him, thinking about his friends. If they didn't happen to have a handy Treegirl nearby, they'd be stuck with sign language and grunting if they met anybody. Of course, out in the wild woods, meeting somebody would be a stroke of luck. And even greater luck to meet somebody friendly!

Fiorlen had a travel pack full of food. They ate together, and it wasn't until Stanley was through his third apple and a small loaf of black bread that it dawned on him that the Treefolk ate the same food as humans. Why this shocked him, he didn't know. What had he expected them to eat? Dirt?

When Blue Time fell, Fiorlen Sang her Translation Song over Stanley—it was a different Song from what Ysgafn had Sung, and it didn't seem to be quite as powerful. But she explained that the effects of the Singing were cumulative, and the Translating would stay with him longer and longer each time. It was as if his brain needed time to be modified by the Singing magic.

They spent the first hour of the evening sharing what they knew about Ysgafn and the others, which wasn't a whole lot. Stanley explained how they had broken contact with Ysgafn while coming through the Veil. Emery and Genevieve had come through together. Audrey and Ysgafn. Quinn and Nolan. And Stanley had come through alone.

Fiorlen was ecstatic to learn that Quinn was in possession of the Love Verse, but she wouldn't elaborate further, either because she didn't know or because she didn't feel she should. Stanley didn't press her for details. Instead, he focused on learning as much as he could about this Otherworld he found himself trapped in.

"So, if my friends met someone here, they wouldn't be able to understand him now, huh?" Stanley was breaking twigs and tossing them into the small fire encircled by stones that Fiorlen had started with a short two-line Song before Blue Time ended. Useful, this magic stuff!

"By now, I would think the Song's effects would have worn off, yes," Fiorlen said. "It did for you. The Aossí's language is based on ours; they're very similar. But without the Song of Translation, they would be stuck trying to draw or make gestures." She frowned.

It was dark by now, and Stanley was feeling sleepy, sitting next to the warm fire with a full belly. Fiorlen had even used some medicinal leaves to soothe his itching ant bites. He found he wasn't terribly worried for Nolan and the others. If he had made it through the Veil and his first night, they should have, too. But he did feel a little guilty snuggling up next to the warmth, talking to the Treegirl, when he didn't know if his friends were shivering in the dark. Still, searching for them at night seemed to have a very small chance of success, even with the help of a Coeduine. She'd found him entirely by accident.

"Who are the Aossí?" Stanley asked, curious.

"Well, they are like you. They are Men, but they live on our Side of the Veil. There is a village that I will take you to tomorrow. We Coedaoine have kept out of the direct affairs of Man for almost a century, so they will be as shocked to see me as they will be to see you. But the people of this village are kind-natured; we keep watch over them from afar. And given how rarely a person from your Side of the Veil is permitted to cross over, I think my father would want me to take you to the Aossí. There is a chance your friends would come across the village, and, at the very least, Aneirin can organize a search party."

"Who is Aneirin?"

"He is the leader of Arshúil, the only human village for many, many miles. My father once told me that it was founded more than a hundred summers ago, with our help, but had been abandoned for quite some time, until about ten summers ago. There was a war between Men and some of the Corrupted in the Forest. I think Father said there are about a hundred or more Aossí living there now. I'm not all that certain, as I have only seen the village from afar, and they don't venture into the Forest for very long."

"What's a Corrupted?" Stanley didn't like the sound of that.

Fiorlen sighed, poking at the fire with a stick. "We Coedaoine are Shepherds of this Forest. Our Songs can Awaken anything that draws breath, be it plant or animal. This Awakening changes it, makes it larger, more intelligent, capable of speech, able to choose between right and wrong. There are levels of Awakening, though. The more advanced of my race can fully Awaken a creature, but I am a Sapling; my Songs are limited.

"Every once in a while, an Awakened being chooses the path of evil. These are called Corrupted. My father is a seeker of the Corrupted; he destroys them whenever he finds them."

While Stanley could guess that a Sapling was a Coedaoine youth, he wasn't sure how old Fiorlen was, nor if she would be offended if he asked. Cultural relations between humans and legendary creatures weren't part of Stanley's normal repertoire. Still, he ventured to ask, "How long do the Coedaoine remain Saplings? Do they live a long time?"

Fiorlen smiled. "This is the first time I've ever been asked such a question. It isn't something we Coedaoine give much thought to. But I am seven summers old. The Coedaoine live much longer than Aossí, at least, so says Rhydderch. He says the Aossí live about one hundred and twenty summers, and he is pretty old. But my father is almost seven hundred summers, and he is considered young by my race; for the Eldest, Crannhyn, is thousands of summers old. I'm not sure when we are considered elderly, for Crannhyn doesn't look much older than Father. Maybe his hair is grayer."

Stanley started. The Coedaoine, then, were virtually immortal. Fiorlen was a baby by their reckoning. Humans lived a hundred and twenty years here? And who was this Rhydderch person?

Actually, who was *Crannhyn?* Stanley had gotten goose bumps when Fiorlen had mentioned his name.

He had so many questions, and his mind was racing through theories and probabilities. But what he ended up asking was, "Why do you reckon time by seasons? Do you have days? Months? Years?"

Fiorlen waited for the Translation Song a second, then nodded. "Oh, yes. Today is *Déardaoin*." It was Translated "Thursday" in Stanley's head. "The Aossí and Coedaoine share the same calendar. We follow the moon for thirteen months, but Father says we must add days now and again to correct the time. I don't know when that happens, but I do know we start a new year every summer."

Fiorlen didn't seem all that interested in the way things worked on the Other Side of the Veil. She asked very few questions about Stanley's home, which was just fine with him.

"You ask strange questions, Stanley," Fiorlen remarked. He could tell by her tone that she didn't mean it rudely.

"It's the way my brain works," Stanley explained. "It helps me understand about the Otherworld."

She smiled. "Actually, *you're* from the Otherworld."

Stanley chuckled for the first time since arriving in Tírcluddaithe. "All in the perception, I guess."

The Coeduine didn't mind long silences. Fiorlen seemed to be attuned to the Forest on levels Stanley could only guess. As humanlike as she was, Stanley was aware her faculties far surpassed his, and she was of a wholly different race—as separate from Stanley as an elephant or an oak tree. And yet—in some way, she wasn't so different from a kid Emery's age. It made his mind reel, wondering about their Coedaoine taxonomy. He thought of Lewis Carroll again. *Are you animal, vegetable, or mineral?* He wasn't sure the joke would translate well, and he didn't want to offend her, so he waited until she spoke again.

"We have a long walk tomorrow," she said finally. "You should rest. I will build the fire to last through the night. Have no fear; you are safe, for I will watch from the trees for Corrupted." And without any "Good night" or "Pleasure to have met you," the Treegirl stood to her feet and prepared to climb into the boughs of a tall elm. Stanley assumed she slept in the trees.

"Wait," Stanley called out to stop her. "I didn't get a chance to thank you."

"For what?" she asked, cocking her head.

"Well, for finding me, for giving me food."

"I didn't find you; I wasn't looking for you. My food I would share with anyone in need—the Laws of Hospitality require such. Still, if you are thankful,

I am glad to make you welcome." She turned again to grab a branch and was ten feet off the ground before Stanley could ask the question that was really on his mind.

"Can you send me back?" he asked anyway. He knew the answer to the question, somehow, deep down, and he knew he wouldn't leave Nolan and the others, anyway; still, he had to ask, had to hear it from her mouth.

Fiorlen stopped her climb and looked over her shoulder, down at the strange human she'd found in the woods. "No, Stanley, I'm sorry. Only Father can send you Sideways."

It didn't quite Translate; "Moving Sideways" had something to do with passing through the Veil. But the effect was the same: They were stuck here until they found Ysgafn. Stanley nodded and sighed, staring at the fire.

Fiorlen moved further up into the tree. After several minutes of silence, he heard her far above him. "Do not despair, Stanley. The Aossí will help us find your friends. And then we will find my father. I have much faith that, as long as your friends are with the Love Verse, no lasting harm shall befall them."

Stanley took little encouragement from that, but he nodded anyway. He was sure she could see him, even from the treetops. So basically, his life as he knew it, and the safety of his friends' lives, all revolved around a magic Song stuck in a diamond. Hadn't they made a kids' movie with creepy Jim Henson Muppets about this kind of stuff?

Oh, and a seven-hundred-year-old missing Treebeing was the only person who could send them home again.

Great. Nothing to worry about, then.

11

Sign Language and Cold Pheasant

Just great, Nolan, really flippin' great." Quinn took a swing at him, livid, but the weapons maker held them apart, one in each of his hands, looking confused. He probably hadn't expected them to start fighting each other.

"I didn't *mean* to get caught. Ow, dude, cut it out!" Resisting the man was impossible; he just tightened his grip, and Nolan's neck felt like it might snap. "'Course this guy'd be as big as your father! Ouch!"

"No one *means* to get caught, ya idiot!" Quinn tried to lunge for Nolan again, and this time the Aossí, completely perplexed, spun her around away from him. "All right, ya oaf, I get it!"

"*Leyn vo folin cabeth?*" their captor demanded.

The people around him seemed just as dumbfounded as they watched two kids scrap at each other. What were they saying?

"Look, we can't speak your language! Not from here. No talkie the Aossí. Ow! Quit it!" Nolan's voice cracked, and someone laughed. But several people started murmuring—they understood the word "Aossí," but the rest of his speech was lost on them.

"*Glaoan ve lucféagwyl,*" the man grumbled to the crowd. Some younger ones ran off into the night, calling "lucféagwyl," and Nolan just knew that had to mean "cops."

But Quinn wasn't letting up. Now she was kicking dirt at Nolan and the weaponsmith. "Just smashin'. Of all the harebrained, idiotic…. What were ya thinkin'?"

"Quinn, not now—Mister Gentle, here, wants to hurt us."

"Aye, and it's all yore fault!" She slapped at her captor's hand, but he just tightened his grip.

"Well, why didn't you run into the Forest?"

"Why d'ya always want me to *run into the Forest*, for Pete's sake?" She shrieked so loudly, even their captor blanched. "What *good* does that do, Nolan? Like I'm gonna come bust ya outta jail?"

Nolan stopped struggling and held up his hands in surrender. "Okay, stop, Quinn—just *stop*! Look, man, we are not from Tírcluddaithe. Do you understand? The Coeduine. Right? Coeduine. He brought us here. We are not like you. We are not Aossí."

There was a collective intake of breath from the crowd, and then they were perfectly silent. Only the crackle of the fire and some crickets in the fields could be heard. The large man slackened his grip ever so slightly.

"Coedaoine?" he questioned, holding Nolan out at arm's length as if he were contagious. The people started whispering and mumbling.

Nolan nodded. *That must be Treepeople instead of Treeperson.* "Yes, Coedaoine. The Shepherds." It was a horrible gamble, but he knew only three or four words in their language. He just hoped they weren't at war with the Trees. He pointed toward the Forest. "Coeduine. Ysgafn Droed." Then he pointed at the crowd. "Aossí. Fair Folk." Finally he pointed at Quinn, who had stopped fighting for the moment. "No Tírcluddaithe. No Morsden." He made unintelligible gestures with his hands, trying to convey that they weren't from around here. Quinn jumped on board and did her best to shake her head emphatically, to show she agreed with her companion.

"We…are…from…the Otherworld." She made a ridiculous hand gesture, like the humps of a camel or something, to show they were from far over the Forest.

Nolan raised an eyebrow. "What the heck did *that* mean? It looked like you were hailing a cab."

"Shut up! Ya didn't do any better!"

The crowd parted, and four armed guards in the black cloaks came rushing in, jabbering in their throaty speech. The weaponsmith answered, and then the others started speaking all at once. The men held up their hands, and when there was silence, they started asking questions of Nolan and Quinn, their words unintelligible.

They both just shook their heads and held up their hands.

"I'm sorry," Nolan said. "We don't understand."

After several more seconds of back-and-forth, the weaponsmith turned them over to the guards. They were marched toward the center of town, not rudely, just forcefully. The sword maker and the eager crowd followed, all speaking at once. Two of the guards held wicked sharp pikes, and it looked like they knew how to use them. One of the men swatted down a buzzing insect with the tip of his spear without breaking stride. The other one used the butt end to keep Quinn and Nolan a few feet apart from each other. The other two men carried long swords, and Nolan had no doubt they were equally proficient with their weapon of choice.

Their all-black uniforms were quite drab compared to the townsfolk's clothing. But the eagle's head on the left breast of each cloak, with its screaming beak stitched in silver, looked just like the symbol on Nolan's stolen belt. He assumed it was the village's coat of arms, or whatever it should be called. His knowledge of heraldry began and ended with *Ivanhoe*.

In front of a large, low cabin with a raised stone dais, the children saw a tall, middle-aged man with long blond hair and sharp eyes. He held a staff capped with a gold eagle's head. He, too, wore a cloak with the embroidered symbol, but his was ornate and blood red. It seemed likely he was some kind of town leader. The guards bowed, saluted, and said something as they pushed the weaponsmith forward. He proceeded to tell his tale, with the townsfolk adding bits and pieces to the story.

Finally the elder raised his hands for silence and stepped forward to study the kids. "Aneirin," he said, pointing to himself.

"Um, Nolan," Nolan replied, then pointed to Quinn. "Her name is Quinn."

"Hi." She waved.

"Nolan," Aneirin sounded out the name. He touched his chest in a salute, then turned to speak to a young page standing at his side. The youth disappeared into the cabin and returned with a horn of ink, a scroll of parchment, and a quill pen. Several men stood around him holding torches to cast light on the paper. Aneirin drew something on the parchment and then held it out for the children to see. It was a rather good drawing of a Treebeing.

Nolan nodded. "Yes. Ysgafn. Coeduine. This Treeman brought us here, but we lost him." He realized he was making stupid signs, and Quinn mocked him. He ignored her and made a motion like he was looking for Ysgafn.

Aneirin smiled and said something to the crowd. Several gasped, and some scoffed. One or two gave a small cheer. He continued speaking to them for about a minute, and then they all started to disperse. No one questioned his authority, no matter how intrigued he might have been. One of the guards returned the sword to the weapon maker, who approached Nolan and Quinn.

"Cadfan," he said, thumping his chest.

"Erm, nice to meet you. I think." Nolan smiled.

The big man guffawed, saluted Quinn, then slumped off. He was joined by several townsfolk, and they all began talking at once, shooting the occasional glance over their shoulder at the children.

The guards motioned for Nolan and Quinn to enter the main wood-and-stone building, and Aneirin followed. Inside was a long, sparsely decorated hall with low ceilings. There was a pit in the center with a hole in the roof above, but there was no fire. Benches lined the walls.

It was a waiting area, Nolan guessed. Candles and lamps hung from the log walls, which were dressed in a few tapestries similar to what he had seen at the clothes tent. They showed scenes of battle, giant eagles hunting prey, men on horses. Some showed creatures, like animals—lions, elephants, tigers, deer, and beavers—and some were plants and flowers; but they were all walking on two legs like humans, wearing clothes, and holding weapons. That explained the humanlike wolf! In these tapestries, there was usually a Singing Treebeing with an intelligent, gentle face. Shepherds of the Forest.

Several doors branched off the back of the hall. The guards directed the children through one on the left wall, which led back outside into a kind of a small courtyard enclosed by a tall fence. Across the way was another low building, adjacent to the waiting hall, and then they proceeded through another door that led to…cells.

They were being locked up!

"Aneirin," Quinn said, gesturing to the cells, "don't put us in there. We're not criminals! I mean, not *usually*," she pleaded with a worried look on her face.

The town elder thought for a second, said something they couldn't understand, and made a gesture. He drew his arms to his chest, as if holding something tight, and then slowly raised his hand and pointed out the door. Nolan thought he might be referring to the rising sun.

"I think he means just for tonight," he said to Quinn. "Like he's afraid we'll run away. Or for our safety, maybe."

"That's what ya got out of that? How can ya tell?" Quinn asked.

"I can't. Just seems that's what he's trying to say. And it's not like we have a choice, anyway." Nolan eyed the guards' spears. He sighed and entered the cell.

It was a long rectangle with four bunk beds covered in straw mattresses. The floor was clean, and there were two windows sporting iron bars. The walls were wood, and off in the far corner was a wood box seat that obviously was meant to serve as a privy.

At least it wasn't a dungeon with rats.

Aneirin also entered the cell and motioned for the children to sit on the beds. He remained standing, with a guard positioned behind him. Another guard he dismissed with a short sentence. Moments later, that same guard returned with two long cloaks, which he handed to Nolan. It was clear they were meant to be used as blankets.

"*Leyn daoineil?*" Aneirin asked, pointing to Nolan, then to Quinn, then to two or three invisible people next to them.

"I think he's askin' if there are more of us," Quinn supplied.

Nolan looked to her. "Tell him the truth?"

"I think we should. He could send out search parties, maybe. Better all of us here than Gran, Emery, and Stanley out there alone."

"And Genevieve."

"Ah, yeah...her too."

Nolan nodded. "Aneirin, there are four others." He held up four fingers and made shapes of invisible people. "Two boys," he said, pointing to himself, "Stanley and Emery, my brother. And one girl"—he pointed to Quinn—"Genevieve." Then he pointed to Quinn again and said, "And her grandmother, Audrey." He stood up and stooped over, shuffling like an old person hunched over a cane.

"She's not decrepit, Nols. Come on."

"Like to see *you* do a better job!" Nolan snapped.

Aneirin's eyes widened. "Stanley, Emery, Genevieve, Audrey." He did pretty well pronouncing the strange names.

"Yes, that's right," Nolan confirmed. "Stanley is like me, Emery is little, Genevieve is tall. Audrey is older." He made the appropriate sizes with his hand, then drew his arms to his chest like Aneirin had, as if holding something tight. "Our friends. We have lost them." He made like he was looking for someone. "Can you find them?" He pointed to Aneirin and made the same looking motion.

"*Ie.*" Aneirin clapped his hands and gave instructions to the guards on the other side of the cell. They left. Aneirin made hand gestures of eating, drinking, and sleeping, then turned to leave.

"Wait. Aneirin."

The elder turned.

"Are there any Treefolk here? Any Coedaoine?" Nolan pretended like he was singing, then touched his ears and mouth.

Aneirin frowned. He shook his head and made a motion with his hand, like pushing something away, over and over. Nolan thought maybe he understood—"far, far away" or "long, long ago." Then Aneirin said something that probably meant "not for many, many years" and, after a pause, "*Leyn jyn dío.*" The expression on his face needed no Translation. He was saying he was sorry. Nolan and Quinn were crestfallen.

The town leader shrugged and said, "*Brearych muid ve Coedaoine anois.*" Nolan understood "Coedaoine," but when Aneirin made the same looking gesture Nolan had made before, like searching through a long glass, he figured it out.

"They're looking for the Treefolk, too."

Aneirin made the saluting motion again and bid them good night. Then, as it seemed to Nolan, he ordered the remaining guard to bring them food and drink. And to lock the gate.

Torches were set outside the cell, and a dim orange light splashed on the wooden walls, flickering. The two children were outright exhausted. Goblets of wine and water were brought, as was cold pheasant (something Nolan had never had before; he thought it tasted like gamey chicken), bread, boiled red potatoes, and hard-boiled eggs on brightly stained wooden plates. It wasn't a bad meal, all things considered. It never occurred to the children that the food might be poisoned or anything—Aneirin, while not exactly friendly, didn't seem to want them dead, either.

They ate in near silence, yawning every few seconds. Finally Quinn admitted to being still a little angry at Nolan but said there didn't seem to be any use in holding a grudge; what was done was done, and she felt that Aneirin would have a better chance of finding her gran and the others than two foreign kids traipsing through the Forest, nightgowns or not.

They took turns staring out the cell's iron gate so the other could use the wooden box seat (and some cottony type of gauze that was apparently the equivalent of toilet paper). The guard stationed outside the gate also turned around respectfully. They soon found it wasn't any good asking him questions—he might as well have been mute. But he did eye them with a kindly expression and watched them with obvious interest.

They each chose one of the lower bunk beds. As they lay down, Quinn couldn't resist one more shot at Nolan. "See, Nols, should've just come to 'em in the first place. No need to sneak and nick food and stuff. Ya should listen to me more often. I'm older 'n ya, and I *am* a queen's great-great-granddaughter, after all!"

"Yeah, yeah, yeah. Go to bed, Your Highness. Hope there's no peas under your mattress…." He had been about to say, *'Cept now we're in a jail cell and can't look for the others*. But, of course, it wasn't *her* fault they were in jail now, so he kept quiet. Instead he sighed. "I'm sure your grandmother's okay. She was with Ysgafn when they crossed through."

Something in his tone must have made Quinn feel bad, because she said, "And I'm sure Emery and Stanley are just fine," with a touch of compassion creeping into her voice and eyes.

Nolan nodded, then chuckled. "And maybe Genevieve."

"Her, too…maybe." She snickered.

And with that, they both fell into a deep sleep.

12

Fiorlen

Morning sunlight streamed in through the windows, casting shadows from the bars on the swept dirt floor. What woke Nolan was the excited jabbering of children outside, trying to peek over the window ledges at the "newcomers." He saw little bobbing heads as they tried to climb on each other's shoulders, and then several pieces of some kind of candy flew through the windows and landed on the bunk beds. He grabbed one, smelled it, and took a nibble of the sugar stick. It tasted like honey and mint. It was good, so he stuck it in the corner of his mouth, sucking thoughtfully. He heard a guard outside approach the kids and shoo them off. Quinn stirred, stretching with a loud, rude yawn.

"What're ya eatin'?" she asked in a thick voice.

"Candy. Some local kids threw it through the window. Try one. They're good."

"How d'ya know it's safe to eat?" She picked up one of the light brown sticks and smelled it.

"I don't think the kids are trying to kill us. It tastes fine."

A guard opened the door and brought in two trays laden with breakfast foods: a bowl of porridge, more eggs, toast, butter, grilled onions, and little strips of bright red mystery meat, kind of like bacon but not made of pork. The guard bowed to the two children as he laid the trays on the two empty bunk beds in their cell. He had a pitcher of water and another pitcher of cool, thick milk with two empty wooden cups.

He smiled when he saw the candy and pointed at the sticks. *"Elgaet."*

"Sweets," Quinn said, then popped the stick in the corner of her mouth with a smile.

"Sweets," the guard repeated, saluting her before retreating.

They ate well and used the water to wash up afterward. Quinn was no longer acting cross toward Nolan—she said it did no good to stay mad at him for getting them caught. And she felt maybe it was for the best that they'd made contact with the villagers, anyway; it was their greatest hope of finding the others. If only Aneirin would let them go.

They dozed awhile, ate lunch, and then around midday, after the changing of the guard, tried asking the new one how long they were going to be kept locked up. He just smiled and saluted, but they could get nothing out of him, no matter what signs they used. Nolan thought it was maddening how everyone just saluted.

Some more local children showed up outside their window, chattering and jumping up to the window ledge to get a look at the foreigners. They were soon chased away by an adult, but Nolan wished they'd at least tossed in some more candy first—he and Quinn had already finished off what had been delivered that morning.

As far as he could tell, the afternoon was waning, and Blue Time was only a short time off. The slant of the sunlight through the windows seemed at a low angle. They had seen no one but their guards, yet they were fed well and had plenty of fresh water to drink. It was so boring that they started making up elaborate escape plans, just for fun, each one more desperate and implausible than the last, until there was a clamor in the distance.

Something exciting was happening, but it was several minutes before the noise got louder as it approached the cell block. The door from the courtyard swung wide, and several Aossí entered, dressed in forest-colored garb, kind of like camouflage—not the bright colors the villagers usually wore.

They were followed by Aneirin and, lastly, a tall, slender Treegirl!

Quinn gasped and grabbed Nolan's arm. He was wide-eyed with surprise. It hadn't occurred to him that there must be Tree-women if there were Tree-men, but the sight struck him as odd. She was different from Ysgafn: much smaller—in fact, only a little taller than Quinn—and her features were youthful and fresh, not weatherworn and aged. She was much younger, perhaps even a child by Coedaoine standards. Her yellow eyes were wide with wonder, or perhaps there was even a hint of fear.

No, it wasn't fear, Nolan decided. She was excited to see them. She was dressed in a simple earth-toned smock and no shoes; her long, willowy hair was tied behind her back. Her bark-skin was lighter than Ysgafn's, but she had the same intelligent look about her.

Aneirin was beaming, as if he'd just struck gold. He pointed to the Treegirl and said, "Fiorlen." Then to the children, "Quinn *onkustus* Nolan."

The cell door was unlocked, and Aneirin motioned for them to come out. They both approached the Coeduine maiden. She gave a small, sheepish smile and said just one word: "Ysgafn?"

Nolan nodded. "Ysgafn." Then he made a series of complex motions that he hoped would communicate that they had been brought through the Veil by him.

Fiorlen clapped her hands and jumped up and down, giggling. She reminded Nolan of a young kid excited about a trip to the zoo or a new toy. It was a peculiar sight to behold, and soon Nolan and Quinn found themselves laughing at the Treegirl's enthusiastic delight.

"*Leyn Ysgafn m'atadir*," Fiorlen said, her eyes bright with excitement.

"Hey! I know *athair*," Quinn said eagerly. "Means 'father' in Irish. I think Ysgafn's her dad."

Nolan gaped. "Dumb stinkin' luck," he whispered. What were the odds of the first Treeperson they met in Tírcluddaithe being Ysgafn's daughter?

After she quit dancing, the Treegirl inclined her head, as if listening to something only she could hear. Then she reached for Quinn's hand and held it just a second, still listening. With one of her long, twig-like fingers, Fiorlen touched Quinn's purple tunic, over her heart, and gave a very slight nod. The diamond was virtually undetectable under the thick fabric, but somehow Fiorlen could sense it. The Coeduine raised her mossy eyebrows, and her yellow eyes held Quinn's for a couple heartbeats.

If this seemed like an odd action to the Aossí, they didn't show it. They were probably as clueless of Treefolk behavior as the children were.

Fiorlen stepped back and turned to Aneirin, and there was excitement in his voice as he said, "*Canadhan ve mercaíln ahenocht.*"

"Okay, I didn't understand that at all," Quinn said.

Fiorlen crouched down and, with her finger, drew a setting sun in the dirt of the cell floor (she was quite an artist), and then she sang a few bars. Her voice was beautiful, high and lilting, and it made Nolan want to listen all day to whatever she wanted to sing. Nothing else mattered but the singing. Fiorlen touched her mouth and then her ears. It was at this point that Nolan noticed the Coeduine had pointed ears that were larger proportioned than a human's. *The Coedaoine must be able to hear very well*, he mused.

Then he realized what she meant by the gesture.

Relief poured through his veins. "She can Sing the Translation Song! Tonight, at Blue Time."

Finally! They would be able to ask questions and get some answers. Quinn looked overjoyed. But before Nolan had time to revel in the idea, Aneirin was talking animatedly, gesturing back toward the main hall, motioning for them to come.

"Now what's he saying?" Nolan asked.

"Why're ya askin' me?" Quinn responded.

It appeared Aneirin had no intention of keeping them locked up any longer, so they followed him a little sheepishly through the narrow courtyard and back into the main hall.

There, at a wooden table below the tapestries of humanlike animals, next to the fire pit—dressed in local garb, clean and safe and dry, scarfing down what looked like roast beef and carrot stew—was Stanley. He swallowed and jumped up, grinning widely.

"Are you kidding me?" Nolan shouted. His voice broke, but he didn't care.

"Aneirin wanted to surprise you," Stanley said. "So…are you surprised?"

There were several minutes of hugging and laughing. Even Quinn hugged Stanley, and he seemed to hold on to her a little too long, which Nolan thought was a little odd. But when she pulled away, they both laughed and grabbed Nolan in a three-way embrace.

As excited as he was to see Stanley alive and well, his presence only reminded Nolan that the others were still missing. They had wasted a whole day locked in the cell. "What about Emery and Genevieve? And Audrey?" Nolan asked as he pulled out of the hug.

Stanley looked down at the floor. "I'm sorry, Nolan, I don't know. Aneirin's sent teams out looking for them."

"I'm sure they're all right, Nols." Quinn reached out and squeezed his hand.

The wooden doors of the main hall stood open, flanked by Aossí in black cloaks. The sunlight coming through was low; it would be dark within the hour. They couldn't venture into the Forest tonight. Nolan's trepidation for his brother and Gen and Audrey was almost physically painful, but there seemed to be nothing he could do about it tonight.

Nolan gave Quinn's hand a light squeeze in return, then released it. "No matter what Aneirin says, we leave tomorrow at first light," he resolved. "Agreed?"

His two friends nodded.

Aneirin cleared his throat. He made a low bow to the children, made an even lower bow to the Coeduine, then said something as he motioned them toward the open doors.

"He says it's almost time to eat," Stanley supplied. "We're having a feast with the whole town. Just when I'm finally full...."

"The Translation Song works as well for the Aossí language as the Treefolk's?" Nolan asked.

Stanley nodded. "Their language is very similar to the Coedaoine's; it's actually a proto-Gaelic, so Quinn might be able to pick up bits and pieces even without the Song."

They went outside, where a hundred or more Aossí were waiting for them. Some of the people even cheered. Fiorlen looked sheepish, but Stanley didn't seem to mind the attention.

"We're kinda like celebrities," Stanley said. "Our world is a legend to them, and no one's seen the Treefolk here in ninety years, so they're just as excited about Fiorlen. Sorta like meeting a guardian angel or something."

They were swept along in the crowd toward the fields by the river, which Stanley called the Rhrushden. Quite literally, the "River Roaring," he said; even though, at this particular spot, it was just a wide, mellow purr. He was explaining how *den* meant "-ing" in the First Language, so Morsden Forest was "the Covering" or "the Shrouding," but *mors* also meant "death," so it was kind of a clever play on words.

Aneirin had told Stanley that none of the townsfolk had ever heard of children being alone in the Morsden and surviving to tell the tale. Stanley abruptly fell silent, likely remembering that Emery was still missing and that Nolan was probably thinking of him.

A dozen long wooden tables were set on the grassy field before the River Roaring. Several Fair Folk women were spreading out bright tablecloths, and they saw Cadfan the weaponsmith sitting on a large stump, tuning a fiddle that looked miniscule in his behemoth hands. Several other musicians were sitting near him on their own stumps, getting ready to play. Cadfan chortled and said something as the children approached.

"He says, 'Hail, Otherworlders.'" Stanley waved at him. "'Especially the feisty girl.' He means you, Quinn. Why's he call you feisty?"

"Long story," she said, smiling back at Cadfan. "I wonder if they're gonna make us pay 'em back for the things we nicked."

"I don't think so," Stanley said. "They have these Laws of Hospitality, which mean they give visitors anything they need. Soon as I got here, they gave me these clothes." He was dressed in a bright red tunic with yellow checks, sea-green trousers with blue stripes, a wide brown belt with the screaming eagle, and brown ankle boots. He pushed his glasses up on the bridge of his nose. "They've got wild taste, huh?"

"I think it's fun," Quinn said, gesturing to her own clothing. "The Celts back home used to wear outfits like these as a status symbol. The louder the clothes, the richer ya were."

As they walked down the middle of the rows of tables, Aneirin motioned for them to take their places at the head table—positions of honor. The town's elite were already seated around it. They stood when the children and Fiorlen approached. Every eye was upon them, faces showing expressions of awe or, perhaps, concern; maybe even a little fear. It made Nolan uncomfortable to be the subject of such scrutiny, and Fiorlen seemed awkward with the attention, too. After a few moments, she drifted down to the water's edge and stared out into the setting sun.

"They're kind of an aloof species," Stanley remarked.

Aneirin spoke several sentences to the children, then saluted them all before turning to give directions to a couple of the feast organizers.

Stanley thanked him, then told the others, "They're going to wait till *gylináma*, the time-between-times, to start the feast, so Fiorlen can Sing and we can understand each other. He's honored and excited to be hosting this historic occasion. It's the first time in any of their lives they will have heard a Coeduine Sing. He's asked the townsfolk not to bother us until then, and he says we should relax and catch up."

"So who's this Aneirin bloke?" Quinn asked. "Is he a good guy?"

Stanley shrugged. "You've known him longer than I have. I met him only an hour ago. He's the town's leader; Fiorlen said they are elected every two years by the people, and he answers to some guy named King Dubric in a country called Tírsor—that means "Southlands"—about a two days' journey from here, across the Culais Strait.

"Dubric's brother is the High King of Tírcluddaithe—Alaric the Gracious, he's called. But the royal city, called the Citadel, is days from here to the northeast, across the ocean. Fiorlen was told the city's carved out of alabaster, but she's never seen it."

"Wow!" Quinn said. "A High King! That's like the Hill of Tara in old-time Ireland."

Stanley nodded. "Nolan would know that, too, if he'd paid attention to me on the flight over from Boston."

Nolan made a sour face. "No, no, I got it. Hill of Tara, one guy in a skirt, king of the other guys in skirts."

"Only the Scots wear skirts, Nolan," Stanley corrected him.

They shared a small laugh, and it felt good to smile again.

"Anyway," Stanley continued, "this village is called Arshúil, which means 'Away,' and it's the first settlement here at the southern tip of the Covering. The Aossí generally steer clear of the Forest proper—they call it the Deep. You're lucky to have found the only settlement in fifty miles."

"How does Fiorlen know all this if the Greenmen and the Fair Folk haven't seen each other in almost a hundred years?" Quinn asked.

"Fiorlen's dad is one of the guardians over Morsden, one of the Shepherds, so he keeps tabs on the people here, too, but the Coedaoine haven't made themselves known for decades. It's kinda like they have as little to do with the Aossí as possible, and vice versa. Most people revere the Greenmen as almost mystical beings—and some don't even believe in them. Of course, I guess that'll change now."

"Fiorlen seems…young," Quinn said.

"She's seven summers. Er, that's how they reckon age. For a Coeduine, that's like a toddler. They're called Saplings—isn't that cute? Far as I can tell, they're almost immortal. 'Least, no human's been around long enough to see one of them die of old age, and the Aossí live longer than we do. It's not uncommon for one of them to live to a hundred and twenty or so. And did you notice their ears are a little tipped? I mean, they're clearly human, but they're taller than us…and paler.

"Oh, and get this: The words for 'child' and 'wealth' are the same in the First Tongue. That's why there's so many kids here. The more children you have, the richer you are. That's what Ysgafn meant when he called me the 'wealth of Aossí.'"

"But yore not one of the Fair Folk," Quinn pointed out.

"Technically we're *all* Fair Folk. These people's predecessors were our predecessors—but they've been hidden for thousands of years by the Greenmen. In fact, your ancestor, the one Ysgafn called the Embroidery Queen, was one of the first Aossí."

At the mention of the Embroidery Queen, Fiorlen approached them whisper-quiet. The villagers were giving her a wide berth, though a few of the younger children would run up close, smile, wave, and then run back to their friends, giggling. Some of the adults looked at Fiorlen like she was an alien. Nolan figured their cautiousness made sense; it'd been almost a hundred years since anyone had seen a Treeperson.

Fiorlen sat next to Stanley and smiled at the people around the table. She leaned in to whisper something in Stanley's ear.

He said, "Uh, once 'she Sings, I guess we're not supposed to talk about your ancestor, Quinn. She wants to talk to us in private after the feast about all that."

Quinn nodded. "Okay."

"I guess you still have the, uh, *thing?*" Stanley asked her.

"Yeah." Quinn's hand brushed where the diamond lay under her tunic.

"Really lucky Aneirin didn't have you searched," Stanley said.

Fiorlen clicked her tongue, even though the Aossí had no way of understanding what the children were talking about, and Nolan interpreted the sound as an indication that it was time for a change of subject. He grabbed a twig off the ground and started twirling it between his thumb and forefinger. "So how come the Treefolk can Sing only at Blue Time?"

"The magic works only for about an hour a day, at dusk," Stanley explained. "Any other time, nothing magical happens. Just the way the universe works—Fiorlen calls it the Law. Like gravity, or thermodynamics."

Fiorlen spoke then, smiling, and Stanley interpreted: "She says the Law is stronger than gravity. They're pretty serious about it."

Quinn smiled at Fiorlen and asked Stanley, "What else did she tell ya 'bout the Songs?"

"Um, she told me the effects of the Songs are cumulative. If more Treefolk are Singing, the magic is stronger. And the older ones have more power. Their Songs can Awaken plants or animals…like, *evolve* them into something more intelligent, more anthropomorphic. Quite a few of the wildlife living in the Morsden are Awakened creatures, but there seem to be levels of Awakening."

"Yeah, we know all about that!" Nolan told Stanley about the Awakened wolf, for that was clearly what that creature had been, and about the moving plant.

Stanley's eyes got wider as Nolan continued. When he finished, Stanley said, "Oh, man! All I saw was a great big mushroom." He grabbed a piece of yellowish-green fruit from a bowl in the center of the table and gave it a sniff before taking a bite out of it. "Mmm. Tastes like a milky banana." He swallowed before continuing. "Did you know some of the most Awakened creatures have their own nations and kings? The Aossí have made alliances with them, and they all answer to King Alaric."

"That's amazing," Nolan put in, trying to picture an organized nation of Awakened animals and plants.

"It is," Stanley agreed. "But those kinds of Awakened beings are much rarer. Only the most powerful Coedaoine can fully Awaken a plant or an animal—and for some of the creatures, it takes several Treefolk Singing.

"Ysgafn is several hundred years old, he's very advanced in Singing. He's so powerful, he's one of the few who can raise the Veil separating our world from Tírcluddaithe."

That last sentence hung in the air a moment as Nolan realized what Stanley was saying. "Wait. So that means *she* can't send us home." He sighed and tossed the small branch down on the ground. "Great! That means we're stuck here without Ysgafn."

13

A Fair-Folk Feast

Yeah. Part of that universal Law is, it takes the Greenman who brought you over to send you back." Stanley shrugged. For once, here was a topic he didn't know much about. "I couldn't understand all of what Fiorlen was trying to explain, they call it 'Moving Sideways' between our world and this one. It has something to do with the individual Coeduine's memory. Ysgafn *remembers* how to take us back home. But if Fiorlen tried to take us back, we could end up stuck between the two worlds—we could end up anywhere, or *nowhere*."

The Treegirl nodded but didn't speak.

Quinn was thoughtful for a second. "That makes sense. Kinda. If ya think about it, it would be like someone drivin' ya to a theater they'd never been to."

"Couldn't they stop and ask for directions?" Nolan frowned, but he was only half serious. This stuff went way over his head.

"Huh?" Quinn apparently hadn't gotten the joke, for she felt a need to defend her explanation. "I know it's not *exactly* the same, lads. Crossin' the Veil's not like cruisin' down the M25."

"Hey, you're the one who started this whole driving analogy." Nolan winked at her to show he was kidding.

"No one *cruises* down the M25 anyway. I hear it's a glorified parking lot." Stanley chuckled.

Fiorlen spoke in her high voice, and Stanley gave the interpretation: "She said even if she could raise the Veil and remember where to take us home, she doesn't know where there's any *portanuam*...I don't know, the Song's struggling for a Translation. Er, what's a portanuam, Fiorlen?"

She gave an explanation in the First Tongue.

"Ah," Stanley said. "That's 'doorways.' Like, places where the Veil is thinnest between our world and here. Uh, I guess she's talking about ley lines, geomagnetism, quantum physics, M-theory...that kind of stuff."

"I've no idea what ya just said." Quinn scratched her head.

Fiorlen gave a short quip, and Stanley laughed, setting the core of the weird fruit down on the table. "She said, 'Me, neither.' Well, it's like the doorways are hidden all over the place, like what's at the Rathdowns cairn. Bottom line, you have to be at a portanuam to raise the Veil."

Nolan was suddenly pensive. He felt guilty making small talk when his little brother was out there in the Forest somewhere. "Doesn't matter anyway. We're not leaving without the others. When we find Emery, Gen, and Audrey, we'll find Ysgafn, too."

Fiorlen commented on that.

"She says something is preventing Ysgafn from finding *us*," Stanley interpreted. "To find her father and the others, we will need to ask Crannhyn for help."

At the mention of the new name, Nolan and Quinn looked at each other. There almost seemed to be a breeze that passed between them, some electrical charge in the air, that made the hair on their arms stand up.

"You've mentioned him before," Stanley said to the Treegirl. "Who's Crannhyn?"

Fiorlen's face adopted an almost enraptured expression, as if she were speaking of a favorite uncle or grandfather. Someone she thought was angelic and could do no wrong. The other children leaned in to hear, and even the Aossí seated near them could no longer feign disinterest.

"He is the first," Stanley translated, his voice just barely audible. "The Eldest of the Coedaoine. The eldest of *any* living thing. Only the rocks are older than he. Crannhyn was here to watch the dew settle on the young green grass when the sun rose on its first morning. It was he who created the Veil, and he who Awakened the first creatures of the Forest. He is Crannhyn the Mighty."

One of the Aossí who had been eavesdropping laughed and returned to his ale. The rest soon followed suit.

"That was rude," Quinn observed. "Firs' time I've seen any discourtesy from the Aossí."

Fiorlen waved her slender hand in a dismissive gesture and spoke. Stanley said, "Crannhyn has become a myth to the Fair Folk." The Treegirl didn't seem perturbed by the Aossí's reaction. "She says we could probably find Emery and Genevieve, but she doubts we will be able to find Ysgafn and Audrey. Something prevents her father from seeking her in the Deep, and yet she feels within herself that her father is alive, and that your grandmother is with him. This is why we must get help from Crannhyn."

They were all silent for several moments. Not far from the tables, Cadfan was drawing a few notes out of the violin. Aossí children romped in the fields under failing light. The sun was just about to touch the horizon, and Nolan saw the first twinkling stars appear. Blue Time was moments away.

He gave Quinn a reassuring nod. "We'll find them." He spoke so only she could hear. Quinn nodded back at him, a determined look etched on her face. They both realized Fiorlen was talking and that Stanley was trying to piece together what she said.

"I don't know what she means," Stanley admitted. "Crannhyn's bird is the village? Huh? It's *his*, um, bird...no, *eagle*, that's the name of Arshúil—the town's named after Crannhyn's eagle? Er...what? (Sometimes the Song takes a while to pick the right words.) Fiorlen, I'm sorry, but I don't understand what you're saying."

Fiorlen grew frustrated. She raised her hands and said loudly, "Tintreach!"

Many of the Aossí startled and looked to the sky, and children ran to their parents. From across the field, Aneirin eyed the Treegirl sharply.

"I understood that!" Quinn looked up. "She said 'lightning.'"

"But the sky's clear," Nolan commented.

From the edge of the Forest, a winking greenish-yellow light came zooming over the River Roaring like a ball of, well, greenish-yellow lightning. Children screamed and ducked. Nolan heard Cadfan's voice over the tumult, but of course, he didn't understand what he was saying.

The lemon-lime light hovered in front of Fiorlen's outstretched hand, and it dawned on Nolan what he was looking at.

It was a Firefly. A giant lightning Bug, the size of a football. Its head and black eyes were massive; its body was black and red. Its wings vibrated, and its soft, fat tail flickered on and off. What was weirder, it was talking to Fiorlen. She nuzzled it affectionately, and it settled on her shoulder like a parrot.

"She says its name is Tintreach," Stanley said as she resumed speaking. "That's appropriate." Several of the braver Aossí were now gathering nearer to her so that they could see the enlarged Insect. "Um, the Bug says it's pleased to meet us.

"She says this is her Awakened, and she practices Singing on Tintreach. They're companions. Her father's Awakened is Bassett, who should be coming soon. Uh, Bassett's a 'Ball of Light'? Hmmm. That doesn't quite Translate. A butterfly, maybe? Crannhyn's Awakened is an eagle—oh, I get it!" Stanley stood to his feet in excitement. "They named the village after Crannhyn's eagle, Arshúil. I understand now, Fiorlen."

"That's *so* cool!" Quinn said. "*I* wanna Firefly for a pet."

"How come you didn't show me Tintreach yesterday?" Stanley asked the Treegirl.

Fiorlen was speaking to several of the Aossí children and invited them to come touch the Firefly. Tintreach seemed to be eating up the attention as Fiorlen turned her head to answer Stanley's question.

"I was asleep," he explained, "when Tintreach returned in the middle of the night, and then she sent him with a message to Rhydderch to meet us here. (I still don't know who that is....) A friend of Ysgafn's, she says."

Aneirin came up to them, smiling, bowed low to Fiorlen, and held out his hand. He offered a wedge of apple to Tintreach, which it consumed greedily. The town chief said something to the Coeduine in a voice that sounded respectful and a little overawed to Nolan.

"He says gylináma has fallen," Stanley said.

And Nolan knew Aneirin was right: It was Blue Time. He felt it in the pit of his stomach even before he looked to the sky. Dusk had come, the magic hour, and Aneirin clapped his hands, calling for silence and for all the Aossí to gather around Fiorlen.

When a hundred-some-odd Fair Folk had encircled the Treegirl and her lightning Bug—the three travelers in front of her, next to Aneirin and Cadfan—everyone sat on the grass and waited as Fiorlen began to Sing.

No one breathed. At first, Nolan could hear only the *Chéad Teanga*—the First Tongue—but then, right in the middle of the second line, it popped in their heads what she was saying. It felt as if her Song wasn't quite as powerful as Ysgafn's, but that didn't make it any less enrapturing. It was mournful, melancholy, and yet cautiously hopeful.

Nolan could've listened for hours on end, with no thoughts of food or drink or sleep. He thought only of the Singing, and he realized that this was merely the Translation Song; how much more powerful other Songs must be! What would it be like to hear the Coeduine Sing of Awakening or raising the Veil? What if several Coedaoine were Singing all at once? He imagined it must be like listening to the Elves in old stories.

> *"Cébod leyn jyn saibhristyn holc,*
> *Roithyg tand clus domi.*
> *Ddweud jyn…the tale of understanding,*
> *What it is to hear and see.*
> *A thousand times a thousand,*
> *And a thousand years ago,*
> *We shared one speech,*
> *One Song, one joy, one land,*
> *And one sorrow:*
> *For it was your doom to fight and lie,*
> *To cheat and steal, and kill.*
> *The Veil was raised, in hopes it may*
> *From doom to keep us still.*
> *But there was hope to be rejoined,*
> *A curtain to be raised;*
> *Our Songs weren't lost on ears of stone,*
> *Just hidden in a haze.*
> *The years have driven, the seasons raced,*
> *At last the time has come*
> *To reunite the separate ones*
> *And see us all back to home."*

The last notes faded and echoed across the River, which seemed to silence itself for her Song. The Covering seemed to shimmer, maybe even shiver—Nolan couldn't decide which—but as the Song rippled across the grassy field, everyone was touched by it, and the Aossí bowed their heads in reverence.

"That was different from Ysgafn's," Quinn whispered to her companions.

Stanley nodded. "When she Sang to me last night, she said it's not just the words, it's the Song itself that matters. I think if she Sang about a soda can, we'd still understand it. The magic comes from Fiorlen, an act of will—the Singing just puts it into action."

After several respectful moments, the townsfolk broke into a collective cheer, and a spirit of frivolity returned. Aneirin stood on a bench and waved his hands for silence.

"Fellow citizens of Arshúil, we have guests. Now that they are known to be friends, and now that they should be able to understand our speech"—here he bowed low to the Treegirl—"the Laws of Hospitality prevail upon our humble village to provide them with everything they need. You have all heard the old tales, but I, like you, never expected my eyes to witness legends come true. I foresee a new time is turning: the spring yields to summer, the Coedaoine have come again, and they have brought Otherworlders that need our assistance. I expect it of each of you, and thank you in advance. Welcome, Nolan, Quinn, Stanley, and Fiorlen...and, of course, the Awakened Tintreach—"

The townsfolk interrupted with shouts of welcome, but Nolan noticed that not all the faces in the failing light seemed to be as convinced about a new time turning and spring yielding to summer. It appeared to him that not all the Aossí were excited that this Treegirl and her Otherworlders had shown up out of the blue.

Aneirin held up his hands. "Tomorrow to business, but tonight...we feast!"

Cadfan, who had slipped back to his tree stump, shouted, "Lively now, lads!" and the meadow erupted into riotous, joyful music that made Nolan's toes tap unconsciously.

As trays appeared on the tables, Nolan recognized one thing the Aossí women were exceptionally good at: food! However, despite his own excitement and sudden hunger, he felt a twinge of regret, as he remembered that Emery, Audrey, and Genevieve were out in those woods, possibly starving. Quinn and Stanley, though, were diving right in, offering him roast goose, a mug of strawberry-honey mead, and a wooden plate loaded high with roasted potatoes, carrots, onions, and grape tomatoes.

Rhythmic clapping broke into his reverie as Cadfan's band started up a vigorous tune that was apparently a crowd favorite. The Fair Folk began forming small circles of young men who passed the village maidens between them, spinning them so that their brightly colored dresses twirled like spun sugar. In the early twilight, white teeth gleamed behind wide smiles, and the field was filled with the sounds of laughter and jokes.

The unbridled merriment around Nolan broke through the dark cloud of his anxiety and concern, and he noticed several heaping plates of food in front of Stanley. Apparently his friend wasn't so full that he couldn't drag four platters of meat and sauces toward himself.

Nolan found himself relaxing and glad to be by his best friend's side again. He reasoned they wouldn't be able to do anything for the missing people tonight, and the odds of them also stumbling across some creature like the Wolfling seemed remote, if very few Greenmen were able to Awaken things like that. Perhaps good fortune had found the others, as it had also found him, Quinn, and Stanley...he hoped.

First light, he told himself, promising Emery he would find him.

Quinn was telling Stanley more about their ordeals since passing the Veil, in between mouthfuls of wonderful "nosh," as she called it with a laugh. The Song Translated the word as "light snack." It didn't surprise Nolan that the Translation Song worked for British English as well as American English.

As divided as Nolan was, his spirits couldn't help but rise as the feast turned into an all-out Fair-Folk festival—the music; the mead; the men breaking into spontaneous challenges of wrestling, stone throwing, archery, and sword fighting; the children in their bright clothes, beacons of joy in the bonfire's orange lights; the women dancing in complicated steps, stiff-armed and yet spinning, spinning, without dizziness, mimicking the stars that came out, huge and twinkling and spinning.

With no Boston lights to damper its glow, the Milky Way streamed across the blackness as if some careless giant had tipped over a glass of diamonds on a black velvet board, which reminded Nolan of Quinn's pendant. He looked for the barely discernible bulge of the necklace under her tunic as she reached for a plate of spicy sausages smothered in onion gravy sitting atop what looked like flat dinner rolls.

"Oh, yum! Toad-in-the-hole!" she exclaimed without further explanation.

Nolan decided it was better not to ask about toad-in-the-hole and soon was wondering what exactly they were going to do. After finding Emery and Genevieve, they were still stuck here; and, as nice as *here* was, it wasn't *there*, which is where he should be. Would Crannhyn be able to help them find Ysgafn and Audrey? Would they figure out what this diamond Verse did? Nolan felt as if the real adventure hadn't even started yet, and it frightened him.

Fiorlen's lightning Bug landed with a thud on the bench next to Nolan, scaring him half to death, its tail end blinking on and off. Quinn shrieked, sausage still in mouth, and spilled her mug of mead. Stanley laughed as he dug into his second lamb chop.

Nolan stared sidelong as the Insect cocked his head (it was a male Bug) to look at him and buzz-clicked. In Nolan's head, the noises were changed to English, albeit with a strange drawl. He had a hard time placing the accent. It almost sounded…Minnesotan. The Bug's words sometimes trailed off in a whirring sound. It was the weirdest experience he'd had so far in Tírcluddaithe.

"*Bzzz*. Fiorlennn would like to have a worddd when you are finisheddd," Tintreach said as he pointed one of his antennae at the children. He stood there on his wiry back legs, using his middle legs to steady his body against the table, as his front legs reached for two raspberry tarts covered in cream. The children stared, openmouthed.

"Nice to have buzzeddd in your bonnettt," Tintreach said with a mouthful of tart, then flew off.

Everyone was silent for several seconds until Stanley quipped, "Waiter… there's a bug in my tart!"

The table burst into roars of laughter, and several Aossí clapped Stanley on the back. Nolan raised an eyebrow and pulled a curry vegetable dish toward himself. The music was getting much livelier now that the mead was flowing and bellies were full, but the dancing was becoming sloppier and sluggish.

Just when the travelers thought that they couldn't eat another bite and were getting ready to go find Fiorlen (and her sweets-eating lightning Bug), a fierce call split the night.

The music dropped silent, and all eyes darted to the tree line of the Morsden, where two shadowy forms came running out of the Forest, calling for Aneirin.

"Runners from the search parties," Cadfan yelled over the tumult, looking at the Otherworlders with worry in his black eyes.

Nolan's full stomach fell into his boots. *Emery….*

The two young men ran into the crowd, gasping for breath. Aneirin also began pushing his way into the center of the gathering. He spoke in low tones to the runners, then called for the children and Fiorlen.

Turning to Nolan with a look of tense apprehension in his deep-set eyes, Aneirin held up a small white object. "The searchers have come across evidence of Tërimrush about a day's journey through the Covering."

The foreign word shuffled through the Otherworlders' minds before settling on "she-bear," but that didn't seem quite right—as if the Song had found the best approximation.

In a daze, Nolan seemed to watch himself take the small white object. He stared at it for several seconds, not realizing what it was; and then with a start he dropped it to the ground and took several shaky steps backward. Cadfan reached out to steady him as Quinn looked down at the item, puzzled.

"Oh, my..." she managed as her hands flew to her mouth.

There on the ground, glowing in the red light of the low fires, torn and smeared with blood, was a little boy's sneaker.

14

Cloaks and Daggers

Fiorlen seemed to be listening again to music she alone could hear; her eyes were closed and her head was cocked to one side. Nolan thought it must have been a kind of quiet meditation, tuning in the voices of the Forest, listening to the trees and the wind and the River. She seemed to be weighing differing sides of a noiseless conversation, analyzing different predictions and possible outcomes, prophetic statistics. Stanley could probably understand that kind of analytical logic, even if her mind was attuned to some mystical force even he couldn't hope to comprehend.

Her eyes flickered open, and they seemed to glow yellow in their own light. "I do not believe your brother or your cousin has perished," she finally said. "We should find them. I will accompany you for the Song of Translation tomorrow evening. And Healing for the others…if needed."

"Then let's go now," Nolan managed faintly. He believed her, or at least he *wanted* to believe her. Emery was *not* dead.

"In the dark, that is unwise, my friend," Aneirin ventured, placing a halting hand on Nolan's shoulder. "You may not understand how virtually impenetrable the Deep can be."

"I don't care!" He shrugged out of Aneirin's grasp. "If there's a possibility that Emery and Genevieve need our help, then we need to leave now! I'm not going to wait until morning—"

"I agree with Nolan," Quinn put in. "I think we should leave immediately. If they say it's a day's journey, we might could make it by dusk tomorrow if we hurry."

Aneirin gave them a grave look. "There are many Corrupted in the Forest, Tërimrush being one of them. And your family could be anywhere. Not to mention the need for whatever daylight that can penetrate the forest canopy in order to find them. At night, the blackness of the Deep closes in on all sides and threatens to smother."

"But the sooner we leave, the sooner we can find them!" Nolan persisted.

Aneirin stood for a moment, deep in thought, and then nodded. "You must at least rest awhile; we need to outfit horses and gather supplies. I do not recommend making so long a journey on foot. Our runners are set on relay routes every couple of leagues, but to travel miles into the woods on foot is as dangerous as it is unwise."

He motioned for the two runners, who were hastily eating the remains of the feast. "Rest one hour, then find the relays at the old post by the Broken Rock. Try to get a message to the search team as swiftly as you can: The Otherworlders are on their way with the Coeduine. Await their arrival; assist them anyway you can. I have spoken."

"We are ready now, Aneirin," said one of the young men eagerly, taking a deep gulp of air. "An easy jog through the Morsden."

His companion laughed, tossing a chicken bone into the fire. "Like a summer stroll through clover fields!"

"Then depart now with protection on you both."

"Hail, Aneirin! And hail, travelers!" The men saluted and offered an Aossí blessing, "Swiftness!" then headed into the night. They were at the tree line in moments.

Fiorlen inclined her head to Tintreach, who was perched on her shoulder. "My friend, find Rhydderch and Bassett. Tell them to make haste to meet us at *Brisdwn*." The word was rendered "Broken Rock" to Nolan.

The lightning Bug nodded and took off into the Forest, glowing as it flew. It soon left the runners far behind.

Aneirin raised his eyebrows. "Rhydderch? You know the monk, Singer?"

"He assists my father in keeping watch over Arshúil."

The town leader chuckled. "He sometimes comes to the village for supplies, but we've always considered him to be mostly harmless and somewhat of a fool—begging your pardon—but anyone who willingly lives in the Deep of Morsden must be a little mad."

Fiorlen smiled. "Rhydderch is a very good actor."

Cadfan approached. "Aneirin, I will go with the Otherworlders. They will need my help." He smiled at Quinn. "Ever ridden a horse?"

She nodded.

"Good, 'cause trekking through the Shrouding on horseback is not the easiest task!" His wild eyes twinkled, and he stalked off toward his storefront, humming a tune.

"Shouldn't we go by foot?" Quinn asked. "The Deep can't have very good horse trails."

"Nay," Aneirin said. "The Coedaoine move through the Morsden like smoke, but the Aossí are much slower. The search team is a day's march through the Covering on horseback. Maybe forty miles. And you may need the horses to carry back the others, if…*when* they are found. There are few paths, so it can be troublesome for the horses, but there is protection in the saddle. Rest now, my friends. We will be ready to depart in two hours."

It was sad to watch the feast melt away. The Aossí no longer seemed cheerful and gay, now speaking quietly as they cleared the debris and called for children to get ready for bed. Nolan was sorry the party ended on such a somber note, but his own worry for Emery and Genevieve overpowered any other feeling. While he was worried about Ysgafn and Audrey, his immediate concern was for his brother and cousin.

"What is a Tërimrush?" Stanley asked Aneirin. "The Song Translates it 'She-bear,' but it seemed to take a while."

"It is a proper name meaning Tërimrush." This time, when Aneirin said the word, the Song Translated it "Roaring Insanity" instead of "She-bear."

"Fascinating," Stanley mused. "The Song seems to Translate the *intent* of the words, not just their literal meaning. Connotation and context are also conveyed. I'll bet even 'skyscraper' and 'spaceship' would Translate into something the Aossí could understand."

Aneirin continued, "Often, when a she-bear has lost her cubs, she goes insane and becomes exceedingly violent. If she happens to taste man-flesh, it will be all she seeks until she finds more or starves. This is called the bloodlust, and the bear must be destroyed for the safety of the people.

"In the last few weeks, we have heard random reports of a giant Corrupted she-bear in the woods from the few people who dare live in its depths—mostly monks and madmen, like Rhydderch. One of our own, a trapper named Grwn, went missing a fortnight ago, and we suspected Tërimrush the culprit. We have kept close watch yet have found nothing so far. But tonight, the scouts saw spoor and claw marks on several trees, and, of course, the shoe."

"Wish I hadn't asked," Stanley replied, looking forlorn. He placed a hand on Nolan's shoulder.

"It is possible the signs of the Bear may be unrelated to the missing Otherworlders," Aneirin conceded. "It is most possible the Coeduine is correct, the scouts are mistaken, and your friends are perfectly well." He bowed to Fiorlen. "She will be most valuable assisting you in either case."

With that, Aneirin led them all to his home, where they were given mattresses filled with clean straw, along with furs and pillows, the best the leader could offer. He apologized, but Nolan was too distracted to care. The elder left to finalize arrangements, promising to come for them in two hours.

Fiorlen slept outside; Stanley said the night he'd spent with her, she had climbed into a tree branch.

None of the kids slept, neither did they talk much. They lay on the pallets, staring up at the thatched ceiling, while Nolan remained withdrawn.

When Aneirin returned two hours later, the air was cold and still. The crescent moon was hanging just above the trees of the Morsden. The River rumbled like muted thunder in the quiet night.

Several Aossí had collected to send them off, and a lady and her teenage daughter came out of the crowd to stand before the Otherworlders and the Sapling.

"My name is Ffion, and this is my daughter, Delwyn. We are tailors," the mother said. "You are wearing our clothes."

Quinn blanched. "About that, ma'am...we're very sor—"

"No, traveler, you misunderstand." The woman shook her head. "We are honored you would deign to put on our simple garments, and we come to offer you a gift, as is custom according to the Laws of Hospitality. It is not much, but please accept these as a token of our desire to extend a hand in friendship."

Delwyn unwrapped a large package and produced three cloaks. "These will keep you dry and well-hidden in the Shrouding," Delwyn said. "They are lightweight but warm and made of very sturdy material. It is the best of our ability in making such cloaks." She handed one to each of the children, lowering her head.

"Th-thank you," was all Nolan could say. The cloaks were amazing, a muted greenish gray, like the forest floor—unusual compared to the loud colors most Aossí wore. They were perfectly tailored for each child, although no one could guess how the women could have gotten the sizes so exact. They went over the head like a poncho and, once put on, fit like gloves. They allowed free range of motion, yet were tight enough to keep all but the wettest weather out. Hoods could be pulled low over the eyes to conceal the face, and the hems fell to mid-thigh. The material felt strange, like a cross between wool and leather.

"Wow, this is awesome." Stanley beamed. "Thank you, seamstresses."

"We hope to repay yore kindness someday," Quinn added.

The two ladies bowed and took their place with the rest of the group.

"Well, of course, I don't have a cloak like that!" Cadfan said as he approached, leading four horses laden with supplies. He whistled, startling the front two animals, then placed his giant hands on their necks and shushed them. Addressing the two boys, he said, "You lads know how to fight with a sword or shoot a bow?"

Stanley and Nolan looked at each other, then shook their heads.

Cadfan's huge face bunched in a smile. "You sought to steal a sword, Nolan, and yet you have no knowledge how to use one? Perhaps you planned to clean under your fingernails with it? Well, 'tis no matter. I had thought Otherworlders would be great warriors, but it is something that shall be remedied."

The weapon maker chuckled and settled the horses again before producing two leaf-bladed swords like the one Nolan had tried to steal. He handed one to each of the boys, who held them at odd angles.

"Don't slice off a finger. They're sharp," he warned.

While neither Nolan nor Stanley knew the first thing about swords, they could tell Cadfan thought these were works of art, and they were—gorgeously etched, double-edged, glinting in the pale moonlight. The weight and length felt right, somehow, in Nolan's hands.

"Dude, it's like we're in *The Legend of Zelda!*" Stanley said. He stared at his sword and whistled, giving the weapon a quick turn with his wrist and nearly shaving off an ear.

"The legend of who?" Cadfan asked, then turned to Quinn with a twinkle in his eye. "M'lady, it is considered unbecoming for the fairest to hold such a crude weapon, even if my swords *are* the best in the lands; and yet, it is improper to enter the Covering without some form of defense. Therefore...."

He handed her two beautiful daggers, each about a foot and a half long, with etched silver handles and bloodred stones faceted to look like roses in the hilts, sheathed in a leather belt that would hold both knives at the small of her back.

"I have taken the liberty of naming them already, for every good weapon should have a name," he said. "These are Lively and Spirited. May they serve you well, Quinn."

"Uh, ta.... They're brilliant." She buckled the belt on and drew the daggers with a ringing hiss. Already she looked capable of taking on a she-bear herself.

To Fiorlen, Cadfan inclined his head. "You would prefer to touch no metal weapons, I know, unless the need be dire. But would you condescend to carry one of my bows?"

The Treegirl curtseyed. "Aossí, I would."

Cadfan gave her a yew longbow taller than Nolan and a quiver of arrows fletched with eagle feathers. The arrowheads were severe and serrated, carved from bone. Fiorlen slung the quiver over her shoulder and pulled back the bow-string, letting it go with a powerful twang that startled the children.

"It is an outstanding bow," Fiorlen remarked. "Thank you."

"I've no doubt you could shoot out a fly's eye at one hundred paces in the dark," Cadfan responded.

Fiorlen smiled. "Don't let Tintreach hear you say that."

Cadfan rumbled with laughter and sank into the saddle of the largest horse, a red stallion a full foot taller than Nolan at the shoulders.

"I have selected calmer mounts for the younger ones, but make no mistake; they will serve their riders well. I know a thing or two about horses; I'm from Tírsor originally." The enormous weaponsmith clicked his teeth, and the steed whinnied.

Nolan assumed the people of the Southlands were known for their horses. It didn't surprise him that Cadfan had gone all "Riders of Rohan" on them, although he would've thought finding a horse big enough for the giant man to ride would've been a hard task. Nolan looked like Little Joe sitting on a horse next to Hoss.

Quinn, who had some experience with the horses at Audrey's estate, tightened the saddle on a black-and-white mare and patted her neck. "What's yore name, bonnie?"

Cadfan said a word that came out in Nolan's head as "Ink Blot," then proceeded to name the others. His own, the monstrous roan, was rightly named "Red." Nolan's brown gelding was Whimsy, and Stanley's was something that, for one reason or another, didn't quite Translate, but Cadfan explained it was akin to alcoholic buttermilk, sort of like eggnog.

Nolan had expected more *manly* names for the horses—things like Thunderhoof and Barbed Wire. He'd ridden only once before, and that had been at a dude ranch in Montana with a simple, circular trail.

Sheathing his new sword at Whimsy's side, he was proud he remembered how to mount and get his feet in the stirrups, but Whimsy must've sensed he was an amateur because the animal stuck back its ears and gave Nolan's left boot a little nip.

"Sorry," Nolan told the horse, correcting his posture so the toe of his boot wouldn't dig in its rib cage.

Stanley was the most miserable of all. He'd managed to get the sword put away, but now he was going round and round in circles with the wrong foot in the wrong stirrup, trying to climb on backward.

Cadfan chuckled. "Your other foot, right? No, your other foot, lad, in *that* stirrup. Buttermilk, don't hie, old boy; stand still, will you? Easy now. Stanley, swing your free leg over his back. No, you're still going to mount him backward, son, see? You can't stare at his backside for fifteen leagues. I thought you'd said you could ride a horse, lad!"

"*Quinn* said she could ride," Stanley murmured. "*I've* ridden only once, and it was a Shetland pony, and I was five. And it was tethered to a walker." He looked at Nolan and then Quinn, face flushed with embarrassment, aware that the eyes of the villagers were watching him with mirth. Quinn blatantly stifled a laugh. Stanley, being overweight, was out of breath and starting to sweat, muttering a few select words that the Translation Song had difficulty putting into the First Tongue.

Cadfan rolled his black eyes and dismounted. Moments later, Stanley was correctly astride Buttermilk, and Cadfan had retightened the saddle.

"Hold the reins like this. To stop, to go, to move left, to move right. Aye, you've got it. Don't hold them too tight or too loose, and don't kick him in the flanks; he'll take off like an arrow and leave you in the pine needles. Raise your butt up, like you're standing in the stirrups; keep your back taut and sit up straight, otherwise you'll be in pain before you know it. Done. Now you look like a rider!"

A few of the villagers applauded, and color rose to Stanley's cheeks. He waved to them from the height of his horse and nudged Buttermilk forward just to show he could turn in a circle.

"Now we are ready." Aneirin clapped his hands for silence. "There are supplies for a couple of days, plus bandages and healing herbs. When you return, we will discuss what to do next. May you be protected and return safely. Swiftness!"

"Swiftness!" the townsfolk repeated, and Cadfan nudged Red forward.

"How'll Fiorlen keep up with us?" Quinn asked, glancing over her shoulder.

Nolan followed her gaze and saw the Treegirl walking behind them toward the Forest.

Cadfan looked back to wink at Quinn. "Watch!"

Suddenly Fiorlen was *ahead* of them, and with a salute, she disappeared into the trees and was gone.

"Never mind," Quinn said.

"She'll keep an eye on us, no doubt, but I'll bet three *quorins* she's waiting for us at Broken Rock," Cadfan said.

15

Searching for Emery

It was easy following the trail of white stones for the first few miles, but then they plunged into the trees. It was shadowy black under the canopy, and Nolan understood why Aneirin had suggested they wait until morning to delve into the Deep. It was much more enclosed than where they'd appeared in the Morsden that first night. An orange glow flashed to life ahead of them as Cadfan struck light to a torch with flint and fire steel.

Although Nolan had spent a horrifying night in the Forest before, this time seemed more *oppressive*. It was almost claustrophobic how the trees pressed in on all sides, and he felt his lungs threaten to rebel. He could see only about five yards in any direction, even with his excellent night vision. White trunks towered like pillars to the skies, jumping into view with every labored tread. Branches whipped in his face; vines tried to entangle him. The horses whined and snorted, their noise sounding amplified in the eerily quiet Forest. This time around, there weren't the normal nighttime sounds of a woodland teeming with life.

As silent as it was, Nolan noticed lots of eyes in the black, reflecting with so little light. Yellow, green, and red slitted animal eyes, winking and disappearing. Dozens of them. They were by no means alone out here, but to what shapes the eyes belonged, Nolan dared not guess. For all he knew, they could've just been floating *eyes* without bodies! None of them seemed to reflect the intelligence of an Awakened animal, however, and he took some relief in that.

"Bassett approaches!" They were maybe half an hour outside Arshúil when they heard Fiorlen's voice break out from above their heads in the trees, and the children let out startled shrieks.

"Sorry, my friends," the Treegirl said. "Well met, Bassett! *Shdritn ve wybrán!*" (Which the Song Translated as, "Shine on the path!")

Instantly a bright white ball lit up the blackness and zoomed to the head of the troupe, shouting, "Well met, seekers! Follow me!"

The Pêllys did some loops around each of their heads. In Bassett's light, the rest of the Forest grew absolutely black; but in front of them, they could now see ten yards.

"I'll be," Stanley marveled. "It *is* a ball of light!"

"A Will-o'-the-wisp," Cadfan explained. "A wee person with clear butterfly wings about the size of a forearm. Never believed in 'em till now." He shook his head. "The stories say they change color."

Bassett burst into pink light. "Do you like this one, Aossí?"

"Aye, small one!"

"Bassett, what news?" Fiorlen was still invisible in the branches above.

"Rhydderch sent me on ahead. He makes his way to Arshúil with that new apprentice of his following dutifully behind."

"This news frustrates me," Fiorlen replied. "I have sent Tintreach to fetch Rhydderch to Brisdwn."

"If they make a fraction of the noise these Otherworlders make, he will have no trouble finding them. In fact, they should beat us there!" Bassett did some lazy loop-the-loops.

Up in the trees, Fiorlen chuckled.

"Come, let's close up and keep near; the path's wider here." Cadfan broke off three straight branches, each as thick as a broomstick, as he let the horse follow the light in front of them. "Nolan, Stanley, Quinn—catch!" He threw the sticks at them. Stanley dropped his. Cadfan laughed and broke off two more sticks. This time, Stanley caught his, and Cadfan kept one.

"First thing to know 'bout sword-fighting is a strong wrist, loose arm. Don't be tense the whole time, white-knuckled; you'll tucker out before you start, and you'll end up dead. Only tighten your arm when you strike. Like this."

Cadfan had them practice different moves in the saddle until they thought their arms would fall off. While they practiced, he also shared the rudiments of archery and knife-wielding. Nolan couldn't tell if he was actually learning anything at all; the stick was much lighter than a real sword, and he couldn't hack at anything except the air in front of him. Once, he swatted Whimsy lightly on the head, and the horse turned and nipped him on the leg.

Four hours later, they reached Broken Rock: a man-made clearing around a massive boulder the size of a house, cracked right down the middle as if a giant hammer had split it. When they entered the clearing, Fiorlen was already standing in front of the fire, speaking with an old man. A teenage boy stood at his side, and the two runners from Arshúil were there.

The old man was asking the Sapling, "And news of your father?"

The Coeduine maiden shook her head. "It appears he is with Audrey Redding, but Tintreach and I have found no clue as to their whereabouts."

The old man was resolute. "Ysgafn is tough. He will be all right, and he will protect Audrey." Then he turned to Nolan and the riders. "Hail, Otherworlders; hail, Cadfan, you are well met!"

The children mumbled tired hellos as Tintreach buzzed on Fiorlen's shoulder, clearly happy to be reunited with his Treegirl.

"This is Rhydderch, my father's friend," Fiorlen said.

Rhydderch looked to be in his late sixties but very fit and spry. His thick white hair was cut short, his white beard was trimmed, and his clothes were simple: a traveling cloak over breeches and tunic. In his right hand, he held a walking staff of birch, and in his left was an elaborate tobacco pipe with glowing bowl. From his belt hung a sheathed dagger and a waterskin. He wore old-fashioned-looking wire-rimmed spectacles, and Nolan wondered where the man had gotten them; he hadn't seen other Aossí wearing glasses thus far.

Rhydderch had the appearance of one who'd spent the majority of his life squinting at small print, poring over ancient tomes of knowledge. He was a bookworm, Nolan decided.

Yet something in his blue eyes warned Nolan that looks could be deceiving. The monk looked like he knew how to use the dagger he carried. Whether he was a madman, as the villagers of Arshúil thought, or not, Nolan could only guess.

"Heilyn." Rhydderch snapped his fingers at the teenager standing beside him. "Don't neglect your manners! Help the lady out of the saddle."

The young man snapped to attention and hurried to Quinn's side, reaching up with his hand to help her off the horse.

Quinn appeared not to know what to think of the courtly attention. She thanked him, but he didn't respond, keeping his head bowed. He seemed to be about seventeen and was of average height but very trim, with longish, curly chocolate-brown hair. He was dressed plainly in gray trousers and a faded maroon shirt.

"Yore name's Heilyn?" Quinn asked, forgetting that he wouldn't be able to understand her without the Translation Song. After a few seconds of silence, she said, "Can ya speak?"

"Yes, m'lady," he said, raising his eyes.

And what remarkable eyes they were! A champagne gold, something Nolan had never seen before. They were fiery eyes that didn't belong in the head of a beaten-down servant boy—they were the eyes of someone intelligent and impulsive.

"Ya've very pretty eyes," Quinn said.

Heilyn blushed and looked down. "Thank you, m'lady."

"And he's speaking English," Stanley pointed out.

Quinn started, as if she hadn't realized Heilyn was not speaking the First Tongue.

"I am teaching your language to Heilyn," Rhydderch explained. He was speaking it, as well, with a soft British accent.

"How is it *you* speak English?" Quinn asked him.

"I know your grandmother. When we were about your age, she traveled to the Hidden Lands frequently with Ysgafn Droed, and we became good friends. Over the years, Audrey taught me English and brought over many, many books, for my passion has always been the study of the Other Side. I so wanted to visit it with her; but, alas, the Coedaoine rarely permit people to cross the Veil. Your grandmother, of course, was a special case."

Quinn looked stunned. "But how d'ya know she's me grandmother?"

"You look remarkably like she did all those years ago." Rhydderch smiled as if recalling a happy memory.

After a few pleasantries, they rested for an hour, though no one could sleep. Rhydderch spoke in low tones with Fiorlen around the other side of Broken Rock, but Nolan could not make out the details of their discussion.

As the first inkling of sunrise drifted through the canopy above them, they bid farewell to the runners, who would remain behind to await news from

Cadfan once the boy and the girl were found. Already saddle-weary, the troupe left Broken Rock and plunged into the domineering thickness of the Morsden Deep.

The Forest turned a muted rosy gray from the morning sun that was struggling to break through the oppression of the trees. Fiorlen, Rhydderch, and his apprentice were on point, followed by the children, and Cadfan brought up the rear.

When it was light enough that Bassett's glow was barely noticeable, the children got a good look at the little manlike creature: about a foot or so high, curiously dressed, with pointy ears and an earring, fluttering with a pair of crystalline butterfly wings. His solid black almond-shaped eyes were insect-like, large on his face with no pupils.

"Are you an Awakened being?" Stanley asked, wide-eyed.

Bassett flittered in front of him and landed on Buttermilk's saddle horn. "This is correct, Otherworlder," the creature said with a bow. "We were one of the Eldest's first creations. Very few of the Coedaoine could Awaken such a one as me; as such, there are only a few of my kind."

"So are ya a butterfly made to look like a human? Or are ya a human made to look like a butterfly?" Quinn was trying to understand.

The Pêllys became stern. "M'lady, it is the greatest violation of the Law to Sing over a human, for they were already Awakened by the Composer, and they are too easily Corrupted. The last human who was Corrupted is hunted by the Coedaoine to this very day."

"You mean Agenor?" Cadfan supplied.

"You know of the Foul One?" Bassett took off from Stanley's saddle and floated in front of the weaponsmith, showing great curiosity on his small, elfin face. "I didn't think the Fair Folk knew of him."

"We have stories to frighten children into obedience," Cadfan explained. "Agenor is the boogeyman, the malevolent Boarman. No one really believes he exists. In fact, it's been so long since we've had dealings with the Coedaoine, some of my kind don't even believe *they* exist."

"That's the problem with humans," Bassett said. "If you can't see it, it's not real. But I assure you, your Boarman is real and is a malicious, violent fiend. He is hideously disfigured by his Corruption and seeks pleasure only in destruction and suffering."

Nolan's skin crawled as Bassett spoke of this Agenor. He trembled to think the monster might be in these woods, looking for a morsel to snack on. It was a faceless fear, different from an Awakened wolf, because it was a human being who'd been Corrupted. The thought gave Nolan the shivers.

The hours melted away—miles of treacherous poking through under-growth, up knolls, down berms, under low-hanging branches, over rotting logs, and among snagging brambles. They passed four more relay outposts, each one more spaced out than the last, pausing to rest briefly before pressing on. The runners at each post were waiting nervously, with nocked arrows on their bow-strings, and they seemed grateful to be sent back toward Arshúil with news that the team was safe.

Toward evening, the Forest grew so tight and mottled with thick branches, the horses had difficulty finding space to proceed. There was almost no light piercing the crown, and the ground was covered in moss and lichen, for nothing larger could grow in so little sunlight.

Nolan must have fallen asleep while still on the horse at some point in time. For how long, he didn't know, but he woke when he started sliding side-ways out of the saddle.

"Cadfan, we need a rest," he grumbled, and there were sighs of relief from the other children.

Cadfan seemed about to push them just a little further, but after looking them over, he nodded and reined his horse to a stop. The kids fell out of their saddles, not even bothering to tether the reins to a branch. The weapon maker let them rest while he tended the horses.

Rhydderch and the teenager pulled away from the group and spoke in low tones with Fiorlen. Nolan, Quinn, and Stanley were too tired to talk, but they took long pulls from their waterskins and munched on dry biscuits and jerky. By the time Cadfan was finished with the horses, the children were asleep against the tree trunks.

16

Tërimrush

Grumbling is what woke Nolan. Like a hungry belly that wasn't his. But he wasn't fully awake until Fiorlen dropped out of the tree above his head, landing in a crouch, arrow taut on her bow. The Sapling's yellow eyes glimmered in the failing light as she peered into the Forest's depths, Tintreach and Bassett hovering above her head. Nolan was about to ask her what was wrong, but the Pêllys motioned for silence.

There was the grumbling noise again, and Quinn stirred next to him. Stanley was lying down with his head at an awkward angle against the tree trunk. Cadfan was crouched over by the horses, watching the Treegirl intently, sword in hand. Rhydderch had his dagger out, and Heilyn had a bow at the ready.

The grumbling was followed by a rooting, shuffling noise, and something sniffed just out of eyesight. Nolan rolled clumsily to his feet, fighting light-headedness, and nudged Stanley and Quinn. He then crept to Whimsy's side and unsheathed his nameless sword, giving Cadfan a puzzled look. Quinn and Stanley awoke and were shushed by Tintreach before they could question what was going on. Nolan motioned for them to arm themselves and nodded toward the Forest.

There was a sharp *snap-hiss* as Fiorlen let loose the arrow into the falling darkness. An angry roar split the air, and the Sapling cursed, "Madán!" She nocked another arrow so quickly, Nolan couldn't even see her hands move.

"It did not penetrate the hide," she mumbled grimly.

But Nolan didn't have time to ask what she meant, because a woolly mammoth seemed to have broken through the trees, bellowing in rage. Quinn screamed and raced toward the horses. Ink Blot reared in panic, and her companions jerked at their tethers, eyes wild with fear, teeth bared, ears flat against their heads. The slender branches they were tied to snapped, and the horses tore off into the Forest, bucking and kicking, almost trampling Quinn and knocking Nolan to the ground. Cadfan lunged after Red, but the stallion was gone.

Yet it wasn't a mammoth—it was a Bear! Nolan thought his eyes deceived him as the beast stood on its hindquarters, towering fifteen feet in the air, a hundred times more frightening than the Corrupted wolf that had hunted them. The Bear opened its bright red maw, baring yellow teeth inches in length, and roared at the Sapling. Another *snap-hiss* was her reply, but the arrow glanced off the Bear's chest and clattered to the ground, useless.

"Incredible," Cadfan murmured in disbelief.

The Bear charged Fiorlen. A muscular hump jostled between its shoulders as its enormous paws pressed down into the mossy floor, and Nolan had a split second's view of brutal, curved claws nearly a foot in length. His heart stopped, and his throat closed up. A sharp intake of breath almost threw him into an asthmatic fit, but he forced himself to his feet.

Fiorlen was in the trees before the Bear was halfway to her. Tintreach and Bassett both swooped down upon the brute, calling and yelling to distract it, flashing different colors of light and tossing small stones, which did nothing more than antagonize the monster. The Bear snarled in frustration and took a swipe at the lightning Bug, who barely dodged the attack.

It was then that the Bear noticed Stanley and Quinn.

A golden-red light flared as Cadfan struck his fire steel to a torch. "Oi, beast. Oi there, beastie!" he yelled, jabbing the torch toward Tërimrush.

The She-bear backed up a step and roared at the flame. Cadfan had to jump in the air to ram the torch into her snout, which proved to be a mistake. She swatted him with her paw, shaking her head in fury as the torch lurched from his hand. Cadfan flew into a maple trunk and crumpled to the ground, senseless. Nolan dimly registered three long gashes on the side of the weapon-smith's broad face.

"Shoot her!" Rhydderch yelled to Heilyn, and the apprentice's bow went *snap-hiss*. The metal arrowhead found its mark in the neck of the giant Bear, but it seemed only to infuriate her the more. It would take twenty arrows, at least, to bring her down.

Something welled up in Nolan. Whether it was a fight-or-flight response, or anger for his missing brother, or simply adrenaline pumping because he knew he and his friends were about to die, he didn't know. He didn't feel brave or heroic, but he was uncommonly clearheaded, and time seemed to slow down. In fact, he felt petrified—his legs were in molasses, and his spine seemed flimsy—but he forced himself to move.

In his left hand he held the sword, and he was shocked to hear a battle cry pass his lips as his voice broke into a shriek. Tërimrush must have been shocked, too, because she looked down to see him and didn't immediately attack.

With her face so close to his, Nolan raised his arm in slow motion and brought the sword across the Bear's maw, just as Fiorlen materialized out of thin air with Cadfan's sword and swatted a gargantuan paw away before it could maul Nolan's head.

Tërimrush bellowed in pain and recoiled. Her foot was cut by Fiorlen, and Nolan's sword had sliced her nose, spilling crimson on the forest floor.

"Her neck," Fiorlen grunted. "*Vrastë ei muin!*" There was no time to listen to the Translation Song, and there was no need, for the Coeduine reared back to plunge the blade into the She-bear's jugular.

"Stop! Stop! No! Don't!"

It was something out of a dream, and Nolan wondered if he were already dead, because, as Tërimrush reared on her back legs, Emery rushed under them, slipping on the slick moss, and tackled Nolan. The little boy was on his feet before his older brother even knew what had knocked the wind out of him.

Emery stood between the Bear and the Treegirl, waving his hands frantically. Fiorlen seemed just as puzzled as Nolan, but she began to lower her sword.

Tërimrush planted her paws protectively over the boy, bringing him to her chest, as he gave a muffled yell. "Please, don't kill her! She's my friend!"

Nolan stared, openmouthed, at his one-shoed little brother being cuddled by a six-ton grizzly Bear. Faintly, he registered Genevieve standing by a tree a few yards off, filthy hands to her mouth. Both she and Emery looked like they'd taken a mud bath, but they didn't appear to be seriously harmed. Tërimrush, on the other hand, was moaning from the slices on her paw and muzzle. Heilyn's arrow seemed to have broken away. Cadfan was unconscious, but Nolan saw his rib cage rise and fall. The whole scene was surreal.

Heilyn had another arrow on the string, but Rhydderch had sheathed his dagger.

Quinn broke the silence. "What in the flyin' blue blazes is goin' on here?"

No one answered, and Nolan sensed in his stomach that Blue Time had fallen. The Bear kept her paws in front of Emery but did not show signs of aggression. She watched Fiorlen with an intelligent, questioning look, and Nolan realized she was expecting the Treegirl to Sing.

"Genevieve? Are you all right?" Stanley asked.

The fifteen-year-old burst into loud wails and staggered toward Quinn. Awkwardly, Quinn put her arm around her future stepsister's shoulder and gave Nolan a bewildered look.

Cadfan rumbled as he came to. The three claw marks on his face were furrowed and bleeding. On his hands and knees, he turned to look around, blinking, confused.

"Wh-what happened?" he managed.

"Emery, what is going on?" Nolan asked. "You *know* this Bear?" He realized his sword was still drawn, ready to strike, and he lowered it warily.

"We've been looking for you," was his brother's reply. "All over the woods. For days. Where have you been?"

"Oh, buddy, I'm so sorry. We've been trying to find you. There are dozens of people looking in the Forest for you." Nolan laid the sword on the ground and knelt, holding out his arms. "Emery. Thank God you're safe. Come here."

The Bear let Emery go, and as the boy raced into his brother's hug, liquid relief coursed through Nolan's veins: Emery was safe!

"I'm sorry, Nolan," he said with his face buried in his brother's chest. "I lost my shoe. Genevieve and I fell down in the mud a lot, and I cut my ankle bad from slipping on a rock, and my shoe stuck in the mud. I couldn't find it."

"Never mind that. We'll get you other shoes and make sure the cut is not infected, okay?" Nolan squeezed him again, and then they both turned toward the Treegirl. "Can you Sing the Translation Song?" Nolan asked her.

Fiorlen Sang softly, and everyone was mesmerized by the tune, even Genevieve and Tërimrush. For a few minutes, the only sound was Fiorlen's flittering voice like two birds falling madly in love. As the Song floated away, Tintreach and Bassett flickered on and off, making Emery squeak with delight.

"That was beautiful. Now will you heal my wounds, Coeduine?" It was the Grizzly. She spoke the Chéad Teanga.

Emery gasped. "I can understand you!"

The Bear lowered her enormous head to stare at the boy. "I have always spoken, but you could not follow. The Coeduine's Song has made us comprehend one another, cub. You should thank her."

"Now, hold on." Cadfan was on his feet, clutching his face. He still seemed angry, though he was in no condition for further battle. He addressed Fiorlen. "If you're going to heal the brute, heal me, too!"

"And Emery has a gash on his ankle," Nolan put in. After all he'd seen the last couple days, talking about a Coeduine healing someone's wounds wasn't far-fetched. He almost sort of expected it.

"Brute?" Tërimrush growled, and Nolan realized she was responding to Cadfan.

"Yes, *brute*. You slashed me open like a fish," the sword maker said.

Somehow the Bear adopted a hangdog demeanor, which made Nolan want to laugh. Her face was as expressive as a human's, and he had no idea how her mouth moved to make the sounds of the First Tongue. "In my defense, you shot at me first with your pokey stick-launcher. I merely responded to the attack."

"That was the Sapling," Cadfan protested.

"And you jabbed me with flames."

"All right, all right." Cadfan waved off her retort. "Fiorlen, please, can you fix us? *All* of us?"

The Treegirl nodded. "Of course. Well, I think so.... All of you come stand before me."

They shuffled in front of her, and she raised a timber hand to each of their cheeks in turn. Her Song was different from any the children had yet heard, short and clipped; the words were not poetic, as if Fiorlen wasn't used to this type of Singing. It felt almost as if she were asking for a favor in her Song. When it was Tërimrush's turn, Fiorlen gingerly pulled the broken shaft out of her neck and let it fall to the ground.

Moments later, she lowered her hands, and all their wounds were healed. Only tiny white scars hinted on Cadfan's face, and Emery was bouncing around, testing his ankle. The Bear, the boy, and the weaponsmith gave their thanks.

"Wow." Stanley blinked. "Did you know she could do that?"

Nolan shook his head, cradling Emery in his arms. "Not exactly. Maybe." It was yet another reminder that they knew next to nothing about the Coeduine's power, next to nothing about the world they were stuck in, next to nothing about what to do next; and they'd been here four days. Four days? That was all? Nolan looked down at his brother and squeezed him.

"My healing Songs are limited," Fiorlen said. Her voice sounded tired, as if the Singing had taken a lot out of her. "Wounds beyond simple cuts are above my ability to repair."

Quinn had been holding Genevieve during this time. She let her go and asked gently, "What happened when you and Emery came through?"

Genevieve seemed to be calm enough to begin telling their story: how panicked they'd been, how her cell phone hadn't worked, how they'd almost died, freezing, that first night in the dark woods. And how Tërimrush had found them the next day as they wandered, screaming out for anyone to hear them. How the Bear had taken a shining to the boy, and Emery had been insane enough to approach her. How Genevieve herself had thought the Bear would turn on them, until Tërimrush had brought them nuts and berries. They'd been unable to communicate, but they could tell the Bear was intelligent. The whole story poured out like a frothing torrent, with Emery tossing in little points here and there.

"We must camp here tonight," Cadfan said as Genevieve took a shuddering breath during a pause in her story. "The search teams had orders to return for Arshúil tonight; perhaps they will stumble across us. I will start a fire, and Fiorlen, can you help in recovering the horses?"

Fiorlen nodded and turned to Heilyn. She gave him a small smile that struck Nolan as a little odd, although he couldn't say why. She hadn't acknowledged the teenager much at all throughout the day, but it was as if she knew Heilyn better than she had let on so far. "Heilyn, will you accompany me?"

The assistant looked to Rhydderch, who nodded his head. "Of course, m'lady of the woods," Heilyn said with a bow, then followed Fiorlen and her two glowing companions into the Deep.

Cadfan and the monk began gathering wood for a fire, while Quinn asked Genevieve and Emery, "Are ya hungry?"

"Starving!" Emery said.

Some of Genevieve's tetchiness returned as she grumbled, "Thought you'd never ask."

The next half hour was spent arranging a makeshift camp around a fire ring, which soon crackled with burning orange warmth, somewhat cheering the dismal tyranny of the Shrouding. Fiorlen and Heilyn returned with the horses, and the Treegirl sat with the humans instead of leaping into the canopy. They shared a simple meal and told each other their stories.

Tërimrush remained behind Emery the entire time, a warm brown mountain of maternal love. She did not eat, nor did she speak much, until Cadfan said, "What's your story, mother Bear?"

The She-bear made a rumbling sound somewhere in her chest, and Nolan couldn't tell what it meant. Perhaps a chuckle, or maybe she was just clearing her throat. No, he thought it was a noise like someone would make who was asked a question he would rather not answer—an uncomfortable sound like, "Mmm...well...."

When she spoke, it was with controlled emotion, as if she were trying to keep her deep voice steady and free of rising anger.

"If you would care to hear, my story is a simple one. Some few years ago, before I was Awakened, my two cubs were taken from me, cut down by a murderous Aossí hunter for no other reason than vicious sport. Perhaps he was a criminal turned away from his home, a hateful man whose time in the Deep had stripped his mind. He was more animal than I, utterly savage, devoid of humanity. He was...Corrupted.

"It was early spring, and my cubs woke before I did, scampering, full of life, romping in the sun, testing their light claws on the bark of Morsden trees...."

Tërimrush paused at the memory, and her expression was tinged with great sadness. "If any of you have children-wealth and know the pain of losing them, you will understand. If you do not, there is no way I can make you comprehend.

"I heard them cry out. Their deaths were not quick, for the Aossí toyed with them, delighting in their suffering. I burst forth from our den...I will not describe what I saw. In truth, I saw only red, and I fell upon the man. The crunch of his neck, the salt of his blood, his quick cry silenced as I tore him to pieces.... His death was quick compared to my children's, and his broken body was left to the carrion birds....

"I went mad. For two summers, my grief was swallowed in my rage. I sought the few Aossí who lived alone in the Morsden; I killed and ate without remorse. I would have consumed myself in frenzied wrath were it not for Afanen."

Fiorlen looked at Tërimrush. "You know Afanen?"

"Who's Afanen?" Stanley asked.

"A Caevnaóir," Fiorlen replied, using the word for "Shepherd," the Treefolk's proper name. "She is the daughter of one of our leaders, Lord Mabon."

Tërimrush nodded, and Emery pushed into her warm fur and stroked her gigantic paw, which was now healed.

"A wonder Afanen has never mentioned her meeting you," the Treegirl said.

The great Bear shrugged her shoulders, much like a human would. "Afanen gives the impression of one who keeps her own counsel on most things."

Fiorlen agreed with a small smile. "That is most true. She is private and aloof, even for the Treefolk."

"In any case," Tërimrush continued, "Afanen coaxed me into a deep sleep with her Singing. I tried to fight it, but her words were a soothing balm to my broken heart and fractured mind. She drew me out of madness with the caress of her words.

"When I Awoke, the maiden told me I now had a choice. I could continue to take steps that would lead to further hurt and eventual ruin, or I could struggle down a path that would lead to wholeness once again, but it would not be easy.

"Several times in the months that followed, she Sang over me. I believe she foresaw that if I chose the right direction, my loss would be restored, and my destiny would be fulfilled."

Here the Bear stopped speaking, lost in thought, until with a great, rumbling sigh, she said, "Eventually, she stopped coming to see me, as if now the decision were solely mine. So I have tried to take the right steps ever since, and I begin to see her prophecy was correct." She smiled down at Emery.

"I'm glad you chose the right path," he said.

"Indeed, little cub." This time her rumble was definitely a small laugh. "Man-flesh is much too tough for a stomach as sensitive as mine."

Stanley blanched. "Was that supposed to be a joke?"

Cadfan and Rhydderch laughed along with Tërimrush. Apparently it *was* a joke. Maybe.

"Thank you for telling us your tale," Fiorlen said. "I am glad you fought against Corruption. Very few do."

Tërimrush nodded her immense head and spoke no more. She seemed to be dwelling in a reverie of the past, but she nuzzled Emery from time to time, and her great red tongue caused his hair to stick up at a funny angle.

Cadfan piled more broken wood onto the flames, and, one by one, they dropped off to sleep. It took Nolan quite a while, what with a monstrous, man-eating grizzly Bear snoring like a diesel engine not twenty feet away—even if she had reformed!

But if she had wanted to harm them, she would've done so already. And Fiorlen soon left the group and was up in the trees with the Pêllys and the lightning Bug, keeping an eye on the children below.

Heilyn offered to take first watch and he climbed into a lower branch, whispering with the Treegirl. The children were to sleep through the night. Cadfan curled up with a naked sword in his grip. Rhydderch had his dagger a handsbreadth away.

Nolan tucked up next to his brother on a bedroll that had been tied to Whimsy's saddle. The forest floor was still uncomfortable, but at least Emery had a blanket now. It seemed like a luxury after all he'd been through.

Soon, the fire burned low, and the dull orange-red glow of hot coals and spent embers reflected off the weary sleepers.

Part III

The Real Quest

17

History Lessons and a Fistfight

Exhaustion and the soft, muted light of the Morsden kept everyone sleeping well after sunrise, until they were gently awakened by Fiorlen. Tërimrush had been up for hours and delivered four large salmon for breakfast, from some estuary that only she knew of, for Cadfan was surprised there could be that much water flowing so deep in the Covering.

The fish were cleaned and soon sizzling on a freshly banked fire. The smell was tantalizing; but, more than food, they all longed for clean clothes and a hot bath.

"I wish we'd thought to bring some coffee," Cadfan griped as he turned the salmon on sharpened sticks to cook them evenly.

"Do the Aossí grow their own coffee beans?" Stanley asked.

"Aye," the large man answered. "The Alabaster Mountains produce the best coffee in the world! We bring it down all the way from the King's City—it's one of our few luxuries. I wish we had some for you to try. More's the pity."

"One shouldn't complain with such a pleasant surprise for breakfast," Rhydderch admonished him. To Heilyn, the monk said, "Feed the horses, lad, and be quick about it. Then have the Bear show you the stream to refill the waterskins."

After the salmon breakfast, rounded off with butterless bread and apples, the horses were saddled, the weapons were fastened, and a grudging group of sore children climbed aboard their mounts and turned the reins toward Arshúil.

Ever since the uncharacteristic emotional outburst of last night, Genevieve had reverted to a sullen, despondent attitude; and her terse comments belied a seething anger at their situation that was just under the surface, waiting for a reason to bust out. She whined and murmured under her breath at having to ride behind her future stepsister on a flea-bitten hack like Ink Blot. The horse didn't seem too thrilled at the prospect of toting two people, either.

Emery, on the other hand, was a kid on Christmas morning. The overpowering She-bear lowered herself to the ground so the boy could clamber onto the hump between her shoulders. He was twelve feet in the air as Tërimrush loped along, far behind the horses, so as not to frighten them. It was one of the most madcap visuals Nolan had seen so far in Tírcluddaithe. Emery almost had to shout to be heard.

"So what do we do when we get back to this village, uh, Arshúil?"

Fiorlen's voice answered from the treetops on their left-hand side. "We must find Father and Audrey, and the best person who can help us do so is the Eldest. Father knows the Morsden better than just about any creature alive; he could find us anywhere in the Forest—so there must be something that prevents him from getting to us."

"And you think that something is Agenor?" Quinn asked.

"Agenor is just a puppet," Rhydderch said. "He is enslaved to Bàsisolc."

At the mention of this second name, Nolan's skin crawled, and it felt as if a chilled air blew down his back. The name conjured up even worse images of fear than Agenor.

"Who is Bàsisolc?" Stanley asked. He gave his best friend a look that told Nolan the name affected him the same way.

"Well, you probably know Crannhyn is called the Eldest because he is the oldest living thing on the planet, aye? The second-oldest living thing is his brother, Bàsisolc—"

"Ah, Rhydderch," Cadfan interrupted with a small grin tugging at one corner of his mouth, "come now, let's not scare the children-wealth. Bàsisolc is a fable, a myth. The most evil, the bringer of death, the devil himself—there's no such thing, kids, just like there's no such thing as Agenor; just like there's no such thing as Crannhyn."

"My dear Cadfan, there is, I assure you; for I have met all three," Rhydderch replied. "Agenor and I have a lot of bad blood between us."

Cadfan rolled his eyes but said nothing more, so the monk continued, "When the world was made, it was decided that mankind, and *not* the Coedaoine, would have dominion over the earth. Crannhyn, always benevolent and compassionate, gave to mankind the Master Song."

"And what is the Master Song?" Stanley asked.

"One thing at a time, dear boy. I'll get to that. And I'll thank you all for no more interruptions." Rhydderch took a swig from his waterskin and handed his horse's leader to Heilyn, who trotted beside him. The apprentice led his master's horse along the broken trail, as if quite used to Rhydderch plunging into long tales and paying no attention to the way before him.

"There, now I can tell my story." He spoke as a master bard, a true historian of the Hidden Lands, and his words took on an almost musical quality.

"The world was made by the Great Composer many, many summers past. From the start His world was inhabited by the Treefolk—wonderful Shepherds who watched over the kingdoms of the animals and the plants. To them was given the duty and the pleasure of cultivating the world around them. In the twilight of the evening, they Sang beautiful Songs that made everything that drew breath become aware of itself and its surroundings. The music was always there from the Composer, you understand, but the Treefolk added the words.

"After many summers—more than you or I would care to count—the world was full of these Awakened beings. The animals talked, and the plants moved, all responding to the Songs of the Coedaoine.

"But the Composer decided to turn His world over to Man's dominion, for better or worse. The Humans were the Composer's greatest work, and they quickly spread across the face of the earth. When they came to Crannhyn's dominion, the Treefolk named them Aossí: the Fair Folk.

"Crannhyn the Mighty was delighted with the Fair Folk. The Eldest rushed to them with open arms, to offer his wisdom and to Sing for them. He taught the Humans how to build and cultivate and to speak the Chéad Teanga, the first language.

"But Crannhyn's brother, Bàsisolc, was jealous of Man's special favor in the Composer's eye, for he himself wished to be in that place alone. He wrongly believed the Composer had grown tired of the Caevnaóri, His Shepherds, and would supplant the Treefolk with these small, soft Men.

"In secret, Bàsisolc was able to convince many other Coedaoine that soon they would all be servants to Mankind, and they joined him in his iniquitous plan to enslave the Aossí before it happened to them.

"Soon the Fair Folk, too, listened to Bàsisolc's discordant notes, his double talk. He convinced them that Crannhyn would subjugate the Fair Folk, turning them into slaves for the Coedaoine.

"Of a truth, it was Bàsisolc who sought to betray Humanity, but the harmony between the two races was already broken, for Mankind is easily deceived.

"Bàsisolc was able to Corrupt many men with his vile Songs. He Sang to them false words, playing to their egos, puffing them up, while slowly pitting them against Crannhyn's loyal Coedaoine, and in time these Men became savage and cruel; they became barbarous and nomadic and warlike.

"The loyal Treefolk recoiled in shock and took their Songs away from Men. It was a hard lesson for them to learn, that Mankind was pliable and easily swayed by whatever wind, foul or fair, blew his way. The music of the Coedaoine was too powerful for human ears, even if Sung from a pure heart and with good intentions, so Crannhyn ruled that the Treefolk could Sing over Humans no more. It pained his heart to withdraw from the Aossí.

"Secretly Bàsisolc convinced the Corrupted men that Crannhyn was now working against them—that he had taken the Songs away out of spite and jealousy, to keep the Aossí in the dark, and not out of concern for Man's well-being.

"And, like so, a heartless tune was played, for Mankind made war with the Trees. After all, the Aossí thought, the whole world was under their command; therefore, so should the Trees be beneath them. The Fair Folk planned to subdue the Coedaoine and *force* them to Sing at their beck and call.

"This was called the Woods' War, and the whole earth was darkened in sadness and despair—yes, it spread across all lands. For a hundred years, there was groaning under the travesty of murder in the name of selfish gain. The Treefolk had something the Aossí wanted, and the Aossí were determined to take it by force.

"After this fashion, it was the Fair Folk who taught the Treefolk to fight, for they had never needed to defend themselves before. And yet, they were quick learners; soon they became warriors, and Crannhyn's loyal fought against Bàsisolc and his minions, and the Aossí, as well.

"The rivers of earth were overflowing with blood; the land and the seas were polluted by Bàsisolc's scheming. He now determined that not only would the Humans kneel before him, but so would his brother and all who had sided with him. They would kneel, or they would be crushed.

"What ended the War were the Awakened—those creatures given the discernment to choose between good and evil. Some chose the path of Corruption and worked for Bàsisolc, but many times more sided with Crannhyn and turned the tide of battle: the *Leucis*, noble Awakened great cats; the *Loxon*, massive and wise elephant-men; the Thornsword Brethren, a numberless multitude of Awakened flowers; and many, many others. They all came to the aid of the loyal Coedaoine.

"When it was clear Bàsisolc could not defeat his foes, he fled into the wastelands, the deserts far south, many days' travel beyond Tírsor. His Treefolk, those that remained, fled with him as banished outcasts.

"An Alliance was made between the Trees, the Men, and the most advanced of the Awakened creatures. The land was divided into kingdoms, and the Trees agreed to keep to themselves in Morsden Forest. Man spread across the whole earth and took it for his own.

"Still, through it all, Crannhyn the Mighty never stopped loving Humans. It pained him to take away all the riches of Singing from them. So he wrote one Song, and one Song only, for Mankind to Sing for themselves—the one Song the Coedaoine could not Sing.

"It was his greatest work, the most perfect Song, and he gave it away, because Crannhyn believed that if Man's heart would open to the music, it would heal their warring minds; it would strengthen them to rise above Corruption.

"Seven virtues—seven Verses—were put into this Master Song: Love, Wisdom, Might, Valor, Kindheartedness, Devotion, and Meekness. These seven qualities, when perfected, could help Mankind learn to control himself.

"The Master Song was given to the first High King of men, Hynfel, who is called the Old King and who was the best friend of Crannhyn.

"Hynfel had seven daughters. He was benevolent and good, and wisdom and love flowed in his veins. He let the Song work through him; however, he knew one day men could use the seven virtues selfishly, for even the Verses can be Corrupted if Sung with a greedy heart. Indeed, Love, the greatest virtue, could become obsession; Wisdom could become control; Might could become brutality; Valor could become pride; Kindheartedness could become manipulation; Devotion could become fanaticism; Meekness could become frailty. And all the world would suffer.

"The Song was too powerful in the wrong hands, so Hynfel had Crannhyn separate the virtues of the Song into seven stanzas, and he placed the power of each virtue into a different gemstone.

"Hynfel gave one jewel to each of his daughters, bidding them to expand their kingdoms and build on each virtue respectively. In this way, no one Human could wield the total power of the Master Song, and yet each virtue on its own could be developed, and the Aossí as a race would be blessed.

"To his oldest daughter, known as the Embroidery Queen for her proficiency in spinning, he gave the Love Verse. Her kingdom became the greatest, and her sisters were jealous.

"After many years, Bàsisolc and his cohorts stole back to the Seven Kingdoms, hidden in the shadows of the Deep. When he learned of the Verses, he coveted that power for himself, and through his spies—wicked Treefolk—he began to turn the sister queens against each other. They listened to the poisoned honey-whisperings of the deceiver, who bred the seeds of rivalry, and soon, war among the Aossí threatened their destruction. Bàsisolc knew that only the queens could Sing to open the virtues, and he sought to manipulate them for his own machinations—like a puppet master, hidden in the dark places of the Forest, pulling strings.

"Upon learning of his brother's maneuverings, Crannhyn realized he must step in to protect the queens and their Verses. He convinced the sisters to return the gemstones for their own safety, and the Treefolk would contrive a way to guard the power of the virtues until Bàsisolc could be found and dealt with.

"Crannhyn decided the world would be split in two. The most accomplished of the Shepherds gathered to Sing, and the Veil was created—a partition that would hide the Verses throughout the earth, so that no one Coeduine, not even the Eldest, would know where all the Stones were concealed. Some of the gemstones were on one side of the Veil, some on the other.

"The Embroidery Queen decided to live on the Other Side of the Veil, where Crannhyn was working to set up his domain. Some Aossí chose to follow their queen and crossed the Veil with her; they settled a part of the Otherworld, which, in your tongue, eventually became the British Isles.

"And, thus, you now know the origins of the Master Song. May its virtues once again hold sway over the Aossí!

"My tale is finished."

Everyone remained silent, even Cadfan, long after Rhydderch stopped speaking. The only sounds to be heard were the horses' hooves, the clanging of their gear, and the padding of the Awakened she-bear.

"Where is Crannhyn now? Is he still around?" Quinn asked after several moments.

This time Fiorlen answered, her voice calling down from the trees. "His domain is in a special part of the Veil, like the Temples where the virtues of the Verses can be released. A place-between-places, neither entirely on our side of the Veil, nor on yours. He reigns at the northern tip of Morsden, where the Spiacánacha Mountains meet Scáthán Lake, at the mouth of the Rhrushden River. From there, one can enter his Sanctuary during gylináma."

Spiacánacha was Translated "Jagged," and *Scáthán* came out as "Docile" or, more literally, "a Mirror."

"The mouth of the Rhrushden? It takes days to cross through the heart of Morsden Deep," Cadfan pointed out. "And I've rarely heard of Aossí doing so. We skirt the woods to the east, through the outposts on the fringe, and still it would take six, maybe seven, days just to reach the northern tip of the Forest. Unless you wanted to sail around the Forest to Mhórrónta."

"I've heard it said the Icelings are having a wonderful season with scalps," Rhydderch returned with a snort. "No, thank you."

Nolan had no idea who the Icelings were, but the idea of them taking his scalp was a little unappealing.

Quinn was thoughtful. "Fiorlen, can we take the Rhrushden through the Coverin'? Like on a boat? That'd be faster than hikin' through the Forest."

"It is a possibility, but it will not be an easy journey," Fiorlen answered. "The River is aptly named Roaring in some places, but the Docile Lake is a mocking name. Scáthán is anything but placid, and fearsome Awakened creatures live there. They are fierce, and for some, their loyalty to Crannhyn is questioned." She shifted to another tree.

Rhydderch added, "All the while, we must keep a lookout for Bàsisolc's own Corrupted. He would like nothing more than to capture you, Quinn, I'm sorry to say. I fear Agenor will soon learn that Otherworlders have returned to the Hidden Lands, if he hasn't already—and he will hunt us down."

Cadfan looked puzzled. "Why would Bàsisolc or Agenor—and I'm not saying I believe they exist, mind you—but why would they care a cat's whisker about the lass?"

Fiorlen dropped out of the treetops, and Cadfan pulled up short, while the rest of the group stopped in a loose configuration as close to a half circle as the narrow trail would allow.

"Quinn is the last descendant of the Embroidery Queen," the Treegirl answered. "Her grandmother Audrey, along with Rhydderch and my father, found the Love Verse many years ago, right before Bàsisolc did. Crannhyn decided to give it to Audrey for protection on the Other Side of the Veil, and now Quinn has it."

Cadfan looked at Quinn, then at Fiorlen. "Singer, you are saying *she's* the last descendant of the Embroidery Queen…? And forgive me, Quinn—I'm not impugning your heritage—but you have to understand, most of the Fair Folk believe that all this about the Seven Queens and the Master Song is an old-time fairy tale."

Quinn shrugged.

It *did* sound hard to believe.

"It is no fairy tale," Rhydderch countered. "I will say it again: I have met Crannhyn, Bàsisolc, and Agenor. I have held the diamond with the Love Verse in my palm."

Cadfan held up his hands. "Look, I've never had problems believing in Treefolk, like some thick-skulled folks have. The Awakened and the Corrupted had to have come from *somewhere*. And obviously the Veil exists, because here before my eyes are children from the Other Place. But to say there's one ultimate good being, one ultimate evil being, and a Master Song of amazing power—my dear friends, these are tales told to children-wealth before bed. We've all heard them. And to say this spirited young girl is the daughter of some legendary Embroidery Queen…well, it's a little hard to swallow, is all I'm saying."

"I assure you, she is," Rhydderch said, wearing a confident expression.

"And I assure *you*, monk, if that be truth, High King Alaric would bust a royal stitch, as she would have more right to the throne than he. Come now, aren't these old wives' tales?"

Fiorlen cocked her head, and it reminded Nolan of a dog that was puzzled. "I don't understand that expression, 'bust a stitch.'"

"Have a cow?" Emery offered from the Bear's shoulder hump. Tërimrush rumbled a short laugh through her muzzle, sitting on her haunches at a cautious distance from the horses.

"Ah," Fiorlen said as the Translation Song found a close equivalent. "We would say 'snap his twig.'"

"We would say 'flip his wig,'" Nolan tittered.

"Or birth kittens," Stanley said.

"Poo a brick," Quinn added.

"That's gross, Quinn," Genevieve muttered. It was the closest she would come to joining in on the fun.

The children had fun testing the limits of the Translation Song by spouting more euphemisms, each one cruder than the one before, until Cadfan eventually held up his hands in surrender, and they all resumed plodding through the makeshift path with the occasional last-minute pun or joke thrown in. Fiorlen continued walking alongside Red, petting his mane.

"So you are saying Quinn has a Verse of the Master Song," Cadfan put to the Treegirl.

"I am."

"*The* Master Song?"

"Is there another?" Rhydderch asked.

The weaponsmith whistled through his teeth and scratched his tangled beard with his free hand. "It's just all a little overwhelming...." His voice trailed off as he mulled over this new revelation.

Fiorlen said, "I agree, Cadfan. To know this is the Love Verse—I can sense its power radiating off Quinn! *The* Love Verse, the strongest of the great virtues! The chorus of the Master Song, the jeweled star of the blanketed night—"

"The cream of the crop," said Stanley.

"The bee's knees," said Emery.

"The mutt's—"

"Enough!" Genevieve interjected. "Can't you all be serious for one minute? Don't you realize our predicament? We are *stuck* in another world, with giant man-eating bears, and talking trees with talking bugs, and whatever that butterfly thingy is. And some gormless, pikey swordsman, with some *monk*, for crying out loud, traipsing through a black forest with no road in sight, to find some fairy-tale creature! It's like a twisted, screwed-up version of *The Wizard of Oz*—and you lot are makin' jokes!"

"I say...gormless pikey?" Cadfan looked like someone had slapped him across the face.

"And Tërimrush wouldn't eat people," Emery protested.

"I have done, man-cub," the Grizzly responded. "Just not *these* people."

Nolan thought she looked like she might make an exception in Genevieve's case. And at the moment, he wasn't quite sure how he felt about that.

Quinn looked over her right shoulder. "What would ya like us to do, Gen?"
Genevieve's eyes glittered. *"Don't* call me Gen."

"Look, I'm sorry yore gonna miss some phone calls, and there's no
Sainsbury's up the road for ya to buy more makeup; but we're doin' the best we
can, so why don't ya lighten up, or just keep quiet? Okay...? *Gen?"*

The fifteen-year-old yelled and grabbed Quinn's hair. Quinn cried out and
flung her head back to hit Genevieve but missed. Ink Blot startled and bolted,
throwing both girls onto the moss-strewn floor, where they rolled over yellow
pine needles, gray feldspar, thorny brambles, and black dirt. They were a blur
of tumbling, tangled hair, and fists.

"Okay, now. Really, girls." Cadfan dismounted.

Nolan and Stanley clambered off their horses, not quite sure what to
do. Fiorlen slinked over to Tërimrush and Emery, whispering to them both.
Heilyn was off his horse, trying to reach into the fray without getting struck,
with Rhydderch offering suggestions from his horse.

Tintreach and Bassett seemed to enjoy a good, old-fashioned tussle. They
egged on the girls by tossing little pebbles at them.

Nolan realized it was getting out of hand and said, "That's enough. Quinn!
Genevieve! Stop!" He jumped to his left to avoid the rolling mass as a random
leg lurched out and almost tripped him.

"Hail, Cadfan! Rhydderch! You are well met!" boomed a deep voice from
behind them. Everyone froze in hilarious poses like a game of Statue, and all
heads turned in unison toward the sound.

It was the search party.

Nolan wasn't sure which group looked more surprised: his own motley
crew staring wide-eyed at the six men on horseback, who'd materialized out of
nowhere; or the six men staring wide-eyed at the elephant-sized grizzly Bear
with a tiny boy on its back and the set of wild Otherworlder girls wrestling in
the dirt and underbrush.

Nolan would've put his money on the search team.

"That you, Yale?" Cadfan asked, addressing the lead man. Once again,
Cadfan caught Quinn by the scruff of the neck and held her at arm's length as
she kicked and spat at Genevieve, who was twisting around in the brawny met-
alworker's other hand. Finally they stopped kicking and twisting, and Cadfan
released them. Genevieve stormed off behind a nearby tree, holding a sleeve of
her shirt to her split lip, and Quinn moved to stand next to Nolan and Stanley.
She had the making of a shiner over her right eye.

"Well, flame me," the man named Yale chortled. "What've you got going on here, mate?"

"Misunderstanding between the Otherworlders. Out of their systems now, I hope." Cadfan grinned.

"And what, pray, is *that?*" Yale pointed at Tërimrush. "Is it tame?"

The grizzly Bear growled. "I am called Tërimrush by these humans." But they did not understand what she said, for she wasn't speaking the First Tongue. Still, her growls were Translated by the Song to Nolan's group.

"This is the She-bear we have heard rumors about," Cadfan supplied. "Tërimrush is a friend of the Otherworlders."

"If this is one and the same, then she is a man-eater and should be destroyed," Yale said.

Tërimrush gave a low growl, and Emery held his breath.

"I will vouch for her," Cadfan said. "She is not enraged with the blood-lust—at least, no longer. And we have no proof she has attacked any Aossí."

"I most certainly have!" the Bear protested in a burst of rash honesty, but Cadfan gave her a *shut-up* look, and Emery patted her between her enormous ears.

Yale sighed and gave a slight shrug. "It's on your head then, friend. But if she even looks at my men wrong, we'll be feasting on bear meat at the village tonight." He turned his attention to the Treegirl. "Singer, you are well met."

Fiorlen nodded.

Nolan realized it was the first time any of the search party had seen the Coeduine. It had to be a bit of a shock, even to the Aossí, since none of them had seen a Treeperson in his lifetime. Kind of like meeting Santa Claus on Christmas Eve.

Yale greeted Rhydderch, gave only a casual glance at Heilyn, and then saluted the Otherworlders. "I must admit," he said, "these are strange days in which Aossí are in the Deep of Morsden, running into visitors from the Other Place, a Coeduine maiden, and a giant Awakened she-bear. We met a contingent of Catfolk yesterday on their way to Arshúil, but they were not inclined to say *why*.

"And let me tell you, Cadfan, they're an *odd* lot of creatures. Eight-foot-tall Catmen, but seemingly as civilized as we. Though it does take one aback when they occasionally lick their hands, and the way their ears and tails seem to twitch at random, just like a kitchen cat looking for a scrap of fish." His men chuckled. "Yes, strange days, indeed." Yale spat on the ground as he finished.

"Speaking of Arshúil," Rhydderch said, "shall we proceed? I fancy a hot bath and a cup of strong tea. I'm also in need of refilling my tobacco pouch."

Yale smiled. "Indeed, monk. You will find your fill." He turned in the saddle to the two men on his right-hand side. "Ofydd, Paderau—yours are the fastest horses. Hasten to Arshúil and give word that the Otherworlders were found and we return."

The two men nodded and shouted, "Swiftness!" before nudging the horses into a trot. They were soon lost in the green-gray distance of Morsden Deep.

"Well, then," Quinn said as Genevieve skulked back to the group. "Gen—rather, I mean, *Genevieve*. Shall we?" She held out her hand to help her up.

"I'd rather walk," Genevieve replied.

"She can ride behind me," Heilyn said with what seemed to Nolan as a tinge of reserved eagerness. It was the first time they'd heard him speak in hours. Rhydderch might have picked up on the subtle interest, because his eyes narrowed on his sheepish-looking apprentice, but the monk made no comment.

Genevieve glanced over at the servant boy with the thick hair and striking eyes. While she probably wouldn't give most help-staff a second glance, this young man must have given her pause, because she threw Quinn a sarcastic look and grasped Heilyn's muscular outstretched arm to climb on behind the horse.

"Thanks," she said to Heilyn, who nodded and clicked his tongue at the horse.

"Right, then." Cadfan cleared his throat, one eyebrow slightly raised. "Let's go home."

18

A New Enemy

The horses seemed to sense that the village was close. Cadfan told the children to hold the reins tight to keep them from running the last few miles. The path opened up, white stones lining the way. They could hear the Rhrushden through the trees, and the sounds of a typical forest came to their ears: wind, insects, birds, and small rodents. After the stifling silence of the Deep, it seemed as loud as a train station. Everyone was dog-tired and looking forward to a hot bath and deep sleep.

Blue Time fell while they were yet a couple miles outside the village. Fiorlen Sang the Translation Song, but the words were simple and not poetic, as if she were merely stating facts: the Otherworlders needed to understand the First Tongue.

But no Translation was needed to understand the screams emanating from the village.

Cadfan, Rhydderch, and the search team urged their horses into full gallop, with Quinn not far behind them. The other children, not so adept, were soon passed by the loping She-bear. Fiorlen blew past them all, followed closely by Tintreach and Bassett. Nolan yelled after Tërimrush to wait—he wasn't about to lose Emery again—when suddenly they rounded a bend and Arshúil came into view.

The village was under attack.

From this distance, in the gathering dusk, it looked like pandemonium. What at first appeared to be whirling storm clouds, Nolan soon recognized as hundreds of black Ravens, enormous in size, circling over the fields surrounding the town. He could hear their caws over the tumult on the ground. Every few seconds, several dozen birds would drop out of the sky to skim along the banks of the River. He wasn't quite sure if they were attacking the townsfolk, but another sudden outburst of screams ripped his attention back to the villagers.

Nolan could make out the women of Arshúil herding their children toward underground shelters. Bonfires tossed angry sparks of red and gold into the evening sky. The men in their black cloaks were rallying toward the Rhrushden—some on horseback, others on foot. Even the townsfolk were armed, dressed in their loud, defiant colors.

A few people were splayed along the grasses by the River's banks. Nolan couldn't tell if they were dead, but he urged Whimsy to hurry and pulled his sword out of its saddle sheath. Strangely, he felt little fear, but his heart thumped in his ears, and he worried most for Emery. That maniacal She-bear seemed oblivious to the small child on her back.

One of the black-cloaked *lucféagwyl* let out a blood-freezing scream as he fell to the ground. But what had struck him? The birds? Certainly not; Nolan could see nothing but the River running downstream and a dense fog roiling onto the bank.

A war horn split the dusk, clear and commanding; bells pealed in the village itself, but their cries were unneeded—every villager who could fight was already at the River's edge.

"Tërimrush! Stop! Emery is with you!" Nolan shouted again, his voice cracking. His lungs threatened to seize up, perhaps from the sudden rush of adrenaline, or from fear.

Or was it the black mist that crept up from the shoreline?

What the…?

Disbelieving his eyes, Nolan pulled hard on Whimsy's reins. The horse whinnied and reared back on two legs. Nolan lost control and slid off the back end of the horse, landing on his side. Luckily the sword dropped from his hands so he didn't impale himself. Whimsy bolted toward the stables, and Nolan couldn't blame him.

Someone had set fire to the grass by the water's edge.

Coughing and gasping for air, he rolled onto his hands and knees, scrambled for his sword, and came up crouched. He wasn't more than twenty yards from the bank of the River.

Nolan watched as several Ravens broke formation and swooped down from the swirling mass above. Diving toward the riverbank, they pulled up at the last minute, releasing small, glimmering drops onto the ground below. They passed so close to Nolan, he could see the village fires reflected in their cold black eyes.

But what happened next was beyond Nolan's wildest thoughts. As each drop streaked through the black mist and smote the ground, a fiery red spark shot high into the air, sucking in both fog and dirt like a whirlwind, which materialized into a dark, wraithlike form. Dozens of them began appearing out of the mist.

While Nolan watched in disbelief, another Raven broke rank and streaked down toward him. Instinctively Nolan threw his free arm over his face to fend off the attack, but instead of claws and tearing pain, he felt a cold drop splatter across his forehead. Had the Raven *spit* on him?

But when he reached up to feel the wetness, his hand returned a dark, shiny red—it was blood! The birds were dropping *blood*!

Before he could make sense of what was going on, Nolan realized with a flood of horror that the nearest wraith was advancing upon him. He screamed as the monster's glowing red eyes locked onto his own.

The phantasm was comprised of black mist, wet gray vapor, some muck from the bottom of the Rhrushden, and a foul odor like squalid swamp water. It was humanlike, but its flesh was dead and gray like a corpse. It had two arms, two legs, a torso, and a rather human face, but its penetrating, dark red eyes glowed with hellish light. In its hand was a black sword that, in the firelight, unfortunately looked solid enough to slice Nolan in half. The wraith stood some six feet tall, blade-thin, and the Mist whipped around it like a cloak.

When it stood before Nolan, it spoke with a hollow, toneless voice. Nolan nearly jumped out of his skin.

"We have come for you, Otherworlder," it said in the First Tongue as it reached a long, snakelike hand with four grasping talons toward Nolan. It started gliding along the grass toward him as though it had no feet.

Grabbing his sword, Nolan screamed again and managed to jump to one side just as the rotting talons lunged for him. The sword swung wide and passed unhindered through the gray flesh, whirlwind and all. The monster was nothing more than dust and mist! And yet, it was something horribly more....

As the creature flew past Nolan, it turned so quickly, the top half of its gruesome form twisted 180 degrees before its bottom half flipped around to join it. Before Nolan could even blink, its leprous hand squeezed his throat in a viselike grip, lifting him several inches off the ground.

"You will come with us," it hissed in its airy voice as Nolan's sword dropped to the ground.

Nolan choked, struggling for breath and writhing like a snake in the Mist-monster's grip. He tried feebly to claw at the wraith's hand cinched around his windpipe. White stars exploded at the corners of his vision, and his veins seemed to have been filled with lead. He was dying! He was going to suffo-cate—the most terrifying feeling for a child with asthma.

Quinn came flying through the air with a war cry on her lips, her daggers, Lively and Spirited, in each hand, as she landed on the creature and buried the blades in its back. The monster exploded into black vapor, and Nolan collapsed to the dirt while Quinn fell to her knees over the pile of wet ash.

Even as she leapt to her feet, the dust started swirling on the grass again, spinning like a tiny cyclone, growing larger in a split second, gathering tufts of grass and dirt as it whirled—this time taking on a hulking shape like some kind of giant black wolfhound.

"Oh, ya've gotta be flamin' *jokin'*!" she screamed in defiance as the smoky dog stared her down with its red eyes.

Nolan couldn't gulp down air any faster—his lungs were protesting the rough treatment, and his throat felt feverish where the monster had grabbed him. By sheer will, Nolan forced himself to his feet and picked up his nameless sword. He staggered next to Quinn as they faced off against the hound.

It snarled, showing rotted black teeth. "You will come with us, Otherworlders," the dog demanded.

"Stop saying that!" Nolan's voice was hoarse, and it hurt to move his vocal chords. But he was so angry that it fueled his strength, and just as the wolf-hound lunged, he saw a tiny ripple go through its misty frame and solidify.

Now! his mind shouted, and he rammed the sword into the Mist-dog's open mouth. The blade went straight through, slicing the monster in half. Black smoke exploded around Nolan as if he had divided an incoming wave with his hands, and the forward motion of the disintegrating beast caused the vapor and dust particles to pour out behind Nolan like a flag snapping in the wind.

Instantly the Mist started funneling again behind the children, but this time Quinn was ready. She kicked at the Mist and the clumps of stuff it had sucked up, spreading it far and wide. The creature seemed to be confused and dizzy, buying them precious seconds to run away from it.

"They're easy to put down," she gasped as she pulled Nolan after her. "It's just gettin' 'em to stay down that's the problem."

As they moved a few steps farther away from the riverbank, Nolan realized that the nearest Aossí villager was shouting in a mix of horror, fear, and disbelief as he fell back from an approaching wraith.

"What's going on?" Nolan managed as terrified shouts of "No! No! It can't be you! It can't be you!" filled his ears.

Quinn tried to explain the little that she knew. "I overheard one of the guards say that all the monsters look like a villager who went missin' a few weeks back, voice an' all!" Quinn shouted over the din.

Nolan didn't have enough free brain power to process what she was saying.

"Where's Emery?" he yelled over the battle sounds. His windpipe felt flattened.

There was no need for Quinn to answer. A loud roar pealed through the plains so thunderously, even the Mist seemed to recoil. It was almost dark now; there was maybe twenty or thirty minutes of Blue Time remaining. Nolan desperately hoped that whatever evil was empowering these shape-shifters would stop once the sun went down.

Unfortunately, there was only one way to tell; but if they did linger past the magic hour, Nolan, his friends, and the entire village were all doomed.

Nolan scanned the horizon. Right at the water's edge, Tërimrush had four Mist-monsters clawing at her back paws, two in the shape of dogs, two in the shape of the hapless missing villager. She reared back, and Nolan saw Emery clutching to her shoulders with one hand and throwing stones down at their attackers with the other. But in front of Tërimrush stood a Horse with a flaming mane. Almost as tall as the She-bear, the Horse was the same jet-black as the Mist-monsters, but this most definitely was *not* some smoky shape-shifter. It was a real horse, of sorts, only ten feet tall.

Tërimrush roared again, and her giant paw lashed out at the Nightmare, knocking its head clean to one side. The Horse stumbled under the blow, and the Bear's claws dug deep into the flesh. The Horse howled in pain, but where blood should've poured out, red embers and smoke escaped instead, burning the Bear's paw. Tërimrush reared back again, almost crushing the four monsters at her flanks, and bit down hard into the neck of the Nightmare, shaking it like a dog might a rag doll. Mindless of her burning mouth, she somehow managed to lift the Horse into the air with her jaws and *threw* the beast ten feet into the churning waters.

Nolan had never seen a display of strength like that in all his life.

"Holy—" Quinn swallowed her words.

The Horse broke free of the water with a very humanlike shriek and bolted for the other side of the Rhrushden, fleeing into the Morsden in a trail of smoke.

As Tërimrush came crashing down on all fours again, little Emery clinging on for dear life, she let loose a victory roar at the retreating Horse that reverberated so loudly, the four Mist-creatures in her midst burst into puffs of inky fog and cycloned away. She sounded like a twenty-foot lion, and it shook Nolan to the core.

"Guess the ol' girl can take care of herself!" Quinn said with a slightly shell-shocked look before coming to herself and racing toward the throng of Aossí fighters between the village and the riverbank. Most of the grass was on fire now. Several men lay motionless along the banks. The ringing sounds of metal on metal filled the air, as well as the groans of wounded and dying humans.

"C'mon, Nolan!" Quinn yelled. "Emery's safer 'an we are!"

She slashed one of the Mist-monsters from behind, slitting its throat with her dagger, just as its sword was about to fall upon a black-cloaked guardsman. The Mist had already begun to re-form as the guard shouted his thanks and recovered his footing.

It seemed the shape-shifters remained mist-like and vaporous until the moment of impact, when their weapons and bodies turned solid. Nolan thought maybe they had just enough energy to solidify temporarily, even if that instant was more than enough to wound, maim, or kill. But in that moment, their smoky, wraithlike form was easily broken with a sharp stab or slash, exploding like a smog-filled balloon.

And it appeared that depending on how dispersed the smoke was, it took longer for the creature to re-form, often into another shape. Spreading the cloud seemed to buy a little extra time, but beyond that, the creatures seemed invincible.

The Ravens began to disperse, flying low over the Morsden, cawing in triumph.

Nolan and Quinn surveyed the battle before them. They couldn't see Cadfan, Rhydderch, or Stanley, but what they could see horrified them. The Aossí were losing. Forty or fifty men against a hundred unkillable doppelgängers made out of dust. How could they even hope to overcome?

"D'ya think they'll disappear after Blue Time?" Quinn shouted in his ear.

"Man, I sure hope so!" Nolan yelled back through the pain in throat. He was relieved to see that Quinn was thinking along the same lines. Whatever was keeping the Mist empowered surely had to end when the magic hour was over. Right? Or were the monsters permanently Awakened? Maybe the Treegirl would know. "Quinn, where's Fiorlen?"

She glanced around, then pointed with a dagger. "There!"

The Treegirl stood in the center of a circle of trampled grass about twenty feet in diameter. At least a dozen of the monsters surrounded her, some humanoid, some flying like bats, some slithering like snakes, and some hunched like wild dogs about to strike.

But they gave her a wide berth, for she was Singing. And as she Sang, tongues of flame like little darts leapt out of the burning grasses and speared her enemies. They exploded in clouds of vapor and dust...*and didn't re-form*.

"Fire!" Fiorlen shouted over the tumult. "Use fire!" she yelled, then continued to Sing.

"Fire! They evaporate in fire!" Nolan and Quinn began screaming to the Aossí, but Nolan had to stop because he gagged on the smoke from the grass, and his lungs closed up. He fell to his knees, trying to pull in air.

Cadfan and Rhydderch both drew to his side with arrows in their hands dripping with something that looked like tar. They dipped them down into the burning grass and set the flaming arrows to the bowstrings. The fiery missiles whistled through the air and sank deep into two Mist-creatures that had just taken solid form. They exploded in a shower of fetid water and smoke, and particles of flaming dust floated through the air like burnt paper, the only trace left of the monsters.

Stanley was next to appear at Nolan's side, sword in hand. "Nolan? Nolan! Are you all right?" he shouted.

Nolan nodded, forcing oxygen into his tight lungs. "N-need a minute. Wh-where's Emery?"

"We cannot win this battle," Rhydderch said, nocking another lit arrow. "There are too many...."

But before anyone could reply, another war horn winded, this time from the tree line. Nolan's heart leapt to his throat. Not more enemies!

As if things weren't nightmarish enough, thirty Catmen came bounding out of the Forest without warning and threw themselves into the fray.

But to his sudden joy, Nolan realized the Catmen were attacking the black monsters. And they were *good* at it, too. The Mist seemed to evaporate before their fierce blades, and Fiorlen began shouting at the top of her lungs, "Use fire, Leucis, use fire!"

Nolan's eyes hardly believed what they were seeing. The newcomers were humanlike, but huge and definitely feline—Tigers, Lions, Panthers, Jaguars, Cougars, Cheetahs, and a whole bunch of other species he didn't even know the names for. They were seven or eight feet tall and walked on two reverse-articulated legs. They roared just like great cats and issued challenges and taunts in the First Tongue as they waded fearlessly through the black Mist as if fording a river, swords swinging, lances and battle-axes at the ready, wearing shining armor like medieval knights.

One in particular stood out because of his sheer, white fur that almost seemed to glow in the last moments of Blue Time. He appeared to be the leader, for he was the greatest of the warriors, slewing dozens of the Mist-monsters with a gigantic, butcher-knife-like sword that was aglow with dancing flames. Nolan guessed that the Catman had dipped it in something like tar as he watched it slice through the ranks of vapor-fiends like butter. At least thirty monsters fell by his sword alone.

And then it was over.

Blue Time ended, and without a sound, the remaining doppelgängers disintegrated where they stood, like falling piles of ash, and returned to the earth and vapor from which they had been made. Nolan's hunch had been right: The magic ended after dusk.

He collapsed on the ground, exhausted and struggling for air. Stanley was already calling out to Emery and Tërimrush and Genevieve. Nolan had completely forgotten about her, but he hoped she was all right.

With the battle now over, all that remained were the cries of the wounded, the smells of smoke and blood, and the shouts of victory and agony. Nolan looked out across the Rhrushden and started.

There at the tree line, hidden in shadows but faintly illuminated in the dying firelight, was the Boarman, Agenor. He might have been a normal-sized man, around six feet tall—it was hard to tell—but he was not as tall as the Catmen or the flaming Horse. His body was rotund, covered in what looked like dark, bristly fur. A naked sword hung at his right hip, and his left hand gripped a long glaive with a glinting axe head. Wicked yellow tusks curved upward like a handlebar mustache from his sneering lips; little flames of orange and red danced in the darks of his eyes.

Nolan jumped to his feet, about to sound the alarm, but Agenor faded into the Forest, and Nolan thought perhaps his eyes had tricked him after all.

But deep down, he knew what he'd seen.

"Hail, Orbo King!" Fiorlen cried out as the white Tigerman approached, wiping soot and tar off his sword. "Has there ever been an Awakened that was more well met than you?"

19

The Tiger and the Apprentice

Seventeen Aossí were dead, including Aneirin. The town leader had been one of the first men to engage the Mist-creatures, and he was one of the first to be cut down. His sacrifice had bought a precious few seconds to usher the women and children into the underground shelters, and he was celebrated—deservingly so—as a hero.

The entire village mourned the loss of life: husbands, fathers, and sons. Thankfully, no small children had been killed, but a few of the lucféagwyl had been young men scarcely older than Nolan and Stanley.

Two women had died during the attack: an elderly woman, whose heart seemed to have failed her, and Ffion, the seamstress who had given the Otherworld children their cloaks. Along with Aneirin, she was hailed a hero, for she had gathered several children, including her daughter, Delwyn, and herded them toward a shelter. As they rushed down the stone steps into the underground refuge, Ffion had turned and fought their pursuers with nothing more than a burning stick and a long brass knitting needle. When they had gathered her body, they had found three piles of burnt ash around her. Delwyn wailed over her mother's corpse, clutching the knitting needle to her chest.

As energetic as the Aossí were in their merrymaking, they were as equally ardent in their mourning. The women and small children helped the battered menfolk collect the bodies of the slain, and by midnight, many funeral pyres had been lit.

"They will want you for their leader," Yale said to Cadfan as the two stooped by the River's edge to wash the grime and death from their bodies. The Aossí were ritualistic in their cleanliness, and it was customary for the survivors of battle to purify themselves in the waters of the Roaring.

"And I will refuse," Cadfan returned, grim-faced. "My place is with the Otherworlders. What have I to offer Arshúil beyond steel and horses? I will nominate you, Yale."

"And I will accept," Yale said.

Cadfan nodded.

Nolan, Stanley, and Emery overheard this exchange, also bathing in the chilly waters under the moonlight. The briskness helped clear Nolan's lungs of smoke and sadness.

"Blast, where *is* that slothful boy?" Rhydderch's voice broke through the night. "Heilyn! Where are you, lad? Hang your idleness!"

It was then that Nolan remembered Genevieve was riding behind the monk's apprentice, and neither of them had been seen since the battle.

⌒

DURING THE FIGHT WITH THE Mist-monsters, Genevieve had watched Heilyn intently. At the first sign of trouble, he had directed his horse into a copse of trees surrounded by gorse bushes and underbrush, about a hundred yards from the village entrance.

While she'd had no inclination to rush into yet another life-threatening situation, she had at first thought it cowardice that had motivated him to sneak away from the conflict. But she had been able to see, from his mannerisms and agitated demeanor, that he was actually itching to leap into the fray; and he seemed to be fighting the desire to assist the villagers, for he would look at her over the back of his horse while she stood on one side, and he on the other. His mouth would move silently, and he would shake his head, then turn his attention back to the battle.

Could it be he was trying to *protect* her? Genevieve studied this strange young man scarcely older than herself. Even in the pale twilight, his features were stunning—so refined and well-bred, incongruent with his status as a lowly servant boy to that weird monk. His curly hair was well-groomed, and his eyes were such an unusual shade of gold that she found them almost unnerving; there was an intelligent intensity behind them that made Genevieve want to uncover what he was thinking about at any given moment.

He had hardly spoken to her on their way back to the village, but when he did say something, it was with an air of astuteness and gentility, as if he knew much more than he let on. His English was spoken with a perfect Kent County accent, perhaps from Kingsdown, where Audrey Redding was born. He was by no means fluent, she could tell, but she thought it a kind gesture that when he did speak to her, it was in her native language.

During the battle, he had kept up a soft running dialogue, apparently for Genevieve's benefit. The whole scene had looked like utter chaos to her, and she couldn't even tell whom the Fair Folk were fighting.

"We have taken the northernmost quarter of the fields," Heilyn had explained. "They fight against the Mist, it seems—some form of Corrupted I've never seen. The Sapling has destroyed several! They appear weak against fire, and we press our advantage, but I fear we shall be overwhelmed. Your sister I can just make out; she fights well!"

"Future *stepsister*," Genevieve had corrected him, following his finger as he'd pointed out Quinn in the gathering dark. Genevieve had felt a twang of something—she wasn't sure if it was jealousy or something else—and she had felt an overwhelming urge to rush out into the battle herself. But she had quickly swallowed the bizarre compulsion. It was *madness* on Quinn's part to risk her life for a bunch of people she hardly knew.

A sudden earth-rumbling roar caused Genevieve to startle and bite her lip to keep from screaming. Heilyn placed a reassuring hand over hers as she steadied herself against the horse. That casual touch seemed electrified, and Heilyn held her gaze for a moment before pulling his hand away.

"Apologies, m'lady." He inclined his head and patted the horse's neck to calm it. "Tërimrush has overcome that flaming Horse. I now think we will defeat the onslaught. From what I can see, your stepsister and her young friends are well, and the Sapling has destroyed many of these fiends with fire."

Genevieve saw the brute tearing off into the woods not more than a few hundred yards from their hiding place. The monster turned her skin to goose-flesh. At least, that is what she told herself; because, in the back of her mind, she was thinking it was Heilyn's touch. Just her luck to meet a handsome boy in this nightmare world she was stuck in.

Genevieve was *not* "boy crazy"—in fact, she found most of their gender to be dirty and immature. So, this was not some budding infatuation, but she couldn't help recognizing the guy *was* good-looking.

It was just a few minutes later that Heilyn jerked his head around to the Forest behind them, startling her out of her musing once more. His hand clasped the hilt of a sword sheathed to the horse's saddle.

"What is it?" she asked, petrified.

Moments later, about thirty Catmen approached, armed to the teeth, literally, and led by a stark-white, bipedal Tiger who towered over her by at least three feet. She bit back a scream as Heilyn pulled the sword out of its sheath and held it up to the advancing line of giant creatures.

"Declare yourself!" Heilyn called out in the First Tongue to the white Tiger. He was obviously the leader, for the rest of the great Cats stopped when he held up a fist. "Friend or foe?"

"To the Aossí, we are friends. What transpires here?" the Tiger demanded, brandishing a large sword shaped like a butcher's knife.

As the Tigerman spoke, Heilyn lowered his sword in a salute. "Ah. Hail, Orbo, King Leucis—you are well met."

The Tiger cocked his head, ears twitching back and forth, as his long tail danced left and right. Genevieve, in spite of her terror, almost laughed at this catlike reaction.

"Have we met, lad?" King Orbo asked.

Heilyn gave a small smile as he sheathed his sword. "Once, many years ago. But hurry, the village is under attack from Corrupted—shape-shifters weak against fire."

Orbo looked down at the young man, studying him for a moment, as if trying to remember. Then to his entourage, he spoke over his shoulder, "Leucis, to arms—Arshúil is attacked!"

As he turned to lead his soldiers, Orbo looked intently at Heilyn once more. "We will talk later. Watch after the youngling." And he was gone.

"Youngling?" Genevieve was offended. "You're nearly the same age as me!"

Heilyn gave her a wide smile showing white teeth. He leapt into the saddle and held his arm out for her to climb up in front of him.

"For the Catfolk, m'lady, anyone under a hundred summers is a youngling. Come. With the Cat warriors, this battle will be over in moments."

⌒

"HANG IT, HEILYN, WHERE ARE you?" Rhydderch called out again as he dressed. Nolan was on the verge of starting to worry when a Cat warrior, this one a midnight-black Panther in scarlet-red armor, approached the River's edge where the men were bathing under the moonlight.

"Is there one named Rhydderch among you?"

"There is," the monk replied.

The Catman studied him for a brief moment, then said, "My lord requests for you to join him. He has summoned a young lad and an Otherworlder maiden, and the boy claims to be apprenticed to you. Follow me."

The Panther didn't await a reply but turned to walk toward one of the bonfires, as if he expected Rhydderch to comply. As a result, he didn't see the older man blanch and look nervously to Nolan and Stanley. To Yale and Cadfan, he said, "We will join you at the council in half an hour," and then he walked after the Panther, leaving the boys to shrug their shoulders at each other.

⌒

FARTHER UPRIVER, WHERE THE RHRUSHDEN pooled in a calm eddy partially enclosed by a jetty of land studded with huge boulders that blocked the view from downriver, Quinn washed with the womenfolk of Arshúil. They spoke softly, many in tears, and ignored the Otherworlder. But Fiorlen sat on a stone near Quinn with her spindly wooden legs dangling in the water. Her wet willow-hair was gathered behind her, glistening with droplets in the moonlight.

"What do we do now, Fiorlen?" Quinn asked, squeezing water out of her hair. It felt like a blessing from above to be clean, even if the River was chilly. Her teeth chattered as the wind picked up, making the trees sigh. The Love Stone was wrapped out of sight in her cloak, which lay on the bank beside the Treegirl, who had already dressed in her plain earth-toned smock.

"Our plans do not change. We must make for Crannhyn as swiftly as possible."

"And leave the Aossí undefended?"

Fiorlen allowed a small smile. "I admire your courage, Otherworlder. But six children will not make a difference should the *Capána* return tomorrow evening. Nor do I think they would attack…if we were to leave."

A new word had had to be coined to name these Corrupted shadows; Fiorlen had dubbed them Capána, "the Mistfolk."

Quinn realized Fiorlen was counting *herself* as the sixth child. She seemed so much wiser than the average seven-year-old human, it was hard to fathom that she was the *youngest* of their group. Little Emery was two years her senior.

"It is my belief that Bàsisolc sent the Mistfolk after *you* to recover the Verse," Fiorlen said. "And should you not be *here* at tomorrow's gylináma, the Aossí will be safe."

"So it's *my* fault these people're dead." Quinn stared off into the Forest.

"I did not say that," Fiorlen replied. "People suffer where evil goes unchecked. The Morsden is full of Corrupted who have been here much longer than you have; the Aossí are no strangers to hardship, battles, and death."

Quinn walked along the shoal bottom of the shallow eddy to dry land and dressed in silence. The Fair Folk used cotton, but it was coarsely spun, and their towels were none too soft.

Once sure that no one was watching, she slipped the pendant over her head and clasped the diamond in her water-wrinkled hand to stare into its depths. All *this* for a Song? A *Love* Song, at that? *There's little love here*, she thought as she tucked the diamond under her tunic and sighed; it felt so heavy against her chest.

"Fear not for the Aossí," Fiorlen continued. "The Catfolk will offer their steel; King Orbo swears it to me."

That made Quinn feel a little better. "I shore wouldn't want to brass off those Catpeople."

"Indeed," Fiorlen said, following Quinn back toward the bonfires. "You should see them when they're angry."

As they neared the fires outside the town proper, Quinn couldn't help but stare at the great white Tiger. He wasn't properly albino, she noticed, as he had startling blue eyes with vertical pupils. He was rippling with muscles, still wearing silver battle armor, and a purple cloak hung off his shoulders. His feet were bare, and semi-retractable claws peeked out from under the fur. When Quinn noticed the thin circlet of pale gold set at an angle over his furry ears, she had a momentary desire to run her fingers through his soft scalp. On his furred, five-fingered hands were several rings studded with emeralds and rubies.

His massive jaws moved as he spoke to Rhydderch, showing glistening incisors and a strawberry-red tongue. Quinn spotted Genevieve and Heilyn standing just beside the monk, also engaged in conversation, and she felt a stab of shame that she hadn't thought of Genevieve at all since the attack. Her step-sister seemed just fine, her attention focused entirely on the apprentice, but Quinn wondered what they were talking about so animatedly.

Fiorlen clicked her tongue. Quinn was starting to decipher the Treegirl's mannerisms, and she recognized this one as an exclamation of mild distress and disappointment.

"Madán. I had hoped the Leucis king would not meet with Heilyn. If he recognizes him, no doubt he will inquire after the Red Sword."

Quinn had no idea what that meant or why that would be a problem. "What is the Red Sword?"

The Sapling merely shook her head. As they neared the fire, two Cat warriors moved to stop Quinn, but when they saw she was with the Coeduine, they genuflected and permitted the two to approach the Cat king.

"Ah, there you are, Fiorlen." King Orbo nodded. "I would have sent for you, but none of my entourage is female. What is your role in this business?" He gestured to Heilyn and gave Rhydderch a rather sour glance. "Does the monk speak the truth about the Red Sword?" He lowered his voice when he mentioned the sword.

Quinn watched the exchange, puzzled. She caught Genevieve's eye and gave her a questioning look. Her stepsister mouthed, *"Later,"* but she seemed excited about something.

Fiorlen seemed hesitant to respond. "He does, Your Grace. However, it is not my place, nor *his*"—she meant Rhydderch—"to go into greater detail."

Orbo sniffed, and his eyes narrowed on Heilyn again. "I will not let him out of my sight, then. Rhydderch says you will make for *Suas*."

The word Translated "Up" to Quinn, leaving her more confused than ever. The Song seemed to imply it was a place, not a person, although she couldn't have explained why she knew that.

Fiorlen nodded. "We go now to ask the Aossí for help setting us down the River."

King Orbo gestured with his long arm toward the town. "Then, by all means."

20

Council Fire and a Missing Prince

Nolan was surprised to see Quinn and Fiorlen enter the Great Hall with Genevieve, Rhydderch, Heilyn, and the white Tiger king in tow.

Stanley nudged him in the ribs and whispered, "Looks like we missed something interesting."

The boys were seated with Emery, Cadfan, Yale, and eight other Aossí leaders around the circular fire pit in the main hall. They bunched together to make room for the newcomers, but King Orbo seemed cramped no matter how much space they tried to give him. A hewn log was burning, and several oil lamps were lit, hanging from sconces on the wooden walls.

Yale's face seemed drawn and tired, his eyes rimmed in red. "We meet in council to decide what to tell the village," he began. "The Laws of Hospitality require us to provide safe haven for the travelers, and yet many blame the Mistfolk attack on their presence here; coincidence seems unlikely. Still, I ask myself, *why* would they attack? For pillage? Or were they looking for the Otherworlders? I fear we do not know the underlying reasons *why* the Coedaoine have summoned travelers from beyond the Veil after so many years."

We've come for you, Otherworlder. The attack by the demonic Mist-monster was vivid in Nolan's mind, and the memory sent a shiver through him, even in the warmth of the fire. He reached up to touch his neck, which was swollen with a green-purple bruise in the shape of the Capána's fingers. It felt so tender, he could hardly swallow.

They wanted the diamond, and Nolan knew they would follow him and his friends until they got it.

Yale continued, "Also, from whence come these Mistfolk? By my oath, I've never heard of Corrupted such as these—shape-shifters and monsters made of mud and vapor. The ones I saw looked all the same, like the corpse of Grwn the trapper, missing these past two weeks. But the legends I know speak of Singing only over that which is alive. Is this wrong? I would know this council's mind, but first I would hear from the Coeduine maiden." Yale looked to Fiorlen.

Fiorlen was silent a few moments. She searched for each elder member's gaze. Some held it; some looked away. She said, "I believe the Mistfolk are a new form of Corrupted. I have never heard Father speak of such a creature before. And, Elder Yale, you are correct: The Song of Awakening works only on something that respires, plant or animal.

"This means the Capána are composed of *something* that breathes; and although I cannot say for certain, I believe they come from the grasses along the banks of the Rhrushden, perhaps the amoebae and bacteria in the water itself...and from the skin of the Aossí, their *dust*. Somehow it has Awakened the very dirt and ash itself. This is why they are weak against fire, for the dust burns, and the Corrupted Song fades."

Cadfan cocked his head. "Forgive me, Fiorlen, but dead men don't breathe. I understand the water and the weeds, but I would think the dust would be useless in Singing."

"Yes," the Treegirl conceded, "there must be some other factor to Awakening the dust."

"Blood," Nolan said quietly.

"What?" Rhydderch's eyes narrowed.

"Uh, those clouds of Ravens." Nolan felt uncomfortable when all eyes were on him. "They were dropping blood. Wherever it fell, the Mistfolk came up."

Several of the council members seemed incredulous.

"Hey, I *saw* it." Nolan couldn't bring himself to share what else he'd seen: the fabled, malevolent Agenor.

Fiorlen was thoughtful. "I believe this would be correct. Even shortly after death, the blood holds oxygen, and the dust would respond to the Singing through it. Thus, the blood of the recently dead could become one of the components of the Corrupted, gathering material unto itself, more dust, along with the water vapor and the grasses. The way a tornado gathers strength by picking up the debris around it."

"I know of these tornadoes," Cadfan said. "They are common enough in the springtime on the plains of Tírsor. But they are almost unknown here in the Morsden."

"This would also explain why the Mistfolk look the same," Yale said. "It would have been Grwn's blood used to Awaken them."

The Aossí around him looked as if they'd eaten something distasteful. Certainly, the notion of using one of their brethren's blood to Awaken an army of doppelgängers was revolting.

Rhydderch's eyebrows met together in contemplation. "If Fiorlen is right, and the Song gathers more of the dust unto itself, more of the water, more of the plants surrounding it, then the supply would be virtually limitless, and an army could be raised out of the very ground itself."

This was a very uncomfortable thought for Nolan, who imagined legions of the shape-shifting, wraithlike monsters.

"Provided there was enough Fair-Folk blood," Fiorlen corrected the monk. "If animal blood worked, the Corrupted presumably would have used it."

"Why would that matter?" Quinn asked. "Blood's blood, innit?"

The Treegirl shook her head. "I am speculating, but I don't think animal blood would be effective. Human blood is special because Man was Awakened by the Composer Himself." She was thoughtful for a second. "I suppose Caevnaóri blood would work, too…. But, if I am correct that this Song is activated by human blood alone, that, at least, is limiting, for it is not something readily available."

"Not yet," Cadfan murmured before he asked in a louder voice, "Have all the Aossí been accounted for?"

"The count is done. None of the villagers is missing," Yale responded.

Quinn's face grew pale, and Nolan knew what she was thinking. Her *grandmother* was still missing. They could only hope Ysgafn was protecting her from this new menace.

The Treegirl spoke again. "Whoever Sang the Mistfolk into being is a master Coeduine. I know of none that advanced, save for perhaps Crannhyn and—"

"Bàsisolc," Rhydderch interrupted her. "The same with the Corrupted horse that the She-bear chased off—only Bàsisolc could make something like that."

Fiorlen nodded. "Quite right. I believe it is most probable Bàsisolc murdered this missing Aossí, and from thence the Capána arose. It is evil of the highest order, for it is birthed out of death and not life."

"So they're like zombies," Stanley said when Fiorlen paused to take a breath. The Translation Song took a second to render *zombies* into the First Tongue. To the Aossí, it came out as "the dead who are not dead."

Fiorlen tapped a finger on her lips, pondering this statement. "Yes, Stanley; after a fashion, I think this is right. However, as we saw, this kind of Singing would last only for the gylináma. It is unnatural, an amalgam of many types of Awakening—it is somewhat different from the Nightmare, wherein Bàsisolc started with a normal mare and Corrupted it. Even if the blood of fire and the mane of flames are unnatural, the source material for the Singing *was* natural.

"But the Mistfolk should *not* be. I don't know how it would even work, for the dust is of the dead; and yet, with the blood…there they are. It is…"—here Fiorlen seemed to struggle for a word in her language—"*Morscan.*"

The Translation to the Otherworlders came as "Singing Death" and then, a split second later, "Necromancy." Quinn made a disgusted face.

"What's necromancy?" Emery asked.

"Never mind," Nolan told his brother.

"It's gross," Quinn said.

One of the elders shook his head. "Are we saying we really believe Bàsisolc exists here? I think the devil is a myth, as is Crannhyn."

"Not so, Eurig," Rhydderch replied. "I have seen both with my own eyes."

"Twaddle!" the elder retorted. "This will serve no other purpose than to further frighten an already terrified village. You're known to be a madman to most of the people, and I think living in the Deep has stolen your mind; you see what your eyes make up."

"Peace," Yale said, bringing his hand down in a silencing gesture. "Until a few days ago, I would've said Otherworlders were a myth. What we know and do not know are on opposite sides of a long bridge. Whether there is Crannhyn or Bàsisolc or no, one primary source of what is good and of what is evil, it does not change the fact that our town is in mourning over the deaths of our leader, our family members, and our friends.

"They were killed by a race of creatures that should not exist, and we were spared only by the check of gylináma on the malevolence. I would know *why* the Capána attacked. Again, was it for simple plunder? Or were they after the Otherworlders?"

Fiorlen held up her hands. "I must beg your forgiveness, Aossí friends. It is not my place to explain the whys of my father's actions in bringing these Otherworlders to Morsden. I must present our request, imposing on your goodwill, without further clarification. I do this for your safety, not to withhold information. We need your help in setting us on our way along the Rhrushden; we go to seek Crannhyn, for I know he is not legend. He can help us overcome this new threat."

"You believe the Capána will return?" Yale asked.

"No. I believe they will follow us; but again, I cannot tell you why."

"And if they don't? You would leave us with half our guards upon the pyres whilst you seek what many of us still consider a myth?" The question, posed by a female elder, was not necessarily asked with any ire, but neither was it polished with softness.

"King Orbo has said the Leucis warriors will protect the village in our absence," Fiorlen told her, then turned to the Tiger king, who nodded in agreement.

"This is not my council," Orbo said, "yet I would be heard, if permitted."

Yale inclined his head. "Of course, Your Grace. A king's wisdom will always be welcome at our council fire."

"Then, upon my word, I swear Crannhyn is no more a myth than the shadow-beings we saw tonight. For it was the Eldest himself who Awakened my father's father's father. But that is not all that I wish to tell you." Orbo took a breath. "I fear another plot is afoot, and it is perhaps connected to this tragedy tonight. I find it more than chance that Arshúil is attacked by a new form of Corrupted, just as Ysgafn goes missing and Otherworlders appear.

"To this, I will add, I am here at the behest of King Dubric, having traveled five days with my contingent, across the Culais Strait, for the sole purpose of meeting the High King at Arshúil…only, the High King is not here."

Emery was young enough not to bother with decorum and had no trouble interrupting the Tiger. "Wait, who's Dubric?"

Orbo smiled patiently at the boy, his pearly fangs reflecting the firelight, and Emery gulped. "He is the king of Tírsor, lad, and the Far-Flung Islands; and he is the brother of High King Alaric."

"He is called Dubric the Dark," Rhydderch added, "because of his complexion, and also his disposition. He suffers from epilepsy and is given to great fits of melancholy."

"King Alaric, though, has not been to Arshúil in nigh on five years," Cadfan inserted, bringing the conversation back on track. "Why would he come here unannounced?"

Orbo exhaled. "You are most likely unaware that Prince Chadric has gone missing these past six weeks."

There was a collective intake of breath around the council, and this time, it was Stanley who interrupted. "Prince Chadric is Dubric's son?"

"Nay, Queen Basillia—that's Dubric's wife—is barren," Rhydderch supplied while Yale calmed the council down. "Which is one of the reasons Dubric struggles with depression."

"So then, this Chadric who's gone missing would be the heir to the High King's throne." Stanley, sharp as ever, had quickly put it together.

Orbo nodded his great head. "King Alaric busies himself to distraction in search of his son; his duties as High King have been neglected, and I fear the under-kings will use this to their own advantage, his brother most of all. Indeed, the Citadel City has been left in the stewardship of Dubric, who dispatched me to Arshúil. His Majesty was said to be here, awaiting my arrival, and I was sent to guide him through the Deep, looking for the prince. Dubric has sent the other under-kings on what I believe are equally spurious missions to all corners of Tírcluddaithe—there is not a king within a five-day journey of the Citadel. I fear Dubric has sent me on a fool's errand purposely, and I begin to suspect the Dark King knows more of the prince's disappearance than he lets on."

There was another small gasp from the council.

Astutely, Stanley said, "So Chadric ran away because of Dubric, then."

"Wait," the female elder interrupted. "The prince might have been kidnapped, for all we know."

"With no ransom demand after six weeks?" Cadfan shook his head. "Not unless he was kidnapped only to be murdered."

"Do we have any inclination whether the prince lives?" Yale asked.

Orbo glanced at Rhydderch and Fiorlen; it was subtle, but Nolan caught it, and he raised an eyebrow at Quinn and Stanley.

"I am sure of it, but I cannot explain why." Orbo spread his hands apologetically to the elders. "I share all of this with the council only in case His Majesty should arrive, and for you to be aware of what is going on. I will leave my warriors to protect Arshúil, and they will let King Alaric know I have traveled north with the Coeduine maiden. Perhaps Crannhyn the Mighty can assist us with this matter of the prince, as well as help the Otherworlders; for indeed, I believe the two situations are intertwined."

The council digested all this information for a few moments until Yale brought them back to the matter at hand. "Singer, how, then, can we help you in your journey?"

Soon after the council meeting, the townsfolk gathered to lament the loss of Aneirin and the other Aossí warriors. The mourning of those lost prevented the villagers from showing disdain toward the Otherworlders and their Singer. But from the looks Nolan saw, it was clear many of the Aossí blamed them for the attack.

No one slept that evening. They worked all night to ready two large rafts and gather ample provision. Fiorlen estimated it would take three days of rafting almost two hundred miles down the Rhrushden to reach the Docile Lake—a method that was twice as fast as walking through Morsden Deep, and potentially twice as dangerous. Although to Nolan, they faced possible death on land *or* on water, and he'd just as soon not go under the Covering again.

Nolan was more than a little relieved that the giant Cat king was coming with them, as was Cadfan, who seemed to have thrown in his lot with the Otherworlders, for better or worse.

Genevieve was more reclusive than ever, refusing to help prepare the rafts. She gave one-word replies, and those only to Heilyn, while she stared blankly into the dying embers of the bonfires.

Stanley and Emery seemed almost *excited* about the adventure. Quinn, while perhaps not excited, worked with a grim determination; and only Nolan, it seemed, nursed a growing sense of foreboding.

He wiped down his sword as Cadfan had shown him. He'd officially christened the blade The Sword That Shall Not Be Named; but because TSTSNBN was too hard to say, he simply called it Unnamed—it sounded mysterious. (Stanley had named his Link, after the video-game hero.)

Nolan felt a little overwhelmed, but he didn't show it to his brother and friends. After everything they'd been through, only now was the real journey beginning. And at the end of the journey, they still had to find Ysgafn and Audrey. The tasks ahead seemed insurmountable to him.

There was no room on the rafts for Tërimrush; her weight would've sunk them. But she promised to follow Emery swiftly behind on the bank and to travel overnight, if needed, to catch up to him each morning. In spite of her enormous size, she moved quickly and tirelessly, and she said she'd once traveled as much as eighty miles in a single day.

Her unwavering devotion to Emery was beyond contestation; and again, after seeing how she'd dealt with the Nightmare, Nolan was glad she was coming along. He did, however, mention his concern for her *running* all the way to the mouth of the Rhrushden.

She replied that she didn't tire like they did and could go days without sleep, moving constantly, provided she ate well. Of course, she added, her normal fare of a hapless Aossí was quite out of the question; but not to worry, for she hunted quietly and swiftly, just like a tiger.

Orbo allowed a small grumble of laughter when he heard this. "I've not a doubt in my mind, mother Bear," he chuckled.

Finally the rafts were ready, floating on massive pylons made of airtight casks. The rafts themselves were made of sturdy logs lashed together with thick rope, fifteen feet long and about as many wide; each had a three-sided wooden enclosure with leather flaps in front and a shingled roof, which would provide shelter. They were steered by a rudder in the back and several long poles.

About a quarter mile downriver from Arshúil, where the water deepened and began to pick up speed, the rafts floated low in the Rhrushden, loaded as they were with provisions.

On the shore a short distance away, the funeral pyres were dying. The sun had just broken the horizon, and the world was awash in golden light. The sky was still; the Forest was silent; and the townsfolk continued lamenting their dead. The Otherworlders, too, felt the pang of loss for Aneirin, Ffion, and the lucféagwyl.

After the ceremony honoring the fallen, Yale took his oath of office, and his first official act as town elder was to wish the questers "Swiftness!" Most of the villagers wished them the same, but many had a look of relief—or perhaps even "Good riddance!"—upon their swollen, tired faces.

Delwyn, the seamstress's daughter, made her way out of the crowd. She stood before the children and the Treegirl, her face red with tears.

"Don't yore heart ache for her?" Quinn whispered to Nolan. "To lose a mother! I've no idea what that would be like, but me fear over Gran gives a small inklin'."

Nolan nodded. He wished he could offer Delwyn some consolation, but he could think of nothing to say that wouldn't sound trite.

"I have worked all night," Delwyn began, with her voice thick and pained. "I have made cloaks for the boy and the girl, to match your own." She handed them to Quinn, who was speechless.

"G-gosh. Wow. Th-thank you," Emery stammered from one of the rafts.

"Yes, thank you," Genevieve said as she took the cloaks from Quinn. She sounded sincere. Apparently she wasn't as heartless as Nolan had thought, and he had to give her credit. "Really. *Thank* you."

Delwyn nodded. "Mother would've done the same. I believe you have all come from your world to help us. I am simpleminded, but I sense a great destiny in each of you. You will right the wrongs of this past night. And for that, I am thankful you have come." She raised her voice so the villagers could hear. "So I say, hail, Otherworlders. Swiftness!" And she saluted them with tears running down her cheeks.

Quinn and Genevieve's eyes both flooded with tears, and they ran to hug the girl they hardly knew, as all but a few of the villagers shouted, "Hail, Otherworlders. Swiftness!"

And with that, they were on their way down the mighty River Roaring.

21

The Call of the Flowers

The Rhrushden was clear and cool in the summer sun, about forty feet deep in the very center, where the current was fastest. By the banks, when the water was clear, the children could see all the way to the bottom as rocks and patches of green underwater plants sped by. Fish of any number of species darted out of the rafts' way. They could see huge turtles slumbering on logs by the water's edge. Frogs by the hundreds croaked and plopped into the water. Large birds—some kind of hawk—and a few inland gulls flew overhead. They saw herons, kingfishers, beavers, badgers, water rats, and a type of large mole. Emery swore he saw a ten-foot-long snake, but Nolan doubted it. On the fringes of the Morsden, life was teeming. None of these, of course, was a highly Awakened animal, but it was sort of like going on a safari.

About noontime, Stanley raised his voice to be heard by the travelers on both rafts and asked a question that was on all the children's minds: "What is our plan, Fiorlen? Are we going to stay on the rafts during gylináma or make landfall in case the Capána attack?"

"We risk setting the rafts afire should the Capána attack this evening," Fiorlen said, and Cadfan and Rhydderch agreed. "I do not doubt they could even glide upon the water. I would say a couple hours before dusk, we should make land and prepare for defense. With luck, Tërimrush should catch up with us by then; we could use her help."

The adults nodded, and Cadfan asked, "Rhydderch, do you think it's possible to raft during the night, or is it too dangerous?"

The monk rubbed his white beard and brought his pole aboard, laying it lengthwise along the raft; it was almost as long as the barge itself. "With torches, and Tintreach and Bassett lighting the way, I think we could do it. If we raft through the night, we will hit the rapids mid-morning tomorrow, I would guess. But, of course, that means a second night with very little sleep.... Still, we could save almost two days of rafting if we pushed through the night."

"Then that's what we should do," Cadfan said, "after we get through gylináma this evening."

A few hours later, Nolan and Stanley were discussing who was Huck and who was Tom when Fiorlen called out to them for quiet. They fell silent as the Treegirl listened intently to the sounds of the Forest and the River.

"We need to make land," she said, grabbing a pole and pushing them toward the right bank.

Without questioning, Rhydderch threw a weight tied to a rope into the River to slow the front raft's speed, and Cadfan did the same with the back raft. The extra drag created by the makeshift anchors, helped by the rudders being turned hard to port, slowed the rafts to a slight drift, and within a minute, Orbo leapt to land and tied the front raft to a tree. Soon after, Nolan followed suit with the second raft. For his first time rafting, he was pleased to have caught on quickly.

"Why have we stopped, maiden?" Cadfan asked when all were ashore.

"I felt the call of the Flowers, steelworker," Fiorlen said without further explanation.

"Does that mean she has to go to the bathroom?" Emery asked seriously, and the other children cracked up. "What?" the nine-year-old demanded. "Why's that funny?"

"That's the call of nature, squirt," Nolan managed.

"Okay, what's the call o' the Flowers?" Quinn asked.

"Some of the Thornsword Brethren approach," Fiorlen said.

"That didn't answer the question," Quinn retorted.

But Fiorlen didn't seem to expect an attack or anything. In fact, she looked *happy*.

Seconds later, the Flowers did, indeed, appear out of the Forest.

"What in the *world?*" Genevieve whispered. It was the first she'd spoken in hours. Heilyn, standing beside her, broke into a wide grin.

Of all the strange sights Nolan had seen the past several days in the Hidden Lands, this had to be tops. King Orbo and the Wolfling looked *normal* compared to these guys.

"Wow, that's...uh...that's almost unbelievable," Stanley commented, scratching his head.

"Oh, my word." Quinn's mouth dropped open. "They can Awaken *flowers.*"

Yes, they were Flowers—like a Rose, and a Sunflower, and a Tulip, and a Bluebell, and a Daisy—about twenty of them, all riding various kinds of large, marginally Awakened beasts; some on strange, four-horned, armored Goats, some on wolverine-like Rodents.

The Brethren were about three feet high and shaped kind of like little humans, in the sense that they had green twig-like arms and legs on skinny green stalk-bodies about the thickness of a baseball bat, with broad leaves for hands and wide, flat leaves for feet; but the leaves were creased or cut to make toes and fingers. They were nimble and strong enough to hold or carry swords, shields, and bows, and they were dressed in assorted types of armor made out of tin metal, perhaps—all miniaturized, to be sure, but lethal-looking like a foot-long needle can be lethal.

"What do they use for muscle?" Stanley asked of no one in particular. "They *smell* terrific."

"Wonder if they've got chlorophyll instead of blood," Nolan whispered as a side comment to his friend.

"I think they're freakin' *cool!*" Emery said in awe.

The oddest thing about the Brethren was their heads. Their faces were made of opened petals surrounding the eyes, ears, nose, and mouth, just like a person, but their eyes were all black and beady, like oversized poppy seeds; their noses were little ridges in the folds of their petals; and their lips were slits in the bottommost petals, which were fashioned to look like chins. Their faces were as expressive as any human's, and there was intelligence behind the focus of their black eyes.

The Flowers seemed to be knights of some kind, Nolan realized, and they moved like an organized unit. He wouldn't have been more surprised if a deck of cards came marching through the woods and a fat Red Queen started shouting, "Off with their heads!" while holding a flamingo as a croquet mallet.

"Hail, Fiorlen! Hail, Rhydderch! You are well met! We would've been earlier, but, by my thorns, we were almost trampled by a She-bear four miles yonder, and 'tis truth. She comes soon after at full speed, making a ruckus such as I've never heard in all my Awakened days."

This greeting came in one long breath without pause by the foremost Rose. And what a Rose! The deepest crimson red, his head, or bud, or whatever, was the size of both of Nolan's palms. Around his slender shoulders was draped a bloodred cape stitched with gold trim and emblazoned with a golden sword, though without hilt, and shaped more like a skewer or needle—the crest of the Thornsword Brethren. Along the length of his body, trailing down the stems that made up his arms and legs, were thorns. The Rose held up a closed leafy fist to signal the troops to stop. They fanned out behind their leader.

Stanley nudged Nolan in the ribs and whispered, "They're like Pikmin, dude."

Nolan swallowed a laugh.

"That Bear is my friend," Emery said.

The Rose merely nodded, as if that weren't surprising.

"Good to see you, Lord Boujòn. What news from Suas?" the Aossí monk asked with a genuine smile. One couldn't help *but* smile at the Brethren, not in a mocking way, for Nolan could tell that insulting one of the Flowers would be unwise—but they were awfully darned cute…in a vicious, militant kind of way.

The Rose stepped down off his Wolverine mount (it might have been some type of badger or ferret, Nolan wasn't quite sure) and handed the reins to his lieutenant. Boujòn pronounced it "leff-tenant," which carried through the Translation Song. Though his name sounded French, he had a decidedly British accent, but Nolan couldn't guess why the Song gave him an accent at all—probably for the same reason Tintreach sounded like he was from Duluth.

"Rhydderch." Boujòn made a low sweeping bow. "It does my heart good to see you well, and Mademoiselle Fiorlen. Great Cat King, well met! Yes, Tintreach and Bassett, as well. Hail, Otherworlders!"

"Hi," Emery said, smiling. Nolan and the others waved.

"Were you able to reach the Eldest, Sir Knight? Does he muster?" Fiorlen asked.

The Rose frowned and accepted a small wooden cup of fresh water from his "leff-tenant." The second-in-command was a Lily of the Valley, but he was about twenty times larger than any Nolan had ever seen. His neck was extra slender, so that his bud-like, bell-shaped head drooped down on the stalk and

peered out. His petals were milk white, and Nolan wondered if he was poisonous, as real lilies of the valley were.

Boujòn took a sip of the water after toasting the others. "Sadly, we were
repulsed at the Scáthán, Mademoiselle Singer. The Awakened of the lake dealt
with us violently. Several of my soldiers were injured, four seriously, and my
army has returned to Suas awaiting further orders." He paused to take another
drink of water. "Either Crannhyn has set the guardians of the lake to impede
the progress of any who seek his realm, or Bàsisolc's influence is being felt more
and more among the Awakened of the Morsden. Of a truth, we have seen a
marked increase of the Corrupted as of late.... At any rate, your mother dispatched us, and we were making for the monk's cabin as swiftly as possible,
when, by good chance, we sensed your presence and moved to intercept."

Nolan wanted to ask how the Flowers could *sense* the Treegirl was nearby,
and he wanted to inquire about the Treegirl's mother, but his questions would
have to wait, for now Rhydderch and Fiorlen were discussing the next course
of action.

"Madán," Rhydderch muttered. "I had hoped Crannhyn would've already
been roused. We must press on. Time is against us, especially should the
Capána return this nightfall."

"Who are the Capána?" Boujòn asked, handing the drained cup back to his
second and remounting his steed, which Nolan was now sure was a Wolverine
because of the stripes on its flanks. The Lily's mount was a Badger because of
the stripes on its face. Nolan remembered that from *The Wind in the Willows*.

Fiorlen answered, "The Aossí village of Arshúil was attacked last night by
a new form of Corrupted, made from dust, water, and human blood—shadow
creatures that can shape themselves like tendrils of smoke and mimic many
forms. We also saw the Nightmare my father spoke of, whom Bassett called
Arsoíche."

Nolan almost admitted to seeing Agenor, but he held his tongue, although
he wasn't sure why he just didn't tell them. Perhaps he didn't trust his eyes;
perhaps he was afraid they wouldn't believe him.

Perhaps he was just afraid.

"This is troublesome news," Boujòn replied, reining in the Wolverine as
the slightly Awakened creature pulled at its bridle, seeming eager to be away. "I
assume the Corrupter, then, knows of the Otherworlders' arrival, but I do not
know why Bàsisolc would care, unless...." The Rose let his words dangle, looking to the Treegirl to finish his sentence.

"The full explanation must needs await a more leisurely time, Sir Knight," she replied. "We must be away quickly. Suffice to say protecting the Otherworlders is our top priority, but getting through to Crannhyn so that we can find my father and the missing Otherworlder is our primary objective."

Rhydderch said, "Boujòn, will you select three of your best warriors to accompany us by raft? We could use your help in repulsing the Capána if they attack tonight. The rest of your contingent should make haste to summon the most Awakened of the Forest to gather at Suas and await our return with Crannhyn, with any measure of luck by two mornings hence."

The Rose nodded. "It shall be done."

⟜

WITHIN FIFTEEN MINUTES, THE REST of Boujòn's party was dispersed on their various missions, and the Rose, his Lily lieutenant, a massive Sunflower with an appropriately sized battle-axe, and a serious-looking purple Orchid dressed in a black *judogi*, of sorts, each without his mount, clambered aboard one of the cramped rafts, bringing only their weapons and some small provisions.

As much as Quinn wanted to talk to the Flowers, she also needed to have a conversation with Genevieve. They were on the back raft with the boys and Cadfan, while Rhydderch, Heilyn, Fiorlen, and Orbo were on the fore raft with the Brethren. Tintreach and Bassett flitted between the two barges as they saw fit.

"Genevieve, can we talk?" Quinn motioned for her future stepsister to clamber under the makeshift shelter with her. It was too hot for the leather flaps to be lowered, but it provided a little bit of privacy.

The fifteen-year-old seemed to debate it a moment, but then she nodded and sat down in the shade of the shelter. There were several seconds of awkward silence as they stared at each other, waiting for the other person to start.

Exhaling, Quinn said, "Look, Genevieve, about that fight—"

"No, Quinn," she cut her off. "Look, I'm sorry. You've gotta understand, I'm not cut out for this kind of stuff—adventures and magical creatures and shadow demons and bein' lost in the woods for days. You're...adventurous"—Quinn could tell that she was trying to put it nicely—"but it's too much for me. I—I'm sorry I lost it, okay?"

Quinn nodded. "Yeah. Yeah, me too. Sorry. I know this seems like a nightmare. And I'm sorry ya got dragged into it."

They stared at each other uncomfortably for a while. Apologizing was something Quinn rarely did, if she could avoid it; but here in the Otherworld, it seemed foolish to harbor grudges. After a bit, they both nodded at each other, and that was that.

⁓

GENEVIEVE DROPPED HER EYES. WHY was this was so difficult for her? It wasn't as if she *hated* Quinn. She just…. *Oh, who knows?* Maybe Quinn was more "together" than she was. More *comfortable* with herself, her father, her life in general. Perhaps Genevieve was a little envious of Quinn, though she would never admit it publicly, even if they *were* being cordial with each other at the moment.

She would've left it at that, but it seemed Quinn was trying to reach out, patch things up, so Genevieve forced herself to remain seated.

Quinn managed a small smile. "So, uh, what's up with this Heilyn bloke? D'ya fancy him?"

Genevieve felt her face flush. This was the first time they'd ever had "girl talk," and she felt a little self-conscious. "Oh, Quinn, I dunno. I barely know him, but yeah, he's…uh, well, he's really brilliant…."

"He's not like a monk's apprentice, that's for sure. Not some peasant boy with bad teeth and a Cockney accent." It was a leading statement, and Genevieve tensed.

"You noticed that, did ya?" Genevieve peeked out of the shelter to make sure none of the boys was listening in. They seemed to be paying more attention to the River and their swords, but she lowered her voice to just above a whisper. "Quinn, he's chivalrous and holds himself like he's well-bred; he speaks like royalty—you've not heard him talk much. But…d'ya know what I mean?"

Quinn furrowed her brow. "What are ya sayin'?"

"Can't you see?" Genevieve leaned in conspiratorially. "Heilyn's the High King's son. That jolly great Tiger slipped up and called him 'Your Highness.' I heard him."

Quinn's eyes widened in shock. She looked ahead to the fore raft, where Heilyn's chocolate-colored locks were drifting in the breeze. He stood as straight and square-shouldered as the Tiger king next to him. The confidence, the way he held himself—it was obvious he wasn't a poor apprentice boy.

"Wow," she muttered. "Ya've got a crush on a prince!"

Genevieve smirked. "I don't have a *crush* on him, Quinn; I just think he's nice, and maybe I fancy him. You know, a bit."

"And Fiorlen and Orbo know who he is?"

"Yes. Orbo figured it out immediately. Rhydderch is protecting Heilyn—er, *Chadric*—from his uncle, that sot Dubric. That Treegirl knows; the Greenmen are helping to conceal him, as well." She paused as she read Quinn's face. "But, Quinn, you can't tell the others. I mean, it's not our place to tell them. If Chadric does, that should be his decision, right?"

Quinn thought for a moment, then nodded. "Yeah, but Stanley's smart—he might figure it out on his own."

"Well, at least, *we* shouldn't tell them." Genevieve shrugged. "Agreed?"

"All right. What was Orbo talkin' about, this Red Sword?"

Genevieve looked out at the boys again. "I'm not really sure. I think Chadric stole his father's sword when he ran out. Rhydderch told Orbo the Greenmen had it hidden. It must be something important. Orbo nearly had kittens on the spot when he found out—"

"What're you girls whispering about in there?" Stanley's voice startled them. He was peering into the shelter with a smirk on his face, swinging his sword around like Jack Sparrow—only more drunk-looking. "Is it about boys?" He laughed and gave Nolan a wink.

"None o' yore beeswax," Quinn said, climbing out into the warm summer sun.

"Yeah, why don't you watch where you're swingin' that thing? You're liable to fall overboard, little boy. And it *is* sharp, you know!" Genevieve said it as a joke, and her future stepsister giggled.

"Not nearly as sharp as your tongue, Otherworlder," Cadfan put in with a chuckle.

❧

AS THE AFTERNOON WORE ON, the children grew increasingly somber; they spoke less, and there was no joking. As beautiful as this part of the Rhrushden was, it was lost on the Otherworlders and their companions, who saw the waters only as one more hurdle to overcome before reaching the safe haven of the Treefolk city. And then there were the Mistfolk....

Nolan had a growing sense that the Capána would return at Blue Time, and he was learning to trust his gut instincts—so far, they'd been correct. He was aware of a pressing fear that was like iced hands squeezing his heart. But he didn't think it was so much about facing the shape-shifters, for he knew their weakness, and with so many warriors with the children, he felt they could rebuff an attack.

But he feared Agenor was stalking them through the woods even now. The sense of dread he'd felt the evening before when he'd seen the Pigman at the wood's edge was now like a constriction around his throat. The imaginary tightening made the actual bruises throb even more. With a mounting feeling of apprehension, he wildly thought perhaps the marks on his neck would leave *permanent* wounds, as if it were a poison sapping his strength, draining his courage. He wanted to talk to someone about it—Stanley, Cadfan, Rhydderch, *anybody*—but he was choked off, it seemed, from mentioning what he'd seen the night before.

The group rushed along the Rhrushden's waters, pushing against slick boulders and half-submerged fallen trees. They pulled to shore two hours before gylináma to wait for Tërimrush, for they would need her strength against the onslaught. It was decided that Emery was safest on her shoulders.

"Emery, I've got something for you!" Cadfan was rummaging through a sack and produced lightweight armor of leather and brass that looked like it would fit the boy just perfectly. "Here you are, lad. This should do the trick!"

While it was sort of cool that Cadfan taught him the names for the different parts of armor, Emery still frowned at the jerkin, hauberk, gauntlets, and greaves, clearly disappointed. He was probably expecting something shinier and pointier. "Can't I have a sword?"

The weaponsmith winked. "All in good time, my young man. Even the Aossí don't arm children-wealth of nine summers."

Now, why the Aossí made child-sized armor in the first place, Nolan didn't think to ask, but he was thankful it would provide some protection for his brother. He helped Emery strap the armor on.

The little outcropping of land they'd selected jutted out into the Rhrushden. The area was flat with no rocks, almost like a small, sandy beach, but not as beautiful as the private inlet he and Quinn had found on their first day in the Covering. The earth here was well trampled, as if many animals came out of the Forest at this location to drink. The Morsden itself was pushed back a couple hundred feet. The adults and the Coeduine agreed this seemed as good a place to defend as any they would likely find. At any rate, it would be easy to see the Capána approaching.

They were all terse and tense as they prepared to repel a legion of undead horrors. Tërimrush caught up to them a few minutes before Blue Time, hardly winded, and was given specific instructions from Nolan and Fiorlen to guard Emery with her life, to which she grumbled, "I promise you he won't suffer so much as a scratch." If the She-bear was fatigued from running several leagues through the Morsden, she didn't show it. In fact, she seemed eager to confront the Mistfolk.

King Orbo had unsheathed his gigantic butcher's knife, and the Aossí were smearing their own blades with pitch from a small barrel, while Quinn and Fiorlen dipped several dozen arrows into the black tar.

"I need a weapon," Genevieve said as the sun dropped behind the trees that ran along the other bank of the River. They'd all been so quiet, busily working, that her sudden speech startled them. No one said anything for a few seconds, and she frowned. "What? I'm just supposed to stand around, shrieking like an idiot?" She turned to Heilyn. "I made top marks at school in archery. Give me a bow and quiver."

"Your school has archery?" Stanley asked, though he didn't seem to expect an answer. His naked blade, Link, was resting lengthwise across his knees, waiting for its bath in pitch.

Nolan was shocked at how different his best friend looked, how different they *all* looked, in just a few short days on the Other Side. Stanley, while still overweight, looked somehow leaner than Nolan had ever seen him. But it wasn't just the weight loss or the tan or the outlandish Aossí garb. No, something was different in Stanley's eyes, behind those glasses that reflected the fast-failing sunlight. It was a look of determination. And self-assurance. Quinn had it, too. Even Genevieve.

The Otherworld was changing them, turning them into adventurers. Warriors, even! It was another feeling in the pit of his stomach that Nolan couldn't quite describe. What had his friends become? Heroes of some sort?

Nolan sure didn't feel like a hero. His heart thudded against his rib cage; his mouth was desert dry; his knees shook.

Agenor. The Capána. The Nightmare. *Bàsisolc*. All were against them. And yet, somewhere in the back of his mind, Nolan wondered if his friends could see a similar change in him. He tightened his grip on the hilt of TSTSNBN.

If they were becoming heroes, perhaps he could be a hero, too. He absently touched his aching throat, feeling the puffy finger marks left by the Mistfolk who had tried to choke him. He could master his fear if his friends could master theirs. He could face these threats defiantly and courageously, just like them. He looked over at Emery, who was rubbing the giant Bear's snout and letting her eat an apple from his open palm. For his brother's sake, Nolan could be brave!

Fiorlen had started Singing the Translation Song. Blue Time had fallen. Nolan's heart slowed, he wet his lips, and his knees locked. As the Treegirl Sang, the two fires Rhydderch had started leapt into the twilight with a whoosh. The knots in the wood cracked and popped, sending up sparks of golden orange. The smoke drifted across the clearing, but Nolan breathed deeply—for the first time since coming through the Veil, his lungs weren't tight.

Suddenly a ring of fire erupted around the group, far enough away so as not to be oppressively hot, but it was a tight enough circle to keep them close together. Fiorlen's Singing kept the flames about waist high, so they could look out into the falling twilight and launch over the ring as needed, but it would be an extra deterrent for the Capána.

King Orbo held up his pitch-coated sword and roared a challenge to the evening. Tërimrush joined him, as loud as any lion ever roared. Cadfan and the monk beat the hilts of their swords against the bosses of their small bronze shields. The Thornsword Brethren joined suit, raising a battle cry that even drowned out the humans. For Flowers, Nolan would have said they were fiercer than the eight-foot Tiger or the elephant-sized grizzly Bear. There was a wildness about them that was utterly inhuman, and yet their loyalty to Fiorlen and her eclectic group was unquestionable. They would fight to the death.

The Forest was still and quiet around them; even the Rhrushden seemed to await the moment. Stanley and Quinn came to stand silently by Nolan's side, their weapons in their hands. Emery shifted in his perch atop Tërimrush, who was outside the ring of fire. Genevieve, Heilyn, and Fiorlen had arrows nocked and ready to let fly. The Sapling was still Singing in a low voice, almost like a chant. She was speaking protection and speed, courage and accuracy, honor and power, might and wisdom, over the entire group: a blessing before battle.

The anticipation was palpable. Everyone seemed to know the enemy was coming. But they were ready and up to the challenge. As if on cue, roiling clouds of dust and black Mist started swirling in from the River onto the shore of their little beach. Nolan gripped Unnamed more firmly and swallowed hard, the pain in his throat throbbing to the rhythm of his heart. *No fear*, he told himself. *This is your chance to be heroic!*

"Excellent," a haughty voice dripping with sarcasm said out of the Forest. The piggish snort that followed froze Nolan's blood. "All the sheep gathered in one fold!"

By the edge of the Forest, leaning against a tree as if he were waiting for a friend, stood the Boarman. Orbo growled and dipped his sword into the ring of fire. The others followed suit, and when they raised their weapons, drops of flame fell to the trampled earth of the cove they had selected to defend.

Undaunted, Rhydderch retorted to Agenor, "Why, Old King Hynfel, long time, no see! You don't look a day over five thousand. What's your secret?"

The whole Forest was silent. Even the churning Mist seemed to flatten. Emery's small voice called down from the Bear in a stage whisper, "I thought the Pig guy's name was Agenor."

22

Old King Hynfel

On the branches of the tree supporting Agenor were a few dozen slightly Awakened ravens, each about the size of a large house cat. They were eerily silent, and Nolan knew it was because their mouths were filled with the human blood that would call up the Mistfolk.

"Rhydderch, you salty, fatherless old dog," Agenor was saying. "I'm glad you're here. I shall enjoy watching you bleed to death."

Agenor's demeanor was arrogant and a touch effeminate, and Nolan was surprised by the high pitch of his voice. A scent of perfume from his shiny, well-groomed fur wafted over the smell of burning wood. His coat was thick and wiry, the color of a roasted chestnut; and though he wore no armor, he was dressed in kingly finery: an ermine-lined traveling cloak that defied any blotch of mud. His royal dress seemed incongruous with the surrounding scene.

None of this, though, made him any less terrifying; yet it was his eyes that made Nolan shiver. Soulless and cold. Not dead eyes, no; they glittered with hatred and cruelty, and enjoyed watching pain and suffering. Nolan believed Agenor found torment thoroughly entertaining.

The Boarman offered a malicious grin that revealed more of the yellow tusks at the corners of his mouth. "It figures you'd throw in with this rabble of misfits—a handful of dirty Otherworld children, a Sapling, some Weeds, and an albino Leucis."

"Misfits?" Genevieve bit out. "Look who's talkin', ya furry freak."

King Orbo rumbled a short laugh as Heilyn pulled back on his arrow, taking aim at one of the Ravens.

"Don't waste the shot," Rhydderch cautioned him. "We can't hit forty birds, and they'll just take to wing."

The apprentice adjusted his aim directly at Agenor, but the Boarman didn't seem to flinch. Instead, he stifled a yawn and studied his fingernails. Nolan noted he had only two fingers, shaped like a pig's foot with an opposable thumb.

"Wait, I'm still confused," Emery said. "So, the Pig guy's really the old king with the seven daughters? Isn't that, like, from a super long time ago?"

"That's the nature of his Corruption—he's enslaved to Bàsisolc for eternity," Rhydderch replied without looking at the boy. "His narcissistic foppery… well, that's learned behavior."

The monk spit on the ground.

"I amend my previous statement," the Boarman returned, his grin falling as his eyes narrowed into a murderous glare. "I shall enjoy watching you bleed to death. *Slowly*. In fact, you know, Rhydderch, I *had* toyed with the idea of sparing the children and leaving them to the Deep. But I believe I have now decided to torture them and let you watch before you die, just because you vex me so."

"Enough." Fiorlen cut off Rhydderch's retort, her hand hovering over the flames of one of the fires, prepared to Sing at a moment's notice. "What is it you want, Foul One?"

"Oh, don't act like you don't know, daughter of the woods. You're young—not *stupid*." Agenor snorted. "We want the girl and the Love Stone. Give them to us." He paused as if revolving something around in his mind. "Give them to us, and you all can just walk right out of here, no matter how much Rhydderch irritates me. I give you my word."

"Devil take you," Boujòn said, brandishing his sword.

Agenor smirked. "Too late, dandelion."

As he spoke, two tall Treefolk appeared out of the woods behind him. Their very presence exuded a sense of death and Corruption that even the human children could feel. Their bark skin was ashen and sallow; the leaves of their hair were yellow and brown, like humus. Mold clung to them in great white-green clumps, and their smell was one of rot and decay. The Forest seemed to grow darker around them, but their yellow cat's eyes glowed with menace, directed at the Otherworlder children.

Rhydderch glanced toward Fiorlen.

"I've not seen them before," the Sapling responded to his unasked question. "They must have turned to Bàsisolc before my time."

Agenor waved her comment away as if it were unimportant, then addressed the rest of the group. "We're burning gylináma here. Shall we proceed with the abortive attempt at negotiations, or should I just start the attack?"

"There will be no negotiations," King Orbo growled.

"I was hoping you'd say that." Agenor threw wide both arms, and the Ravens took wing, streaming toward the riverbank just as the dark Treefolk began to Sing.

Fiorlen's Translation Song either could not or *would not* Translate these words, and Nolan was actually grateful; the notes of the Greenmen's Singing seemed to ooze with vileness, and it burned in the pit of Nolan's stomach. It wasn't fear that he felt; it was anger. Anger that these Treefolk would dare blaspheme the First Tongue with their demonic incantations.

"Can you Silence them?" Nolan could just hear Rhydderch speaking lowly to Fiorlen.

The Treegirl shook her head as the Mist coming off the Rhrushden started whipping itself into an agitated frenzy in response to the Corrupted Song. There was a hint of true fear in her small voice as she said, "No, they are far beyond my skill."

The Greenmen broke off into different Verses of their abominable Song, each of them Singing different words in a haunting two-part harmony that caused gooseflesh to break out over Nolan's skin.

"Augmented fourth," Stanley whispered, but Nolan didn't get a chance to ask him what that meant because Fiorlen started screaming, and their ring of protective flames sputtered down to shin-height, turning a sickly and sad kind of blue.

Nolan spun to see what was wrong with her and heard the *snap-hiss* of bowstrings. In spite of Rhydderch's warning, Heilyn and Genevieve both loosed arrows that found their marks, and two of the Ravens fell like stones. Another one came too close to Orbo's flaming blade and was sliced in half. But many more flew to the edge of the Rhrushden, where the dirty black Mist was churning, and dropped their mouthfuls of blood. Just like the previous night, red sparks leapt into the air, and out of the whirlwinds, the Capána began to rise.

The defenders' paltry ring of fire was useless now. But before Nolan could register why Fiorlen was doubled over, clutching her abdomen, Quinn's panic-stricken scream nearly made his heart stop. He jerked his head around to see the teenager grasping her chest and falling to one knee. He followed her frozen, terrified gaze and saw one of the Mistfolk solidify.

It was Audrey Redding.

But this was an Audrey Redding that had decayed: the skin was leprous and bleached white, and the hair was matted with grime. And the eyes glowed with the same nefarious red as those of the Mistfolk from the previous evening.

"Surprise!" Agenor said, his voice dripping with spiteful sarcasm. He seemed to feed off their fear—it was *exquisite* to him.

In a moment, Rhydderch was at Quinn's side. "That is *not* Audrey, Quinn. That's not your grandmother!" As if to prove his point, he jumped over the faltering flames just as the Mistfolk approached and raised its black sword overhead with both hands. Rhydderch stabbed it in the midsection and ripped his flaming sword upward to the neck. Black Mist and river muck sprayed from the throat wound as the Capána exploded, leaving trails of dying embers floating in the breeze.

That seemed to bring Quinn out of her shock. She spun her daggers, Lively and Spirited, in her hands and, with a desperate war cry, fell upon the next Audrey clone that materialized.

The battle was joined. King Orbo sprang from a crouch, over the blue flames, his sword grasped in his right hand, his left hand pawing the earth for traction, as he leapt upon one of the Mistfolk who had formed into a wolfhound shape. Orbo's powerful jaws clenched down on the back of the Dog's neck the second it went solid, then he stood to his back feet, shaking the squirming shape-shifter. An instant later, he brought the massive sword up into its abdomen and gutted the Mist-creature from rib cage to tail. As it exploded, the Tiger king used his giant paws to sweep the dust and debris into the spluttering flames. The remains of the monster crackled into sparkles of fell blue and poisonous green.

Heilyn and Genevieve took careful aim at two Audrey-like Mistfolk, waiting for the moment of solidification, when they were able to be attacked. Two flaming arrows found their marks, one striking a shape-shifter in the head and pitching it headlong to the dirt, the other arrow punching through the sternum of the remaining Capána to stick into a tree beyond.

The Mistfolk retreated into churning clouds by the water's edge, regrouping. It gave Nolan and Stanley time to stoop over Fiorlen, who was on one knee, retching. Bassett and Tintreach were flittering around her in agitation, unable to help.

"Fiorlen!" Stanley shouted. "What's wrong? Fiorlen?"

Nolan saw ten, fifteen, twenty or more, lacerations and boils bubble up on her bark skin, oozing a viscous, sap-like blood.

"Do you like the tune, little boy?" Agenor taunted over the tumult. "Leaves quite the *impression*, does it not?"

One of the dark Treefolk broke into an odd, hollow-sounding refrain, and Fiorlen's yellow eyes went wide with fright and pain. She was able to garble, "Morscan," and icy panic prickled down Nolan's spine to the backs of his legs.

He heard Orbo shout something in the First Tongue to Heilyn, who grabbed a protesting Genevieve and started pushing her toward the She-bear. The Translation Song wasn't working anymore!

"Don't shove me!" Genevieve thundered, her eyes flashing at the apprentice.

"The Song of Words works no longer," Heilyn managed in English. "The Sapling is harmed."

"He's right!" Rhydderch switched to the Chéad Teanga and shouted to the weaponsmith, "*Cadfan, abhrúle chun nimór dúinn Fiorlen! Ionmosod an y Coedaoine Truillygru!*"

"Behind us!" Stanley cried, and Nolan whirled around to see three hazy Capána gliding along the riverbank. They shifted to a flying bat-like shape, splitting into four, then eight, of the creatures and swooping into the air with hair-raising shrieks.

"Fiorlen, we need the flames! Sing! *Please* Sing!" Nolan exclaimed, his voice breaking, as the vague Mist-shapes dropped into a dive toward them. He realized she couldn't understand him, but it didn't seem to matter.

The Treegirl raised her eyes to the evening sky, her cheeks blistered and bubbling. She managed to mutter a few words, and weak spears of blue flame shot out of the waning fires on either side of her, slicing through the air with a whistle as they gathered speed and strength. Six of the nasty little beasts momentarily formed, preparing to assault her; but instead they were impaled by the needlelike flames, and they disintegrated into crackling ashes. The remaining two broke off their attack and zoomed out toward Nolan and Stanley, congealing to pounce on them.

Raising his sword, Nolan caught a glimpse of the shape-shifter flying toward him—it was a hideous imp with claws on its leathery wings and three talons on each foot. A long black tail darted out to correct its course as it came upon him. It was a cross between a small dragon and a bat, with the same glowing red eyes of the Capána. With a yell that seemed to split his bruised throat, Nolan slashed down with Unnamed, sheering off one of the monster's wings. It squealed and barreled into the sand, exploding into Mist, and then began to reform.

He turned to see if Stanley was all right. His friend had batted the other Mist-creature out of the air and was stamping it into the ground with his boot. Stanley slashed once, and the thing's head came flying off with a snarl. As its body started to collapse into Mist, he kicked the headless dragonet into the dregs of their fire circle, where it shriveled and burst into green-and-blue flames.

Just as Nolan was going to congratulate Stanley on his kill, Tërimrush let loose an earthshaking roar, and Nolan's mind jumped to Emery. Turning his head, he saw the mother Bear with his brother on her shoulders. She was surrounded by no fewer than a dozen vaporous Mistfolk. They seemed to be gauging whether it was worth leaving the security of their semitransparency in order to throw themselves at the Bear.

Nolan was going to shout to Emery, but it appeared unnecessary. The She-bear's paws were as dexterous as human hands. Tërimrush snaked a claw into the chest of one of the Mistfolk at that singular moment when it could be grabbed. She hauled it up to her open mouth. It wriggled like a fish, squealing, and before it could dissipate into Mist, the Bear bit down on its head. Had it been a human being, the scene would've been gruesome; she tore away its head and shoulders, flinging the twitching torso and legs into the feeble flames at the children's feet.

"Sick, dude, she *ate* it," Stanley muttered in disgust.

"Half of it," Nolan corrected him as he watched Tërimrush grab two more Mistfolk that had hardened, and eviscerated them on the spot.

Boujòn and his fellow Flowers were shouting directions to each other in the First Tongue, but it was apparent to Nolan that they were coordinating a direct attack on the two Singing Treemen. Several of the Capána had formed a shadowy half circle in front of the chanting Greenmen and Agenor.

As Orbo, Rhydderch, and Cadfan were preparing to throw themselves at the Mistfolk guards in a reckless attempt to silence the Greenmen with steel, Cadfan was visibly startled as Boujòn swung up the big man's knee, climbed onto his shoulder, and launched his Flower body over the heads of the Mistfolk like some kind of fierce monkey. Two other Brethren followed suit, using Rhydderch in the same fashion: the Lily of the Valley and the Sunflower with the battle-axe, who was actually *laughing* like a maniac. The lithe Orchid in the gi flipped himself over the Capána without any assistance. His vertical leap was well over six feet.

The valiant Flowers charged to engage the towering Treemen and the Mistfolk single-handedly, but the Coedaoine erupted into a new, virulent strain of their Corrupted Singing, once again in odious harmony. As soon as the notes hit Nolan's ears, he dropped to his knees with a shriek, Unnamed falling to the dirt at his side. He *sensed* rather than saw his best friend fall to the ground next to him, clutching his stomach and screaming in agony.

With an even greater sense of trepidation than he'd experienced yet, Nolan realized Stanley was calling out for him; but the words were garbled, as if Stanley were speaking Greek or Spanish or even the First Tongue. Nolan tried to respond, but his own words sounded foreign. They couldn't understand each other!

It was with that panicky realization that the fire erupted out of Nolan's belly and started crawling up his arms and spreading down his legs. A poisonous, burning sensation, similar to the feeling of injected serum wending its way through your veins, only thousands of times worse. Everything painful he'd experienced in his life was condensed into the liquid fire that burst out of his skin in lesions and boils. His throat closed off where the Capána had grabbed him the night before, and he struggled to breathe.

All around him, though Nolan was almost in too much pain to notice, his compatriots collapsed, writhing, as boils burst and oozed with a sickly sweet smell. He heard a girl—Genevieve or Quinn—cry out, and he thought of poor Emery.

Nolan managed to turn his head, trying to find his little brother and Tërimrush, but instead his streaming eyes spied Agenor standing over Rhydderch, who was clutching his stomach and thrashing at the Boarman's feet, spouting unintelligible words from a bleeding mouth. Orbo and Cadfan were writhing nearby.

Somehow, they all understood Agenor's words.

"Are you surprised?" he asked. "Did you all think you could *win*? You couldn't hope to understand the power at my command." He leered at the monk, and a string of manic drool collected at the corner of his piggish mouth.

"Rhydderch, you fool, you've brought *children* to their doom. Do you understand that? I want you to die with the knowledge that this is your fault. With one snap of my fingers, the Treemen will kill them—all of them—just like *that*."

Somehow, in the throes of tormenting pain, Nolan noticed that the word "children" wasn't "children-wealth." He also noticed that the Flowers were wriggling in the hands of one of the Greenmen, who was still chanting his sick Song. He held the Orchid and the Sunflower in one hand, Boujòn and his lieutenant in the other.

Agenor snapped his pig-fingers and glanced at one of the dark Treemen. "Kill the Brethren, then the Leucis king, and then that cursed Bear."

To the other Coeduine, he ordered, "Grab the girl." And to the Capána, he said, "Kill the whelps, but save the monk for last."

The Capána, in their almost transparent, mocking Audrey-guises, were drifting around the group in a swirling, dizzying circle of blackness, their eyes glowing with wild excitement, as the Corrupted Treeman threw the Orchid and the Sunflower down and stomped them flat into the earth. The crushing, squelching sound could be heard over the moans of pain and the rushing whirl of the Mistfolk and the soft, sinful chanting of the Coedaoine.

Nolan heard Fiorlen wail, but he couldn't see her. Another wave of fire threatened to consume his entire body, and he blacked out for a moment. Every breath was an exercise of sheer will, and for those few seconds of unconsciousness, Nolan's brain toyed with the idea of just not breathing again. It was a half thought of Emery, and then of Quinn and Stanley, that brought him around, and he gasped for air.

Through bleary eyes, he saw the Treeman fling Boujòn into a patch of brambly undergrowth, the Rose's inert body twisted at an odd angle. Only the Lily remained, burbling defiance at his murderer—though no one could understand what he said—until the Coeduine stretched the Flower with both hands and rent his stalk-body in two. The Flower's bell-shaped head fell limp. And through it all, the Greenman had kept up his foul Song.

In an unbelievable act of strength and willpower, Orbo overcame the pain of his cuts and boils and lunged for Agenor's ankles; but the Boarman sidestepped him and brought the butt of his glaive into the Tiger's side with enough force that Nolan heard a rib crack, and the Leucis king crumpled back to the dirt.

"What do you think you are doing?" Agenor admonished him. Once assured Orbo was down, he turned back and continued gloating to Rhydderch.

The other dark Coeduine scooped up a flailing Quinn. Heilyn, who was doubled over nearby, tried to make a grab for his giant hand, but the Greenman simply batted the apprentice away. Nolan heard Stanley yelling, and he felt himself doing the same as they watched the Treeman fling Quinn over his shoulder.

His Song changed once again, and somewhere down into the woods, a pale green light glowed. A portanuam had opened. In other circumstances, they might have been surprised to find an access point through the Veil in such close proximity. As the Treebeing started stalking into the woods, Quinn managed a scream and made a feeble attempt to break free of his iron grip.

His comrade had turned his sights on Tërimrush, and he seemed concerned with how he was supposed to kill an elephant-sized Bear, even though she was roaring from her wounds. His eyes drifted to King Orbo as he tossed the Lily's corpse aside. The Tiger lying on the ground seemed a marginally easier target.

As the Treebeing turned to finish off the Leucis, Orbo struggled to his feet once again, clutching his chest with one bleeding paw. In the other paw was his sword, no longer flaming but still smoking. The Tiger king spat blood on the ground and raised the sword to attack the Treeman.

"Kill him already!" Agenor screamed. It seemed the Boarman preferred others to do his fighting for him, and the Coeduine begrudgingly moved to obey.

The Tiger's sword strike was slow and off-balance. The Treeman easily batted the flat side of the blade away, and it fell to the ground. He grappled with Orbo and landed a solid wooden knee into his broken rib. The Tiger howled in pain as the Coeduine struck him again, wrestling to get the king into a bear hug.

But Orbo's desperate plan had worked. The Treeman had stopped Singing, distracted with the scuffle.

And as his Song trailed off, Fiorlen wasted no time. Her voice was wavering and weak, but she was Singing; and all of a sudden, with his eyes closed, Nolan could understand.

> *"In the bleak of night, hope for the morning sun remains.*
> *In the grinning face of death, the smile of life is returned.*

In the weakness of flesh, the courage of spirit pushes out.
In the midst of our pain, the strength of will continues.
Rise up! Rise up! Rise UP!"

And they did. Somehow, the pain lessened—it wasn't gone, by any means—but Nolan was able to force himself to his hands and knees. He spat blood on the sand from his split lips, and his lungs were thorny brambles in his chest, but he staggered to his feet, clutching Unnamed in his trembling hands.

Surprised by the Treegirl's sudden outburst of power and Song, Agenor turned away from the fallen monk a split second, and he was beginning to say, "Imposs—" when the point of Rhydderch's sword pierced him through.

The monk was standing. He had been aiming for the Pig's heart, but Agenor had turned, and the sword had gone through his shoulder instead. The word died on Agenor's lips, and he let out a shocked cry of pain. He looked down at the bleeding wound as the old man pulled his sword free.

Rhydderch stumbled, his body covered with lesions and pustules, but he managed to leer at the Boarman. "Surprise!" Rhydderch slurred. Fiorlen's Song was working, and everyone could understand once again.

"Kill them all!" Agenor shouted at the swirling Mistfolk, then turned to hurry after the Treeman who'd left with Quinn. Rhydderch was too weak to take up the pursuit, and he almost fell, but Heilyn had struggled to his feet and was weakly supporting his master. Cadfan was there a moment later, lending his hand to keep them both from collapsing.

"Somebody stop him!" Heilyn shouted, and Genevieve turned her bow on the Boarman. She loosed a hasty arrow that might have struck home, but her wounds had prevented her from drawing the string fully. Instead, the arrow whizzed just inches to the left of the back of the fleeing Agenor. One of the Capána had solidified at the last moment, and it took the arrow to the chest as its master blundered past.

Grunting with frustration, Genevieve managed to nock her last arrow and swing her bow back to the Treeman who was now lifting the smaller Tiger king off the ground in a bone-cracking embrace, intent on crushing Orbo's back. The Coeduine started up his infernal Singing once again, *enjoying* his gruesome work.

In that moment, something seemed to click inside Genevieve. With a look of rage Nolan had never seen her display before, she wiped away blood that was dripping off her eyebrow and took careful aim, arms quivering, then pulled back on the bowstring. Nolan hoped she wouldn't hit Orbo.

Exhaling, she let the string fly.

The arrow sliced into the Coeduine's throat, *just* missing Orbo, the feathers tickling his nose. The Treeman's yellow eyes went wide with shock as his Song was cut off mid-note by the gurgling sound that escaped through his bloodied mouth.

"Shut up already!" Genevieve shouted as the Treeman dropped Orbo and staggered backward, hands clutching at the shaft protruding from his throat, mouth making garbled, gasping noises.

"Agenor! Stop him, Nolan!"

Nolan registered that Boujòn had crawled out of the bushes where he'd been hurled and was shouting at him. The Rose's body was twisted at a painful angle, like he'd been bent in half, but somehow he was still alive.

Nolan had no time to marvel at this, however, because Stanley was already beside him, pulling on his arm. He realized that they were the closest to Agenor's path of retreat. It was possible they could catch him and the Treeman before they reached the portanuam.

Maybe.

"Nolan! *Quinn!*" Stanley shouted, pulling him toward the woods where the Boarman had retreated.

In front of them was a veritable wall of Mistfolk protecting Agenor's escape, though they seemed hesitant to attack Nolan's group now that the remaining Coeduine was choking to death on his own blood with an arrow protruding from his throat.

"Nolan! Come *on!*" Stanley was still shouting.

But Nolan couldn't move. Or he *didn't* move. He stood rooted to the spot, looking blankly at his best friend as if he couldn't understand what Stanley was saying—as if he were speaking the First Tongue, and the Translation Song wasn't working. But he understood just fine. He knew what Stanley was saying; knew he should be racing after Quinn, doing whatever he could to save her. Fight off the Capána, crawl on his hands and knees, do *something*.

But he couldn't. He couldn't make his body work. It didn't respond to Stanley's screams. Nolan wasn't sure if it was fear, exhaustion, cowardice, enervation, or simply being overwhelmed. Probably a bit of everything. But he couldn't move. He just couldn't! Even though his mind was roaring in syncopation with Stanley's shouts, telling him he had to try to save his friend, he just stood there. The Unnamed sword went limp in his hand.

They had to get to Quinn!

But then he realized it was true: It wasn't exhaustion, it was *fear*. As much as his body ached from the cuts and boils, he was *afraid* more than all that.

It was paralyzing, and, in a way, the emotion was worse than the physical pain he felt. The swallowing, drowning feeling that he was too scared to go after his friend who needed him. His friend who might *die* if he didn't act.

He was weak and worthless.

"We have to get to Quinn!" Stanley was shouting hysterically now, his eyes fierce and wild, screaming in Nolan's ear as Nolan sank to the ground in a heap. "Get up!" With his free hand, Stanley grabbed Nolan's collar and tried to jerk him to his feet. "What's wrong with you, you coward?"

The green light of the portanuam faded away, and Quinn was gone.

23

Weakness

Stanley was furious with Nolan, an emotion he'd never felt toward his best friend. But before he could dwell on it, he was tackled by a solid Capána. He went down with a cry that snapped Nolan out of his stupor.

⌒

RETURNING TO HIMSELF, NOLAN LET out a wild shout that vented all the frustration and embarrassment buried in his chest. He lashed out with Unnamed, and the Mistfolk exploded in a spray of watery soot that splattered over Stanley.

Brandishing his sword brought a wave of pain throughout Nolan's body, and he was aware that while Fiorlen's Singing had saved their lives, it by no means had healed them of the myriad gashes and ulcers that pocked their skin.

He held out his hand to help Stanley to his feet, but his friend scrambled up on his own without so much as a thanks. Nolan didn't know what to say. He sighed and turned to make sure Emery was still safe on Tërimrush's back.

There were more than a dozen immaterial Capána circling around the battered group, and Nolan's heart sank in despair. They were in no condition to hold off the Mistfolk until Blue Time ended.

King Orbo seemed to grasp their situation, and with a cry of pain, he rammed his butcher-knife sword down into the Treeman's chest, piercing the odious being clear through to the earth beneath him. The blade quivered a moment in the twilight as the Corrupted gasped a last bubbling breath and then died.

Nolan was shocked the Greenman had still been alive; it wasn't like in the movies, where the bad guy fell over and that was it. Genevieve had shot him at least a minute earlier, and he'd been slowly suffocating ever since. Nolan shivered. *How horrid.*

But as he stared at the corpse, the memory of the Treeman's comrade kidnapping Quinn came over Nolan like a suffocating blanket, and he gasped for breath as anger and shame coursed through him. They had Quinn! All of this was for nothing! And he'd let them take her without so much as raising a hand to save her. Nolan cursed himself.

With a ghastly whooshing sound, the Capána crumbled into dust and twirled away on a foul-smelling wind like so many ashen leaves.

Immediately Fiorlen's fires leapt up, and the Treegirl quickly called for everyone to gather close. Orbo reclaimed his sword and exhaled. "I had hoped their existence would be tied into the Coeduine's." Boujòn was crawling toward Fiorlen, and Orbo lifted the knight gingerly into his arms. Heilyn was supporting his master as they shambled toward the warmth of the fire ring. Genevieve seemed somber and withdrawn as she followed with Cadfan a half step behind her. They looked like they'd been thrown off a cliff onto razor-sharp rocks far below.

Tërimrush whimpered as Emery scrambled down her side, his grubby face lined with tearstains. Nolan put his arm around his little brother and held him gently. Emery looked up into Nolan's face, searching for some sign that everything would be all right—that Tërimrush would be all right, that Fiorlen would heal their wounds, that Quinn would be fine, and everything would go back to normal. But Nolan couldn't bring himself to convey any of that with his facial expression.

"It'll be okay," the nine-year-old said, and Nolan just nodded as Stanley pushed by him and collapsed in front of the Treegirl and her fires.

"I will do my best," Fiorlen said, wincing from her wounds. "I—" She faltered as her eyes fell on the grisly corpses of the mangled Flowers. "I don't know how much good it will do, though."

"It will suffice," King Orbo said in a firm tone. He motioned for Heilyn to help him collect the Brethren. In a respectful silence, they gathered the twisted pieces of the Lily, the Sunflower, and the Orchid and laid them side by side.

Fiorlen's Singing didn't sound overly powerful. That now-familiar feeling of ancient authority didn't seem to carry much weight in their current circumstances. Her words were plain and petitioning, as they'd been when she'd healed Emery, Cadfan, and Tërimrush once before. The worst of their wounds closed at least partially, the bleeding lessened, and the pain seemed to grow distant, as if they'd all been given a dose of morphine. They weren't, by any stretch of the imagination, *healed*; it just wasn't in the Sapling's range to Sing that kind of healing.

But, as Orbo had said, it would suffice. It had to. They needed to press on, no matter what wounds still remained.

After a few bars of a new Translation Song, Fiorlen focused on Boujòn the longest. It seemed as if his back—or what equated to his back—had been bent double by the dark Coeduine. Nolan had no idea how Boujòn was still able to move; in all honesty, he hadn't really understood how the Flowers were able to move to begin with. The physics of bipedal foliage were lost on him.

There were audible crackles and pops as Boujòn's stalk-body straightened, and the knight groaned with pain, despite his best efforts to remain stoic.

Fiorlen sank to the ground in exhaustion—the fight and the Healing Song had taken every bit of her strength. Her body was drenched with sweat as the last glimmers of Blue Time faded away. The fires settled down, burning naturally instead of being fed by her Singing. Everyone slumped where he was. The sky was fully dark now; stars twinkled, and the moon was breaking over the horizon of trees. Bassett the Pêllys burst into light, and the Firefly blinked now and again. Peacefulness was returning to this corner of the Morsden, and a soft summer night was unfolding like a tranquil evening primrose. Nolan was almost angry at the evening's pretense—the night was anything *but* peaceful. Stanley sat away from him, next to Genevieve and Heilyn, refusing to look at him.

"There is a slightly Awakened herb," Rhydderch said after several minutes of silence. "Bassett, do you know *Perleighis* plant?"

"Perleighis?" the Will-o'-the-wisp returned. Nolan had never heard of it either; it must have been an exclusively Otherworld herb.

"Pearlmint," Orbo supplied.

"Pearlmint—aye, it's a *weed*," Bassett remarked.

Tintreach flickered twice, also apparently surprised. "It's a garden menace."

The monk nodded. "Take Heilyn and gather as much as you can. Hurry! It will assist Fiorlen's Healing Song."

Nolan raised an eyebrow as a sense of déjà vu washed over him, and he looked up at Stanley. "Isn't that Tolkien?" But Stanley acted as if he hadn't heard, and Nolan fell silent. Thinking of Tolkien suddenly made him remember Quinn—talking with her about Shire leaf when they were outside the village of Arshúil. That seemed *ages* ago.

As the apprentice left with the two Awakened creatures, Rhydderch shambled away from the warmth of the fire and knelt beside Boujòn, who had taken the Lily's arms and folded them across his chest, laying his short sword lengthwise in his leafy hands. The Lily's lower half had been placed below his torso. Had he been human, it would've been a gruesome sight, but the Flowers didn't seem to bleed regular blood.

The Sunflower and the Orchid had been laid with reverence next to their lieutenant. They were crushed completely, blossoms trampled underfoot; their features were disfigured and covered in grime; and yet, even in death, they retained something of a proud, warrior-like quality on their faces: defiant and honorable to the last.

"I am sorry, Lord Boujòn. From what I knew of them, they were true knights and died bravely," Rhydderch said.

That didn't make Nolan feel any better. Even *Flowers* had fought more courageously than he had.

"What are the Brethren's customs for dealing with their dead?" King Orbo asked, standing to his feet with a wince.

Boujòn also stood, visibly fighting off the pain. He was only a little taller than the kneeling monk. His back had been mended, more or less, but he had a stoop, and Nolan wondered if it would heal completely in time. The Rose touched the wilting, once-white petals of his lieutenant. "His name was Majalis. He was of thirty-four summers, and served faithfully as my aide de camps for sixteen; of a better warrior, I have met very few. He died with honor, and that is enough."

Indicating the two slain soldiers, the Rose said only, "Helian and Leata acquitted themselves like true Brethren. They will be remembered."

They buried the Flowers in shallow graves on the banks of the Rhrushden, under the guarding branches of a ramrod-straight black alder tree, its long catkins swaying above the overturned earth in a perpetual salute of the interred warriors. A brief testament to their remembrance was carved in a piece of drift-wood and set at the base of the tree.

⌒

THE CORRUPTED GREENMAN WAS LEFT where he had fallen, and Genevieve found herself, against her own wishes, wondering if the corpse would rot like flesh or like wood. Would there be a skeleton underneath? Or just pith? She shook the morbid thoughts away. This place was *getting* to her, she realized. She'd helped *kill* that creature, and that notion didn't bother her nearly as much as she thought it should. In fact, she was *glad* she'd loosed that arrow....

⌒

THE TIGER KING HAD TAKEN a few moments to scratch out a warning onto another bit of driftwood with a dagger. The sign was rammed into the ground next to the Coeduine, and it said in the First Tongue: "All heed: Such is the price of Corruption. I declare it justly exacted by my lady Genevieve's bow. —Orbo III, King Leucis."

Soon after they'd buried the fallen Brethren, Heilyn returned with the Pêllys and Tintreach, laden down with armfuls of an herb that looked like ordinary spearmint to Nolan, excepting its opalescent sheen that seemed almost to glow in the dark. Rhydderch began preparing a concoction at once, as they needed to be away soon if they had any hopes of reaching Crannhyn by tomorrow's gylináma.

"We're not going after Quinn?" It was the first time Stanley had spoken in nearly an hour. A shocked expression hung on his face as he watched Cadfan and Heilyn, with Emery's help, begin unloading one of the rafts. The plan was to leave behind as much as could be spared and have everyone pile onto one raft.

Fiorlen sat up long enough to look over at the boy, cocking her head. "How should we follow them, Stanley? Even if there were a means for me to raise the Veil outside of the time-between-times, I have no idea *where* they went. We could end up on opposite sides of the Hidden Lands. I'm sorry, Stanley. Our only hope of rescuing Quinn is to get to the Eldest as quickly as possible."

Stanley's face grew scornful, and he reluctantly joined the workers in toss-ing items onto the beach. His grimace showed pain and frustration. "Wouldn't *have* to if Nolan had any guts."

Nolan thought that wasn't really fair. There was no way to know if he and Stanley would've been able to rescue Quinn. In their current state, and against Agenor and a Corrupted Greenman? They were just boys, after all. Nolan thought someone as smart as Stanley should've recognized *that* little fact. Deep down, though, he understood how Stanley felt.

They should've at least *tried*. Nolan had chickened out, and Stanley's verbal barb had been deserved; though to hear it come from his best friend's lips was a kind of pain that cut deeper than any of the slashes and boils on his arms and legs. Tears threatened, stinging his eyes, and his chest ached with remorse. He cast his gaze down at his feet.

"Tread softly, Stanley," Orbo said in a cautionary tone as he handed Stanley a pile of cloths to make into strips to bind their wounds. "These words are unworthy to use on a friend."

"Whatever." Stanley rolled his eyes. "He should've *done* something."

Boujòn stretched his back and made a sound like clicking a tongue. "Young master, my warriors fought in many battles, and they were killed by the Truillygru tonight without even a chance to raise their blades."

Stanley turned on the Rose. "You're the one who told him to go after Agenor! Would *you* have wimped out when your friend needed you?"

Cadfan's brow creased, and he looked like he was about to respond, but Fiorlen cut in first: "Enough. It is done. If we start to point fingers, we are defeated before we begin. We bear one another's burdens, and we press on. That is all." Her tone softened as she looked back and forth between the two boys. "Come, this potion of Rhydderch's tastes like toadstools, but it works. Drink, and let's be on our way."

They drank, and after spitting and sputtering, fighting the gag reflex, they began to feel warmer, and somehow *lighter*, even though their tongues were stinging as if they'd swallowed a glass of nettle wine. But the potion did, indeed, work; their pains lessened, and a blanket of heaviness was lifted off the group.

Everyone piled onto the one raft, though it was a noticeably smaller group of adventurers than what had originally set out. Still, with seven humans, a Flower, a Treegirl, and a six-hundred-pound Catman, the raft was low in the water. It wasn't very deep at this point, but it sped along on powerful currents near the center of the River.

"To Suas, then, young ones," said the Cat king with a determined voice. "One of the true wonders of the Deep! Never will you find a greater work of craftsmanship, artistry, and practicality formed into one."

Fiorlen smiled. "King Orbo, you flatter our abilities. It's really just a bunch of trees...." She paused and sighed. "It's home," she added with a longing glance downriver.

The children were supposed to sleep through the night, but Nolan took his turn at lookout without comment, using the lights of the lanterns posted at the four corners of the raft, supplemented by the brighter glow of Tintreach and Bassett flying ahead, to look for boulders and half-submerged trees. It was a futile exercise; if they came upon something that might dash them to pieces, they'd scarcely have time to turn the heavy craft out of the way. Yet Nolan didn't mind the quiet. He stole an occasional glance up at the stars as he held the rafting pole in his hands.

Emery, Genevieve, the Cat king, the Rose, and Rhydderch were sleeping in a great pile in the center of the raft. Orbo didn't seem to mind the human children bundling into his warm fur; it was such a safe feeling, nestled next to the huge sovereign, that they slept and didn't stir.

Fiorlen was manning the tiller, and Heilyn and Cadfan were keeping watch on either side of the raft, careful not to upset the precarious balance. Somewhere behind them, Tërimrush was trundling through the Forest, more slowly than before, but still determined to keep up with the rafters.

The moon, bright and almost green in the clear summer sky, was overhead when Stanley appeared at Nolan's elbow, balancing precariously as the raft sliced through the dark waters. Nolan sighed, resigning himself for the argument he knew was coming.

"I just want to know why, Nolan," Stanley said in a quiet voice. "I know it would've been dumb...we might have gotten kidnapped with her, too. Or worse. But that doesn't matter; we should've done *something*. Why didn't you move? Why didn't you at least *try?*"

"I...I don't *know* why." Nolan spoke with his back turned to his best friend, under the pretense of being watchful of the River, but he didn't want to face Stanley. Not out of humiliation, Nolan realized, but he didn't want to lose his temper. Stanley was asking a question he didn't have an answer to, and that really troubled him.

"Would you've let them take me? Or *Emery?*"

Nolan spun around to face his only real friend, the one person who'd understood him and all his oddities, his strengths and his weaknesses. The one person who *got him*. And here he was, what? Accusing him of being a coward?

Nolan struggled to keep his voice low as he hissed, "Get off my back, Stanley! I told you I don't know why!" It was pretty much the truth. He *didn't* know why. Was he afraid? Yes, of course; they all were. You'd be stupid not to be. But was he a coward? Nolan didn't think so. Who was Stanley to look down his nose at him?

Stanley shook his head and sighed. "Fine. I'm not going to blame you. But you better figure out why. Things are just going to get worse—you've seen what we're up against and what's at stake. This is our *lives*, Nolan. And they have Quinn. Who knows what she's going through now? And I gotta know that when it comes down to my turn—or even your *brother's*—you won't leave us hanging. Foolish or not, if my life's on the line, you better come and get me. 'I don't know' just doesn't cut it."

Nolan stared at him. He was right, and that was what upset Nolan the most. Of course he was right. If it had been Stanley—or, God forbid, *Emery*—would Nolan have just stood there in a panic? No. He was sure of it. Wasn't he? So why hadn't he gone after Quinn?

Nolan exhaled sharply, and though his teeth were clenched in frustration, he managed a meager, "Fine."

Stanley shook his head again and turned on shaky legs to lie back down among the pile of bodies in the center of the raft.

Nolan forced his breathing to slow. His ears were thudding, his lungs ached, and it didn't help that he still had twenty or more semi-healed cuts all over his body. He was exhausted, like everyone else. At least, the kids were; maybe the adults were used to this kind of thing. But they were all on edge. He tried not to hold on to his anger. Fiorlen was right—they bore one another's burdens. That's what friends did.

He turned back to watching the River and spat into the water.

"It isn't your fault, you know." This came from the monk's apprentice. He'd been quiet through the exchange, and now his voice floated over to Nolan at the front of the raft.

"The lad's right," Cadfan added. "You shouldn't blame yourself. We *will* rescue Quinn."

Nolan wasn't sure if they saw him nod, but he said nothing. Deep down, he knew it wasn't his fault—if he and Stanley had raced after the Treemen, they'd likely be dead now or would have been kidnapped, as well—but it still *felt* like it was his fault. He should've at least tried to help her. But when it came down to it, he'd been afraid, and that was weakness.

And, yes, he also knew they *would* save Quinn; of that he was resolutely convinced. But the earliest they could get to Crannhyn's was Blue Time tomorrow. That was hours away. What would they do to her in the meantime? What if they were hurting her? He'd never forgive himself.

He stroked the bruises on his neck, the cuts on his arms, the boils on his hands. He wasn't a coward. No. He would prove it to himself. And to Stanley. Next time—*next time*, he wouldn't let his friends down.

As if to make his point, he stabbed the rafting pole down into the black water and pushed savagely off the River's bottom, urging their raft onward.

24

The River Roaring

Heads up! Here comes the last stretch—these're the worst, lads! Hold on tight! Here we go!"

A spray of cold water soaked the raft, threatening to plunge it under the whirlpools in front of the huge submerged rocks that littered this section of the Rhrushden. The River was living up to its name, the Roaring. Nolan figured no true white-water rafting company would dare to take a group of tourists on an adventure like this. And here they were on a wooden raft with *poles*, and nary a life vest between them.

Poor Emery was clinging for dear life to the makeshift shelter, looking like he was about to vomit, and now Nolan was kicking himself for not sticking his little brother safely on the back of the man-eating warrior Bear. Even though she was trudging through the Corrupted-infested Deep, it *had* to be safer than this lunacy!

They'd all been soaked to the skin since sunup; the water this far north was icy cold, much bluer than normal, and Rhydderch had explained that it was due to snow runoff from the Spiacánacha mountain range, which encircled the northern and western half of Morsden. The heart of this range—the seat of Crannhyn's domain—was not more than twenty-five miles dead ahead. Several tributaries and smaller rivers merged here near the mouth of the Rhrushden, and the swollen summer current was pushing the raft along at twice its normal speed, whipping the melting glacial headwaters into a virtual frenzy before they spilled into Lake Scáthán, where, more than likely, any number of unnatural creatures would try to kill them.

In other words, it was shaping up to be just another typical day in the Hidden Lands.

"Left, left, left!" Heilyn screamed himself hoarse to be heard over the roaring waters. To keep him from being pitched overboard, one of his hands clasped a leather strap lashed to a lantern post at the front of the raft, and he was shouting out directions as best as he could, while Cadfan and King Orbo both leaned against the tiller, trying to maintain some control over the vibrating watercraft.

"Too far, too far!" the apprentice roared, jerking his free hand in the opposite direction.

"As if we can thread this monstrous death trap through the eye of a needle!" the Tiger king hollered in response, but he and the weaponsmith leaned their combined strength the other way, to compensate for the shouted directions.

There was a sickening *crack!* as they clipped a boulder; a second later, the raft was in a spin, buffeted by the crashing waves, and twirling counterclockwise. Nolan slipped on the wet wood and dropped to his hands and knees, scrambling and clawing for purchase as he slid, his left leg dangling in the water, the current threatening to drag him off the side of the raft. The searing temperature set fire to his partially healed wounds. Stanley and Emery grabbed at his arms and managed to haul him up, but the whirling of the raft was making them all dizzy, and they were slipping, too.

"Man overboard!" Boujòn's high-pitched voice called over the tumult, and Nolan looked up and realized they were now barreling down the river *backward*. He saw the valiant Rose, crooked back or no, pitch himself into the water.

"Genevieve's fallen in the water, too!" Stanley spluttered, and then the raft slammed its left side against another partially submerged boulder, and the wood splintered. The ropes lashing it together snapped and whipped into the water with a loud smack, like high tension wires popping, and the raft started coming apart.

With no time for a second thought, Nolan grabbed his brother and his best friend in a vicious embrace as they tumbled into the water.

Everything was bubbles and icy cold. Emery let go of his brother and latched on to a timber beam, but Nolan's grip slipped off Stanley as a countercurrent ripped him away, further under the wreckage. All of this was understood only vaguely by Nolan, who saw flashes of Stanley's brightly colored clothes but nothing more distinct than that. It was only animal instinct that kept Nolan from swallowing a lungful of glacial water.

Some part of the raft slammed into Nolan's back with a painful explosion of golden stars behind his closed eyelids, but he managed to push off and down toward Stanley. He clawed blindly for his friend, and when he sensed his numb, wounded fingers close around something solid—Stanley's shirt, he hoped—he hauled up with all his might, kicking for the surface.

They both broke the water, coughing and spluttering. The cold was like knives against their already raw skin.

It took Nolan a split second to recognize that they were still barreling down the rapids, surrounded by various bits of their shattered raft. He saw Emery still clinging to a piece of wood, and his heart warmed with some degree of relief. *Thank God!*

He managed to scramble toward a piece of the shelter that was floating just ahead of them, pulling Stanley along as best he could. They both threw their arms over the wreckage, struggling to keep their heads above water as the world turned topsy-turvy. The roar of the water was deafening, and Nolan had no idea how long they zoomed down the River. He heard shouts from the others, and after what seemed like hours, although it was probably only minutes, Cadfan's booming voice rose above the crash of the water.

"Eddy up ahead! It clears up ahead—just hang on!"

Soon, pieces of their woebegone raft were bumping into the shoal-lined shore. Nolan and Stanley made their way onto the smooth, flat rocks. Just behind them, Emery kicked off and waded to shore, where he flopped down next to his brother. A few feet away, there was Genevieve, retching water. Nolan couldn't see the others, but he heard them shouting as they gathered the scattered remains of their supplies and hauled them ashore.

Emery rolled on his back with a groan, and Stanley shuffled into a kneeling position, wiping water out of his eyes. Before they'd entered the rapids, he'd wrapped his glasses several times in a soft cloth and hung them around his neck with a piece of leather strapping. Miraculously, after all they'd been through, the lenses were still intact.

Nolan was lying on his stomach, shivering. "D-d-does th-that an-answer your q-question?" he asked Stanley.

Stanley coughed up water and glanced at his friend. "P-p-possibly." He managed a small smile, though his teeth chattered uncontrollably.

"Someone start a ruddy fire before we all get hypothermia!" That was Rhydderch's voice.

"Here come the weapon barrels!" the Rose shouted. "Thank the Composer they still float!"

Nolan heard more scuffling as the adults continued dragging stuff to shore. Soon Fiorlen was standing over him. He saw her bare feet in front of his face, her wooden toes seeming to grip the spaces between the rocks, and he noticed she had toenails made of paper-thin bark, neatly trimmed. He forced himself to sit up.

"Are you injured?" the Treegirl asked. She was dripping wet and wide-eyed.

"I—I don't think so. Is e-everyone else s-s-safe?"

"About the safest we've been all morning," she replied with a slight giggle. "Lord Boujòn rescued Rhydderch, and everyone seemed to be able to grab hold of a piece of the raft. We were very near the end of the rapids, and here by the shores of Suas, the water calms a great deal."

"Well, *that* was pleasant," Genevieve snorted. "Remind me to send a strongly worded letter to the White Star Line." She stomped up to the boys and the Treegirl, wringing out her hair.

"How far is Suas?" Stanley asked, trying to find something dry to use on his glasses.

"Not more than a couple hours' walk that way," the Treegirl replied, gesturing toward the Forest. "If the raft had survived, we could have pulled right into the harbor. Still, once we've dried out and collected our breath, we can be on our way. Breakfast will be waiting for us there; my mother has sensed our coming."

Nolan wanted to ask how it was the Treefolk could sense each other over long distances—he figured it must be like the call of the Flowers—but instead he dragged himself to his feet and started shaking water out of his ears.

If he'd stopped to think how very near they'd all come to drowning, he would've felt sick with fear, but now all he felt was a fiery resolution to get to Crannhyn before Blue Time this evening. No more weakness; for his friends, he'd be the hero.

"Come on, Emery, Stanley. Long day ahead of us, and Quinn's waiting," he said, sloshing off to help tally their scavenged belongings.

Hiking through the woods, they dried quickly, and it was late morning as they approached Suas. An entourage of stern-looking Greenmen, dressed more fancily than any the humans had yet seen, stood in a line by the edge of the Morsden where the city began. The Coedaoine didn't come out to greet the travelers.

The children looked up and up and up, and their mouths fell agape. Here the Forest turned into unbelievably tall trees, sequoias of some kind; but obviously they'd been Sung over for centuries, for they were hundreds of feet tall, some as big around as houses.

Nolan had seen pictures of the redwood forests in California, but *these* trees were unlike anything he could've imagined. A sense of vertigo stole over him, and his breathing quickened, making him wish for the hundredth time he'd been smart enough to bring his inhaler.

And Suas itself wasn't some pioneer village; it was a *city*, hung in the trees, one, two, hundred feet above the Forest floor. It went on for as far as the eye could see, miles into the Deep of Morsden. Even from this distance, it looked like Suas was home to thousands upon thousands of Coedaoine.

Emery whistled as they took in the sprawling vista, and Stanley, always the sci-fi geek, commented, "They're like Wookiees on Kashyyyk."

"How tall do you think those trees are?" Cadfan asked, clearly just as astonished at the sheer scope and magnitude of the city.

"The tallest tree in all of Morsden is the birthplace of Crannhyn," Fiorlen answered. "It is named Talaf and is revered by all in Suas as a holy place. Talaf is thousands of summers old, and it reaches"—here she gave a dimension that was Translated "three quarters of a mile in height."

"Impossible," Stanley muttered.

Fiorlen shrugged. "Most of the trees in the city are about four hundred feet tall, and the city itself averages one hundred and fifty feet off the ground, but it is spread across three levels. The bottom level holds the working areas of the city; the middle level is the housing level; and the very top is the communal level, where meals are taken, Saplings are instructed, and the government council sits. Suas is home to over fifteen thousand Caevnaóri, most of whom are young like me. Like the Aossí, Treefolk believe their wealth is in their children."

Nolan's mind reeled. *Fifteen thousand Treefolk!*

The group started approaching the Treefolk who were waiting at the entrance to the Forest city, and when they were within hailing range, Nolan heard a female voice echo across the distance.

"Fiorlen, you and your comrades are well met!"

The Treegirl broke into a wide smile, showing her bright white teeth. "Sorry I'm late, Mama. We fell into the River." She said it as if it happened all the time. "But, see, I have brought Father's Otherworlders!" Fiorlen broke into a run and jumped into the arms of a slender Treewoman wearing an elegant cream-colored dress trimmed with gold thread and adorned with red glass beads resembling holly berries.

"Friends, this is Mama," Fiorlen said as her mother squeezed her.

The Treewoman was pretty, Nolan supposed, by Greenmen standards. She was about nine feet tall and held herself with great poise and feminine grace, not condescending, but as someone who is used to being obeyed. He had no idea how old she was, but her face seemed young, even similar to his mother's. Her yellow catlike eyes were bright and intelligent, as were all the Treefolk's; but her bark-skin was lighter than any he'd yet seen, almost a pale ash, and her hair was ringlets of yellow leaves like a quaking aspen's.

"Greetings, Otherworlders and Aossí and Awakened alike! Rhydderch, old friend. Lord Boujòn, my heart is warmed to see your safe return so soon. Welcome, welcome all, to Suas!" The Treewoman inclined her head to King Orbo. "And Your Grace is most welcome."

The Tiger king bowed low, stifling a grunt of pain. His rib still had a hairline fracture, and his numerous other wounds were only partially healed. With any luck, he would get a Song of Healing from the Coedaoine lords this gylináma—if there was time.

The mother's gaze fell on Heilyn, and she nodded to him before introducing the six other Treemen around her. "I am called Tegwyn. These are the council members of the Caevnaóri: my lords Trahaearn, Mabon, Rheinallt, Meurig, Illtyd, and Pryderi."

Nolan and Stanley looked at each other, trying not to chuckle. As if they could remember a slew of names like that! The humans could hardly tell the Greenmen apart, except that Trahaearn looked somehow older than the others, grayish, and his bark-skin looked as hard as iron. Mabon held himself with a prim air of superiority, and Nolan recalled that it was his daughter who'd Awakened Tërimrush.

Emery must have been thinking the same thing, for he whispered, "Rhydderch, when Tërimrush catches up to us, where will she stay?"

The monk smiled down at the boy and whispered back, "Not to worry. Coedaoine hospitality is legendary, even among the Aossí. After all, it was the

Treefolk who instituted the Laws of Hospitality! Never you worry. Tërimrush will be well looked after."

Tegwyn looked down at Emery and smiled. "Indeed, we will take excellent care of your friend."

"She's a big Bear," Emery hastened to explain.

Tegwyn nodded, as if people made friends with bears all the time. "Then I shall have a special meal prepared just for her, and a place for her to rest." She turned to address the whole group. "Would you like to breakfast? I've no doubt you are all starving after your adventures, and we have much to discuss. Come, friends, let's go Up."

25

Suas

The Treefolk's city was mind-boggling. Under the thick canopy of enormous redwoods, it always seemed to be on the verge of twilight. Suas was lit by thousands and thousands of translucent, teardrop-shaped lanterns, which cast an eerie and yet strangely *calming* greenish glow over the city.

Stanley, of course, was intrigued by how the lanterns worked, and Fiorlen explained it was a natural mixture provided by Awakened lightning bugs.

"You squish Fireflies?" Emery asked, sounding appalled. But Tintreach, who was resting on Fiorlen's shoulder, buzzed with laughter.

"Heavennsss no, child-wealth," the bug responded. "We onnnly makkke it. It'sss a concccoction of various elemennnts: herbs, sapppp, roots, and minnnnerals. We use ssseveral types of ssslightly Awakkkened mushroommms, as well."

"They probably use some species of *Armillaria*," Nolan added, referring to the mushrooms.

Stanley looked at him and allowed a small smile. After Nolan had saved his life in the River, he seemed to have rationalized that it was counterproductive to stay angry at him.

Nolan was thankful their bedrock friendship was stronger than that. He smiled back and nodded, letting him know they were going to be all right.

"So it's a chemical reaction," Stanley explained to Emery, turning his attention back to the lamps. He showed the nine-year-old that there was a small flask attached to the back of each teardrop lantern. "It's called chemiluminescence. See? Gravity causes the chemical compound from the flask to drip every once in a while, and it mixes with the chemicals in the lantern, giving off light but no heat. Sorta like glow sticks back home."

"That's kinda neat," Emery said, probably understanding most of the process. He was pretty good at science.

"*Kinda* neat?" Stanley shook his head. "It's ingenious for a society that has no electricity!"

"It's a similar premise to how I light up," the Will-o'-the-wisp remarked and then chuckled. "But of course, I make my *own* light."

The group continued on. Besides the sprawling structures in the trees, a lot of the city was on the ground, as well: pens for livestock; armories, where primarily wooden weapons were crafted; acres of planted fields, with the main crops seeming to be edible fungi, potatoes, and foodstuffs that grew in little sunlight. Fiorlen explained that between here and Lake Scáthán was a lot of land used for pasture along with fields of wheat, rice, and corn.

For access to the city itself, several dozen of the straightest trees had enormous spiral staircases wrapped around their trunks. The stairs were bolted onto collapsible scaffolding resembling a massive spring some twenty stories high. Counterweights were used to raise and lower the staircases, like an elevator of sorts. A steady stream of Treefolk, Awakened creatures, and supplies were ferried from the ground and back by these constructs.

The group of travelers lined up on one of the impressive stairways and staggered across a few Coeduine-sized steps. Moments later, they watched the counterweight slowly descend from the top, and their staircase creaked and began climbing up, up, and up around the colossal tree trunk, bringing them to the first level of Suas.

The children were surprised to find that the Treefolk *did* use metal, but they relied on the *Keras*, a race of Awakened rhinos bigger than King Orbo, to work as blacksmiths in forges on the Forest floor; for the Coedaoine seemed to have no proclivity for metalworking themselves.

Even so, their understanding of architecture was astounding. The "buildings" of Suas were organically shaped, grown, and Sung right out of the sides of the trees and, in many cases, even *through* the trees.

Circular verandas, strung with lanterns and roofed with thatch, commanded a 360-degree view around the trunks. These were the primary homes of the Treefolk families, and every bit of their architecture was aesthetically pleasing, etched with artistic whorls and designs and the odd-looking glyphs and runes of the Chéad Teanga.

Wooden walkways (not flimsy rope bridges) and smaller versions of the mobile staircases connected the city together; so far, this was the only frightening thing about Suas, seeing as none of the catwalks or staircases had a guardrail. This was spooky for the humans, who weren't as sure-footed as the Coedaoine or their Awakened comrades.

"Careful not to look down," Rhydderch warned the children. "We're a hundred feet off the ground, and a sense of vertigo can make you stumble."

"Brilliant," Genevieve sniped as she glanced down. "Thanks for reminding us."

Nolan gripped Emery tightly as they made their way through the city, even though the catwalks were built to Treefolk scale, and the children would've had to make a mad dash to get to the edge of the walkway. It was just the *thought* of being so high up with nothing to hold them in place except for a two-hundred-foot-long wooden *plank*.

Stanley started calculating aloud how long a person would spend flailing through the air before becoming a permanent addition to the Forest floor. Thankfully, he didn't share the final number.

Even Cadfan appeared a bit overwhelmed, not so much because of the height as due to the vast amount of city to take in. The place was buzzing with activity, and the inhabitants seemed to move in a chaotically organized way, a blur of motion, yet somehow synchronized, like a complex dance set to an equally complex arrangement of melody and counterpoint.

Dragonflies with three-foot wingspans flittered overhead, carrying written messages to various parts of the city. Many Awakened lizards, anthropomorphic like King Orbo but much smaller, scurried here and there. Fiorlen explained that the *Uropsid* enjoyed stonework; they fashioned all the ornate basins for water and fire in Suas.

Nolan thought there had to be a lot more workers hidden somewhere, because no visible surface in the city—wood, stone, or metal—was left untouched by artistic designs etched or carved with amazing detail. Even the floors were stained in bright colors and marked with intricate knot work. The furniture, from the simplest kitchen stool to a luxuriant, Treeman-sized bed, was as richly detailed as any antique from the Victorian era in the children's world. Hundreds of banners flapped in the breeze from poles jutting out over the Forest below, embroidered with the colorful crest of Suas or with pastoral scenes of Treefolk Singing. The whole city was a breathtaking, living work of art.

But what seemed to impress Stanley the most was the plumbing—piping made from narrow, flexible trees, moderately Awakened and somehow hollowed out with time and Song, running down into the black soil hundreds of feet below, where wastewater was leached into the mushroom fields.

"Check this out," he was saying as he analyzed what looked to Nolan like a spiderweb of some kind of bamboo. "It's a system of vacuum pumps and convection currents running through an advanced capillary system. Looks like they use both the wind *and* the sun to bring up groundwater from reservoirs under the city."

"Uh, right," Nolan said, trying to act like he comprehended. "Ingenious."

"Wait, what's a conviction current?" Emery asked. "Is that like an electric chair?"

Nolan groaned to himself as Stanley plunged into a detailed explanation.

Stanley stayed in full-on science wizard mode when he discovered the wooden plumbing was sealed inside and out with a resinous scarlet varnish secreted by lac bugs that were roughly the size of dinner plates. To Nolan, who couldn't view them quite as scientifically as Stanley, they were simply hideous-looking bugs, like enormous cockroaches; but they were peaceful, industrious creatures, Awakened just enough to understand their cohabitation within Treefolk society. They seemed happy as far as insects went, and they were apparently well fed, but Nolan was quite glad to leave them to their secretions.

Finally, the travelers were brought with great pageantry to a hosting room on the middle level, not far from Fiorlen's family's house. This room was one of the strangest they'd yet seen, for it was fashioned out of the center of a living sequoia. It gave Nolan the sense of being inside a cabin, with its wooden walls, floor, and ceiling. And yet he didn't feel claustrophobic about going *inside* a tree that was as big around as a house. In fact, it felt kind of *homey*.

The circular walls were a creamy color of shellacked wood, decorated with tapestries and beautiful knot work. Nolan hoped the etching was a product of Singing and not done by hand, for it would've taken centuries, as intricate as it was—and this was just *one* room.

The furniture was human sized: plush futon-like sofas and papasan-like chairs, with a serving table in the center. Along the walls were shelves lined with leather-bound books, all written in the First Tongue. While Fiorlen's mother called for breakfast, Stanley experimented with the Translation Song by seeing if he could read some passages that were apparently on Treefolk etiquette. To his astonishment, he found he could understand the glyphs if he stared at them long enough.

The lords dallied as long as required by the Laws of Hospitality and then excused themselves to gather for council. If they were surprised at the sudden appearance of the Otherworlders, and the news that Ysgafn had not yet turned up, they seemed to hide their emotions well. Nolan was left wondering if perhaps the Treefolk had a bit of premonition, or perhaps the way they could "sense" each other over distances was a kind of mental communication between them.

In any case, Tegwyn didn't seem shocked to find her daughter in the company of an Aossí weaponsmith, a monk and his apprentice, some Flowers, the king of the Leucis, and a bunch of Otherworlder children-wealth. Oh, and a mountainous She-bear waiting somewhere down below....

A momentary sense of the absurd washed over him as he realized who all of his traveling companions were.

Fiorlen showed them to a polished granite basin where they could wash up. Ice-cold water scented with hibiscus and rose petals poured out of the faucet, which everyone found quite refreshing. On the opposite wall was similar stonework: a pit set into the floor where a fire could be set for warmth or for cooking. An iron flue hovered over it, attached to the ceiling.

Soon after they had washed up, breakfast was served by two Awakened raccoons, whose nimble hands were well designed for carrying trays and pouring cups of coffee. They even wore kitchen aprons. Nolan was getting so used to the idea of walking, talking animals that he didn't even do a double take when one of them handed him a plate of steaming eggs with sautéed mushrooms. There was toast and marmalade, bowls of porridge, and fresh fruit. It was the best meal the travelers had eaten since the Fair-Folk feast a few days earlier, and they gorged themselves as politely as possible.

After they had eaten, Rhydderch leaned back against his papasan and exhaled. "Lady Tegwyn, your cooks are some of the finest in the kingdoms, and your hospitality is impeccable as always. I thank you." He produced his long pipe, lit the bowl, and began making satisfied noises as he smoked.

Cadfan and the children also gave their thanks, and Lord Boujòn made a sweeping bow, then excused himself, saying he would meet them at the council meeting. He had four of his wounded soldiers to check on, and he needed to inform the Brethren of the loss of their comrades. Stanley was interested in visiting the infirmary and seeing some of the Treefolk's healing practices, but he told Nolan he would feel odd leaving his friends to go follow a Rose with a crooked back and a needlelike sword through the twists and turns of Suas, so he let the Flower depart.

Tegwyn seemed to be a fountain of patience as she waited for the humans to begin discussing business, as if there were no sense of urgency in the fact that her husband had been missing for several days.

Rhydderch drew on his pipe, collecting his thoughts; then, after exhaling a cloud of smoke, he explained everything from the beginning, when the children first arrived in the Hidden Lands, to this morning's misadventures on the raft.

All things considered, it wasn't a very encouraging tale.

As Rhydderch shared how Quinn had been kidnapped, Nolan felt a flush of red creep up his neck at the memory of his inaction the previous night. The wounds from that cursed Song itched, and the bruises on his neck twinged. He reached up absently to touch them.

When Rhydderch had finished, Fiorlen's mother was thoughtful a few moments before speaking in a clear, firm tone. "I believe my husband is being Silenced by Bàsisolc. These new Corrupted, these Capàna taking on the form of Audrey Redding, confirm to me that both she and Ysgafn, and now her granddaughter, are being held by the Evil One. And yet, had Ysgafn perished, I would have sensed his passing. It is my thinking that Bàsisolc will try forcing Quinn to break the Love Stone by using Audrey as an incentive."

"Quinn would never willingly work with Bàsisolc," Stanley interjected, and Nolan nodded his head in vigorous agreement.

"Indeed," Tegwyn said. "However, Quinn's attachment to her grandmother is quite possibly a stronghold which Bàsisolc will use to coerce her into action. Mark my words—this is how the Evil One operates, through the families of those who oppose him. He can be *very* persuasive."

"What happens when the Stone is broken?" Cadfan asked.

"The Verses, when Sung by a Human, will grant to that Human the greatest expression of their corresponding virtue—in this case, Love. But even Love can be Corrupted, and Bàsisolc will wield its power through Quinn by exploitation and control. Love, when used with an impure motivation, becomes manipulation and obsession; and indeed, he is obsessed with securing the power of the Master Song for himself. The love of *self* is the most dangerous love of all."

Tegwyn paused and took a deep breath. "Yes, he possesses a perverse kind of genius, but it is a genius nonetheless. And for someone with his faculty, he could use the Corrupted virtue to pit one kingdom against another, for what ruler doesn't desire to have more power?" Then the Treewoman looked at King Orbo with apologetic eyes. "Your Grace's own integrity suffers no censure, of course."

The Tiger bowed his head graciously to show he took no offense.

"But Bàsisolc is a master of subterfuge," Tegwyn continued. "With the Verse, he could incite civil war, and while the kingdoms were destroying one another, he would simply rise up through the ashes to take over the whole of Tírcluddaithe, especially with the High King missing and otherwise preoccupied."

Here she glanced pointedly at Heilyn, and Nolan didn't overlook the nonverbal communication that passed between them.

"But how is the diamond even opened?" was Genevieve's question. "Does Quinn or Audrey know?"

Rhydderch replied, "Written records do not describe the process. Only Crannhyn or some of the very oldest Coedaoine would know; Agenor, too, perhaps—those who were there when the Stones were made. But the real question is, does Bàsisolc know what will happen when the Sanctuary is un-Veiled?"

Lady Tegwyn inclined her head. "More than likely. He would be foolish in the extreme to open the demeglwys without an army at the ready. While no one but Crannhyn—and now my husband and Bàsisolc—knows *where* the Temple is Shrouded in Morsden, it is fairly common knowledge among the Caevnaóri as to *what* protects it."

"*Lupír*," Fiorlen said with a tone of reverence.

"What's that?" Emery asked.

"An Awakened vampire bat," Cadfan answered, his face serious. "Another legendary creature that apparently isn't as legendary as I once believed."

"A Bat doesn't sound so scary."

"It does when it's large enough to blot out the sun."

"Wow, that's a big Bat." Emery fell silent.

"Not quite *that* large," Rhydderch amended. "His wingspan is maybe fifty, sixty, feet, or so the history says. Lupír has been Veiled in Sleep for the last few thousand years, so very few would know firsthand; but once the Sanctuary is revealed, Lupír will cast off his Slumber and defend it to the death."

"What would a Bat be like after being locked up for three thousand years?" Emery wondered aloud.

"Hungry," Stanley said, poker-faced.

"Look," Nolan said after a few people chuckled at Stanley's quip. "This is great information and all, but I wanna know what we're gonna do about rescuing Quinn and Audrey and Ysgafn. We all need to get home again."

A heavy silence fell on the room.

Lady Tegwyn's voice adopted a sympathetic timbre. "I am sorry that this has come to you and your friends. Of the many questions I have, one of them is *not* my husband's intentions in bringing Quinn over. I am confident he meant the best, but perhaps he reacted hastily to the news of Bàsisolc's uncovering the location of the Temple. I am not sure how he was planning to deal with Lupír—maybe he thought the guardian would submit to his Singing, though I find it too foolhardy to believe he would have entertained such a thought. He should have returned to Suas to receive counsel. Prudence has never been Ysgafn's strongest quality; however, loyalty to Crannhyn and his family *is*."

Nolan nodded. "I'm sure Ysgafn acted with the best of intentions. It isn't his fault we got separated crossing the Veil. But what can we do to save them?"

"The council will convene in a few minutes. We have much to discuss, but I have no doubt we will muster a contingent of warriors and attempt to reach Crannhyn during this evening's gylináma. Once he has been informed of the situation, I believe the Eldest will move swiftly and decisively. It's likely he will move on the demeglwys tonight."

"What do you mean, *attempt* to reach Crannhyn?" asked Heilyn, who'd been silent up to this point.

Tegwyn sighed. "Crannhyn has become withdrawn. It saddens him that he is unable to work with Humans like the Caevnaóri once did, for he is very fond of Mankind. But while Bàsisolc remains at large, Crannhyn has decided it is best for him to keep the knowledge he possesses concerning the Master Song out of his brother's reach. Thus, he has exiled himself to his domain at the mouth of Scáthán Lake, which is fiercely guarded by several powerful Awakened creatures. One does not simply *walk* up to Crannhyn—one must approach the Eldest with caution. And perhaps with a great show of force.

"Lord Boujòn, while possessed of many fine qualities like my husband, lacks shrewdness and prefers action over calculation. Rather than seek our council, he attempted to approach the Eldest on his own, and his entourage was…*rebuffed* by the guardians. They are not evil, mind you; they simply follow their duty to keep *everyone* away. They are not in a position to make distinction between friend and foe.

"So when we approach Scáthán, we must do so carefully. A contingent will have to keep the Awakened occupied, while a smaller, less obvious, group raises the Veil to access his domain."

"*Occupied*…great," Nolan snorted. "That means more fighting."

By the time the travelers arrived with Lady Tegwyn to the uppermost level of Suas, Boujòn and the Greenmen lords were already gathered.

The council dais was immense in size, a long rectangle straddling the open space between two of the largest trees Nolan had yet seen. He wasn't quite sure what supported the vast floor underneath, seeing as they were some hundred and fifty feet in the air. He imagined giant pillars, since the floor was made of polished white marble, inlaid with humongous golden flakes (which Rhydderch said was *real* gold) and shards of obsidian. But it was entirely possible that *nothing* supported the floor of the council hall, save for the magical Singing of the Coedaoine.

A wall waist-high to Nolan ran the length of the chamber. He could see out in any direction, looking over the breathtaking vistas through the inconceivably tall trees.

A Treefolk-sized table carved from a solid piece of oak—one singular tree trunk, that is—was the main piece of furniture. The top of the table was above Nolan's head, but the legs and sides were etched with glyphs and knot work. When he stared at the glyphs, he realized he could understand what they said: "All who would hope to attain these seats of power, let only justice, mercy, loving-kindness, and wisdom prevail."

In other words, you can't sit here and be a jerk, Nolan thought.

"Again, welcome, Otherworlders. King Leucis, Lord Boujòn, and Aossí friends: welcome. I trust you have been given time for refreshment." This greeting came from Lord Trahaearn, the steely gray Greenman whose stern face looked like it had been carved out of iron, and Nolan wondered if he'd ever smiled in all his long life. The boy thought maybe the Treeman's face would crack and splinter if he were to break into a grin.

"Lord Trahaearn, thank you for your hospitality," Rhydderch replied. "M'lady Tegwyn provided a most wonderful breakfast." The monk made a little bow, and the lord inclined his head while everyone sat.

Human-sized chairs had been arranged just off to one side of the enormous table, next to where Boujòn was seated, far enough away so the smaller people could see the faces of the larger, and yet close enough to feel like they were included in the meeting. Even though King Orbo's chair was appropriately sized, it creaked under his eight-foot frame.

Once they were all seated, Lord Trahaearn said, "Then perhaps our honored guests will forgive the slight breach in etiquette whilst we proceed directly to the matters at hand. Afterward, there will be opportunity to rest before gylináma this evening."

Lady Tegwyn gave a succinct, yet no less disconcerting, account of what had transpired so far, and the lords listened without interrupting.

"This is most disturbing news," Lord Mabon decided once Lady Tegwyn had finished. "A new form of Corrupted is in the Deep, fed off the blood of the Aossí; Lord Ysgafn is taken hostage and Silenced; and it appears beyond reasonable doubt that Bàsisolc is now in possession of not only the Chorus of the Master Song but also the only two Otherworlders who are capable of opening it. And he knows where the Temple is Veiled. This is distressing news, indeed."

The lords began grumbling among themselves, and Trahaearn called them to order. "Lord Mabon speaks concisely, and it appears to me that our only true course of action is to seek out the Eldest. We must reach his domain before nightfall tonight if we are to be of any benefit in these matters. Are we agreed?"

The assent was unanimous and swift, and Nolan wished all forms of government could agree that quickly.

"The Sealwyrí must be marshaled," said one of the lords. The word was Translated "Hunters" or "Seekers" in Nolan's mind, but it carried the connotation of warriors.

"One additional item must be addressed before this council is brought to a close." Trahaearn motioned for an aide, who had been waiting in the shadows near the entrance of the hall. As he approached, Nolan realized the Treeman was only a teenager, about seven feet tall.

The lord whispered to the lad, who nodded without a word and quickly disappeared into the walkway that connected the council hall with the rest of Suas.

When he returned, he was ceremoniously carrying a long sword in both arms as if it were a precious treasure. It was a very odd sword, for it was completely red, from the pommel to the grip to the cross guard to the sculpted scabbard—and, Nolan assumed, to the blade, as well; a deep crimson red, like blood, with a large, glittering ruby set in the hilt.

Cadfan gasped, and his great head whipped to his left, as if to see whether the other Aossí were as shocked as he was. They weren't. Rhydderch was stoic, and Heilyn seemed most uncomfortable as the aide bowed at the waist with the sword resting lengthwise on his open palms, as if he were offering the sword to the monk's apprentice.

Nolan glanced over at Stanley, and he could see that his friend's mind was working overtime. Then he seemed to have figured it out, because he grinned at Nolan and muttered, "Oh, man, this should be good!"

"My son, Fallon," Lord Trahaearn said, indicating the Coeduine youth.

"'Tis my great honor to present to His Highness the Red Sword of the Citadel," Fallon said, still bending at the waist.

His Highness? Nolan gaped, and Emery gave him an astonished look. Out of the corner of his eye, Nolan noticed Genevieve was looking at Heilyn rather proudly, as if this hadn't surprised her much.

Hesitant and solemn, Heilyn reached out with both hands to claim the sword. He drew the blade from its scabbard with a clear ringing sound, and the steel shimmered red.

Once the blade was held aloft, Cadfan and Rhydderch slid out of their chairs and knelt on one knee before Heilyn. Lord Boujòn stood and drew out his skewer sword, saluting the monk's apprentice with his blade held straight before his flower face. Nolan was dumbfounded.

King Orbo also stood and saluted, though he did not kneel. His deep bass voice rumbled, "Behold: Claídear!"

Part IV

The Love Verse

26

The Army of the Caevnaóri

Though everyone else was seemingly able to grab a few hours of solid sleep before it was time to depart for Docile Lake, Nolan just couldn't. His mind was racing, and he tossed and turned on the mattress prepared for him in Lady Tegwyn's house. A number of things were flickering through his mind in disjointed fashion, and he bounced from thought to thought as he drifted in a semiconscious state that was more tiring than just being awake.

One of the myriad thoughts was that Heilyn—well, *Chadric*, actually— was a prince! Only those in the council hall knew his identity, and it was agreed that this little bit of important information should remain a secret for as long as possible. That magnificent sword, *Claídear*, had been wrapped in deerskin, and as soon as they'd left the hall, His Royal Highness had become once again little more than a humble servant boy.

Once back in Lady Tegwyn's house, Rhydderch had explained how he'd come to watch over the heir to the Hidden Lands.

"His Highness had been hiding in the Deep for the better part of a week when Ysgafn found him. It was either divine intervention or a rush of dumb luck the Corrupted didn't find him first! In any case, Ysgafn brought the prince to me and asked that I conceal him by taking him on as an apprentice, which is somewhat of a lark, seeing as how I'm not a very devout 'monk' by any stretch of the imagination! Certainly not good enough to have my own apprentice."

Chadric had chuckled. "Indeed, *monk* is not a word I've heard bandied around concerning you! I've heard tales you were a raving madman who ate the flesh of small children at every full moon. It was only because of my father's good report of the Caevnaóri that I even trusted Lord Ysgafn to lead me to you."

"Nay, I eat meat and potatoes." Rhydderch had laughed. "'Recluse historian' might be a better description of my occupation. Nevertheless, none of us knew the intricacies of some underlying political conspiracy; so while the Coedaoine attempted to gather information, I hid His Highness, and they kept careful guard over the Red Sword."

"Why did they give you the sword back now?" Stanley had asked.

The prince's face had clouded. "With Father missing, it is important for the Aossí to maintain control of Claídear."

"The sword is the symbol of the High King's authority," Rhydderch had explained. "Its very presence commands obedience from the Aossí. Should King Alaric not turn up…well, it would be devastating for the Red Sword to fall into the hands of anyone other than the king's heir."

"Why's it red?" Emery had asked.

"The material is otherworldly," Chadric had said.

"His Highness doesn't refer to the Other Side of the Veil," Rhydderch had clarified—"*your* Side, rather—but truly *otherworldly*. Claídear is crafted from some meteoric material that can be fashioned only by Song."

"The metal is indestructible and can never dull," Cadfan had put in. "The story goes, it was a gift from Crannhyn himself, given to that wretch Old King Hynfel before he was Corrupted, and it's been passed down through the millennia to each High King thereafter."

"Indeed," Rhydderch had told the children, "the history of Claídear is a magnificent tale, but it will have to await a more leisurely time. For now, I suggest we all get some sleep."

But, by afternoon, Nolan hadn't gotten any real sleep. He moaned, rolled out of bed, and tapped Emery and Stanley on the shoulder. "Guys, get up—we've gotta go get Quinn."

It was thoughts of Quinn that had really consumed his thoughts, keeping him from sleep—not Chadric's celestial sword, cool as it was. No matter what was going on between Alaric and Dubric and Chadric, the children's primary goal was to rescue Quinn, Audrey, and Ysgafn—and then get the heck back to *their* Side of the Veil.

Simple. Nolan sniffed and shook his head. *Save the girl, save the Trees, go home.* Just a normal day's work for a twelve-year-old geek. He had the sudden realization that his life was becoming more and more like a video game. He wondered if there was a cheat for unlimited lives or something.

He stroked the fingerlike bruises on his neck, wondering why they were still so vivid against his skin, almost as if they were getting *darker.* And the blasted scabs from that hideous Song weren't helping, either.

There was a sense of fear that he pushed far back into the corners of his mind. But somehow, despite his best efforts, his body reacted *physically* to the emotion of dread. He felt almost displaced, out-of-body—detached, in a way, from what was going on around him. It was difficult to explain. Like he was on autopilot or something.

He only hoped that when the time came, when they were actually rescuing Quinn, he wouldn't freeze like he'd done before. This time, he had to be someone she could count on. He needed to be a hero.

Yeah, simple.

The boys joined Genevieve and the Aossí in Fiorlen's living room, where the Treewomen were waiting. They ate a quick meal, though Nolan barely recognized what he was putting in his mouth. Some kind of chunky soup.

Genevieve talked with Chadric—er, *Heilyn*—in low tones throughout the meal. Nolan watched them huddled over their steaming bowls, trading smiles back and forth. He wondered if something *unusual* was happening between the two of them. They seemed closer than two people who'd met just a couple days earlier ought to.

By the time the group gathered outside to head down to the Forest floor, a contingent of Sealwyrí Greenmen were assembling on the fields just outside Suas, about twenty-five warriors in all. With them were the Thornsword Brethren mustered by Lord Boujòn: dozens and dozens of them, maybe a hundred, or even more. They seemed to be pouring in from the surrounding woods.

Every kind of flower Nolan knew, and several he didn't—some tropical species, some perhaps native only to this side of the Veil. Beautiful Flowers, and all armed to the teeth...if they *had* teeth. From Nolan's vantage point on the middle level, the floor of the Morsden looked like a moving carpet of rainbow colors as they marched in rank and file.

There was a Flower cavalry riding about two dozen armored Goats. The foot soldiers carried spears, and there was a contingent of yeomen archers (mostly the Daisies, for some reason). The officers were mounted on slinky, Awakened wolverines that moved wicked fast and looked capable of pulling down a human warrior by themselves.

As more Flowers marched in, Nolan thought they were at least two hundred strong now, maybe more. No matter what happened at tonight's Blue Time, the Treefolk were preparing for battle—first with the guardians of Scáthán Lake, if necessary; and then, if things went like they all hoped, against Bàsisolc himself.

The Flowers weren't the only Awakened creatures in the amassing army; there were also Loxon, Keras, and Uropsid—Elephants, Rhinos, and Lizards, respectively—about a dozen of each.

The Loxon were *huge*, as tall as the Treefolk, maybe taller: bipedal, anthropomorphic Elephants, heavily armed and armored with curved swords reminiscent of their ivory tusks on either side of their long, plate-armored trunks.

The Keras were a little smaller, but not by much. Also on two legs, they had dreadful horns on their snouts and wielded great double-edged battle-axes.

The Uropsid were much smaller, about four or five feet high, and their company comprised numerous lizard species, from rainbow-colored Geckos to crested bright-green Basilisks to some kind of black Lizard that reminded Nolan of a Komodo dragon—these ones were the largest. While they were known for their stonework, the Lizard warriors seemed equally at ease with metal. They carried these odd, circular throwing weapons that Stanley said were like *chakram* or wind-and-fire wheels, though Nolan had no idea what either of those was.

There were a few Awakened warriors Nolan had never seen before: half a dozen birds of prey and several rodents of unusual size—Rats, Squirrels, Woodchucks, Weasels, Chipmunks, and, Nolan thought, maybe even a Beaver—because when someone stepped on his flat tail, the brown rodent with enormous teeth raised a fit that could be heard from all the way up in the trees. One of them seemed to be a Sugar glider with vast eyes bulging from his head, and flaps of loose skin connecting his armpits to his knees. Nolan wasn't sure what kind of mobility that gave him. Perhaps he was a paratrooper or something....

The birds of prey were unique: an Eagle, two Hawks, a Raven, a Falcon, and an Owl. They walked on their clawed feet like humans and had feathered arms with five-fingered hands that grasped spears below powerful wings sprouting from their shoulders. They wore very little armor, seeming to rely on speed and dashing attacks rather than brute strength, and they were armed with some kind of throwing knives.

"Like *shuriken*," Stanley remarked as the Raven dived toward a target dummy and loosed half a dozen little glinting blades. Each knife found its mark dead center.

"Why in the world would Birds use ninja stars?" Emery asked.

Nolan shrugged. "Makes sense. Attack from a distance, faster than a bow and arrow. Swoop in, toss a bunch of knives, and—*zip!*—ninja-vanish."

Emery giggled.

Once Nolan and his group were on the ground, the noise was deafening with the clamor of so many Awakened voices and the clattering of armor and weaponry.

"Forget the Birds." Nolan pointed ahead of them. "Check out the Frogs!"

The growing army was rounded out by the appearance of about fifteen Awakened amphibians, of all things. But when Stanley pointed out the strategic advantage, it made sense: They were going to a lake; it would help to have some aquatic fighters on hand.

Like Nolan had said, most were some kind of Frog or Toad, but a few were Newts with their tufted, external lungs looking like frilly Shakespearian neck collars. None of them wore armor; and, to be quite honest, they all looked like a band of highwaymen, armed mainly with daggers and crossbows. The leader of this group was a Frog about four feet tall and four feet wide that reminded Nolan of Emery's Pacman, Glynis (she was a girl frog, they thought), at home.

"Man, that's a *fat* Frog," Stanley whispered to Nolan, who was staring at the creature's impressive girth with an open mouth.

"Can you really get that big just eating flies?"

This confidence man—*Frog*, rather—had a red bandanna jauntily draped over one of his muddy green eyebrow horns, and he was complaining to one of the Treefolk lords as the children got close enough to hear. The Translation Song communicated a thick Cajun accent.

"I don't mean to sound ungrateful or grousing, Lord Meurig, I really don't. We're delighted to lend our services to the Eldest...." He trailed off and adopted a dejected, gloomy expression, one of the saddest faces Nolan had ever seen. "It's just...I was told there'd be pie."

"I guess that answers *that* question," Nolan whispered to Stanley.

"And brandy!" one of the Newts added with a similar hangdog expression.

The Frog nodded to his companion in sympathetic commiseration. "Yes, and brandy. Yes. We were told there'd be pie and brandy, see...."

Lord Meurig looked nonplussed at the pie-seeking Frog and his brandy-sodden friend. "Erm. Quite so, Mr. Tophyrs. We are about to march, but I will see if some pie...and, uh, brandy...cannot be summoned up from the, er, kitchens—"

"Excellent, *mon ami*! Truly capital!" Tophyrs was all smiles now as a jolly red tongue snapped out of his fat mouth and licked one of his giant yellow eyeballs.

"Well," Stanley said, "it's all good, so long as there's pie and brandy, right?"

Another wave of detached absurdity washed over Nolan. It was like stepping into the pages of a Narnia book—all they needed was a huge Lion and a White Witch. He looked around to see if he could find them.

Whom he saw instead was Lord Mabon at the far end of the field, at the head of the army. They heard him wind a large horn, and relative silence fell on the eclectic collection of warriors. At his side was a younger, teenage Treewoman whose long leaf-hair was clustered with bright red-and-orange rowan berries, and her bark skin was a pale mountain-ash color. Nolan assumed this was Mabon's daughter, Afanen, for her name was Translated "Red Berry." He studied her for a second, thinking she did seem awfully prim and proud, yet she must be a good-hearted Treewoman if she had Awakened Tërimrush from her man-eating rage.

The mother Bear had collected her charge, and Emery was once again in his armor of leather and brass. Nolan had considered having him remain behind in Suas for safety, but Stanley had pointed out that when they rescued Ysgafn, they wouldn't be able to go home right away if they had to come back and collect his brother.

Eventually Nolan had relented, realizing that Emery was probably just as safe between Tërimrush's shoulder blades as anywhere else in Tírcluddaithe.

"Friends of the Caevnaóri!" Lord Mabon's voice carried across the field. "I thank you for mustering on such short notice. We march to Lake Scáthán. As you are aware, the Docile Lake is protected by the Eldest's guardians.

"While we don't seek to do battle, we must be prepared to defend ourselves as Lady Tegwyn raises the Veil to approach Crannhyn. After the Eldest is summoned, we will proceed at once to a place in the Deep that Veils the demeglwys of the Love Verse. It is believed that we will meet with great resistance there:

a Corrupted army, led by Bàsisolc himself, intent on releasing the power of the Verse.

"You have been given your defensive positions, and Mr. Tophyrs and his companions will lead the way to Scáthán."

The Frog smacked his lips, consuming a third blueberry pie simultaneously with a steak-and-kidney pie and a large tumbler of Aossí pear brandy. He stifled a belch and called out with his Louisiana Creole accent, "We are ready, my lord!" His entourage shouted in agreement, each drinking and eating his full. Several Awakened laughed at the sight of the amphibians gorging themselves before battle.

Lord Mabon nodded with a small smile tugging his lips. He paused a few moments to regain everyone's attention. When he spoke again, his final words echoed across the plain.

"I trust you will acquit yourselves like the proud Awakened warriors that you are, for this is truly an historic moment. For millennia we have been ever vigilant, and it has all come down to this one night. This evening could decide the fate of our united kingdoms for many generations to come!

"The Love Verse *must* be protected. Our way of life, our *freedom*, hinges on this. So cast off all fear, for in the presence of perfect Love, there can be no temerity. Only strength and compassion for our fellow brethren—we fight for them! We fight for our choice against Corruption, we stand against the tyranny of the Most Evil, and we fight for Crannhyn the Mighty! Serve him willingly, and serve him well!"

Here the army raised a tumultuous war cry, shouting, "Hail, Crannhyn!" and beat their weapons against their armor and shields. The noise sent shivers through Nolan, and goose bumps raised the hair on his arms and legs.

Hang on, Quinn, he thought. *We're bringing the cavalry!*

27

Captor and Captive

Quinn was still kicking and screaming as the dark Greenman hauled her through the portanuam. The cuts and abscesses pockmarking her skin burned like acid, but once she was Moving Sideways, it felt as if all the air in her lungs had been sucked out with a vacuum, and bright, sparkling stars prickled behind her eyelids, drowning out the pain from her wounds. Yet, almost as soon as the suffocating feeling came over her, it lifted, and the burning returned. Gritting her teeth, she hazarded a glance at her surroundings.

There wasn't much to see, for she was still slung over the shoulder of her captor, and turning her head left or right gave only a small view of Morsden Forest. The first thing she heard was the Treeman calling out to his comrades, which made her redouble her efforts to break free; but it was a pointless waste of energy, as he held her in a viselike grip.

"Summon my lord!" the Coeduine shouted as he came crashing through the woods into a darkened clearing. "And call for a healer—Agenor is wounded!"

Behind her, she could see the Boarman tumble through the green portanuam, which faded soon after. He cursed and sputtered, clutching his wounded shoulder and stumbling to his knees.

Quinn thought he was overreacting—her own wounds seemed more serious. She was just about to mock him when something distracted her.

Numerous voices were raised in poisonous Singing, and she craned her neck to glimpse a group of Corrupted Treefolk gathered around an inert form—Ysgafn! She tried to scream his name, but all that came out was a shriek. He seemed to be sleeping peacefully on the grass, though his hands and feet were manacled in iron chains.

Thankfully the malicious words of the Song of Sleep weren't Translated in her head, but the tune gave her a sickening feeling in the pit of her stomach, and she swallowed the bile that threatened to come up.

When her kidnapper approached the group, they switched their tune midnote, and Quinn felt the now-familiar effects of the Translation Song taking effect. However, there was nothing exhilarating about this version of the Song; it carried with it the same nauseating feeling that all Corrupted Singing did.

After a few seconds, they trailed off, and one of the Greenman said, "Hail, Eorden! Happy hunting?"

Her captor's name Translated as "Slowing," which didn't make sense to Quinn; he seemed to move fast enough. She felt him rumble in anger as he replied, "T'was not as easy as I'd have thought, Laret. We've lost Hemre, and Lord Agenor is wounded. Inform Lord Bàsisolc I have returned with the whelp *and* the diamond."

Two of the younger-looking Treemen (she assumed they were younger because they were shorter and not quite so moldy) broke out into a run to summon their master. Quinn shivered. *Bàsisolc!*

To a third Coeduine, Eorden said, "Have a healer brought to the pavilion. This runtling is in need of the Plague Song's effects to be reversed. Now go!" The other Treeman snapped to and disappeared into the twilight.

"A few Otherworlder brats wounded the Boar *and* defeated Hemre?" Laret asked. He sounded surprised.

Just as Laret finished speaking, Agenor broke into the clearing, and the Treemen adopted a deferential stance, hailing him as lord rather than "the Boar." They even expressed concern about his shoulder, but to Quinn, it seemed feigned.

"Not just the Otherworlders," Eorden replied; "they were supported by the king of the Leucis, the largest She-bear I've ever seen, and *this* one's Sapling"— here he kicked Ysgafn—"as well as some Aossí, including that monk, the crazy one who lives in southern Deep. It was he who wounded Lord Agenor."

"With trickery, not with skill," Agenor amended, wincing as one of the Greenmen offered him a human-sized goblet.

"For the pain, m'lord," the Treeman said with a bow.

Agenor grabbed the goblet. "Bring me a healer immediately! And inform my lord Bàsisolc that I will await his summons, but apprise him of my dire situation! I crave his pardon." The Boarman shambled off with the Coeduine, murmuring curses between great gulps from the goblet.

Once Agenor was out of earshot, Laret snorted. "I'm sorry to hear of Hemre; he was a fine warrior. As for Agenor, too bad it was just his shoulder!"

The group chuckled. Apparently Agenor wasn't well liked among the Corrupted, either. Of course, Quinn realized, traitors usually weren't—even if they deserted to *your* side, they were still turncloaks.

She was lifted high in the air and then set on her feet, facing Eorden, who kept such a grip on her shoulder that needles of pain shot down her arm, overriding her aching wounds. She cried out and tried to crumple to the ground, but he held her in place, slackening his crushing grasp only ever so slightly.

"Girl," Eorden said, looking down at her, "I want to take you to Lord Bàsisolc walking under your own power; it has a certain amount of class to it. So I will *allow* you to walk, but only if you do not attempt to escape, for I am also quite content to carry you to my lord *after* I break your skinny legs. Do we have an understanding?"

Quinn gave him her most defiant look but said nothing, finally nodding in resignation.

"Laret, fetch us a leash," Eorden said. Then to Quinn, "Pity you humans are so wretchedly ugly, and you look like rubbish, to boot. The Plague wounds can be cleaned, but I wish we could make you more presentable for my lord." He sighed. "Alas, one cannot polish excrement."

Quinn reached back with her right foot and kicked Eorden in the shin, spitting out a few choice words that she hoped the Translation Song would do justice to.

Eorden blinked in surprise, then burst out laughing with his comrades. The kick hadn't even made him wince. "Upon my word, girl, you kiss your mother with those lips?"

She spat on the ground. There was a bit of blood mixed with her saliva. "Don't call me *girl*. I am the granddaughter of the Embroidery Queen!"

"I like your spirit, human!" Eorden said as he took a long length of rope from Laret and proceeded to tie it around her wrists, tightly but not cruelly so. He barely had to stoop to reach her with his long arms. As he worked, he said, "But I was there when the Embroidery Queen left for the Other Side of the Veil. She fled her subjects when war was upon them, leaving them all to be butchered, saving her own neck with a handful of her court by hiding under Crannhyn's skirts. If I were you, I'd not identify with such cowardice—fat lot of good the Love Verse did *her!*"

Quinn felt herself blanch. His tone had a ring of truth to it.

After he finished tying her leash, he flashed an evil smile and said, "Now march, *girl.*"

A sprawling pavilion the color of midnight had been erected at the far end of a perfectly circular plain covered with ankle-high grass. The plain was large enough to house a small army; and, indeed, there seemed to be a battalion camped there.

Tents and fires and piles of weaponry surrounded a couple hundred Aossí with tan, weather-hardened skin. Theirs looked different from the overly fair complexions she'd seen thus far, and it occurred to Quinn that these people may have been from the Southlands that Cadfan had talked about.

Remembering the conversation around the council fire in Arshúil, she thought, *Is Dubric supplying conscriptions to Bàsisolc?* It made sense, then, why Chadric would flee Citadel City; Dubric was working with the bad guys.

While she pondered this disturbing connection, she saw there was also a number of unholy creatures who were given a wide berth by the Aossí contingent, including two that looked awfully similar to the Wolfling that had chased her and Nolan on their first night in Tírcluddaithe.

Along with the Wolflings were three hideous Snakemen, with no legs that she could see, but powerful arms on a humanoid torso and coiled tails about ten feet in length.

Her skin crawled as they spoke the First Tongue with a raspy lisp. They seemed to be discussing the unsavory habit of the Aossí who cooked their meat instead of consuming it raw. Even in the low light of the fires, she could see their jet-black eyes, beady and murderously cold. Long serpentine tongues flicked between their scaly lips as Eorden marched her past them. They were *tasting* the air around Quinn, sampling her flavor, sniffing for her blood. Goose bumps besieged her arms and legs, and she visibly trembled. That brought a hideous snicker from the Snakemen.

"Coeduine," one of them hissed, and Eorden drew to a stop. "Have you brought usssa feassst?"

Eorden jerked Quinn's leash to bring her next to him, and she was actually grateful. He growled at the Snakeman. "Hardly, worm! A gift for His Highness, not for you lot—now, get *back!*" He took a menacing step toward them, and they recoiled onto their tails. Their necks puffed out like a cobra's hood, but Eorden was undaunted.

"Pity," a truly haunting voice whispered just behind Quinn and to her left. "She smells utterly *delectable.*"

She didn't want to, but she couldn't help looking over her shoulder. When she did, she stifled a scream.

Four giant Spiders had gathered behind her, each as massive as a small elephant, with glistening fangs and eight eerie eyes on a shiny, sleek black body. They were widow Spiders, complete with red hourglasses on their bulbous abdomens.

The hairs on the back of her neck stood at attention, and she broke out in a cold sweat. Wolves and snakes she could handle, but only some thoroughly evil being would create Shelob-like monsters such as these.

"So tender!" one of them said, and the Snakemen murmured in hungry agreement. "Scrumptious."

"Such soft, pink flesh," said a third Spider, and a string of drool dripped off its mandible. "And *pints* of sweet blood. Mmm. Eorden, once Lord Bàsisolc is done with her, may we have the leftovers?"

Eorden snarled. "Dectus, be duly warned, if any of your brood so much as takes a step forward, I will ensure that each of your legs is plucked off one at a time. And then I will personally tear out those gluttonous fangs and watch you starve to death. Now get *back,* all of you! Naea, to me!"

This last sentence brought a swift sound like a silken rustling, and Quinn startled as a collection of Corrupted plants rushed in from her right. Several were Flowers—mainly orange-and-blue Bird of paradise—but there were two giant, venomous-looking Venus flytraps that were as frightening as the Spiders in their own way. They were seven feet tall and a dark blood red (at least, they seemed that color in the light of the cooking fires).

In spite of her fear, Quinn thought of Nolan; he would know the exact species, she felt sure, and the realization somehow brought a small, comforting smile to her face.

"Something amiss, my captain?" the Flytrap, who was apparently named Naea, asked. He had no face that Quinn could identify—it must have been hidden amid the tangle of his leaves—but he was able to move around almost silently and blinding-fast on prickly feet; and he had several long tendrils of arms that glistened with a sticky sap, like he was some kind of hybrid between a flytrap and a sundew.

The Spider Dectus shrank back from the Plants. "No need to get snippy, Eorden. We merely jape. We are able to control ourselves, do not worry. We're not *animals*."

The Spiders and the Snakemen gave nervous chuckles and started slinking off one by one into the evening.

"Naea, escort us to Lord Bàsisolc's pavilion." Eorden doled out a little slack to Quinn's leash. He added, loudly enough to be heard across the plain, "And if anyone interrupts us, kill him on the spot."

They started walking again. Quinn looked straight forward, but out of the corner of her eye, she saw more Corrupted: Opossums, Owls, Skunks, Armadillos, Warthogs, Buffalo, and a handful of anthropomorphic *Deer*, of all things. They looked impossibly odd, bipedal and muscular, with racks of antlers atop their velveteen heads. It was hard to view them as evil, but they clearly were, sharpening scythe-like blades in preparation for a coming battle.

Along the edges of the field, right at the tree line of the imposing Morsden, stood tall wood-and-iron machines that Quinn could only guess were some kind of catapult or siege engine—they seemed to be able to launch giant spears or fling heavy objects into the sky. It appeared as if Bàsisolc's army was expecting an attack from above.

As determined as Quinn was, she couldn't help but swallow a lump of raw fear that seized her throat as Eorden marched her through the campsite, flanked on either side by the Flytraps. They halted in front of the dark blue pavilion, where four armed guards were standing in front of the heavy fabric flaps that presumably led into Bàsisolc's chambers. Virtually no light escaped from within, and Quinn felt her pulse quicken. A cold sweat dripped from her neck down her spine as she tried to force herself to breathe regularly.

The two Greenmen that Eorden had sent on ahead emerged from the pavilion with a flash of light that made Quinn squint.

"Captain," one of them said, "my lord commands you to bring the prisoner in at once."

His companion grimaced and said, "We are to wait upon Lord Agenor and bring him later."

The flap opened a second time to reveal a willowy dark Coeduine. This was the first Treeman Quinn had seen whose eyes didn't seem to glow yellow, and she wondered if perhaps his eyesight was failing. He stared at Eorden for a moment, as if trying to place him, and ignored Quinn entirely.

Eorden wasted no time on pleasantries. "Llygwyn, the girl is Plagued." He pulled her leash forward to show the Greenman her numerous wounds.

The Coeduine healer looked down at her, as if seeing a human for the first time. He seemed puzzled. "*This* is the keeper of the Verse? I must admit I find it baffling. This looks like a soiled washrag."

"Llygwyn, we are in a hurry; gylináma is set to expire."

"You cannot undo the Plague?" Llygwyn asked pointedly.

Eorden sighed. "You are the healer, not me. Now, Sing! Lord Bàsisolc is waiting."

Llygwyn shrugged and began Singing in a clear, low voice. The words, once again, weren't Translated, but the effects were immediate. Quinn's wounds itched and began closing up. The Coeduine Sang for only a few moments, but the relief felt miraculous, and Quinn shivered. She fought the urge to thank the Treeman.

"The wounds will heal in time, but there may be some scarring, if that matters." Llygwyn looked as if he couldn't care less.

"The poor girl," Eorden teased as one of the younger Greenmen pulled Llygwyn away, saying, "Come, the Boar needs a Song, and we have but moments."

As Llygwyn allowed himself to be led off, Quinn heard him mutter, "If we're lucky, the wound will fester, he'll take fever, and we'll be rid of the great oaf for once and all."

"Come!" her captor said, prodding Quinn in the back. He urged her through the open flaps and into the lions' den.

28

Bàsisolc the Most Evil

It took several moments for Quinn's eyes to adjust from the relative darkness outside to the blinding brilliance inside. Not only was there a central fire blazing, but dozens of odd lanterns that glowed with a greenish hue were hung from supports along the lush fabric walls. The rectangular tent was long and narrow, with a thirty-foot ceiling, and it was divided into at least two rooms, probably many more, the front section being a receiving area with a heavy wooden table and several chairs, some human sized. Behind the table was a gilded throne set on an intricately carved deck.

On the other side of the throne, there was another partition of heavy drapes, also with four guards, that Quinn assumed led to Bàsisolc's private chambers. She shuddered to think of what he did behind those curtains, and her reaction brought a chuckle from Eorden.

"Our decorations are not to your liking?" he grunted. "Sure, this pavilion may be a little *rustic*, but I doubt you've seen much nicer since you've been on this Side. The Aossí barely live above squalor until you reach their king's city. And the animals of the Forest often don't have enough sense to disregard their own ordure—so *that* can't be all that pleasant." He chuckled again, and Quinn was starting to hate his laugh.

"Well," she said with a calm she didn't really feel inside, "if the Awakened of Morsden know enough to leave *you* alone, I don't mind if they wallow in their own—" Here she used a not-so-nice word. "It's probably cleaner'n you."

Eorden narrowed his glowing eyes. "You know, *girl*, if you don't find a bit and bridle for that tongue of yours, I just may have to relieve you of it."

"Just don't use yore hands to do it, ya filthy bugger. I dunno where they've been."

The Treeman hissed and reared back a hand to bring it across her cheek, which, with the difference in size between them, would've done some serious damage. Quinn flinched and closed her eyes, but before he could strike her, she heard a voice that could only be described as an Aeolian wind harp wrapped in silk, crackling with electric power. It was suave, subtle, commanding, and decisive, all at once—like the murmurings of a brook and the roaring of an ocean, soft and strong at the same time.

"Eorden, for shame." There was the sound of a clucking, reproving tongue, *tsk-tsk-tsk*. "Honestly. Tell me you weren't about to allow yourself to be goaded by a thirteen-year-old human girl. Such violence is beneath a warrior such as yourself."

Fearful of doing so, yet unable to stop herself, Quinn cracked open one eye to see the being who possessed this beautiful voice. She had been steeling herself to suppress a scream once she beheld Bàsisolc's hideousness; she'd expected him to have horns and a forked tail and cloven feet, disfigured by sin and Corruption.

In truth, he was one of the most handsome creatures she'd ever seen; he was better-looking than most humans, if she ignored the fact that he was almost twenty feet tall.

His bark-skin was a rich, flawless mahogany color, smooth and almost *polished*-looking. His face was as close to human as a Tree could get, with a high forehead; a regal, straight nose; lips like two crescents just a shade lighter than his skin; and a well-trimmed beard like black lichen.

But his eyes were what most surprised Quinn. They were huge, almond-shaped and luminescent, with the cat's pupils of all the Coedaoine, only Bàsisolc's eyes glowed with liquid green instead of the traditional yellow. His dark eyelashes were so long, they touched his prominent cheekbones when he blinked. His hair, straight and dark brown, seemed to be made of corn silk and was pulled back in a trimmed ponytail that hung to his shoulders.

The Most Evil was dressed in linen-like trousers dyed a royal blue. The front of his matching shirt was open at the chest, displaying well-defined musculature, and a single golden chain boasted a medallion etched with details that Quinn couldn't quite make out. He wore two identical rings, one on each index finger, of entwined gold and silver adorned with diamonds.

Quinn realized that he was dressed in his *pajamas*—he was ready for bed. Granted, they were royal jammies that looked as fancy as any Egyptian cotton on her Side of the Veil.

Her half-formed retort to Eorden evaporated on her tongue, and she clamped her lower jaw shut when she realized it had been involuntarily left open.

Her kidnapper bowed low. "I'm sorry, m'lord. It shall not happen again."

Bàsisolc waved off the apology as if it were an annoying waft of smoke. "Before you are dismissed, what is this I hear about Hemre?"

Eorden cleared his throat. "Lord Bàsisolc, we were beset by the king of the Leucis and a large Awakened she-bear, as well as several well-trained Aossí swordsmen. Ysgafn's daughter knew of the shadows' weakness to fire and used it to her advantage. We were able to acquire the girl once Hemre began the Plague Song, but Lord Agenor was wounded, and we were forced to flee. It is believed that Hemre fell, since he did not follow us through the doorway."

"We call them the Capána," Quinn said—not because she thought they cared but to show them she wasn't afraid. "That poncey Pig made 'em look like me gran. Where is she?"

Bàsisolc didn't answer, but he looked thoughtful for a moment. "Excellent name—*Mistfolk*. I like it! Has a certain ethereal ring to it. That is what we shall call them from now on."

Quinn frowned. "Oi, *mate*, I asked you a question! Where's me gran?"

Eorden yanked on the leash, dragging her backward till she fell on her posterior. "You will *not* address his lordship as common!"

Bàsisolc cleared his throat. "Eorden, please! What do you expect from the impetuousness of youth? Untie her." Eorden's lips tightened, but he hastened to obey as Bàsisolc continued, "I am sorry to hear of Hemre's loss. But you were correct in leaving to bring the girl to me, though I think Lord Agenor reacted selfishly. He should have remained to finish them off; from what I have been told, his wound was not life-threatening."

"It is as you say, my lord." Eorden replied with a bow, holding Quinn's untied ropes in his hands.

She considered making a dash for it, but there were eight guards between here and the entrance, not to mention Eorden and the Most Evil himself. If he was concerned about her escaping, he wouldn't have had the bindings removed.

"Then, once again, our esteemed Lord Agenor has prized saving his own skin over the needs of our cause, and our enemies still live." Bàsisolc sighed. "Very well. Thank you for your services, Captain. They will be remembered. You are dismissed."

"Thank you, m'lord." Eorden saluted and backed slowly out of the room. He gave Quinn a parting glare as he slipped out into the night, but not before she gave him the Longbowman's Salute—though she wasn't sure if the Translation Song worked for rude finger gestures.

Bàsisolc considered Quinn for a moment, as if just noticing her for the first time. "You're awfully small, aren't you? And quite *dirty*."

"And yore wearin' jammies, so I wouldn't talk."

The Treeman gave her a smile filled with bright white humanlike teeth. "A little spitfire, too. But I'll have you know *these* are my lounging attire. I enjoy comfort and don't stand so much on ceremony, except coming from my subjects. Why, when my great victory comes tomorrow, I may very well be in a bathrobe."

Quinn shrugged. "Whatever suits ya, mate. Y'could be *in* the bath, all I care—I came over in a nightgown. So, what's yore 'great victory'?"

She was terrified, and her stomach twisted with nerves; but, standing in front of this tyrant, she drew on a strength she didn't know she possessed. She was determined not to let him see her fear.

"Oh, it will be revealed in good time. For now, won't you join me for a little refreshment?" Bàsisolc gestured with an open hand to a human-sized chair. "We have something to discuss."

Quinn thought about making some snappy remark and refusing to sit, but really, all this banter meant nothing. He was holding all the cards, and she had to play the game, whether she liked it or not. So she sat.

"Excellent! There's a mature young woman!" Bàsisolc clapped his hands, and one of the guards disappeared into the interior of the pavilion, presumably to summon food and drink. "What is your name, spitfire?" he asked, gracefully sitting down on his throne.

No harm answering, she thought. "Quinn Taylor."

"Mmm, right, after the Embroidery Queen. 'Tailor.'"

"No, it's me father's surname. Just a coincidence."

"I find there are very little true coincidences. I knew her, you know—the Embroidery Queen."

"So'd that git Eorden, or so he says. Jolly good for ya, er...." She realized she didn't know what to call him, so she just said, "Bàs."

He cocked his head at her. "That means 'Most.'"

"I know. How's it feel to have a name that means 'Most Evil'? That's gotta suck."

"It's a title, Quinn Taylor. My true name is lost to the ages, just as my brother's."

"Could call ya *Bob*, if it makes ya feel better. I want to see me grandmother."

"How do you know she is still alive?" There wasn't any menace in his voice; it was simply a question.

"I dunno. I just do."

"Hmmm. Quite so. Well, yes, your grandmother is, indeed, alive, and otherwise in pretty good shape, excepting a little blood we needed to use to make the Mistfolk. In fact"—he gave a dramatic pause—"she is in this very pavilion as we speak."

Quinn darted to her feet. "Where? Let me see her!"

Bàsisolc seemed to consider this a moment, and then he said, "All right. Why not?" He clapped his hands again and ordered another guard to bring in Audrey and "the others," whoever *they* were.

As the second guard slipped deeper into the pavilion, the first guard returned with two servants—Awakened potbellied pigs (causing Quinn to think perhaps Bàsisolc had a thing for swine)—who began setting cold dishes and goblets on the table. There were dates and grapes and apples and nuts, some sandwiches, cheeses, and a few dainties to nibble on. Bàsisolc grabbed several red grapes and popped them in his mouth, one at a time, even though they were the size of small raisins to him.

"Normally my board is a trifle more sumptuous, but I didn't know we were going to be successful in collecting you tonight," he explained. "Agenor's been looking for you the better part of a week now, and—let's be honest—he *is* prone to failure, so I hadn't set my sights overly high. Otherwise I would've had something more suitable prepared."

"Don't put yoreself out on my account," Quinn said. She debated with herself for a couple seconds but then decided it was pointless to refuse to eat. Reaching for a piece of cheese, a golden apple, two sandwiches, and a goblet of red wine, she realized how ravenously hungry she was. She wasn't worried about Bàsisolc trying to poison her—right now, he needed her alive, and she needed her strength.

"You summoned us, Lord Bàsisolc?"

Quinn had half a bacon sarnie in her mouth (trying not to think about the Pigs who'd just served her pork) when she turned to see who'd come into the room. Somehow, without even hearing his name, she knew this was Dubric, the king of Tírsor and brother of High King Alaric, just as she'd known before that he was in cahoots with the Corrupted.

She could see why he was called Dubric the Dark. He was tall and broad, with shoulder-length jet-black hair; dark, intelligent eyes; heavy eyebrows; and a trim beard around his thin mouth, which had a regal turn. He looked like an under-king that never shirked a hunt in the sun or a battle in the summertime; he was deeply tanned and seemed to bathe in perfumed oil, as if to keep his skin smooth, because the scent was wafting over to Quinn. His hands and forearms were tattooed in blue ink—whirls and swirls that she figured were symbols of his royal majesty, second in the land only to his older brother.

Beside him was the *palest* woman Quinn had ever seen—obviously his wife, Queen Basillia. While Bàsisolc and Dubric were of a darker complexion, this woman was so pasty, it was freakish. She had black hair like her husband, but her coal-black eyes were so dark, there were no discernible pupils, and her lips were frighteningly red. Her brows beetled with disgust as her eyes fell on Quinn, and the thirteen-year-old recalled that Her Hideousness was barren. She must have it out for kids everywhere.

Quinn tried to remember the name of the witch in *Snow White*. *Mirror, mirror on the wall....* That was *this* lady, and it occurred to her that some stereotypes were actually true.

Bàsisolc oozed superciliousness. "Ah, King Dubric and the charming Queen Basillia. Thank you for condescending to join us on such short notice. I trust your evening meal was to your liking." He indicated Quinn, still stuffing her face. "I have the pleasure of introducing Quinn Taylor, the last descendant of the Embroidery Queen, and heir of the Love Verse."

Quinn waved at them, unimpressed. "S'up."

Basillia shook her head with ill-hidden contempt, and her husband wasn't much better; he didn't even look at Quinn as he said, "Delighted. Lord Bàsisolc, how can we be of service?"

At that moment, Quinn's grandmother was let into the receiving area. Quinn lurched to her feet with a cry, and the two ran into each other's arms, talking over each other. Gran did look all right, perhaps tired and more gaunt, but not tortured or starved.

"Oh, my dear," Gran said, with tears streaming down her cheeks. "I'm so sorry. I'm so sorry to have let this happen. I had hoped they'd be unable to find you."

Quinn shook her head. "It's not yore fault, Gran. Not yore fault. We're gonna be all right—the others will rescue us. They're comin' for us."

Bàsisolc chuckled. "One can only hope, my dear child-wealth. Now, would you be so kind as to show us the Love Stone?"

Quinn looked at her grandmother. What was the point of keeping it hidden? They obviously knew she had it, and they could just take it by force, if so inclined. She reached down her tunic and drew out the diamond on its heavy chain. She hoped that if they did take it, it would burn their hands or melt their faces off.

The enormous stone caught the light of the fire and the lanterns, sparkling in an array of colors. It really was a beautiful gem—seemed a shame to break it open and release the Verse, however *that* was supposed to be accomplished.

Queen Basillia sucked in a breath, and her husband's brown eyes gleamed like the gemstone—his look was one of hunger, and Quinn found herself thinking, *If you only knew what a nightmare this diamond has been.*

And she knew deep down that if there was a way she could trust Bàsisolc to release her and her grandmother, she'd probably give it to him.

The stone didn't elicit the same desirous response from Bàsisolc; he seemed to view it analytically, coldly, his mind perhaps working out schemes to turn the power of the Verse to his favor.

He said, "The Love Verse, the Chorus of my brother's greatest achievement, the Master Song. M'lady Basillia, what does love mean to you?"

The spiteful woman thought for several seconds. "Love is a feeling, an overwhelming passion. I have heard our wise men say it is a process of the brain releasing a type of bile into our blood, which causes us to burn as with fever for another."

Bàsisolc nodded his great head, taking another handful of grapes. "Indeed, wondrous queen. Well said. And King Dubric? What does love mean to you?"

"I don't know about processes of the brain, but I do understand all-consuming passion. I love my wife, and I love my throne. I would do anything to further my wealth and power in order to secure both."

At least the man answered honestly, Quinn thought. She had expected him to quote a sonnet, although she knew Shakespeare was probably unheard of on this Side, except perhaps by Rhydderch.

Again, Bàsisolc nodded, chewing a singular grape. "Admirable sentiment."

"And you?" Gran asked. She had wiped away her tears, and now that Quinn was at her side, her granddaughter saw a bit of her strength and fight return. The older woman was a spitfire, too. "What does *love* mean to you, Most Evil?"

"Hmmm. I seek power; I do not seek to understand love. I shall leave that for the poets. It is a source of power to me, nothing more, nothing less. It is an obsession leading to possession, which leads to control, and I desire to control all that I see."

"That is lust, not love," Gran replied. "You crave power like a drug, and it matters not what you would destroy in order to achieve that which your heart covets."

Bàsisolc inclined his head a third time, accepting the reproof with grace. "You are most likely correct, woman. My title is, no doubt, appropriately given. What I desire, I will have; it is a simple enough equation. But what about your granddaughter? What do you think love is, young Quinn Taylor?"

Quinn stared into her grandmother's eyes. It was a question she'd never been asked before, and she didn't want to give a flippant answer. *What is love?*

"At my school back home, we study ancient languages. The word *passion* comes from the Latin term that means 'to suffer.' Love is somethin' yore willin' to suffer for, to put another person over yore own needs and feelin's, to prefer that person's happiness even over yore own. When ya love someone, yore willin' to die for 'em. Fact, Someone from our Side once said, '*Greater love has no one than this, than to lay down one's life for his friends.*' And soon after, He did just that."

King Dubric snorted. "And look where it got Him. What happened after that?"

Quinn smiled at her grandmother. "The Composer raised Him from the dead and seated Him on a throne at His right hand."

The silence was palpable for several seconds.

Finally Bàsisolc cleared his throat and said, "King Dubric, m'lady Basillia, I wanted to let you know that immediately upon your return to the Citadel City tomorrow evening, our rather perceptive young lady, here, is going to enter the demeglwys to unlock the Verse within that most wonderful diamond."

Basillia barked a laugh. "And how, pray tell, do you intend to force her to do so, m'lord?"

Bàsisolc looked down into Quinn's eyes, and she held his gaze defiantly. "Simple. If she doesn't comply, I will kill her grandmother. Then we will see for whom she is willing to suffer."

29

The Guardians of Scáthán Lake

Aren't you a little concerned that Tophyrs and his crew will be intoxicated by the time we get to the Lake?"

Lady Tegwyn looked down at Stanley and then over at the Awakened frog, who was guzzling another tumbler full of pear brandy, and she grinned. "I don't think there is enough brandy in all of Suas for Mr. Tophyrs and his companions to get drunk, young one. Though it's rather moot, seeing as how we've now arrived. Look!" She spread her arm expansively as the Otherworlders reached the crest of a hill.

Before them, at the base of the hill they'd just climbed, was a perfectly still lake, maybe two miles across, like a steel-blue slice of quicksilver along the valley floor. It did seem like a docile lake, a mirror giving an exact reflection of the mountains surrounding it, which came right up to its banks. On this side of the Scáthán was a stone beach, but the water was so still, no ripples lapped against the shore at all.

The Jagged Mountains were ominous and foreboding. Capped with a light dusting of snow on their very crowns, they ran like serrated shark's teeth, iron gray and reflecting the bright oranges, reds, and pinks of the setting sun. Blue Time was minutes away, and the view reminded Nolan of a photo he'd once seen of Mount Moran reflected in the stillness of Jackson Lake up in Wyoming.

He'd managed to convince himself this wasn't going to be that scary—have a friendly chat with the Awakened guardians, get Crannhyn to come out of his hidden domain, and they'd be off to rescue Quinn. *Then* Nolan could be scared. But *this* part here would be a walk in the park. It *had* to be.

That line of thinking seemed to hold firm until Tophyrs drained his last tumbler and whispered something to Lord Mabon, who then nodded to Lady Tegwyn.

Tophyrs saluted, perhaps a little wobbly; but then, he'd consumed at least a gallon of liquor on the march over, not to mention a large number of pies.

"Cake tare, Wotherurlders," the Frogman said to the children. "Best o' lake to ya all." He started shuffling down the hill toward the lake, his comrades fanned out behind him. They'd *all* had their fill of pie and brandy.

"Where are you going?" Emery called out from Tërimrush's shoulders.

Tophyrs looked over his shoulder and winked at the boy. "'M goin' to pick a fight, *mon cher!*" He smiled a big, toothy grin and shot out his long red tongue to lick a bulging eyeball.

His group entered the water and within moments had dived below the surface, shattering the serenity of the glassy Lake with bubbles and ripples as they swam down to the guardians.

Nolan thought Mabon had been pretty clear: The idea was to stall for time, not necessarily to pick a fight.

"You're right," Tegwyn said to Stanley, amending her previous statement. "He might be a *trifle* drunk."

"I'm so glad this entire plan relies on an alcoholic Frog who's eaten his weight in blueberry pie." This was Genevieve's contribution, and Heilyn chuckled, standing behind her with the Red Sword on his back, still wrapped in deerskin.

Tegwyn shook her head and turned to her daughter. "Fiorlen, I want you to promise me you'll stay here with the Otherworlders."

The Sapling crossed her arms in frustration. "Mother, I believe I am perfectly capable of going with you!"

Tegwyn sighed. "I know you are becoming a wonderful Singer, my dear, but outside of Moving Sideways, this will be some of the most advanced Singing there is. Crannhyn's domain is well guarded for a reason, and if things go ill with the guardians of the Lake—"

"But, Mother—"

"—I need you to look after the travelers, protect them. Can I trust you in this, or must I find someone else?"

Fiorlen huffed. "Fine, Mother, I shall do as you say."

"Promise me." Tegwyn's gaze narrowed on her daughter.

Fiorlen rolled her eyes. "Yes, all right—I promise."

"Good girl. No matter what happens, your father and I love you, and we are extremely proud of you. The Healing you gave for the Song of Plagues was well above your summers." The Treewoman bent down to hug her daughter and kiss her forehead.

"Love you, too." Fiorlen's tone sounded a little petulant.

Lady Tegwyn and the other Coedaoine lords began to pick their way down the declivity toward the right side of the Lake.

"Wonderful," Rhydderch said. "This should be fun. I think we could've thought this through just a little better."

"Make ready!" Lord Boujòn shouted to the two-hundred-plus Flowers arrayed behind him on the hill. The rest of the army had begun streaming down the left side to take up defensive positions on the small beach at the water's edge, while the flying Awakened had taken to the evening skies. The noise of the now-stirring army was deafening.

It was close quarters, for sure, but Nolan hoped their display of superior numbers would be a deterrent to whatever came out of the Lake. That is, if they *had* superior numbers.

Thank God they wouldn't be fighting undead Mistfolk tonight. Still, an unknown enemy was even more frightening, in a way. At least they knew how to deal with Mistfolk.

Hopefully, within a few minutes, it wouldn't matter.

Blue Time fell; Nolan felt it in his gut, as usual. The fallen sun was to the far left of the mountain range, a burnished line of fiery red and cool purple. To the east, the first of the stars winked into existence, and the moon was already a quarter into its journey through the sky.

The center of Scáthán Lake started churning violently. From their vantage point atop the hill, looking down at the army strewn along the beach, the children exchanged glances.

"Fiorlen," Stanley said, "what *exactly* is in the Lake?"

Before she could answer, Tophyrs and his fellow merry amphibians burst out of the water, hightailing it to shore. The Newts went scrambling over the rocks on all fours, while the Frogs hopped like Armageddon was chasing them; and even over the noises of the whirlpool that was forming in the water and the army that shifted restlessly on the beach, Nolan could hear Tophyrs ribbit and cry out with his throat sac fully distended: "Right-o! *Allons-y*, that riled her right off! Step lively, now; here she comes!"

Stanley had just enough time to murmur, "When-the-Toad-came-home," before the Docile Lake erupted into a shooting fountain of frothy water, and something *massive* barreled toward the shore.

"Kayim," Fiorlen said. "The guardian of Scáthán. The Kype and the Escre will follow her shortly."

"Uh, i-is that an *alligator*?" Stanley stuttered.

Only this Alligator was nearly thirty feet long, black-green with a broad, flat, U-shaped snout and rows of yellow teeth. What was even more terrifying than her size was that as she reached the shallow waters leading inland, she stood on her trunk-sized hind legs and pointed with a huge arm at the fleeing amphibians while bellowing in frustration.

"That's not an alligator," Emery managed to say. "That's Godzilla."

As Kayim stomped to shore and saw the veritable army spread out before her, rather than drawing up short, she seemed to become all the more enraged. She snapped her jaws with a reverberating *clamp!* as dozens of forms began rising up out of the water behind her.

What Nolan saw, he couldn't very well reconcile in his brain. As with the Flowers, his earthbound mind tried to reject what his eyes were showing him.

They were Awakened *fish*—sockeye Salmon, actually; he saw their hooked jaws in side profile and registered their red-tinged flanks. And yet they were six feet tall, with vague appendages ending in foot-shaped pelvic fins that allowed them to shamble somewhat vertically, although Nolan wouldn't have called them strictly bipedal. Their tails bent out behind them at an odd angle, but their pectoral fins were a little more definitively shaped, protruding on a kind of stubby, armlike appendage, so that they were able to grasp short brass swords, which the water had tarnished to a sickly green.

With them were anthropomorphic Crayfish, some four or five feet tall. Their chitinous exoskeletons were an electric blue with tiny purple-and-yellow spots that Nolan's hawk eyes didn't see until they were much closer, and they scuttled onto the rocky beach on two pairs of segmented legs, with two more pairs grasping tarnished daggers, not to mention their two giant claws.

Though the Coedaoine army outnumbered the Lake dwellers, Nolan would've said they were evenly matched; in either case, the potential losses were staggering.

"How long will it take them to reach Crannhyn?" he shouted to Fiorlen as the first of the Crayfish reached its Salmon comrades.

"I don't know. Five minutes? Maybe ten?" She shook her head. "But he is the only one the Awakened will answer to."

"This might be over by then!" Nolan exclaimed.

"They need our help," Stanley said, pulling his sword from its scabbard.

"Absolutely not!" King Orbo rumbled. "Fiorlen, watch over the children-wealth—under no circumstances are they to participate in this fight. Tërimrush, sit on them if you have to. All of you, obey me in this. Please."

He had his butcher-knife sword in his right hand, and his tender rib, only partially healed, was wrapped tightly under his tunic; but with the rib and the scabs of the Plague still lingering, it was too painful to wear armor. As he started making his way down to the army, he turned and said, "Rhydderch, I will expect you not to fight; His Highness must be guarded."

Heilyn frowned and looked as if he was about to protest, but Rhydderch gave him such a stern look that the prince kept quiet.

"Peace," the monk said, nodding. "We will have enough fighting once we reach Bàsisolc."

This entire exchange lasted mere seconds, and soon Boujòn's voice, amplified by a brass speaking-trumpet, was heard over the tumult as both sides lined up. "Hold! We do not wish to fight!"

"*Baliverne! I* wish to fight!" Tophyrs interjected. With that massive throat sac, he was able to be heard over the din. In his hands were two short swords, and his Newts were armed with halberds.

The Rose lord turned his trumpet toward the Frog. "Someone shut up that drunken louse!"

"Who challenges the guardian of the Lake?" Kayim demanded in a voice that boomed out over the armies. She was truly terrifying, and Nolan realized that if the situation turned sour, their defensive position a hundred yards up a small hillside would be a mere minor deterrent for the monster.

"We come in the name of the Caevnaóri," Boujòn told her. "Stand down! We seek access to the Eldest."

The knight was stalling for time, clearly hoping the army arrayed on the beach would distract the guardians long enough for Lady Tegwyn and the other Coedaoine to raise the Veil and get to Crannhyn.

"Impossible," Kayim returned. "We are tasked with the protection of Lord Crannhyn's domain. None may approach. I give thirty seconds for you to lead this army back from whence it came, or I shall order the attack."

"I'm afraid that's not possible, Lady Kayim," Boujòn said after a pause. "We *must* get to Crannhyn."

"Then that pickled Frog shall have his wish. Twenty seconds...."

The Tiger king had come to stand by the Rose, towering over him by at least five feet. Orbo's voice was able to be heard without the trumpet, and he called up to the Alligator, "Lady Kayim, I am Orbo the Third! I order you to stand down so we may approach Lord Crannhyn in peace! We do not wish to fight the guardians of Lake Scáthán."

Kayim turned her great head so that one yellow eye was looking down on Orbo. "King Leucis, you are well met! I have no fight with the Catmen. Command this army to retire, for our orders from Lord Crannhyn brook no disobedience, even for a king. You have ten seconds."

Orbo tried one last time: "Be reasonable, my lady. We have no wish to cause you harm, but you are outnumbered, and you cannot hope to win this engagement."

"We shall see," the Alligator replied. "Five seconds."

Orbo grumbled and gnashed his teeth. "We're out of time, Boujòn. Organize your main attack against Kayim, but try to disarm the Lake soldiers—we want as little loss of life as possible."

"For *us*, or for *them*?" Boujòn mumbled. Then he shouted into the trumpet, "Defensive positions! All ready, disarm the soldiers, target Kayim!"

"This was a really bad idea," Nolan muttered just before the two sides threw themselves at each other.

The initial assault was like two tidal waves crashing together, mixing power with destruction. The Lake dwellers were outnumbered two-to-one; and yet, with that gargantuan Alligator, the strength of the Salmon, and the speed of the Crayfish—whose movements were so fast, they looked blurry in the dusky light—the Coedaoine army took the first losses.

Viewed from the hillside, the pandemonium seemed surreal. The reverberating clash of metal on metal, the screeches of the flying Awakened as they dived to converge on Kayim, the bawling of the Keras, and the trumpeting of the Loxon mixed into thunderous mayhem.

Kayim struck first, lunging the length of her body on all fours faster than Nolan would've thought possible for a cold-blooded reptile of her size. She snatched out with her jaws and grabbed hold of one of the Uropsid, shaking the screaming Lizard like a rag doll before tossing him aside. He landed in a torn, bleeding heap.

An Owl retaliated by loosing three throwing knives to the top of the giant's head, but they reflected harmlessly off her thick skin. Kayim's jaws, now stained a gleaming crimson, snapped at the Owl as it pulled out of its dive, missing its wing by a mere couple inches.

The Kype were not very agile on land, but they made up for this disadvantage through brute strength. Nolan saw four of the Flowers lunge upon one of the Fish warriors in an attempt to drag it down and disarm it, but this proved to be a mistake. The Kype arched its back with a growl and threw its arm appendages wide, sending three of the Flowers floundering through the air. It grappled with its remaining attacker—an unlucky yellow Tulip—and managed to grab its head in one finlike hand and its flailing legs in the other. The Salmon stretched and bent the Tulip almost double until its body cracked. The victor then tossed the limp form aside and stooped to retrieve its sword, looking for another challenger.

The Escre were *wicked* fast on land, scuttling forward in a phalanx formation. Their claws shot out from behind a row of brass shields as the wedge of Crayfish drove forward, doing more damage than the daggers in their second set of hands.

But the Coedaoine army was also able to press through the ranks of Lake dwellers, leaving their own small victories in their wake. Nolan saw one of the Kype fall with at least six arrows protruding from its chest. These had been launched from a line of Daisy archers not far down the hillside from where the children stood. A Loxon warrior, easily twelve feet tall, stamped a stray Escre to the ground with its colossal elephant's feet, crushing the Crayfish's shell and leaving the mangled form in a quivering pile on the smooth rocks.

After the initial onslaught, the Awakened army began to disregard its orders to try to spare as many of the Lake dwellers as possible. Things had quickly escalated into an all-out battle for survival.

Lady Kayim, for her part, was proving indestructible. Nothing seemed to penetrate her hide, and the knobby, hornlike protrusions around her reptilian eyes would deflect all but the most perfectly aimed shots.

"Nolan, can you see the Greenmen?" Stanley shouted over the roar of the battle.

The sky was darkening rapidly, but Nolan's exceptional eyes were just able to pick out the glowing sheen of a portanuam on the far side of the river. The shapes of the Treefolk were indistinct, but they seemed to be standing in a semicircle before the doorway, most likely Singing.

"They've raised the Veil!" Nolan exclaimed.

"Then they better hurry!" Genevieve said in exasperation. "We're not going to last much longer!"

"Look!" Emery cried from his high vantage point on the back of Tërimrush. "Orbo's gotten to Kayim!"

The Cat king was surrounded by a host of injured Kype and Escre, but it appeared he wasn't attacking to kill, only to put them out of the fight. He had carved a swath through the Scáthán guardians and now stood within snapping distance of the Alligator's powerful jaws. Her maw was given a wide berth by both sides of the army, so Orbo found himself relatively alone before her. It appeared that the Tiger and the Alligator were *conversing*, as if Orbo was trying to reason with Kayim.

"I think they're *talking*," Nolan shouted, "but I can't hear them."

Off in the distance, on the right-hand side of the lake, a flash of light shot out of the portanuam, catching the attention of several of the combatants. But Kayim didn't seem to have noticed.

"My lady!" one of the Escre shouted over the tumult, gesticulating with its segmented legs toward the flashing doorway. "They've raised the Ve—" But it didn't get to finish, for it was attacked by a charging Rhino. The Crayfish was bowled over roughshod and nearly trampled, but it managed to flop out of the way, gasping for breath.

In the meantime, the negotiations appeared to have taken a turn for the worse. King Orbo bellowed in rage as Kayim lunged out and snatched up the unprepared Tiger in her deadly jaws. The only thing that saved him from getting crunched on the spot was that great sword of his, which he rammed vertically in the Alligator's mouth.

And now they found themselves at an impasse. Kayim could snap her jaws shut, forever silencing the crouching Tiger, but her skull would be impaled by his sword—and thus the thrill of her victory would be short-lived.

The battle slackened to a standstill as both sides stood gawping in awe at the scene before them: an eight-foot-tall Tiger hunkered down in the gaping maw of a thirty-foot Alligator with the butt of his sword firmly entrenched between her sharp yellow teeth, the tip pressed against the roof of her mouth, threatening to puncture the soft white flesh.

"Was this part of the plan?" Emery asked.

"It appears we are stalemated," Orbo managed to gasp in the ensuing silence. "What now, my lady?"

"I've half a mind to close my jaws, Cat king," she managed to garble.

"And, as humiliating as this is, I've half a mind to let you, Lady Kayim."

A flash of white-gold light erupted down by the portanuam, making the evening as bright as day, and every eye was averted from the blaze. The armies gasped in unison, and the children shielded their faces, while notes of crystalline music echoed across the Lake. The tune was melodic and beautiful, yet not wholly *warm* but rather ethereal, unearthly, and haunting, in a way.

Nolan then realized it was the *light* that was making the music, and he was just about to hazard a glance when a mellifluous voice charged with power thundered across the entire lakeside.

"Stop!" the voice boomed, echoing across the water and the distant hills.

It seemed to Nolan that the word was uttered by many voices layered one over another in multipart harmony, like a choir speaking in perfect unison. The word itself was like a Song.

"Cease!" the voice came again, as the light dissipated and the long shadows of Blue Time fell once again. Everyone stood frozen, the battle now forgone and forgotten.

Though his eyes smarted with the afterglow, Nolan could make out several figures walking briskly along the Lake's edge. In the center was an outline twice as tall as the others. *Crannhyn!* Nolan's heart started drumming in his chest. Lady Tegwyn and the others had done it!

Somehow, the dulcet voice was in the midst of them, and yet Nolan still couldn't see its owner clearly. It called out, in a mixed timbre of tenor, baritone, and bass, "What has happened here?"

Silence reigned for several seconds, until Kayim managed to say, "My lord, there is a perfectly reasonable explanation."

Nolan heard Crannhyn chuckle in his multilayered voice. "Lady Kayim... pray, is that the *Leucis king* in your mouth?"

30

Crannhyn the Mighty

Nolan wasn't quite sure what he'd been expecting the oldest living being on earth to look like. He supposed he'd pictured a bent-over old Treeman with a long white beard, a hawkish nose, deep creases of knowledge around his yellow eyes, and gnarled knuckles clasping a birch staff for support. Like Merlin or Gandalf or Dumbledore...maybe with a pointed hat or something.

But Crannhyn wasn't like that at all. First, he was more than twenty feet tall, towering over the other Treefolk lords by eleven or twelve feet, at least. And, second, he was rippling with muscles, like some kind of action-movie hero. If Nolan had to take a guess, he would've said Crannhyn looked like a father in his late thirties, maybe his early forties—a very *fit* father.

He was dressed in some kind of silken black trousers, barefoot as all Treefolk seemed to prefer being, and a matching shirt that was open at the chest. At his waist hung two naked cutlass swords fashioned from some type of *wood* that glistened like steel. Nolan could see the grain of the wood, and yet he felt certain the swords would cut like metal.

The Eldest's bark-skin was rich, polished rosewood with fascinating swirls of darker and lighter hues mixed in with the burnished red, ranging from shiny black to a light blond. The knotting and grain of his flesh accentuated his musculature.

His hair was a close-cropped cluster of round leaves, heavily veined, that Nolan identified to himself as some kind of *Dalbergia*. His face was smooth with a rather broad nose and a wide smile with full lips, set off by a rounded chin and the tipped, oversized ears of all Coedaoine. His cheekbones were high and perfectly symmetrical, giving him an almost feminine quality, further complemented by large, almond-shaped eyes, which glowed not with the traditional yellow of the Greenmen but a liquid white-gold that spoke of power and wisdom.

For all his soft features and good looks (to Coedaoine standards, at least), no one would've been foolish enough to say he looked girlish, for it was those same eyes that conveyed an intensity and depth that Nolan found unsettling. Looking into those ancient eyes was like searching the glorious face of an archangel. Should his gaze be turned on Nolan, how could a mere human of twelve years hope to stand under such scrutiny?

Not to mention the mountainous piles of muscles in his arms, legs, and bared chest. His *forearms* were as thick around as Nolan's torso.

In fact, Crannhyn would've scared Nolan if he didn't chuckle so much. The Eldest seemed to find humor in many small things. He was by no means flippant or jocund, nor did he ever seem to laugh uproariously. But he had a habit of looking around at things and giving a small chortle, as if thinking of a private joke he wasn't inclined to let others in on. Not some hysterical joke, but something moderately amusing.

Crannhyn was still chuckling over this latest joke as Kayim finally opened her mouth wide enough for Orbo to clamber out. There was a bit of shuffling and jostling, but eventually the Alligator was free to work her jaws a few times, while the Tiger king scrambled to his feet and saluted the Eldest with his great sword.

"Hail, Crannhyn the Mighty!" Orbo managed to muster up some dignity, clearing his throat and straightening his tunic, which was rather sodden with Kayim's saliva and perhaps a little blood, as well.

All the Coedaoine, the Awakened, and the Aossí bent to one knee in unison. The Otherworlders followed suit a moment later—it just seemed like the right thing to do, and even Genevieve looked a little awestruck by the Eldest.

"Hail, Crannhyn!" over three hundred voices shouted with reverberating echoes across the dusky Lake, once again still now that the battle had ceased.

"My apologies," Crannhyn said. "This is my fault. We must devise a better way of protecting my sanctuary and yet still allowing my trusted friends to reach me when in need. Have we…come too late?" His luminous eyes surveyed the scene before him, and he sighed. "How many casualties? Who is injured?"

It took another twenty minutes to reorganize the troops and sort out who needed a Healing Song and who was to be mourned. The fatalities were few, considering. And even though he felt guilty, Nolan was impatient to be under way to rescue Quinn. The hour of Blue Time was half over, though Crannhyn seemed to be in no rush.

Once the simple ceremony for the slain was complete, and wounds had been tended to (including Orbo's rib, finally—though the scabbed wounds from the Song of Plagues had to heal naturally), Crannhyn turned to the Tiger king and Lady Tegwyn. "Where are the Otherworld children-wealth?"

"Here, my lord," Tërimrush answered for them, and she nudged her way to where Crannhyn and the Treefolk elders, along with Orbo, had gathered for a hasty council.

"Welcome to the Hidden Lands," Crannhyn the Mighty said by way of greeting. "Lady Tegwyn has apprised me of the situation."

Once again, Nolan wondered what kind of mental connection passed between the Greenmen that allowed such an exchange of information in so short a time. But, whatever the means, he was grateful it worked so fast.

Crannhyn continued, "I am sorry for your great misfortunes, and I apologize for them. While it is true Lord Ysgafn acted rashly, I should have sensed the Love Verse's return to Tírcluddaithe, as well as my brother's consolidation of power. I have allowed myself to become too focused on protecting my knowledge of the Master Song. By distancing myself from Bàsisolc, I have isolated myself from those who need me, and I have neglected the crisis that has arisen in my own Forest. All have suffered for my inattention, including Otherworlder children-wealth. I am at fault here, and I ask your forgiveness."

Nolan was floored, and he could tell that the others were, as well. Someone so powerful and ancient and wise as Crannhyn the Mighty was asking the forgiveness of his subjects and a group of dirty *kids*?

Perhaps Emery had the best handle on the situation; he summed it up as only a nine-year-old could: "No problem, Mr. Crannhyn. We all make mistakes. At least you can fix this one. We need to rescue Quinn and Audrey and Ysgafn so we can go home. Will you help us?"

The Eldest studied the small boy on the back of the prodigious mother Bear for a few seconds, and then he chuckled. "Just so, little one. Let us right this wrong."

He tilted his head up toward the dark blue sky and whistled. His multifaceted voice carried on and on, and the moment the echoes faded, a reply was heard from the base of the mountain, over a mile away. It was the cry of an eagle, only it was so loud that many startled and clamped their hands over their ears.

In the evening twilight, the armies turned as one to watch Arshúil the golden Eagle stream down from his eyrie, scarcely flapping his wings as he glided over the face of Lake Scáthán a mere foot or two above the glasslike water. He lazily dragged a giant yellow claw with vicious talons through the water.

Arshúil's wingspan was well over fifty feet, and his body was easily the size of a prop plane. His feathers were a beautiful mix of rich brown and yellow-gold with mottled white on the wings and tail, and his curved beak was bright yellow tipped in a grayish-blue.

As he drew up his wings to land a safe distance from the armies on the rocky shore, gusts of wind blew sand and even small stones in all directions. Arshúil's yellow eyes glowed with the intelligence of an apex predator, intense and deadly. This was no pet, and he was most certainly a *wild* Awakened animal. He sharpened his beak once or twice on the edge of a boulder and then said, "Welcome back, my lord."

Crannhyn chuckled. "Hello, my old friend. It's been too long."

The proud Eagle dipped his head. "I see the Lady Kayim has encountered some difficulties."

"Once again, my brother is the troublemaker here. I believe he has released Lupír, and we will need your strength. Will you help us?"

The enormous Eagle cocked his head like a pigeon. "Need you ask, my lord? The buffalo along the plains have made me fat, and I'm pining for a decent challenge."

"And you shall have it," Crannhyn assured his Awakened. Turning to the Treefolk lords, he said, "We must make haste. The time-between-times is fading, and we shall have to Move the entire army Sideways at the same time, so let us organize the warriors and discuss strategy."

A flurry of activity surrounded the Otherworlders, who were left without much to do, while the Treefolk talked in a tight circle and the captains mustered their forces. Nolan paced with impatience, and Stanley, unflappable as ever, asked a question of Fiorlen that probably all the children had thought at one time or another.

"How do the Treefolk communicate mentally and over long distances? You've mentioned knowing your father was still alive, you felt confident Emery was all right, and your mother was able to share with Crannhyn in mere moments all that had happened."

Stanley pushed his glasses farther up on his nose. He was a strange sight, a pudgy twelve-year-old in wildly colored clothes with a scabbard strapped to his side. And still his scientific inquisitiveness bled through. In spite of himself, Nolan gave a small smile while he studied his friend.

As Fiorlen gathered her thoughts, she scratched Tintreach behind his antennae, and he was almost *purring* like a house cat. She finally said, "I suppose the simplest answer is, the Composer is *always* Singing; only, His voice is soft and quiet, whispering as a lover in the ear. The Caevnaóri are attuned to His voice, as was once the race of Men. Sadly, Corruption in all races has muted His words. But by listening carefully, we can...*sense* the information we are looking for. I don't know how else to explain it."

Nolan would have liked for Stanley to ask several follow-up questions, but Crannhyn was suddenly standing over the children, peering down at them.

"We are departing. I believe my brother has already raised the Veil over the Sanctuary, and your friends will be coerced into attempting to unlock the Verse. The guardian of the Temple will have launched an immediate attack on Bàsisolc's forces, and I anticipate he has mustered troops to repel Lupír. A battle is inevitable.

"However, we will use this distraction: A team led by Lord Trahaearn will slip through the ranks to release Ysgafn, for his well-being is vital to sending you home. This might be the harder objective, because we do not know where he is being held; but, once through the portanuam, they should be able to sense where he is.

"I would send you home now if I could, but there are limits even to my Singing—only Ysgafn can send you Sideways. And I know you would be loath to leave your friends behind, in any case.

"Thus, our second objective, equally vital: I will lead another small team in an attempt to reach the Sanctuary before the Verse in unlocked, and rescue your friends.

"Meanwhile, I will ask you to stay here with Tërimrush and Lady Kayim's guardians for your protection."

Nolan, Stanley, and Emery burst forth in a tirade of protests, talking over one another.

The Eldest held up his gigantic hand. "Peace, children-wealth. We have little time to spare. I assure you we will return at gylináma tomorrow, hopefully with Quinn and her grandmother."

"But, Lord Crannhyn," Nolan persisted, swallowing his nervousness while staring up into the ageless face, "Quinn and Audrey are our friends—you *have* to let us go with you!"

"Nay. It is not Caevnaóri practice to take children-wealth into battle. I cannot be concerned for your safety whilst working to rescue Quinn and her grandmother. I am sorry."

Nolan looked crossways at Stanley, who also seemed to be fuming. But what was the use in arguing with one of the most powerful beings under creation?

Crannhyn stood to his full height and turned to King Orbo. "We could use the might of the Leucis king, though I cannot guarantee your safety. If you choose to remain behind, there is no cowardice—you have your people to think of."

"My life and sword are yours, my liege." Orbo inclined his head.

"Very well." Crannhyn nodded, then turned his attention to the Aossí. He gave a small chuckle when his gaze fell on Prince Chadric. "I see you have recovered your sword, Highness."

"Yes, Lord Crannhyn, though I remain in the shadows," Heilyn replied.

"Good. Then remain in the shadows here, as well."

"My lord!" the king's son started to protest.

Crannhyn smiled but gave a slight sigh of impatience. "Must everyone argue with my counsel? Rhydderch, your task remains the same: Watch over the prince. I have no doubt Bàsisolc's scheme is tied into the plot surrounding King Alaric, and I will not place the heir to Tírcluddaithe anywhere near my brother's grasp." The Eldest turned in order to cut off further protesting.

"And I?" Cadfan asked. "I would go, if you permit it."

Crannhyn swiveled back to regard the weaponsmith. "What is your name, Aossí?"

"Cadfan," he replied, puffing out his chest with just a touch of pride. "I have been with the Otherworlders from the start. I would to go in their stead and help to rescue the lass and her grandmother."

Crannhyn the Mighty chuckled once more and nodded his assent before moving on to gather the Treefolk in preparation for opening a portanuam to the Sanctuary. There remained maybe twenty minutes of Blue Time.

"I'll bring her back safely," Cadfan promised the boys, then ran to catch up with Crannhyn.

Once they were out of easy earshot, Nolan asked his compatriots, "So we're going anyways, right?"

"Of course we are," Stanley returned with a grin. "Quinn and Audrey need us. Pri—er, *Heilyn?*"

"Aye. We are of the same mind." Chadric winked.

Rhydderch sighed and shook his head. "If I say no, you'll have me bound and gagged—am I right?"

"Indeed. I've been told you're a mad monk and should be restrained." The prince smiled. "Though I have faith enough in you that I would ask you to watch over Genevieve."

"No way," she protested. "I'm not getting separated from the others again. Where they go, I go. It's no safer standing here next to a thirty-foot-long alligator and a bunch of...*mud bugs* with corroded swords."

Nolan was surprised. He'd expected her to throw a fit and threaten to tell on them. Of course, what she'd said made some sense. He felt he *had* to go after Quinn, more to redeem himself than anything else, but he didn't want the group to be separated again. They should all stick together.

"Tërimrush?" Nolan looked up at the Bear and saw the gleam in Emery's eyes. He knew he'd have to take him, as well, for better or worse.

"I will protect Emery with my life," was all she said.

"Fiorlen?"

She'd been quiet till now, and she seemed to be debating in her mind whether to disobey her mother and the Eldest. "Ysgafn is my father," she said at last. "I go to rescue him." She looked at Tintreach and Bassett, both flying at eye level.

"Well, excellent," the Will-o'-the-wisp said. "We're about to disobey the oldest living being on the planet. How does that make everyone feel?"

"I'm strangely comfortable with it," the Treegirl replied with a shrug.

Nolan thought maybe their bad influence was rubbing off on her.

31

Demeglwys

Quinn and Audrey were placed together in a room within Bàsisolc's massive pavilion. The bare earth had been covered with a rug, and there were heaps of cushions and a human-sized table with two chairs. Wine and fresh water were set out, along with a bowl of fruit and a platter of dark bread and cheese. It appeared that Gran hadn't been starved or left to sleep in a rank dungeon during her imprisonment.

After their reception dinner with the Most Evil, the Dark King and his corpse-like wife had retired to their chambers, presumably elsewhere in the enormous tent; and Quinn was left wondering if *they* had guards stationed outside their door flap and beyond the exterior walls of their room, as well.

She heard their own guards grunting and huffing, speaking the First Tongue with an odd accent that was rendered a base sort of Cockney to her ears. They weren't Treefolk but rather some kind of Awakened, though she hadn't seen what species, as of yet. She guessed they were probably more Pigs, given Bàsisolc's apparent penchant for swine.

As soon as they were in the room alone, Quinn said, *"Mam-gu, a ydych yn iawn?"* It was about the extent of her Welsh.

Her grandmother smiled and reached out her arms toward Quinn, who collapsed into her embrace with a sob.

"I've been so worried," Quinn said through her tears.

"I'm fine, dear, really I am." Gran stroked Quinn's tangled blonde hair and clucked her tongue in a motherly way. "That odious creature has surprisingly treated me with grace as a prisoner. Excepting when they took some blood, I've received no injury."

Quinn straightened, drying her eyes and growing furious. "I can't believe they'd stoop so low!"

She filled her grandmother in on everything that had transpired since they'd been separated while crossing the Veil, especially about Agenor using her gran's blood to summon the Mistfolk that looked so much like the older woman.

Gran seemed particularly excited when Quinn told her they'd met Rhydderch and said that he was with Nolan and the others. "It's been *decades* since I've seen Rhydderch," she said with a wistful look in her eyes, and Quinn realized that her grandmother rather fancied the monk.

"Ya'll see him soon!" Quinn assured her. "I'm shore Nols and the others've gotten to Suas by now and left to summon Crannhyn. We just have to hold on till they get here."

Quinn felt sure their conversation was being listened in on, so she didn't mention Prince Chadric or the Red Sword.

Her grandmother's tale took a lot less time to share. While they'd been frantically searching for the children, she and Ysgafn had been overpowered in an ambush of dark Treefolk soon after crossing over; since then, he'd been kept comatose by a Song of Sleep. They'd been under heavy guard, moving through the Morsden, and had arrived at the clearing yesterday afternoon. Though she hadn't seen much, she'd *heard* Dubric's soldiers and the Corrupted coming through numerous portanuam at last night's gylináma as well as tonight's. It seemed they were gathering for a war.

"Do ya know what'll happen when they un-Veil the Sanctuary?" Quinn asked once her grandmother had finished.

"Only what Rhydderch has told me: The guardian of the Sanctuary will attack, and I hope Bàsisolc's little army is ripped to shreds by whatever it is!"

Quinn was quiet for several moments before she asked, "What'll we do when Bàs wants me to open the Stone tomorrow?"

"That's the thing, dear. No one, except maybe Crannhyn, knows how the Verses are opened; even Bàsisolc has no idea. That was kind of the whole point of sealing them in the gemstones to begin with. If one of the Verses falls into impure hands, that's bad enough—but all seven would be unthinkable. They're better sealed away, and I intend to make sure Bàsisolc doesn't get any!"

"How? I won't let him hurt ya!" Quinn's voice was unwavering. "But if I don't figure out how to unlock the Verse, he said he's goin' to kill ya."

"I'm not sure what I'm going to do yet. But, whatever happens, I want you to promise me you'll do what I say."

Quinn didn't respond.

"Quinn...promise me?"

"I won't let him harm ya," she said.

"That wasn't a promise."

Quinn sighed and laid her head on her grandmother's lap. "'Long as it won't harm ya, I promise to do as ya say."

Now it was her gran's turn to sigh as she resumed running her fingers through Quinn's hair, trying to untangle the knots. "You're as stubborn as your mother."

"And grandmother." Quinn smirked. "Learned from the best."

"All right, then, apt pupil, let's get some rest. We'll need our strength for tomorrow."

Quinn yawned and squeezed her grandmother. "I love ya, Gran."

"I love you, too, Quinn."

By Blue Time the next evening, the camp looked like some kind of twisted, evil carnival: about thirty dark Treefolk standing in one corner of the field, chanting around a bonfire; a couple hundred dark-complected Aossí at the ready, swords gleaming in the falling light; Corrupted animals and plants staggered on the fringes, armed and salivating; and the horrendous-looking war machines locked and loaded, pointed into the evening sky. The demonic army made Quinn's flesh crawl, and Gran squeezed her hand in reassurance.

Eorden was giving Quinn the evil eye, hardly focusing on his Singing, and barely concealed a sneer of contempt for Agenor, who cringed at his master's side.

The Boar's shoulder wound had healed only partially, and he had favored it earlier while making a great production of bootlicking the Most Evil.

Quinn had overheard some servants snickering over the fact that, most unfortunately, last night's Blue Time had ended before Llygwyn the Healer could finish Singing over Lord Agenor. They were under the persuasion that Llygwyn wasn't much distressed by such inopportune timing; he was purported to have said, "Pity I was delayed," before leaving the former king to his agony.

Bàsisolc was completely ignoring Agenor now. In fact, he seemed almost catatonic, his eyes rolled back in his head, as he stood, dressed in something that looked suspiciously like a silk bathrobe, and Sang to raise the Veil hiding the demeglwys.

As always, the polluted words weren't rendered out of the First Tongue, but the haunting tone was enough to give Quinn goose bumps on her skin and a sick feeling in the pit of her stomach. Of course, that could've been the nerves.

Not normally one to be overwhelmed by fear—for better, for worse— Quinn was now fighting off a growing sense of panic. She wondered for the thousandth time if she shouldn't just grab Gran and make a break for the tree line. They weren't restrained, after all. Maybe they could make it.

Glancing in the direction of Bàsisolc, Agenor, and Eorden, her gaze fell on a particularly brutish-looking Aossí warrior. First she'd kick him in the shin, then bring her knee up into his groin, and finally use that same knee to break his nose while he was doubled over....

Then the guy standing next to him would stab her in the gut with his curved sword. She shook her head, dropped her eyes, and begrudgingly dismissed any thoughts of escape.

All at once, the Trees stopped Singing, and an eerie silence fell across the plain. It was amazing a few hundred beings could be so utterly quiet—until there was a roar like a jet fighter going ballistic, and a flying monster shot into the dusk. It moved so quickly, Quinn couldn't see anything other than a ginormous dark-brown blur and flashes of some veined wings punishing the air as the creature fired almost straight up out of the largest tree she had ever seen.

It was a vampire Bat! Quinn was able to identify him as he leveled off, but she lost him in the glare of the setting sun, so she turned her attention back to the gargantuan tree that had miraculously appeared in the center of the clearing. The tree glittered with the twinkling lights of the Veil, like millions of fireflies dancing around its boughs. Its diameter was easily that of a city block in width, and it was hundreds of feet tall, towering over the rest of the Morsden.

At the base of its trunk was an opening large enough for two or three Greenmen to enter side by side without having to stoop. From within, the entrance to the Sanctuary glowed warmly with what appeared to be flickering candlelight.

"That's a jolly big Bat," Gran whispered, trying to track the flying blur. "Hope he wins."

"And I didn't know the Sanctuary was a jolly great tree," Quinn whispered back. Now that things were in motion, it was easier for her to swallow her anxiety.

"Nor I," Gran said. "It's enormous."

Bàsisolc was staring at the entrance to the Sanctuary with a greedy gleam in his eye. Without looking at Agenor, he said, "Send Dubric and his queen through the portanuam back to the Citadel City; their presence is no longer needed. Keep constant vigilance to ensure Ysgafn doesn't Awaken, and, above all else, keep that bloody Bat away from us. Try not to fail me utterly, Lord Agenor."

The Boarman swallowed hard and saluted while clearly trying to hide a wince of pain.

Turning to Quinn and her grandmother, the Most Evil made a sweeping bow, though his smile was mocking. "No time to delay, my ladies; Lupír is undoubtedly hungry. Shall we?"

"Incoming!" one of the Aossí mercenaries shouted, pointing toward the horizon where the sun had just set. As the word left his mouth, a noise like an oversized pneumatic rifle drowned out the rest of his cries, and six or eight spears, each ten feet or longer, launched out of the war machines and streaked across the sky.

Lupír came tearing into the glade with a defiant screech that set Quinn's teeth to chattering; it was like nails on a chalkboard magnified a hundredfold. The Bat stayed in one general location as he dodged the spears, and *now* she got her first good look at the creature, though she wished she hadn't.

His furry ratlike body was about the size of a small airplane, almost blond on the belly, a buffalo brownish-black on the back. His leathern wings, spanning at least fifty feet, were skeletally thin, and the tips, following inward to his clawed fingers, were white. His nose was shaped like a broad, flat leaf, complemented by enormous black eyes. His naked ears had ridged tips and stuck straight up from his triangular skull.

The Bat screamed a challenge. A long pink tongue darted out with an explosive *psst!* and a stream of foul-smelling liquid sprayed out over the first line of soldiers. The Bat was spitting at them! The Aossí recoiled from the spray, gagging as the rank smell saturated the entire clearing. It was a mixture of garlicky thiol, oily petrol, and smoldering sulfur.

"Oh, gross!" Quinn coughed and rubbed her watering eyes.

Steeling themselves, several of the Aossí archers prepared to launch flaming arrows at Lupír's gaping maw.

"But wouldn't you think that liquid is ignitable?" Gran managed while holding her sleeve to her nose.

Bàsisolc glared down at her, but then his head darted up, his expression turning confused and then panicked. "Don't, you fools!" he was able to get out before an explosion rocked the front line, and about twenty soldiers were doused in liquid fire. The screams were horrendous, and the line threatened to collapse as everyone scrambled away. Those who were aflame writhed and rolled on the ground, catching the grass on fire, while a few of the braver warriors attempted to stamp out the flames and restore military order.

"My lord, the liquid is flammable!" Agenor shouted with a stupefied look on his face.

"Is it? You imbecile! Bring that flying Rat down, but don't use fire!" Bàsisolc raised his hands in exasperation for a brief moment before motioning for Quinn and her grandmother to lead the way toward the entrance to the Sanctuary. The malice in his glowing eyes squashed any thoughts of disobedience in the teenager's mind.

The malevolence emanating off him was hotter than the physical flames, and Quinn saw a glint of madness in his gaze. *He really is capable of anything!* she realized with an icy stab in the pit of her stomach. He'd stop at nothing; he'd butcher everyone here, including her and Gran, without a moment's hesitation if he thought it would bring him one millimeter closer to his goals.

He was truly *evil.* Quinn had always known evil existed in the world, in an abstract sort of way. She'd heard of people who killed other people for reasons as insane as jewelry or drugs. She'd read about wars and holocausts and great suffering. Since coming to the Otherworld, she'd caught glimpses of evil, especially in the Capána. But now she felt like she'd seen it all—the *source* of evil—in the eyes of a mythical being who was going to use *her* to achieve his mad desires.

The realization of being confronted with the devil himself didn't scare her as she would've expected it to. Sure, she felt fear, but it had more to do with her grandmother's well-being. What she felt toward Bàsisolc was…. What was it?

It was anger, she realized. She was furious to the point of seeing red. He enraged her, and she recognized that perhaps anger wasn't the best emotion to feel when they were about to enter the Temple of the *Love Verse.* She looked into her grandmother's eyes and took several deep breaths to regain her composure. She needed her wits about her if they were to have any chance of surviving.

Lupír was hovering about fifty feet off the ground on flittering wings that pummeled the scorched grass with their drafts. Quinn found herself silently cheering him on, even when he grabbed one the Aossí archers and flipped the hapless man into his mouth, where he disappeared in a splash of gore.

Looking revolted, Gran murmured, "I thought vampire bats ate only blood."

"Technically he *did* eat the blood," Quinn said.

"Get moving, human!" Bàsisolc grumbled, prodding her to move faster.

"I'm goin'!" Quinn bit out, spinning on her heels to stalk off toward the glowing entrance.

Three dark Treefolk followed them as they scurried across the field, dodging lines of Corrupted soldiers. Quinn guessed maybe ten minutes of Blue Time had expired, and she wondered if the Veil would cover the giant tree once the magic hour was over, or if it would remain visible now that Lupír had been released.

When they came into the Sanctuary, it took several seconds for Quinn's eyes to adjust to the candlelight, which was brighter than the dusk behind them. The room they entered was in the hollowed-out center of the living tree, perfectly circular, with walls of polished wood adorned with hundreds of niches in which were large pillar candles that gave off a strong fragrance of wild honeysuckle.

The ceiling was probably forty feet high, of the same polished wood as the walls, and from it hung the biggest chandelier that Quinn had ever seen. It was fashioned of highly polished woodwork, and hundreds more candles lent their brightness to their brethren encircling the walls. It must have been Singing magic that had lit them all, but Quinn wondered whose job it was to *replace* all those candles. There must have been at least a thousand of them.

The ground beneath their feet was hard-packed earth, smooth and shiny like brown marble, with no dust or debris at all, like the well-used floor of a freshly swept sod home.

Opposite the entrance was a raised dais that seemed to grow out of the back wall, as well as an elaborately carved altar that looked like a continuation of the platform itself, as if wall, dais, and altar were one organically solid piece. The altar was a burnished walnut worked over with glyphs and knot work that resonated in the back of Quinn's mind, sending a flash of exhilaration through her tense body. However, on top of the altar was only a plain, empty bowl.

She thought she heard voices murmuring, though she could discern no speech. Rather, they were the breathy whisperings of the Temple itself, seeming to come from nowhere and everywhere simultaneously. It was then that she realized the demeglwys was alive and breathing.

This was the place—the Sanctuary of the Love Verse, wrought by the hands of Crannhyn and his loyal Coedaoine thousands of years ago, and probably never entered since. It was here that the virtue enshrouded in the diamond could be released, by no other hands than her own.

And Gran's, as well, it occurred to her.

Under her sweaty tunic, the Gemstone throbbed like a second heartbeat, as if recognizing that it was home at last. It grew exceedingly warm and started burning Quinn's sternum, so she pulled it out. The Stone emitted a soft hum and reflected the candlelight in prismatic beams that danced off their surroundings.

She felt an almost irresistible pull toward the altar, and before everyone's eyes, a message in the First Tongue appeared on the wall above the dais, emblazoned within the wood itself, as if written by the invisible hand of a master pyrographer. Intricate calligraphy appeared inlaid with gold filigree, and the glyphs seemed to burn with their own fire. As Quinn studied the writing, the Translation Song rendered it into English in her head:

> *The inestimable cost of Love is priceless,*
> *But what it can buy is fathomless;*
> *The illimitable force of Love is boundless,*
> *But what it demands is endless.*

"A *riddle?* What jest is this?" Bàsisolc demanded after reading the words. He turned to his cohorts. "We haven't time for games! How is the Verse released?"

But as the dark Treefolk hemmed and hawed, there appeared a light within the simple wooden bowl. Quinn took a few steps toward the glow, almost against her wishes, but the diamond dragged her forward.

"Ah, yes. Place the stone within the bowl! Good girl!" Bàsisolc nodded his head and motioned her forward.

Quinn cringed at being treated like some performing pet, but she wasn't sure she could even stop herself—the pull of the diamond was more than she could resist.

"You can't let him have the Verse!" her grandmother cried.

"Be silent!" Bàsisolc thundered. "Do as you're told, Quinn Taylor!"

She couldn't stop herself from approaching the altar, whether she wanted to or not. She stepped up onto the dais and pulled the pendant over her head. There wasn't much heat coming from the candlelight, and the temperature in the Sanctuary wasn't very warm; but she was sweating, and her hands were clammy, as she held out the Love Verse by its chain.

Somehow she could see down into the light's depths. There was a niche, a perfectly sized indention for the diamond, where the light was pouring from. Her hand wavered over the bowl, and she struggled against the overpowering pull to return the Stone to its cradle. She looked over her shoulder at her grandmother.

What would they do once the Verse was unlocked? How could they keep it from Bàsisolc?

A fleeting thought raced through her overworked mind: Perhaps they should make the Treefolk kill them. Perhaps it would be better for her and Gran to die than to turn over the Verse to a diabolical powermonger. She could refuse to open the Stone and rush down to her grandmother.

And what if Bàsisolc didn't retaliate? Could she do it herself—take her own life? And what about Gran?

"Hurry *up*, human!" Bàsisolc barked. "Quit stalling and open the Stone!" He reached out and grabbed Gran by the hair. The older woman let out a startled cry as she was lifted off her feet.

"You—" Quinn shrieked, taking a step toward the Greenman. "Let her go!"

In a flash, a long dagger, which was really the length of a sword, was in Bàsisolc's free hand, and the tip, gleaming in the candlelight, was pressed against Gran's breastbone.

"Ah ah ah!" the Most Evil admonished. "That's quite enough, Quinn Taylor. Place the diamond in the bowl, or I run her through. It's as simple as that. Do it *now*!"

"Don't do it, Quinn! You promised!" Gran shouted, then gasped as Bàsisolc twisted his branch-like fingers tighter in her gray hair.

"Shut up, woman! Don't test me. I *will* kill you!"

"Stop it!" Quinn yelled. "You're hurtin' her!"

"Madán! Of *course* I'm hurting her! This isn't a game! Stop being melodramatic, and *open that Verse*! You have three seconds, or I gut her!"

Now Bàsisolc was nearly screaming, close to hysterics.

Quinn didn't debate, not even a second. So much for her plan of self-sacrifice. There was no way she'd let Bàsisolc kill Gran. She lunged forward and slammed the diamond into the niche.

The light flashed out of existence, and she waited in tense anticipation for something to happen. Five seconds. Ten seconds. Complete silence. The Stone just sat in the niche, and nothing happened. She looked back to her grandmother.

"What's wrong?" Bàsisolc demanded. "Where is the Verse?" He seemed so confounded that his grip on Gran's hair lessened ever so slightly. "Why is nothing happening?"

"My lord—" one of the Greenmen stammered.

"Silence, idiot! Quinn Taylor, why is nothing happening? Open the Stone!" Bàsisolc retightened his grasp on Gran.

"I—I don't know what's wrong. I don't know *how* to open the Stone." She was genuinely puzzled. Was there something she was supposed to say? How come *no one* knew anything about this? Wasn't Bàsisolc the second-oldest being on the planet? Shouldn't he know more about this than she did?

Just then, the entire demeglwys vibrated as another explosion rocked the battlefield outside. The sounds of combat were muffled, but Quinn could hear scraps of shouted commands and, more than anything else, the enraged screeching of Lupír.

"Figure it out, you intolerable urchin!" Bàsisolc inclined his head and briefly closed his eyes. "They are summoning my brother. *Hurry!*"

"I can't!" Quinn shouted back. "I have no *idea* how to open the Verse!" She reached down and grabbed the Stone, studying it in her open palm, willing the means to unlock it to enter her mind. But nothing came.

Bàsisolc bellowed in frustration and lifted Gran off the ground by her hair. She grandmother cried out in pain, twisting and grabbing at the Treeman's fingers, clawing the bark-skin, to no avail. Quinn clenched the diamond in her fist and screamed in anger.

"My lord!" one of the Treefolk interjected, holding out his hand. "My lord, I believe I have figured it out!"

Bàsisolc seemed to gather himself, and he set Quinn's grandmother down on the ground again, keeping his fingers entwined in her hair. "If you are right, Cathmor, I will give you your choice of the Morsden once it is mine."

Cathmor collected his thoughts. "It requires a sacrifice: the 'cost of Love is priceless.' What is more costly than life, my lord?"

Bàsisolc rolled this around in his mind for a few moments, seeming to weigh the cost. Then, with a shrug, he plunged the dagger deep into Gran's chest.

Quinn wailed as her grandmother gave a slight gasp, pulling herself away from the blade, and collapsed to the floor, where a crimson pool began soaking into the dirt.

"Now try it again," Bàsisolc said simply.

Quinn screamed and threw herself off the dais, falling to her knees beside her grandmother, the Love Verse forgotten in her hand.

32

The Battle at the Sanctuary

It took a feat of engineering to be able to send Crannhyn's army through the portanuam all at the same time. Seeing as the Eldest was the only one who knew the location of the demeglwys in Morsden Deep, they all had to grasp one another—a daisy chain of heavily armed warriors—as he led them through the Veil.

It was no easy task to figure out a way for some three hundred beings of varying sizes and physiognomies to hold hands and move together as a singular unit, but soon the Treefolk lords had devised a means for everyone to remain linked together, a hodgepodge of holding hands and grasping lengths of rope. Apparently any kind of connection worked well enough. Once this was accomplished, Blue Time was waning away. Nolan guessed they had only fifteen minutes or so left.

Far toward the head of the great column, Nolan could see Cadfan standing like a small hillock next to King Orbo and a contingent of Awakened fighters. The twelve-year-old felt a rush of admiration and pride that an Aossí weaponsmith they'd met only days earlier, and a Tiger king whom they'd known for even less time, were willing to risk their lives, not only for the Stone but for Quinn and Audrey, especially.

Sneaking among the army in order to hitch a ride through the portanuam wasn't difficult for Nolan and his group. The humans were all holding hands, and a length of rope was tied around one of Tërimrush's great paws, while Emery clung to her fur from atop. They were near the very back of the contingent, hidden amidst a group of Rhinos, who seemed to think little of the giant Bear and her clutch of small humans going through the doorway. The only thing the children were worried about was being spotted by one of the Treefolk, but things were rushing along so quickly that they were easily overlooked.

Tophyrs and his multifarious group of amphibians remained behind with Lady Kayim and her guardians. Before the rest of them had departed, the Frog had set to toasting his ladyship's health with the remnants of their liquor and pie, though the Alligator didn't seemed particularly thrilled with her slurring company. Apparently they'd agreed to come only as far as Lake Scáthán. Nolan understood they weren't warriors; they were streetwise con artists, or something along those lines. While they ultimately sided with the "good guys," they definitely straddled a rather gray area. He couldn't help thinking of a wart-covered Robin Hood and his band of golden-hearted thieves, all with a drinking problem.

The Treefolk at the front of the line started Singing, and within moments, the hazy glow of the Veil shimmered into being, the portanuam growing exponentially larger than any Nolan had yet seen, wide enough to swallow the entire army.

"Make ready!" Crannhyn's multilayered voice trilled over them.

"Here we go," Stanley murmured uncertainly. With his left hand, he reached out behind him to grasp Genevieve's; with his right hand, he reached forward to grab Nolan's.

"Don't forget to look both ways before crossing the street," Genevieve admonished them, and Nolan looked back at her and laughed quietly. He was surprised to feel very little fear. He was more nervous than anything.

"I think that's the first time I've ever heard you make a joke," he said.

"And I hope it wasn't a onetime occurrence!" Chadric added, giving her a wink and a smile as they all started marching toward the shimmering portanuam.

Moments later, Crannhyn's army found itself in the middle of a firestorm. As soon as they were through the Veil, the team tasked with finding Ysgafn broke off from the main force and began slinking along the perimeter of the clearing. There were only a few minutes to spare, but they hoped to Awaken

Ysgafn before gylináma expired. He would be a valuable asset on the battle-field, even if still hungover from a Sleep-induced stupor.

By the time the final group was through, including Nolan and his compan-ions, Crannhyn was already shouting to Arshúil to pick up his team and carry them across the field to where the giant tree was un-Veiled. The Eagle, strong as he was, still struggled to maintain altitude with the Eldest and two other Treefolk in his claws; yet he managed to haul them away from the portanuam, and Nolan silently wished them good luck.

There were a few moments of shuffling and jostling as the Veil closed behind them, and then the Rhinos dispersed to join the attack, and Nolan saw the plain spread out before him, with the enormous tree towering over the scene of a horrendous bloodbath.

Nolan was confused. It looked like a major battle had already been fought here, but could a single Awakened bat really cause this much damage to an entire army?

Several fires burned uncontrolled along the clearing, casting plumes of foul-smelling smoke into the evening sky. The place reeked of sulfur, blood, and death. Dozens of bodies, some human, some not, were strewn across the clearing like twisted plastic army men left by some ghoulish child. Nolan saw maybe three or four dead Treemen, probably fifty Aossí, and at least a few dozen Corrupted, including what must have been a grotesque Snakeman, whose rattle had been severed from the tip of his tail, his green-splotched skin pierced through with numerous pockmarks. It looked as if he'd been chomped on several times before being spat out.

Several towering wooden contraptions were launching iron cannonballs and javelin-like spears at a giant brown blur as it streaked through the evening sky. In the failing light, Nolan squinted. Was that…? Lupír. Wow.

Nolan could think of only a few things more frightening on this side of the Veil. The Bat was unnaturally fast for his size, and in the few seconds it took for Nolan to figure out what he was looking at, Lupír had dived upon yet another human soldier, whose screams were quickly silenced as the Bat snapped him up in his fangs. The creature screeched and shot back into the sky, not seeming particularly concerned about the various parts of the warrior that fell off and landed on the ground with surreal thuds.

The noise and the stench of the fracas were unnerving, almost maddening, and Nolan touched the throbbing bruises on his neck, swallowing down a swell of nauseous panic. He had to focus. He needed to get to Quinn. The goal was to carve a swath to the demeglwys before it was too late. He forced his eyes away from the battle scene and looked over to his friends.

Claídear was still hidden, strapped to Chadric's back, but he was armed with a short sword and a buckler shield, his head covered in a leather helmet. Behind him, Genevieve was nocking an arrow to her bow, while Fiorlen's own bow was ready to let fly. Rhydderch pulled out a pair of strange-looking iron pickaxes, small and sharp, capable of being thrown like a francisca or a tomahawk. Stanley's sword, Link, waited in his anxious hands, while Nolan slowly drew Unnamed out of its sheath with the unmistakable ring of cold steel.

The lines of Crannhyn's army moved quickly across the open plain and engaged Bàsisolc's unsuspecting forces. Like a wedge, they pushed through the ranks toward the Sanctuary, raising shouts of "Suas!" and "Crannhyn!" as they fell upon the battle-worn enemy. Lupír, however, didn't seem to make any distinction between Crannhyn's soldiers or Bàsisolc's, and it was but a moment before there were losses on both sides, once-proud warriors littering the grass like tossed-away tissues. Some of Crannhyn's forces turned to do battle with the vampire Bat, and soon there was a three-way mêlée belching mayhem and death throughout the entire clearing.

Arshúil's cry suddenly rent the air, sounding like the fury of a dozen thunderstorms. With his charge delivered to the Sanctuary, he had returned to the skies high above the battleground; and now, dropping like a bolt of lightning, he collided with Lupír. They fell to earth in a tangle of fangs and beak and claws, crushing some unlucky soldiers who hadn't been quick enough in moving out of the way. It was like a small earthquake; the ground shook with their impact, and plumes of rock and debris went flying in all directions.

The sounds of their fighting drowned out all other noise. Lupír broke free and took to the air with Arshúil in swift pursuit. It was like Anzu and Ziz battling for supremacy, two supersonic fighter planes in a vicious, dizzying dogfight, and only one could be the lord of the skies.

"Can anyone see how to get to the Temple?" Stanley shouted over the din of the battles both above and below.

"Not without a fight!" Genevieve returned, loosing an arrow at a freakish Deerman. The beast was quick as he leapt across the plain, but her aim was true. The arrow clipped his shoulder, and he stumbled to the ground, where several of Boujòn's Flowers were quick to finish him off.

"Let's try skirting along the right!" Nolan yelled, mustering his courage. But just as they were about to start off as a group, Tërimrush let out a mighty roar in challenge.

Everyone spun around as something came barreling out of the woods and slammed into the She-bear, knocking her to one side, so that Emery cried out and clasped her fur, just managing to stay between her shoulder blades.

It was the Nightmare, Arsoíche, and close behind her was none other than Agenor himself, surrounded by half a dozen dark Treefolk—three of whom seemed to be female, Nolan noticed. He hadn't realized any of the Treewomen were working with Bàsisolc, but these most definitely were, and they fit the description of "hideous hag" to perfection.

"You!" Agenor's voice rang out, full of loathing but tinged with a touch of surprise. He was favoring the wound that Rhydderch had given him the night before, and his eyes smoldered as they fell on the monk. He quickly recovered his poise. "Kill them!" he commanded his cronies. "Kill them all!"

"Come back for the other shoulder, did you?" Rhydderch taunted, brandishing his pickaxes. "Maybe another piercing for your dainty pig-ears? Come and let my axes whisper sweet nothings, Old King!"

The Boarman smirked, his tusks curving up alongside his evil smile. "For an old man, you sure are histrionic, Rhydderch. Why, I remember the time—"

But Agenor never got to finish his statement. With a massive leap, Tërimrush landed on Arsoíche's back and sunk her teeth deep into the startled Nightmare's shoulder. The Horse whinnied in pain and crumpled to the dirt as Tërimrush rolled off her in a giant ball of fur and claws. Everyone was forced to lurch backward to avoid the flailing bodies of the Mare and the She-bear.

Nolan's eyes darted around until they found Emery standing just behind him. He had feared that the Bear, in her fury, had forgotten the boy was on her back.

"She told me I needed to climb down and stay with you," Emery said. Nolan nodded and pulled his brother into an embrace.

Suddenly it was bedlam. While the She-bear and the Nightmare rolled to their feet and faced off, Chadric used the distraction to slip closer to one of the Treemen and lash out with his short sword, slicing the ten-foot creature across the belly. The Corrupted slumped over with a howl, clutching his abdomen. His two comrades countered by swinging their staves at the prince. Chadric ducked under one of them, and his buckler blocked the other with a resounding clang. Still, the force was strong enough to send him flying to the ground.

He jumped to his feet, shaking off the dizziness, and raced back undeterred to throw himself into the fray.

Rhydderch buried a pickaxe in the ankle of the nearest Greenman and struck out at Agenor with the other. The Old King leapt backward, spinning his glaive defensively to ward off the attack.

⌒

LORD TRAHAEARN AND HIS GROUP of Greenmen had sensed a knot of dark Coedaoine to the left of the portanuam, and within just a few minutes, they cleared a path through the fighting to reach them. In the fire-flecked darkness, eight Treefolk stood in a loose circle, chanting around the prone figure of Lord Ysgafn.

Belting out the first lines of a War Song, Trahaearn broke upon the enemy with the might and fury of a sudden hailstorm. He spun into a crouch, moving like liquid steel, and tossed one of the Treemen over his shoulder, coming up in the midst of the group. He lashed out with his staff, and the words of his Song overpowered the dark chanting of the Coedaoine. Their Singing faltered, and the rest of Trahaearn's team moved to engage the foe.

Had any humans been around to watch, they would have seen a truly rare sight: Treefolk battling Treefolk—not just with weapons of wood and the strength of ages, but with Song, as well. It was as much a battle of wills as it was a contest of martial skill.

Trahaearn started Singing against the Song of Sleep that clung to Ysgafn like a cloak, but one of the dark Greenmen stood against *him* and countered with a Song of Silence. Before he could rise to a crescendo, the enemy was grappled from behind by Trahaearn's son, Fallon, and thrown violently to the ground.

Though Fallon was more than a meter shorter than his foe, he grabbed the Corrupted in a full nelson and struggled to his feet. They wrestled momentarily while Fallon fought to get his arm encircled around the Treeman's neck in a savage headlock; and then, with an amazing burst of strength and leverage, Fallon jerked and twisted the Coeduine around, snapping his neck.

Trahaearn nodded in thanks, then turned to face another enemy, continuing his Song uninterrupted. With a startle of fluttering eyes, Ysgafn twitched awake, and Fallon knelt beside him with a bone knife to spring the locks holding down the great warrior.

"Lord Ysgafn, it is I, Fallon *ap* Trahaearn. We are at battle. Crannhyn is near. Rise, my lord; rise and fight with us!"

But before Fallon could press a staff into Ysgafn's hand, he was attacked from behind and fell motionless to the ground, left lying prone beside Ysgafn with a wooden dirk protruding from his spine.

As they lay side by side, the gaze of the Coeduine lord locked onto the puzzled eyes of the younger Treeman, and they stared at each other in stunned silence. Ysgafn knew the wound was fatal, for the glow in Fallon's eyes began to dim. With a confused look still set on his face, the Sapling's last effort was to place his own staff in Ysgafn's hand.

"It doesn't hurt much," Fallon managed as a trickle of sap-blood fell from the corner of his mouth. "I thought it would hurt more," he finished, and exhaled his last.

"No!" Trahaearn screamed. He kicked out with a foot that caught his foe in the sternum and followed it up with a downward strike of his staff, catching the dark Coeduine between the shoulders and flinging him to the dirt. With a heart-wrenching howl and glowing eyes that smoldered with tears, Trahaearn wrenched the enemy's neck until it cracked like so much kindling.

Looking about through the stream of his tears, he saw four of the dark Treefolk still standing, and another of his team was dead. But now Ysgafn rose to his feet, spinning the staff around to get a feel for its weight and proportions. There was death in his glowing eyes, and whatever power he possessed deep within seemed to flow through him and out into the Forest like an invisible shock wave, pushing back the surrounding Corruption. He stood to his full height, looking every bit a warrior lord.

Still twirling the staff, he pointed with his free hand at one of the dark Greenmen and motioned for him to come, but the coward took one look at the murderous rage in Ysgafn's eyes and dashed into the Forest.

Sparing a brief moment, Ysgafn looked to Trahaearn and bowed his head solemnly. "I am sorry. I offer my life in payment for your son's," he said.

The gray-skinned Treeman nodded in return. "Just make *them* pay for Fallon's life."

Ysgafn nodded resolutely and then, staff singing, threw himself upon the three remaining Corrupted. They were dead before they hit the ground.

GENEVIEVE AND FIORLEN BOTH LOOSED their bowstrings at the same moment, their arrows striking one of the Treewomen in the chest. She fell to her knees screaming, and Fiorlen followed up with a second shot through the eye. The hag fell lifeless to the ground, and the other dark Coedaoine howled in rage before breaking into the Forest.

"Madán!" Fiorlen hissed. She sent another shaft after the retreating forms, but it careened off a tree and went wide. "We can't let them Sing!" she shouted, breaking into a sprint and nocking another arrow on the fly, so fast that Genevieve had no chance of catching up. In the flash of a half moment, the Sapling was up in the trees and lost to sight.

Genevieve turned back to the fight close at hand and tried to take aim at one of the Treemen or Arsoíche, but she held off for risk of hitting Tërimrush or Chadric.

As if things weren't already confusing and dangerous enough, the main battle out in the clearing was now pushing its way closer and closer to the tumbling forms of Tërimrush and that blasted Horse, and Genevieve was losing track of who was friend and who was foe.

Two Lizards were holding their own against a number of Flowers that she was fairly certain were part of the Thornsword Brethren. Two Rhinos and an Elephant were battling a pair of those hideous Snakemen, who lashed out with fangs and swords alike. One of the Keras managed to gore a Snakeman with his horn before the Serpent whipped around and dug his fangs clear through the thick skin of the Rhinoceros. They both fell to the ground with a crash.

Genevieve felt a ripple of air above her. She had just enough time to swing her bow up and fire at a Corrupted owl that had dropped silently out of the trees. The giant Bird screeched as the arrow plunged into its breastbone, and it flailed wildly toward the ground before slamming into the base of a nearby tree. It flopped over once, twice, in a tangle of feathers, and then lay still.

Forcing herself to control her breathing, Genevieve wiped the sweat from her brow. What madness! Snakemen; Pigmen; huge, bloodthirsty Owls! What was she doing in the middle of a battle? She should be *home*, worrying about some boy at school, worrying about her driver's test; and here she was with a bow and arrow, like some delusional idiot! She might actually *die* here in these wretched clothes, fighting against a slew of talking plants and animals.

"I've had it!" she howled in frustration. God help her, anything that got in her way was getting shot through the skull. She nocked another arrow and loosed it at a slithering Venus flytrap. It was dark red and seemed violent, so she assumed it had to be Corrupted. One of the pulsating, bulbous sacs—which she guessed was an abdomen or something—burst open as the shaft passed through, spraying out a viscous white goo. The Plant toppled, writhing and quivering, tentacles slapping meaninglessly at the air, until it heaved once and stopped moving.

Eight more arrows, and only a hundred monsters to go, she thought sourly. *Just fantastic.*

Those war machines that had been launching spears and cannonballs at Lupír and Arshúil had now been retrained on the battlefield. With a low howl of rushing air, a massive boulder slammed into the ground with thunderous reverberation, throwing a huge plume of dirt into the air and flattening three or four Rodents of unusual size. Two of the Loxon warriors, the largest on the field that Genevieve could see, roared a challenge at the looming war machines and charged, bent on tearing them apart piece by piece.

Her attention was snatched back to their own little battle as Stanley gave a throat-cracking cry and swung his sword wide at the kneecap of a Treeman that Rhydderch had already wounded. Though it was an amateurish attack, the sword bit deep; but the Corrupted was fast, and his staff struck Stanley's sword arm in retaliation.

⌇

NOLAN WAS CLOSE ENOUGH TO hear the bone crack. Stanley dropped Link with a cry, rolling to the ground and clasping his arm.

A new rush of adrenaline made the world around Nolan slow down to a crawl, and he realized just how absurd this whole thing was. They were a bunch of *kids* playing weekend warriors with swords they could barely hold, facing nightmarish foes roughly the size of houses who were determined to kill them all. What were they thinking? They should've listened to Crannhyn; they should've stayed at the nice silver Lake with the drunk Frog and the giant Alligator. They weren't heroes; they were middle-school students, for crying out loud!

But then it happened—something snapped inside of Nolan, too. His eyes narrowed on his best friend, who was writhing in pain, and white-hot anger coursed through his body. Without a second thought, Nolan gave a war cry of his own and launched himself at the Treeman who'd struck Stanley.

He was well over twice Nolan's height, but the boy saw only red through tears of rage. Holding Unnamed with both hands, Nolan swung and hacked with all his might at the Greenman's wounded knee. The Coeduine screamed in pain as the entire leg came away with a splash of sap-blood and sinew, and he toppled backward.

Nolan was on him before he even hit the ground. He spun the sword around, grasped it again in both hands, and slammed the blade into the fallen Treeman's chest. As tough as the bark-skin was, the steel slid through and buried itself firmly in the earth below. The Corrupted gave a wet, raspy gasp and was no more.

I did it! flashed through the haze of Nolan's berserk rage. *Dear God, I've killed him! He's dead!* But it was more a feeling of relief than a statement of guilt. He wiped the tears from his eyes and whipped his head around to see Emery cowering at the tree line with his arms around Stanley's waist.

Nolan's attention was drawn to Chadric, and his mouth dropped open. The prince was a dervish of sword-fighting grace, and the remaining Treeman was quickly dispatched, falling under a maelstrom of precision blows. Before the body collapsed, Chadric turned to Rhydderch and Agenor, who were once again locked in a rancorous one-on-one battle.

For an older man, Rhydderch was his own whirlwind of tight, fierce motion, using his pickaxes to attack the Boarman again and again; but Agenor's glaive was a well-suited weapon, and he was able to deflect the blows. Both were huffing and puffing from the exertion, but Nolan thought he detected a flash of panic in Agenor's wide eyes. His shoulder wound was preventing a full range of motion, and Rhydderch was clearly using it to his advantage.

In desperation, the Old King feinted a sweep with the staff-end of the glaive, and Rhydderch fell for it, leaping backward; but Agenor reversed the weapon mid-swing, and the axe head hacked Rhydderch between his neck and shoulder; a few inches deeper, and his arm would have been severed completely. Rhydderch stumbled backward with a cry, and Nolan and Chadric bolted for the monk. But even as they ran, Agenor raised the glaive above his head to finish him off.

"You're mine now, you old prune!" he gloated, glorying in the moment of victory.

But that split second was all Rhydderch needed. Using his good arm, he flung a pickaxe at Agenor, and with a squelching sound, it imbedded in the Boarman's chest.

Agenor rocked backward, surprise and disbelief flooding his eyes as he looked down at the blade buried in his sternum. The glaive was still held above his head, until his five-thousand-year-old body realized what happened, and his hands slackened, dropping the staff.

With a shout, Chadric leapt into view with a backward spin, and Agenor's great head flew off his shoulders. It landed in the dirt and leaves on the Forest floor and rolled to a stop, face up, with the Boar's tusks frozen in a death rictus, as the body slid to the ground.

"Never spare the moment to gloat, you old fool!" Rhydderch managed through clenched teeth before he fell back with a ragged wheeze.

Fiorlen appeared from the Forest at that moment. Her eyes fell upon the corpse of the Old King, and she nodded with a glint of approval in her eyes. "Good riddance!" she said before turning to the others. "One of the Treewomen escaped, but gylináma will very soon be at an end. I think we will be all right."

"Fiorlen, here!" Chadric called out. "Come quick! Rhydderch!"

But the Sapling's path was barred by two hulking forms barreling through the clearing. With all that had happened in the last minute or two, Nolan had almost forgotten about Tërimrush and Arsoíche locked in their own battle.

The She-bear roared and swiped out with her giant paw, her claws raking the long face of the Nightmare. But instead of blood pouring from the wounds, the Corrupted was leaking something akin to molten rock. Both had taken a multitude of wounds, and much of Tërimrush's fur had been singed and was now smoldering, with bald spots of blackened flesh showing through. The Nightmare's mane was a roaring trail of fire behind her, and her double set of fangs were drooling with yellowish-green venom.

The poison from her bites was beginning to affect Tërimrush. She moved sluggishly, and several of her attacks missed completely. Sensing the advantage, Arsoíche neighed and bore down hard, pummeling the Bear with her hooves.

Tërimrush fell back on her haunches and reared to her full height, but she overbalanced and toppled backward. The Nightmare was on her at once, slamming her into the dirt with another attack of those colossal hooves.

Emery screamed and clasped Stanley so tightly, the older boy winced from his broken arm.

Tërimrush was able to push the Horse back with her hind legs and roll shakily to her feet. Just as Arsoíche charged yet again, Tërimrush managed to strong-arm her into a bear hug. She lifted Arsoíche completely off the ground and tossed her to the side, using the momentum to flip over so that she was now straddling the bucking Horse; and with an incredible burst of strength, she clasped onto Arsoíche's rib cage and stood up, her claws sinking into the flesh. Though the smoke and embers burned her terribly, she refused to let go.

The Horse's eyes widened in fear, and she thrashed and floundered, whinnying in panic, but she was held fast by the crushing might of the mother Bear.

Tërimrush jerked Arsoíche's spine toward her great belly and latched her jaws around the back of the Nightmare's neck. A fount of molten blood spewed out of the wound, and both Bear and Horse burst into flames. Tërimrush roared through her clenched teeth, but she still refused to let go.

Emery shouted and tried to make a dash for his friend, but Stanley gripped him with his good arm and held him fast.

A snarl shook the woods. Tërimrush wrenched her jaws one way, the Horse's rib cage the other. With a terrible crack, she broke Arsoíche's back, and the Corrupted horse went limp in her arms. Tërimrush flung the twisted body away from her, and it slid in a crumpled heap, the flames finally extinguished.

Everyone stood dumbfounded as Tërimrush fell to all fours, wobbling a bit. She surveyed her handiwork and then let loose such a roar of victory that the humans clapped their hands to their ears. The Bear stumbled, and Emery raced to her side, tears streaming down his tiny face.

It was painful just to look at her, singed and burned as she was, and woozy from the Nightmare's poison.

"Please help her, Fiorlen!" Emery cried out, stroking the Bear's ear, one of the few uninjured parts on her body.

The Treegirl tried Singing a few notes, but everyone's injuries remained unchanged; so she tried again, Singing with greater inflection, straining the muscles in her throat, pleading for the Song of Healing to work. But, alas, she simply wasn't powerful enough.

As her voice fell away, Fiorlen shook her head sadly. "I'm sorry," she said, looking to Stanley, Rhydderch, and Tërimrush in turn. "These wounds are beyond my abilities to heal."

Stanley grunted, the monk nodded with a grimace, and Emery burst into wails. A noise from behind threatened to bring new misfortune, but Fiorlen's face lit up, and she cried out, "Father?"

Ysgafn bounded into view, followed by the remnants of the rescue team. Trahaearn drew up short, confusion and a touch of anger crossing his face. "What are *you* doing here?" he demanded.

"Father!" Fiorlen shouted again as she raced into his arms. "I knew you'd be all right, I just knew you would!"

Ysgafn gave her a loving squeeze and looked deep into her eyes. "My dear child-wealth, why have you come here? I am both so happy and so furious to see you here, Fiorlen!"

"I am sorry, my lords," Prince Chadric interrupted. "We have but moments of gylináma left, and we may be attacked at any time. Will you Sing over Rhydderch, Stanley, and Tërimrush? They have received serious wounds and need your skill."

CRANNHYN'S TEAM COMPRISED LORD MABON and his daughter, Afanen. Arshúil had been able to get them within only a couple hundred yards of the entrance to the Temple, and precious minutes had been lost battling through a knot of Corrupted creatures, several Aossí conscripts, and a handful of dark Treefolk. Yet they had pressed on relentlessly until they neared the entrance.

And now, Eorden, the last of the guards outside the Sanctuary, lay dead at Crannhyn's feet. The Eldest had known him before he had chosen to side with Bàsisolc, and he allowed a quick moment of remorse to pass through him. He abhorred death in all its facets, and to end the life of a former friend was an especially great sadness. Crannhyn the Mighty sighed and shook himself before making a last dash for the demeglwys.

Above them, Lupír screeched, and Crannhyn glanced up at the darkened sky as he ran. The Bat and the Eagle were wrapped sinuously around one another, struggling to remain airborne, as they fought for an advantage. Arshúil was slightly stronger, but Lupír was slightly quicker.

In all his long, long summers, Crannhyn had rarely seen such a vicious battle. They were literally tearing chunks of flesh out of each other. Lupír sank his long fangs into the shoulder joint of the golden Eagle, and Arshúil cried out in pain and frustration.

But the Bat held on too long, and Arshúil shoved his head under Lupír's neck. He dealt the deathblow with his curved beak, tearing clean through the Bat's exposed throat. Grasping the fluttering creature with his talons, Arshúil slammed Lupír to the ground and stood upon the broken body, wings outstretched, head cocked proudly to the side, screaming a victory cry that echoed far across the plain and out into the early night.

And again Crannhyn sighed, for he had Awakened Lupír just as he had Awakened Arshúil. Even though it was unavoidable, the guardian's death still pierced his heart like the loss of a child-wealth.

Death, it seemed, still continued to rule Morsden Forest. After millennia spent toiling against Corruption, and uncounted centuries after creating the Master Song, death still exuded a power he could not defeat on his own. Was this all that could ever be? A struggle with no final and lasting victory? Or would this all be just a distant memory someday, like the birth of the world?

The Eldest honestly didn't know. With a final glance toward Mabon and Afanen, he stepped grimly into the demeglwys, ready to face his brother, the first and most powerful of the Corrupted.

33

Sacrifice

A strong Song of Binding greeted Crannhyn, Mabon, and Afanen as they entered the Temple during the last moments of the time-between-times. But Crannhyn, as saddened as he was by the senseless death around him, simply pushed aside the darkness with a melodic word, as if it were nothing more than fleeting vapor. The sounds of battle outside were starting to taper off now that Lupír was dead, as was the majority of Bàsisolc's army—though not without significant losses to Crannhyn's side, as well.

The Most Evil didn't appear particularly disturbed by his brother's entrance. In fact, he was scowling at one of his minions. "Well, it seems you were wrong in your assessment after all, Cathmor."

Crannhyn looked down and saw young Quinn Taylor cradling her grand-mother's head in her lap, tears running down her face as she stroked Audrey's gray hair with a hand that still clasped the precious jewel. Blood was seeping through the older woman's shirt like a large red poppy blossom.

"What have you done, Brother?" Crannhyn whispered, his face bunched up into a mask of sorrow and regret.

Only then did Bàsisolc deign to address the Eldest. He sneered and spat out, "Only what needed to be done to control the power of the Master Song, dear *Brother!*"

Crannhyn shook his head slowly. "The power of the Master Song is not for our kind, and this you know. It can be Sung only by humans. What did you expect to gain through all this butchery?"

Bàsisolc looked prepared to provide a scathing retort, but he was cut off by a small, faint voice.

⌒

"CRANNHYN, PLEASE...." QUINN SPOKE THROUGH her scorching tears, not daring to look up into the face of the mightiest of the Coedaoine. "Help me grandmother."

The Greenman sighed and lowered his eyes to the floor. "My dear child-wealth, I am sorry. The time-between-times slips away too swiftly for a Song of Life. I cannot redress such injury in so short a time."

Quinn looked up now through the curtains of her greasy blonde hair, her eyes puffy, her mouth twisted in anger. "I *hate* you," she said in a forceful whisper. "I hate the lot of you. But you, especially, for makin' this Master Song. What power has love in the face of *this*?" She pulled her grandmother tighter in her arms, and the woman gave a little gasp of pain.

"Q-Qui—you...you don't mean that," Gran managed, her eyes fluttering open, bloodshot and glassy.

"And now you see, mighty Brother, that your efforts have been in vain. All your supposed *virtues* boil down to little more than *power*—who will wield it, who will be controlled by it, and who will put false hopes in it." Bàsisolc's voice dripped with sanctimony.

Turning to his underlings, he gathered himself to his full height and exhaled. "Come. The hour has fled us, and we must try to unlock the Verse again tomorrow evening. Now that Lupír is no longer a hindrance, it should prove all the easier." He faced Crannhyn again. "Now let us fight, dear Brother; for once you are dead, as well, I can collect the whelp and console her over the loss of her grandmother."

But Crannhyn apparently had no intention of rising to the challenge. Instead, he cocked his head as if he were listening to a secret from beyond the Veil; and, just as sorrowful as he was moments before, he now gave his peculiar chuckle.

"Gylináma has not yet expired," he said. "Let me tell you a little secret, brother of mine. The power of Love, that greatest of virtues—indeed, the divine energy of the universe—is rooted in something you will never understand: *sacrifice*. Yes, that is true. But not the sacrifice of your servants, nor the sacrifice of your precious time or resources—no! Only through *self-sacrifice* is the power truly released. And now I declare to you, wretched and unlearned: Behold, the virtue of Love!"

Quinn had bent low over her grandmother, their tangled hair mixing together; and as she held her beloved gran tightly, the diamond, still clutched in her angry fist, cut into the palm of her hand. She used the backs of her fingers to caress the old woman's face one more time as she bent even closer.

With her lips a breath away from her grandmother's ear, she whispered so quietly, even the Coedaoine couldn't hear. "Yore right, Gran, I don't mean it… none of it. I love ya, and I always will."

Her grandmother arched her back as she gasped for her last breath, and Quinn lifted her head, swallowing a sob. Her tears splashed down onto her grandmother's face and onto the gemstone still clenched in her fist.

And the diamond shattered.

It broke into a million tiny droplets of glistening light, and the tinkling sound of heavenly music filtered through the air. The pieces sprayed out into a cloud that enveloped Gran's head and continued to grow, surrounding her and Quinn, reflecting the candlelight in glorious hues of gold and bronze, like raindrops in the setting sun of Blue Time. The cloud lifted them both five, ten, twenty, thirty, feet into the air—high above even Crannhyn's towering head.

They were held aloft by the dense fog that partially shaded their floating forms, and the light that emanated from within grew brighter and whiter until Bàsisolc and his minions, even Crannhyn and his companions, were forced to hide their faces from the brilliance.

Inside the light, Quinn could see as she'd never seen before. Colors—such colors in a spectrum beyond the Veil of this world—flared to life, swaying and swirling to the growing volume of music as she and Gran, with her head still in Quinn's lap, began spinning within the cloud. The vivid colors permeated their skin, and a voice began to Sing softly.

Quinn realized it was her own! At first, it was barely a whisper, so that she could just hear it above the music; but soon it grew louder, stronger, and more confident.

From out of her own mouth poured words in the First Tongue that no Song of Translation could ever hope to render. They were words full of bittersweet emotion, sad and yet strangely beautiful, joyful yet melancholy, ultimately sincere and still heartrending.

Indeed, love was a delicate blend of emotions.

Gran was Awake in Quinn's arms. Her eyes were clear, and she reached up to stroke her granddaughter's face.

"I give it to her," Gran whispered. "Let it pass to her."

No sooner had the words left her lips than the cloud of light surged outward in every direction with concussive frenzy. It poured forth with the explosion of a thousand thunderclaps, and the Coedaoine jerked their hands to their tipped ears, but to no avail. The detonation rocked through the Sanctuary, passed beyond the confines of the great tree, and hurtled out over the field, slamming into the remaining combatants and knocking them over.

When the shock wave of power reached Nolan and his friends at the farthest end of the clearing, they were blown backward as if assaulted by a tidal wave of Song—musical momentum that moved unhindered with its own wind and continued to speed its way to the furthest corners of Morsden Deep.

Electricity coursed through their bodies as if they'd been kissed by a lightning bolt. The air between them crackled, and energy leapt in arcs of dizzying color, though it didn't really hurt, fortunately.

Nolan pulled Emery and Stanley closer, but not out of fear. Chadric placed a reassuring hand on Genevieve's shoulder, their eyes wide with wonder. Everyone knew where this divine force had come from: Quinn had opened the diamond.

And then it pulled back in on itself, as if time had shifted into reverse—just as a surging deluge, even a tsunami of unstoppable force, eventually rolls back out to sea. The sound of a mighty wind roared past them and exploded back into the Sanctuary, coiling and pouring into Quinn's body, until Audrey could see every vein, every organ, every particle of the teenager's existence, alight with pure white energy.

And then, with an anticlimactic *pop*, the thunderous noise, the swirling winds, the tinkling music, and the words of the Love Verse were engulfed in deafening silence as Quinn and her grandmother floated softly to the ground to land on their feet.

Gran's shirt still flowered with blood, but she seemed to be feeling better than Quinn remembered ever seeing her. She looked over at her granddaughter, who returned the gaze, and they both burst into outrageous laughter, falling into each other's arms until the tears flowed and their sides hurt, leaving them gasping for breath.

Quinn couldn't have explained why, but it *was* funny. Somehow, it was joyful and dreadfully hilarious; and yet it was so somber and serious, they just had to laugh.

Crannhyn the Mighty, the eldest of all living creatures, cleared his throat and looked on with a smile.

"I'm sorry, Lord Crannhyn." Gran managed to hold up a hand, trying to gain control of her laughter. "I forgot you were there."

"Indeed," the Greenman replied. "Do not trouble yourself. That happens all the time."

Quinn realized his voice sounded multifaceted, like he was always speaking in three-part harmony. It was similar to Bàsisolc's, though much more enjoyable to listen to.

"Goodness, Quinn!" her grandmother exclaimed. "Look at you! Your skin is glowing!" And this set them both to laughing again.

After a few moments of struggling to regain their composure (and failing, for the most part), Quinn finally managed to get out, "What about Bàs and his toadies?"

The thrill of the Love Verse was slightly more manageable now, but Quinn still felt as if all her senses were set ablaze. Sounds were crystal clear, colors were vibrant, and her vision was perfectly sharp. She could smell a whiff of ozone and the fragrance of rose petals hanging in the air, along with candle wax and the reek of stale sweat. She tasted salt and her own bad breath, and for that, she wished the Verse wasn't *quite* so powerful. Her skin tingled with exhilaration, and she felt strong enough to take on the Most Evil barehanded.

Bàsisolc and his cohorts stood in stunned silence, like cattle meekly waiting to see what fearful fate would befall them. It was only when Quinn studied Bàs's eyes that she realized he was blind, as were Cathmor and the others.

"Deaf and mute, too," Crannhyn added, having read the surprised expression on her face. "The Master Song often has that effect on the Corrupted. Of course, *he* wouldn't have known that." He snapped his long, branch-like fingers next to Bàsisolc's ears. "I do not, however, think it will be permanent, unfortunately."

"What d'we do with 'em?" Quinn wondered, her fingers moving to where her daggers, Lively and Spirited, would've been if Eorden hadn't taken them from her.

Crannhyn cocked his head at her. "Well, I wouldn't kill them. Would you?"

Quinn paused and then shook her head. "No. No, yore right, of course. But ya'll see that he's locked up, right? Can ya build, like, a prison or somethin', hidden in the Veil? Not a very nice one, mind ya. Somethin' with rats, maybe? And no toilet."

Crannhyn chuckled and then turned his head, as if to listen to a voice he alone could hear. "I will take care of the situation," he said before turning to the others. "Lord Mabon, would you be so kind as to escort my brother and his sad sycophants out of my Sanctuary, please?"

Before Lord Mabon led the Corrupted out into the night, he and his daughter turned to face Quinn. They bowed in respect.

"Hail, Otherworlder, guardian of the Love Verse!" Afanen said in a clear, high voice.

Quinn gave a self-conscious bow and a nervous little wave, slightly embarrassed.

After they'd led the shell-shocked Coedaoine outside, she turned to her grandmother and said, "Did ya notice that Treewoman's got *berries* for hair?"

Gran giggled. "They're quite lovely, I suppose. *Berry* lovely, one might say." She and Quinn broke into laughter.

"Come, guardian," Crannhyn said with a sweep of his hand, gesturing to the Sanctuary's entrance. "Though we cannot Sing again until tomorrow evening, we must still do what we can for the injured, Corrupted and Awakened alike. Will you accompany me?"

Quinn nodded in agreement and clasped hands with her grandmother.

"Well, at least *some* humans obey me," he said. Then, seeing their puzzled expressions, he added, "Oh, your little friends think I don't know they disobeyed my direct command not to follow us through the Veil. Come, watch me give a stern rebuke to the future king of Tírcluddaithe. It may amuse you." The corners of Crannhyn's mouth quirked into the tiniest of smiles. "It does me."

As they walked together, leaving the demeglwys behind, Quinn noticed a blazing image on the back of her right hand. It was starting to fade, but it left a pearlescent glimmer that could be seen if she tilted her head at a particular angle, almost like a holographic tattoo.

The luminescent image was a single glyph, beautiful and rainbow colored, in the First Tongue.

It said, "Love."

34

Tattoos and Memories

Pyres burned throughout the night, three of them: one for the Awakened, one for the Corrupted, and Lupír was honored with his own, though Agenor and Arsoíche were burned rather unceremoniously on the heap with the Corrupted.

Thus ended the long life of Old King Hynfel, unpitied and dishonored, a source of derision and an object lesson to Aossí children-wealth for many summers to come.

Not very many people seemed to remember that it was a simple historian, one they thought perhaps might be a little mad himself, who had finally put an end to the dreaded Boarman. But Rhydderch didn't seem to mind.

Quinn wasn't concerned about Agenor. The only thing that bothered her was the fact that throughout all the corpses of the Corrupted, none of those hideous Spiders had been found. She wondered if they'd bailed or had somehow survived the battle to sneak away. In either event, it disturbed her to know those monsters were still on the loose. Ysgafn had his work cut out for him, even with the Nightmare's death.

Fallon, Lord Trahaearn's son, was mourned as a hero, as were the Loxon, the Keras, the Uropsid, the Thornsword Brethren, and all the other Awakened who had given their lives trying to protect the Love Verse. It overwhelmed Quinn when she thought of all those who had died trying to get to her, but she didn't feel any guilt, and even a swell of thankfulness washed over her because her gran was miraculously still alive.

Her grandmother and Rhydderch spent most of the next day together, trying to help the wounded, though there wasn't much they could really do. They talked and giggled, and Quinn saw them hold hands briefly, but she decided against saying anything about it. After all, there seemed to be a lot of love floating around, even against the sad backdrop of funeral pyres and injured Awakened. That might have been the Verse working through Quinn, or it could have just been the camaraderie and relief that follow the fevered pitch of battle.

It was probably a little of both.

Stanley's shattered arm was healed, though he said it still ached terribly. Rhydderch's shoulder bore a long pink scar, but he could still use his arm; and in time, he was assured, it would be as good as anyone his age could expect. While the Song of Healing could mend what was wrong, it could not fully remove the marks of an injury. All the children would have some scars that would last the rest of their lives, but they were all right with that, considering the alternative.

Tërimrush seemed to fare the worst. Though the effects of the poison were arrested by the Treefolk's ministrations, and the multitude of burns had been tended to, whole clumps of her fur were gone, leaving behind blistered new skin. Ysgafn didn't know if the fur would grow back or if she'd have bald spots from then on, but the great Bear didn't seem to mind one way or the other. She spent a lot of the day nuzzling Emery and making motherly rumbling noises toward the little boy. She also had a quiet conversation with Lady Afanen, who wholeheartedly recognized the She-bear's turn from Corruption, even if the Treewoman seemed to carry herself a little primly, as if to say, "Could anyone have expected otherwise?"

Cadfan and King Orbo were relatively unscathed. They had wanted to go with Crannhyn, but, as Arshúil had been otherwise detained, they'd made themselves useful by bolstering the army and had acquitted themselves like true warriors. At the memorial service for the fallen, they received a special word of thanks from the Eldest, and Cadfan beamed with pride at having his name mentioned in the same breath as a king's.

The great Eagle had left at daybreak to bring news to his namesake village and then carry word to the guardians of Scáthán Lake. Cadfan had laughed loudly when he imagined aloud what Yale and the council would think when a jolly giant Eagle landed in the cornfields. He made Arshúil promise to mention his commendation from the Eldest.

Lord Boujòn and the Brethren also left at daybreak to return to Suas. Arshúil agreed to let the Flowers bring word of Bàsisolc's capture to the Treefolk city. They had rejected the notion of traveling through portanuam, deciding rather to return home like a victorious, brightly colored army—after all, there were still Corrupted in the Deep, and they were sworn to protect the Forest. That was the Thornsword—always looking for the next glorious battle. Their tenacity made the children laugh, though they were more than a little sorry to see the Rose and his Flowers march off with the rising sun.

The day passed swiftly, and as the sun once again sank behind the ridge of Morsden Deep, Crannhyn gathered all the principal people together. Bonfires were lit for an evening meal, and though it wasn't much of a feast, everyone ate his fill.

⌒

NOLAN WAS ANXIOUS TO BE away. He'd been panicking the whole day, thinking of their return to Ireland—what would they face? Would his mother freak out? Knowing her, the armed forces would've been summoned by now, and the kids' faces would be plastered on every milk carton across the country.

Strangely, other than the mundane things he worried about, Nolan felt no overwhelming fear. Perhaps those demons had been exorcised, for the bruises around his neck had finally started to fade. Instead, he found himself thinking about small things, such as the fact that it had been, what, a week since he'd last used his inhaler?

When he first reunited with Quinn, there'd been a second's awkwardness—on his part, not hers, for she'd been beaming from ear to ear; in fact, she'd seemed to glow.

After he had mumbled an apology for letting her get kidnapped, she'd looked askance at him and said, "How was that *yore* fault? Yore not me bodyguard, Nols—and ya came after me, even though Crannhyn told ya not to. Ya coulda *died*. But ya came after me all the same. That's all that matters, mate—ya came after me."

Then she'd slugged him on the shoulder and smirked. "Lookit, I got a tattoo 'fore any of ya lot did!" She showed the pearly holograph on the back of her hand, receiving several *oohs* and *aahs* from the boys.

A few minutes before Blue Time fell, Crannhyn cleared his throat to get everyone's attention. It wasn't very difficult, considering he was the tallest being around by ten feet, and his unique triple-voice resonated across the clearing.

"My thanks and deep appreciation to all who sacrificed and struggled bravely against Corruption and my hardly lamented brother. I am in your service and debt.

"There remain a few loose ends to address, and with your permission, I will do so now."

Nolan allowed himself a discreet smile. A *few* loose ends?

"First, the High King is still missing, presumably in search of his son. Once gylináma has fallen, we will attempt to speak with Queen Gayle to see how Her Majesty fares at the Citadel City."

Nolan noticed that Crannhyn kept his gaze averted from the monk's apprentice, between whose shoulder blades the sword remained, still wrapped in deerskin. "We will need to begin a search for King Alaric at once.

"Second," he continued, "and just as important, though my brother remains in custody, as do many of his Corrupted, I want to ask you all for advice. Now that the Love Verse is opened and once again under human guardianship, I am of the mind that a quest for the remaining Verses should be undertaken."

Several Treefolk gasped. Nolan noticed their glowing yellow eyes widen in surprise and their bodies grow tense as grumblings were heard around the fire. He wasn't quite sure why there was such a startled reaction among the Coedaoine. To him, it seemed the logical thing to do.

"Lord Crannhyn," Ysgafn said, raising a hand. His wife and daughter were snuggled next to him. "That could prove an arduous task. No one knows where the remaining Verses are hidden."

The Eldest nodded. "That was, indeed, the point. No one, not even myself, has full knowledge of the locations of the other Gemstones. Some are even hidden on the Other Side of the Veil. While the locations of the Temples are all securely up here"—the Eldest tapped the side of his head with a forefinger and chuckled—"and I have a number of excellent guesses where the other Verses may be, I propose that we task Quinn and her friends to collect them—with our guidance and protection, of course."

He looked down at Nolan, and a tiny smile tugged at his lips. "Perhaps they will mind my voice a little better from now on."

"But they're just *children*," Audrey said. "It's too dangerous!"

"Dangerous, yes, but not uncommonly so, at least not with our help," Crannhyn returned. "It isn't as if I'm suggesting we send them out on their own. And if I recall correctly, you were younger than they when you first sought the Love Verse alongside Lord Ysgafn. The stones can be opened only by you or Quinn, after all."

"But, my lord," Mabon interjected, "if Bàsisolc is contained, wouldn't it be best to let the Verses remain hidden?"

Crannhyn was silent a few seconds. "I have given this much thought during the years of my isolation. The Master Song was *made* for the sons of Men. Just because some are easily Corrupted does not mean *all* should be punished. I believe it is time for Mankind to have a second chance. And I, for one, would like to see the Song guarded by the innocent hearts of children rather than by kings and warriors."

He cocked his head to the side and listened a moment. "In fact, I'm *sure* of it," he said finally. "And furthermore, though Bàsisolc is contained, there are other Corrupted out there who I believe are now vying for control of the Master Song. It appears my wayward brother has Awakened a long-sleeping dragon, and the hunt for the Song has been taken up again."

"There's a *dragon?*" Emery gulped.

Crannhyn looked down at the boy with a smirk. "I was speaking metaphorically. I hope to the Composer he's not Awakened a *real* dragon."

"Hold on a tic." Quinn raised her hand. "Yore just volunteerin' us to go huntin' for these other Verses? I'm not shore I wanna risk life and limb again. I just wanna go home. I didn't mean to open the Love Verse to begin with."

"Actually, it was your grandmother who opened the Verse. It was her sacrifice, blended with your tears, that moved the Verse. She simply transferred the Verse's virtue to you."

Quinn started and stared at Audrey. "*You* opened the Verse?"

Audrey nodded. "I was dying, and I didn't want to leave you defenseless against Bàsisolc." Her blush was visible even in the dim light of the fire. "And, to be honest, I *hoped* the Love Verse would spare my life."

"The love of life is important," Crannhyn said. "It is not selfish to want to live; the Verse recognizes that. Your intent is what set it free."

"I hope you're not angry with me, Quinn," the older woman said.

Quinn raised her eyebrows. "Don't be daft, Gran. I'd open a hundred Verses if it would keep ya with me. I just thought it was *me* who'd somehow figured out how to open it."

"And you did," Crannhyn assured her. "Your tears shattered the Stone. But, such as it is, the quest has begun. The Verses will call to one another, eager to be reunited. I cannot say it will be easy, but with our help, I believe it is doable; and, more important, it is *necessary*."

Quinn regarded her friends, who'd gone through trials upon trials just to save her. "Well, what d'ya lot think? Are ya game for a bit more fun?" She smirked at Nolan. "Ya up for another pan galactic gargle blaster?"

Nolan didn't get the joke, once again. He'd been sitting in stunned silence during this entire exchange. He'd been so eager to get home, he hadn't given a single thought to ever returning to Tírcluddaithe, let alone agreeing to subject himself to more danger by searching all over the place for other Verses and invariably coming across yet even more Corrupted *things*.

And yet, isn't that what heroes did?

But what surprised him was that Genevieve responded first. Though her eyes were on Heilyn, she said, "I can't promise I'll come traipsing through the woods with you, nor will I agree to something without fully understanding it, but I'll support you as best I can."

"Th-thanks, Gen—er, Genevieve," was all Quinn could say, and Audrey smiled at them both.

Stanley was rubbing his mended arm. He caught Nolan's gaze, and they stared at each other meaningfully for several seconds. Finally Stanley nodded.

"I think we're all willing," Nolan said.

"Me, too. I'm in," Emery said, and Tërimrush rumbled a small laugh.

Nolan sighed and rolled his eyes. "You can help us do research on the Internet."

The Translation Song must have worked really well, because none of the Aossí or Coedaoine asked what the Internet was.

"Questers, you will have the full support of the Caevnaóri, and, I daresay, the Aossí and Awakened, since this affects all of Tírcluddaithe—and indeed your world, as well." Crannhyn didn't, however, seem disposed to explain just *how* it could affect their world.

"But if you are willing, then at gylináma, before Lord Ysgafn sends you home, we will Sing a permanent Translation Song over you, and a Song of Union, and you will be united as a group."

"Like the Fellowship of the Ring," Nolan said.

"Only that didn't turn out so great for them," Stanley pointed out.

"Nah, no worries," Quinn said. "It worked out all right in the end. But, Nols, ya've gotta read yoreself some *Hitchhiker's Guide*, mate. I'm tired of ya not gettin' the jokes."

"Ain't no hitchhikers in the Veil," he said, still not getting it.

"So, hey…umm, do we get tattoos like Quinn's?" Emery wanted to know.

Crannhyn chuckled. "Only if she gives you one of the Verses."

The moment Blue Time fell, the children and the Aossí and King Orbo were in Bàsisolc's deserted pavilion for a little privacy. The only Treefolk present were Ysgafn and his family.

Prince Chadric sat on a simple stool, and before him in midair shimmered something that looked extremely similar to the Veil, only it was a hazy, see-through oval, like a badly made mirror. Ysgafn Sang a few more words, and it snapped into crystal clarity.

Within the oval, the children perceived an extremely beautiful middle-aged woman. She was dressed regally and had soft, wavy brown hair that matched her son's, but her eyes were a vivid green instead of Chadric's unusual gold.

"Hello, Mother," the prince said breathlessly.

Queen Gayle's hand flew to her chest. "You look as if you're standing in the room with me!" she exclaimed. "Oh, Chadric, it's good to see you!" Tears formed in the corners of her eyes.

"I've missed you, Mother," Chadric said, wiping the back of his hand across his face. "I— You understand why I had to leave, don't you?"

"Yes, I do now," Gayle replied. "Lorne has told me. But I knew you weren't hurt. I just knew it, down in my heart.…"

Chadric's voice cracked as he said, "Is—is Uncle Dubric treating you well?"

Worry lines creased the queen's face. She looked beyond the floating mirror, as if addressing someone else in the room with her. "Lorne, you are sure there is no way my brother-in-law can eavesdrop on this, er, whatever it's called?"

The offscreen voice of the Treeman answered, "Quite so, Your Majesty. Dubric doesn't even know *I'm* here."

High Queen Gayle squared her shoulders and faced her son again. "Your uncle has sent away all the under-kings on worthless errands, under the pretext of searching for you. Your father is somewhere in Morsden Deep, looking for you, as well; meanwhile, Dubric acquires more and more power. I am safe. I feign interest in that wretched woman Basillia. But I fear they seek your life and the life of your father." She paused. "Chadric, *find him*."

"I will, Mother. I swear it."

She nodded and then, as if just then noticing the others in the room, said, "King Orbo, you are well met, sire. And the others...." She inclined her head gracefully.

"I will guard your son's life with my own," the Tiger avowed.

"And we will guard the queen's with ours," Lorne said offscreen.

"May I have just a few minutes alone with Mother?" Chadric asked.

Ysgafn nodded. "Of course."

Fifteen minutes later, they were all gathered around the bonfire with Chadric looking sullen and yet determined at the same time.

"What will you do now?" Nolan asked Cadfan.

"We make for Arshúil and then head into the Deep," the weaponsmith said, holding out his giant hand, and Nolan shook it. "We'll have the Coedaoine send word to you as often as we can. Don't you worry."

Cadfan turned to Quinn and smiled from behind his scruffy beard. "Lass, keep good care of Spirited and Lively! I will see you again soon; I don't doubt it."

"I'll miss ya, Cadfan, and these'll make me think of ya often," she said, patting the knives to show him they were in her possession once again.

The sword maker laughed. "It's nice to be needed. Now, hurry home!" He saluted the Otherworlders. "Swiftness!"

Rhydderch held Audrey's hand. "Too soon, as always."

"I will return, and maybe this time we can convince Crannhyn to let you come see the Rathdowns." Audrey's eyes were welling up with tears.

"I'd like that very much," the old monk replied, giving her a quick kiss on the cheek.

Chadric bowed low to Genevieve. "It has been a great pleasure to have made your acquaintance, my lady. I trust we will meet again soon."

Genevieve blushed. "I can't say I like this place, and I can't say this hasn't been a ruddy nightmare. But I was glad to have met you, Heilyn." She smiled. "Maybe someday." And the fifteen-year-old looked away quickly.

Chadric paid his respects to the Otherworlders and moved to stand next to Cadfan.

King Orbo inclined his head. "Hail, guardians of the Master Song. Of braver children-wealth I have met none. The honor is, has been, and shall remain mine."

"We'll see you again," Stanley replied. "And best of luck finding King Alaric. I'm sure it will turn out all right."

That left only Tërimrush. Emery buried his face in her fur, and she licked his hair with her long red tongue.

"Hush, lad; hush now, my child-wealth," the She-bear consoled him. "This is temporary. When you return, I will be here, back to strength, and ready to find the other Verses with you."

"Nolan won't let me come back!" His voice was muffled by her fur.

Tërimrush looked over at Nolan, then smiled. "If he knows how I will watch over you like my own cub, I'm sure he will."

Emery came to stand by Nolan's side, wiping his eyes and trying to look more like the bigger boys.

Fiorlen tousled his hair, and then, looking to the others, she said, "Are you ready?" Nolan knew she was excited; she'd been talking about how she would be going with Ysgafn and Crannhyn to the Other Side—the first time for her. Tintreach and Bassett flittered around her head, glowing in a dizzy array of colors.

Nolan took one last glance around Morsden Deep. The blue glow of gylináma *did* seem extra magical on this side of the Veil, he decided. He looked at his new friends one last time.

Lady Tegwyn waved good-bye, Tërimrush gave a somber roar, and the Aossí shouted, "Swiftness!"

With a sigh, he nodded. "We're ready."

"Then let's send you home," Crannhyn said, and Ysgafn started to Sing.

⌣

ONCE ON THE OTHER SIDE, it was pretty much how Nolan had imagined it. His mother about had a massive coronary meltdown when he knocked on the huge doors of Rathdowns Manor. She screamed and gathered her children up in her arms, shouting for their father and for Kent and Florence. And then she kept screaming, more and more hysterically.

It was then that Nolan realized she was actually screaming at the giant Treebeings standing in the circular driveway by the fountain, looking rather sheepish.

"I can explain," Nolan began.

⌣

IN THE END, CRANNHYN WAS forced to concede there was just no way the parents were going to be able to accept the truth, try and try as the kids did to explain things as simply as possible. Audrey lost her temper on several occasions when Florence and Darla threatened to phone the police. The fathers seemed the most levelheaded, but that might have been because of the small flask Nolan Sr. had produced and handed off to Kent Taylor, who, pastor or not, had taken a couple swigs.

Very little of the time-between-times was left, and the Eldest had to make a decision. Loath as he was to try to alter human minds, he reasoned that it was similar to the Song of Translation, after all; the brain just needed to be *acclimatized*. And while Crannhyn couldn't exactly implant false memories, he could strongly *suggest* an alternative rendering of the facts.

So he Sang—over all the adults and the staff at Rathdowns, everyone on the grounds. Ysgafn Sang as well, and so did Fiorlen. They Sang about the *possibility* that it was easier to believe the children had been missing only one night, racing off into the Rathdowns Forest after Audrey, who'd had a bout of whimsy, or perhaps a touch of senility, and had gotten lost in the sprawling forest. It was possible, wasn't it?

These children were heroes, Crannhyn suggested. They saved Audrey (which really *was* true), and that was how they'd gotten their bumps and bruises.

Yes, they had saved Audrey. She was a dear, sweet old lady. Perhaps a trifle barmy. (Audrey hadn't liked that, but Crannhyn had just chuckled.) You know how she is with her stories. This time, they just got the best of her. But now she's fine. Look, they're all just fine. They were missing for only a day. Doesn't that make much more sense than a twenty-foot Treebeing from the Hidden Lands?

The adults, save for Audrey, seemed catatonic when Crannhyn, Ysgafn, and Fiorlen quit Singing. There were just a few minutes of Blue Time left.

"Lead them into the house—they'll come to in about ten minutes," Ysgafn told the children.

"I cannot *promise* this is going to work," Crannhyn said. "I've never done it before; and, to be honest, I'm not sure if it was even right to do so. Nevertheless, we'll be long gone if it didn't work, so that should be all right."

"Oh, thanks," Genevieve snorted. "Leave us to clean up the mess!"

Crannhyn chuckled. "This is *your* Side of the Veil, after all." He bowed to each of them. "Children-wealth, I can truthfully say that you are some of the most unique humans I have ever met. I will see you all again soon! Farewell." And without another word, he started walking back to the cairn.

Looking down at the children, Ysgafn shook his head. "I cannot apologize enough. This whole situation has been my fault. I made a promise, and I was unable to keep it. I was rash and foolish. Can you possibly forgive me?"

This time it was Quinn who snorted. "'It's *perfectly* safe,'" she mocked. "'It's a fifteen-minute walk in the woods, love.' Ya stonkin'-great duffer. What exactly were ya plannin' to do with that giant Bat anyway, huh?"

"Technically, it was your grandmother who said it was a fifteen-minute walk. And you *did* end up perfectly safe; it was just the almost dying a hundred times in between that I miscalculated. That—and not knowing Lupír wouldn't listen to anyone, not even Crannhyn. If we had managed to open the Temple, it would've been a very short quest, indeed. So perhaps it was for the best we were separated." The Treeman sighed. "Truly, I *am* sorry."

Quinn smiled up at him. "All's well that ends well, *Lord* Ysgafn. Now if ya'll excuse me, I'm gonna go have a heart attack."

Fiorlen laughed. "I consider you all my friends, and it is an honor to know you." Her gaze lingered on Stanley.

"We'll see you soon," he told her, returning the grin.

Tintreach and Bassett both gave a short "Hail, Otherworlders!" before buzzing off to join Crannhyn.

And then, without another good-bye, Fiorlen and her father saluted the children, turned, and began walking down the footpath toward the cairn.

The children and Audrey stood in silence on the stone steps of Rathdowns Manner for a few minutes. The parents were still catatonic, and Kent Taylor might have even been snoring a bit.

When they turned to herd the adults back inside the manor, Emery said, "I think I got 'duffer,' but what's 'stonking' mean?"

The other boys groaned.

"Oh, never mind," he said cheerily. "Translation Song got it."

"Great," Nolan said, shaking his head. "After all that, there's still two more weeks in Ireland, *and* we've got the wedding to attend."

Epilogue

The Next Quest

The wedding went off without a hitch, and it was actually quite a beautiful ceremony. Quinn and Genevieve were now stepsisters, officially, and Quinn had gained a couple new cousins whom she seemed to like.

There had been a strange, confusing situation when the police arrived, two days after the children had returned from Tírcluddaithe, saying that the search for the kids and the old woman had been called off.

Darla Marten and Kent Taylor had gazed off into space for several moments before saying, "We're sorry, but our children are right here. They've been here the whole time, Officer. They really are heroes, spending a night out in the forest all by themselves to find that dear, sweet old woman. She's a little barmy, you know."

Try as they might to figure out what had really happened, the police eventually gave up and left, scratching their heads. After all, what could they do? There were the kids, right as rain. There was the old woman, and she did seem a little barmy, dressed the way she was.

One of the Irish cops looked to his partner and shrugged as they slid into the car. "Bloomin' Yanks," he said quietly, as if that explained it all. His partner had to agree.

⌣

WHEN SCHOOL STARTED UP AGAIN in September, Boston was still hotter than usual, Jason Dupree was still a jerk, and Nolan didn't know how they were going to handle another semester at Buckingham after all they'd been through. Life seemed to be going back to the way it always was: Nolan the odd one, Stanley the geek; they couldn't tell *anyone* that they were secretly members of a group of questers tasked with finding the Verses of the Master Song. Typical.

One cool thing, though, was the permanent Translation Song. Nolan was assured to get perfect marks in Spanish, and he'd just started taking Latin as an elective because Quinn took it. He could finally understand what was being said during mass. Stanley was trying out ancient Egyptian and Mandarin from a computer program. He was thinking about trying Romanian next. It was fairly easy to learn vocabulary and pronunciation when you could understand everything you read and heard.

They spent all their free time searching the Internet—the Wii and poor Houston the crab were practically forgotten—but there was little about Treepeople and nothing about the Master Song to be found on Google. Stanley decided he needed to work on his hacker skills, saying maybe the NSA had something in its databases.

Nolan hoped his friend was joking—he didn't relish the idea of getting arrested for a national security breach. Weren't kids tried as adults for that kind of stuff?

It was finally Friday, the first weekend after starting back to school, and Stanley was once again spending the night at Nolan's house. They'd had a good meal of Portobello mushroom burgers with crumbled bleu cheese and caramelized onions. And now, Nolan sat at his desk while Stanley sprawled on the bed.

Nolan had noticed that his best friend had lost some weight. Even so, the glasses, the nerdy hairstyle, and the dirty black T-shirt that said, "Clearly I have made some bad decisions," showed he was still just Stanley. Nolan smiled and tucked a lock of his seditious hair behind his ear. He decided he wasn't going to cut it until someone at school made him. Maybe he was going through a rebellious phase.

They both flipped open their laptops to begin writing the first piece of homework for Mr. Shaffer's English Comp class. It was a theme, one thousand words. They looked at each other and burst out laughing as they typed the following words across their computer screens: WHAT I DID ON MY SUMMER VACATION....

A few minutes after Blue Time fell, there was a tap at Nolan's window. Startled, he stopped typing and gave Stanley a puzzled look.

Emery burst into the room uninvited, and before Nolan could yell at him to get out, the nine-year-old said, "Holy smokes! Quick, 'fore Mom and Dad see him! It's the stonkin' duffer!"

He threw open the blinds, and sure enough, there stood Ysgafn, just a little lower than the window. In broad twilight. In the backyard. In Boston suburbia. With Quinn and Fiorlen perched on either shoulder, grinning like maniacs. Tintreach and Bassett buzzed around the warrior lord's head.

Nolan was floored. "How'd he get here through the Veil? Is there a doorway nearby?" he wanted to know. "And isn't it, like, one a.m. in Ireland? What, did they *walk?*"

"Who cares how they got here?" Stanley whispered. "Dear God, some neighbor's gonna see 'em." He leapt off the bed and brushed the wrinkles out of his T-shirt. Nolan saw him smile broadly at Quinn. She did look as good as ever!

Nolan threw open the window and said through the screen, "Uh...hi." He shook his head at Quinn. "You decided to come visit America after all, huh?"

Quinn winked at him. "Hey, Nols. Stanley. And wee Emery." She patted Ysgafn's shoulder, inviting them to climb on. "Ya blokes ready for this?"

Glossary

To the unaccustomed eye, the First Tongue might seem like an inaccessible language, but this glossary should help demystify some of the strange words and phrases.

Remember that stress is normally placed on the penultimate syllable, with a couple exceptions; and the diacritics (´) are acute marks, like the *fadas* in Irish, indicating long vowels.

Sentence structure is verb, subject, modifier; and there is no conjugation—verbs remain infinitive ("to be," "to run," etc.). Thus, *Leyn jyn dío* ("I'm sorry") is literally "to be I sorry." Tense is indicated by modifiers: *Leyn jyn dío cyn* ("I was sorry," literally "to be I sorry before").

⌒

"Abhrúle chun nimór dúinn Fiorlen! Ionmosod an y Coedaoine Truillygru" (Avr-OO-luh KUN NIM-or DO-in Fih-OR-lin! In-MOSS-odd an ih coy-DEEN-ah truh-ILL-grew): "We have to help Fiorlen! Attack the Corrupted Treemen!"

Agenor (uh-JEH-nor): The only living human who was Corrupted by Singing magic; a mutated Boarman; enslaved to Bàsisolc

Alabaster Mountains: A mountain range from which the High King's city was carved; located to the northeast of Morsden, across the Culais Strait

Alaric (uh-LAR-ick): The High King of Tírcluddaithe; husband of Gayle; father of Chadric; older brother of Dubric

Aossí (ess-SHE): "Fair Folk"; humans, in the Otherworld

Arshúil (arsh-OO-ill): "Away"; an Aossí village on the outskirts of southern Morsden; also a giant Awakened eagle

Arsoíche (ars-EE-huh): "Night terror"; a Corrupted mare

Awakened: An animal or plant that has been Sung over by the Treefolk; there are levels of Awakening: The highest level evolves the animal or plant into an anthropomorphic being; usually the Awakened is larger than its un-Awakened counterpart, and Awakened beings have the ability to choose between good and evil (See **Corrupted.**)

Bàsisolc (BAZ-is-alk): "Most Evil"; the younger brother of Crannhyn; the Corrupter

Basillia (Bas-ILL-ee-uh): The barren queen of Tírsor; wife of Dubric

Bassett: A pêllys; an Awakened, incandescent butterfly-like pixie

Boujòn (boo-ZHOWN): An Awakened, anthropomorphic rose; leader of the Thornsword Brethren

"Brearych muid ve Coedaoine anois" (brear-ICK MOO-id veh coy-DEEN-ah AH-nish): "We are looking for the Coedaoine too."

Cadfan (CAD-fan): An Aossí weaponsmith who lives in Arshúil

"Canadhan ve mercaíln ahenocht" (can-UH-yan veh mer-cah-EE-iln ah-EH-nock): "She will Sing tonight."

Caevnaóir (kayv-nuh-OH-er; singular)/**Caevnaóri** (kayv-nuh-OH-rih; plural): "Shepherd," "Guardian"; the Treefolk's name for themselves

Capána (cuh-PAY-nuh): "Mist"; the Mistfolk—Corrupted shape-shifters created from the dust of the dead and animated by human blood

Chadric (CHAD-rick): The only child of King Alaric and Queen Gayle; heir to the throne of Tírcluddaithe

Chéad Teanga (KEE-ahd teh-UN-guh): "First Tongue"; the Singing language of the Treefolk; also, dialects of the Otherworld from a proto-Celtic language

Citadel City: The fortress city of High King Alaric; located northeast of Morsden; carved from the Alabaster Mountains

Claídear (Cluh-EE-dear): "Red Sword"; the symbol of the High King's authority; a gift from the Coedaoine

Coeduine (coy-DIN-ah; singular)/**Coedaoine** (coy-DEEN-ah; plural): Treeperson; an intelligent being with the ability to Sing magic during the time-between-times (see **Gylináma**); guardian of the Veil; Shepherd of Morsden Forest; protector of the Master Song; led by Crannhyn

Corrupted: A being, Coeduine or Awakened, that has chosen the path of evil (See **Truillygru.**)

Crannhyn (CRAN-in): The Eldest of the Treefolk; creator of the Veil and the Master Song; the oldest living being on the planet

Demeglwys (deh-MEH-gliss): "Sanctuary"; one of the Veiled temples where the Verses can be opened

Dubric (DUH-vrick): The king of Tírsor; husband of Basillia; brother of Alaric, the High King

Elgaet (el-GUH-et): An Aossí candy made from honey and mint

Embroidery Queen: One of the first queens of Men in ancient times; ancestor of Audrey Redding and Quinn Taylor; original guardian of the Love Verse

Escre (ES-ker): A race of Awakened crayfish soldiers

Fiorlen (Fih-OR-lin): The Sapling daughter of Ysgafn

Gayle: The queen of Tírcluddaithe; wife of Alaric; mother of Chadric; related through marriage to the Embroidery Queen

"Glaoan ve lucféagwyl" (GLEE-an veh luck-FEEUH-gwill): "Get the guards."

Greenman: A member of the Treefolk (See **Coeduine.**)

Gylináma (gill-in-EH-muh): "Golden Hour"; the time-between-times; the magic hour of dusk; Blue Time

Heilyn (HYE-lin): Rhydderch's apprentice

Hidden Lands: The Otherworld hidden by the Veil, accessible only at dusk; it coincides on our earth (See **Tírcluddaithe.**)

Hynfel (HIN-fell): The first High King of Men from ancient times; the first recipient of the Master Song; friend of Crannhyn (millennia ago); father of the Embroidery Queen and six other daughters

Kayim (KAI-im): An Awakened alligator that serves as guardian of Lake Scáthán

Keras (KER-us): A race of Awakened, anthropomorphic rhinoceros known for their metalworking skill

Kype: A race of Awakened fish soldiers

Laws of Hospitality: An ancient code of ethics that requires the protection of travelers and demands that food, shelter, and gifts be provided to any who journey in peace

Leucis (LOO-kiss): A race of Awakened, anthropomorphic great cats led by King Orbo III

"Leyn daoineil?" (lane DEE-neal): "Are there others?"

"Leyn jyn dío" (lane jen DEE-ah): "I am sorry."

"Leyn tan maefuil saibhristyní? Fójurar!" (lane tan ME-full sai-VRIS-tin-ee foe-JU-rar): "Whose children are you? Thieves!"

"Leyn vo folin cabeth?" (lane vah FOL-in CAH-beth): "What is this foolishness?"

"Leyn Ysgafn m'atadir" (lane is-GUH-fin mah-TAH-dur): "Ysgafn is my father."

Loxon (LOX-un): A race of Awakened, anthropomorphic elephants known for their historical lore and gift of prophecy

Lucféagwyl (luck-FEEUH-gwill): "Guards"; those who protect the village of Arshúil

Lupír (LUH-peer): An Awakened giant vampire bat that serves as guardian of the Temple in Morsden Forest

Madán (MAH-dane): A mild swearword, literally, "My curse (upon it/you)"

Master Song: The greatest of the Songs, and the only one Humans can Sing; it outlines seven key virtues: Love, Wisdom, Might, Valor, Kindheartedness, Devotion, and Meekness (See **Verses.**)

Morscan (MORS-can): "Singing Death"; a most forbidden type of Singing that involves Awakening the dead with human blood (necromancy); it lasts for the hour of dusk

Morsden (MORS-den): "Covering," "Shrouding"; the Forest; home to Treefolk and many Awakened beings

Moving Sideways: The magical means by which Treefolk move through the Veil; the phrase does not directly translate, but the equivalent of "phase" or "shift" is suggested

Orbo (OR-bow): An Awakened, anthropomorphic white tiger; king of Leucis

Pêllys (PAY-liss): "Ball of Light"; an Awakened will-o'-the-wisp

Perleighis (pearl-EH-yiss): An iridescent Awakened herb with healing properties, commonly called "pearlmint" and also known to some as "kingsfoil"

Portanuam (port-uh-NEW-am): "Doorway"; a portal throughout the earth where the Veil can be raised to enter the Otherworld

Quorin (QWOR-in): The principal coinage of the Hidden Lands; accepted throughout the realm, it is a gold coin about the size of the British pound and bears Alaric's profile; a hot meal and a pint at a tavern costs about 2q

Rhrushden (hr-USH-den): "River Roaring"; the river running southeast to northwest through Morsden Forest

Rhydderch (hr-ITH-erk): A monk who lives in Morsden Deep

Sapling: A young Treeperson

Saibhristyn (sai-VRIS-tin; singular)/**Saibhristyní** (sai-VRIS-tin-ee; plural): Child/children; wealth

Scáthán (SCAY-thane): "Mirror"; mouth of the Rhrushden; the ironic name of Docile Lake; the entrance to Crannhyn's domain

Sealwyr (SHALL-were; singular)/**Sealwyrí** (SHALL-were-ee; plural): "Hunter," "Seeker"; one of the Treefolk who track down and destroy the Corrupted

"Sedritn ve wybrán!" (SHED-ritn veh WHY-brain): "Shine on the path!"

Singing: The magical ability of Treefolk to lift the Veil, heal the wounded, Awaken creatures, and so forth, but only at the hour of dusk; some of the results of Singing are permanent, while others fade after the magic hour is done

Spiacánacha (spee-uh-cay-NOCK-uh): The Jagged Mountains; located on the northwest border of Morsden; the entrance to Crannhyn's domain

Suas (SOO-us): "Up"; the Treefolk city in northwestern Morsden Forest

Talaf (TALL-uff): The tallest tree in Morsden Forest, supposedly three quarters of a mile high; the birthplace of Crannhyn the Eldest; a holy place for the Coedaoine

Tegwyn (TEH-gwin): "Blessèd and Fair"; mother of Fiorlen; wife of Ysgafn; matriarchal leader of Suas

Tërimrush (tehr-IM-rush): "Roaring Insanity"; a giant Awakened, man-eating grizzly she-bear

Tírcluddaithe (teer-cluh-DEE-huh): "Hidden Lands"; collectively, the Otherworld; ruled by High King Alaric

Tírsor (TEER-sore): "Southlands"; the plains kingdom of Dubric and Basillia; known for its horses and agriculture

Thornsword Brethren: A knightly order of chivalrous, Awakened flowers

Tintreach (TIN-trick): An Awakened lightning bug

Tophyrs (TAH-firs): A rather sodden Awakened frog with a penchant for pie and liquor who is also apparently a sneak thief

Truillygru (truh-ILL-grew): "Corrupted"; an evil Awakened being

Uropsid (Your-OP-sid): A race of Awakened, anthropomorphic lizards known for their stoneworking skills and artistry

Veil: The magical barrier between our world and the Hidden Lands; it can be opened only one hour a day, at dusk

Verses: When the Veil was created, the Master Song was separated into seven Verses, one for each virtue; the Verses were hidden in seven Stones (See **Master Song.**)

"Vrastë ei muin!" (VRAH-steh ay MUH-in): "Stab her neck!"

Ysgafn Droed (is-GUH-fin droad): "Light of Foot"; a Sealwyr of Morsden; father of Fiorlen; husband of Tegwyn

Acknowledgments

Thanks for reading this novel. I hope you enjoyed it! The earliest ideas and characters that became *The Master Song*, the first book in the Blue Time series, popped into my head more than twenty years ago, even though the book was written over the span of a few months. But during that long time when the story was brewing, there were several influences that shaped it into what it is today, and I would be remiss not to acknowledge them here.

First and foremost, the Lord Jesus Christ. I believe we all have gifts that make us unique, and I would like to think mine is the gift of storytelling. While *The Master Song* is not a Christian novel, specifically, all of my writings cannot help but be influenced by my faith—and I hope that this shows through without my coming across as preachy. The story is told for the story's sake, but my thanks are given to Him for the ability to tell it in the first place.

My wife, Christy. I once read a book on the craft that said an author should write for a specific person, an audience of one. So I write for her, and if she likes the story, I consider it a success. Thank you, love, for your support and patience, and for taking care of our boys during all the long hours I've spent plonking away on a keyboard, lost in Morsden Forest!

My sons, Connor and Christian. I hope someday, when they're a bit older, they'll enjoy their time in the Otherworld and perhaps see a bit of their own virtues reflected in the children.

My parents, James and Joy, for their support and for giving me time off the "serious stuff" to focus on a fairy tale that's been decades in the making.

Don Milam, for finding *The Master Song* and the Blue Time series a home.

Whitaker House, for taking the chance on a wild fantasy series.

Jeffrey Shaffer, for his map and world-class edits, and Courtney Hartzel, as well. Also Brae Wyckoff, for the early read-through.

I write to music, so there's literally a soundtrack that shapes every story. My thanks to Aaron Marsh and Copeland; Adam Young, Owl City, Port Blue, and Windsor Airlift; Better Than Ezra; Colin Hay and Men at Work; Dredg; Emery and Matt & Toby; Eric Nordhoff; Glen Phillips and Toad the Wet Sprocket; Hum; James Morrison; Jimmy Eat World; John Mayer; Josh Groban; Pierce the Veil; Robin Mark; Roger Clyne and the Peacemakers; Rivertribe; and Straight No Chaser.

To the best of my knowledge, all authors love to read. Many thanks to a few of my favorite writers, classic and modern: Alcott, Augustine, Austen, Brontë, Bunyan, Card, Carroll, Cashore, Clare, Colfer, Collins, Cooper, Dante, Davis, Dickens, Dostoyevsky, Doyle, Dumas, Evans, Hawthorne, Hugo, James, Johnson, King, Landy, Lawhead, Lewis, Livy, London, Lu, Lynch, Martin, McIsaac, McKinney, Meyer, Milton, Nix, Paine, Paolini, Poe, Pullman, Riordan, Roth, Rowling, Rutherfurd, M. Scott, W. Scott, Stendhal, Stoker, Stroud, Thackeray, Tolkien, Tolstoy, Turgenev, Twain, Walker, Westerfield, Winfield, Wyckoff, Zahn, and a dozen others I'm sure I've forgotten.

Lastly, to all of you who've read all the way to this page—my deepest thanks. Let's do it again sometime.

—*Andrew Maloney*
Sunset, Texas
January 1, 2014

About the Author

I feel pretentious writing about myself in the third person. So instead: I come from a long line of writers, starting with my great-great-great aunts Phoebe and Alice Cary; my great-grandmother Kathryn Blackburn Peck; my grandmother Dolores Scroggins; my uncle David Alsobrook; and my parents, James and Joy Maloney. It was only natural I'd follow in their footsteps. (How's that for pretentiousness?)

I graduated in the late nineties from the University of North Texas with a writing degree and worked in the real world long enough to know I don't ever want to do that again. So, for the past few years, I've ghostwritten and edited several theology books before turning my attention to novels.

The Elementalists was my first foray into the world of fantasy fiction. I've got several other books in various stages of completion, but it's hard to focus on just one at a time, so you may or may not ever get to read them—not assuming you'd want to in the first place.

Along with my beautiful wife, Christy, I cowrote *Eight Weeks with No Water*, a testimony of our second son's miraculous birth. We have two awesome boys, Connor and Christian, and we live in Texas but secretly hope to divide our time between here and the Pacific Northwest someday.